Trust

I Found My Heart in San Francisco
Book Twenty

Susan X Meagher

Trust

I FOUND MY HEART IN SAN FRANCISCO: BOOK TWENTY

THIS TRADE PAPERBACK ORIGINAL IS PUBLISHED BY BRISK PRESS, BRIELLE, NJ 08730.

FIRST PRINTING: FEBRUARY 2016

COVER DESIGN: CAROLYN NORMAN

ISBN-13: 978-0-9966774-4-8

By Susan X Meagher

Novels

Arbor Vitae
All That Matters
Cherry Grove
Girl Meets Girl
The Lies That Bind
The Legacy
Doublecrossed
Smooth Sailing
How To Wrangle a Woman
Almost Heaven
The Crush
The Reunion
Inside Out
Out of Whack
Homecoming
The Right Time
Summer of Love

Serial Novel

I Found My Heart In San Francisco

Awakenings: Book One
Beginnings: Book Two
Coalescence: Book Three
Disclosures: Book Four
Entwined: Book Five
Fidelity: Book Six
Getaway: Book Seven
Honesty: Book Eight
Intentions: Book Nine
Journeys: Book Ten
Karma: Book Eleven
Lifeline: Book Twelve
Monogamy: Book Thirteen
Nurture: Book Fourteen
Osmosis: Book Fifteen
Paradigm: Book Sixteen
Quandary: Book Seventeen
Renewal: Book Eighteen
Synchronicity: Book Nineteen
Trust: Book Twenty

Anthologies

Undercover Tales
Outsiders

Acknowledgments

My deep thanks to Day, who has edited each of the books in the series. She's always prompt, reliable, professional, and a lot of fun. Her encouragement and helpful comments gave me some badly needed confidence when I was just starting out. If there's one thing I could gift to all new writers, it's that they have their own Day to prop them up and make them believe in themselves.

Dedication

As always, this book couldn't have been written without the support of my beloved wife Carrie. I share Richard Ford's sentiment: "Writing is the only thing I've ever done with persistence, except for being married." I'm very lucky to have both a career and a spouse I love with all my heart.

Chapter One

Jamie Evans opened her eyes, blinked confusedly, then tried to get her bearings. It took only a second to recognize the steady hum of jet engines, the soft rustlings of the cabin crew, and the fact that she was lying not in her bed, but a cocoon-like seating pod. She turned her head, expecting to find her partner, but once again Ryan was missing. A quick check of her watch, and some addition that was harder than it should have been, allowed her to calculate that they'd been in the air for around ten hours. At best, Ryan had been in her seat no more than five. Luckily, flight attendants were trained to put up with hyperactive passengers, but she had to acknowledge that Ryan was probably one of the worst. The woman could neither physically nor mentally sit in one spot for any significant length of time.

Mere moments passed before Ryan slid into her upright seat, which faced the opposite direction of Jamie's, reached across the scant space that separated them, and rested her hand on Jamie's hip. Ryan had either been watching her, or they were freakishly in tune. Either way, she had an uncanny knack for showing up right on cue.

"Hey." Sleepily, Jamie rolled onto her side and grasped Ryan's hand. "Tired of charming the flight attendants?"

"Nah. I could do that all day." She grinned, clearly unrepentant. "But they're getting breakfast ready, and I didn't want to be in the way."

Jamie pressed the switch that returned her chair to the upright position, and tried to appear awake. "Did you sleep?"

"Not much. Can't relax when I'm in the air. I don't want to miss anything." She leaned over and whispered, "Everyone around us is asleep, and the flight attendants are gonna be busy for ten or fifteen minutes.

Want me to sneak my hand under your blanket and give you a wake-up orgasm?"

It was hard to tell if she was being serious or not. Ryan clearly enjoyed semi-public sex, but she liked to tease even more. "We joined the mile high club ages ago. I think I'll wait until I get you home." She patted Ryan's cheek. "Better access to the good parts."

"I was kidding, but you could've talked me into it with very little trouble." Ryan leaned over and took a tiny nibble from Jamie's ear, making her shiver. "We were in a great grove those first two weeks in Australia, but having Mia with us for the last two kinda put a damper on things."

"You got me *good* last night. The farewell party was fun, but nowhere close to that."

"Agreed." She used the Australian accent she'd pulled out on and off for the last month. "I love being down under…you, mate."

"Hmm…" Realizing the spark in her partner's eyes was genuine, Jamie considered their logistics. "Let's go to Berkeley. No one will tease us when we head right for bed."

"It's a deal. We can break the O'Flaherty code and take a shuttle. After I ravage you, we can head home."

Feigning shock, Jamie made her eyes wide. "Really? You don't want to have a family member pick us up?"

The look on Ryan's face showed she'd had to wrestle with the decision. "Well, I *do*, but it's a work day, so none of the boys can come. I'm not sure what Da's schedule is, but he'd move heaven and earth to send someone to fetch us, which is kinda silly."

"If you want a pick-up, I'll call my mom." Jamie patted her, knowing this was, weirdly, important to Ryan.

"Given that we haven't heard from her since she got home, I'm assuming Jennie's keeping her super busy. I don't want to mess up whatever schedule they've got going on."

Chuckling, Jamie shook her head. "I have all of these mental images of Jennie's reaction when she learned she'll never have to go back to the group home again. Every one of them is funny."

"I wish we'd been able to be there to watch her go bonkers, but Jen had to get out of there pronto. We'll go over and have dinner with them tonight to see how they're both adjusting."

Jamie nodded, then pondered the situation for a few minutes. She was certain her mom would be a good guardian, and equally certain it would take a while for her to get used to being responsible for a teenager again. Especially a teenager like Jennie.

They walked into the Berkeley house right at noon. A month's worth of mail was piled up neatly on the table, courtesy of Maria Los, who, much to Ryan's dismay, cleaned the house three times a week—even when she and Jamie were on another continent. "What a load of junk we get!" Ryan shook her head in disgust. "All of those trees felled so millions of people can have their mailboxes filled with crap."

"I'll go through it after we get a snack." Jamie patted Ryan on the butt. "I assume you're hungry."

"Well, yeah." She checked her watch, the cool one Jim had given her to celebrate Cal's College World Series victory. "It's lunchtime."

"Not to your tummy." Jamie patted her belly. "It thinks it's five in the morning—tomorrow."

"Nope. I'm back on San Francisco time. My tummy knows it's lunchtime."

"I should have realized that." Jamie took her hand as they headed for the kitchen. They'd cleaned the refrigerator out before they'd left, but Jamie always kept some bagels in the freezer for hunger emergencies. At the very least they could have peanut butter and jelly.

As the door swung open, Jamie gasped, grabbed Ryan's hand and stammered, "S…s…someone broke in!"

"Shit!" Ryan quickly took in the scene. The window next to the back door was smashed, shards of glass littering the floor. At least the jerk had cut himself. Drops of blood made a distinct trail to the kitchen sink. Her heart was racing, just from adrenaline, but Jamie seemed truly frightened. "Open the back door so you can get out quickly. I'll go make sure the asshole just robbed us."

Jamie grabbed her with both hands. "What do you mean *just* robbed us?"

"Well…" *Damn, that was a dumb thing to say.* "I'm sure that's what happened, but there's a chance…" She looked up towards the second floor, and Jamie did the same.

"Oh, no you don't! If someone's in this house, the police are going to find him." She grabbed Ryan hard enough to leave a bruise and started to drag her to the back door.

"We don't need the police. It'll take them forever if we call in a burglary. I don't want to hang around here all day."

"A dangerous criminal might be hiding in my house!" Jamie snatched the key to the double-deadbolt and opened the back door. "You're not getting away from me until someone with a nice big gun goes through this place."

Ryan really, really wanted to argue. This was a simple burglary. Goldilocks with a Glock wasn't sleeping in their bed. But it wasn't fair to worry Jamie. She'd suffered through enough tense situations in the last year. "All right. But can I thaw a bagel while we wait?"

Jamie grabbed her by the ear and pulled Ryan along behind her. "I'm gonna act like you didn't even ask that."

They went into the back yard and Jamie started to dial 911. Ryan looked up, seeing that their bedroom windows were wide open. Her eyes continued to scan the property, and she noticed the sun glinting off something near the garage. A bicycle. She walked over to take a look, then dashed back across the yard, quickly removing the phone from Jamie's hand.

"What…?"

Ryan pointed. "We know our burglar. That's Jennie's bike."

"What? But why would…"

"Jennie!" Ryan shouted. "Jennie! I'm calling the police in two seconds!"

A sleepy-eyed blonde head emerged from the window. "Don't be mad," she began, but Ryan was already through the door, steaming through the house to reach the kid. Maybe she shouldn't have stopped Jamie from calling the cops. The homicide squad.

By the time she reached the second floor, Jennie was standing in front of their bedroom, dressed in one of Ryan's T-shirts. It was so big that it almost went to her knees, making her look like a little girl. But she wasn't a little girl. She was a teenager who could test the patience of a saint. "What in the holy hell are you doing here?" Jamie was right behind her now. A calming hand landed on her shoulder.

"I had to get away." Jennie sucked in a big breath, then started to cry, something she resorted to rarely. "I had to."

Ryan forced herself to remain calm. To assess the situation before she lost it. While taking in a few deep breaths, she surveyed the girl. Plastic bandages covered a few spots on her hands and arms, likely from cutting herself while climbing in through the window. But that didn't explain the angry purple marks near her neck, nor the dark bruises up and down her arm. Ryan closed the distance between them, took the girl's hand in hers and touched it gently. "What happened?" It was *so* hard to speak calmly.

"Pebbles," she spat through her tears.

"What?" The machinations they'd had to go through to get Jennie's tormentor out of the country flashed through her mind. The kid was supposed to be gone at least a *year*. "She's in Samoa with her grandmother."

Jennie wiped at her eyes with the back of her other hand and shot Ryan a narrow-eyed look. "I *told* you she'd do something. I told you!"

"Okay." Ryan took a breath. "Let's go sit down. We need to sort this out." She put her hand on Jen's shoulder and guided her into the bedroom, with Jamie right on her heels. Jen sat on the bed, and Ryan perched right next to her. Jamie stood near them for a moment, then she sat on Jen's other side. "Tell us what happened," Ryan said. "From the beginning."

Jamie wasn't able to take the patient approach. "Why aren't you with my mom?"

"Your mom?" Jennie blinked slowly. "She's with you."

Jamie's mouth opened and closed. Her eyes met Ryan's, then she got up and left the room, hurriedly.

Jennie's gaze followed her, then she looked at Ryan as if she expected to be struck. "Is she mad?"

"Doesn't matter. Tell me what happened."

Jennie sighed so heavily she looked more like an old woman than a kid. "Pebbles came back."

"When? Today?"

"No." A very annoyed look covered her face. "A couple weeks ago."

"She's in Pago Pago!"

"She didn't like it there. Or they threw her out. When school started, she was back." Jennie's glare was malevolent.

"Oh, fuck. I...I keep forgetting it's September."

"It's *October*," Jennie said. "You've been gone forever."

"Jen," she said, her thoughts banging around in her head, "we thought we'd handled it. Pebbles was supposed to stay in Pago Pago for the whole year. We never would have left you here if we thought she'd be around."

"Well, you did, and she was." Jennie looked like she wanted to bite her.

Ryan leaned back against the fluffy pillows, struggling with shame and anger at herself for not calling Jen even once from Australia. "I'm so sorry," she said quietly. "I…I let the time get away from me."

"You didn't even help me pick out my classes." Her eyes held a shocking amount of anger. This was *very* bad. Bad in ways Ryan couldn't piece together.

"Why didn't you let us know that Pebbles came back? I told you to call if you needed anything."

"What would you do? Other than tell me you'll *handle* it." The bitterness that filled her eyes showed how much faith she had in Ryan's promises. "We're both stuck there until we're eighteen. That's what happens when you don't have a single relative who can stand you."

Ryan was on the verge of throwing up. She'd been working with the kid for over two years, doing everything she could think of to make her feel safe. Yet she'd lost her trust because she'd put her on the back burner when she went to have fun. "Go on," Ryan urged, trying not to look as upset as she was.

"I was doing okay, staying at Ms. Smith's whenever Sandy would let me. Your brother would come over and hang out when he had time. But Saturday morning I had cramps, and I stayed in bed. That asshole snuck in and got into bed with me."

She looked so angry, so outraged that Ryan's heart clutched in sympathy. Then it hit her. Catherine had been home on Saturday. Her anger started to flare and she had to sit on her hands to stop herself from balling them into fists. "Keep going," she said quietly, fighting to contain her growing rage.

"I woke up to see that big, ugly face an inch in front of me." Her eyes nearly closed, lips pressed together. "I *hate* her."

"What happened, Jen? Tell me everything."

"She stuck her hand between my legs and tried to…" She bit her lip, her teeth leaving a dent. "I shoved her, but no normal person could move her stupid ass. She had me pinned up against the wall and her fingers…" Ryan hung on her words, silently begging for a quick end to the story.

"I started slugging her." Jennie punched one hand against an open palm. "I hit her as hard as I could, but I didn't have much room to get any weight behind it. She was moving really, really slow and didn't even flinch when I hit her. I don't know how high you can be, but she was past that."

"Then what happened?"

She closed her eyes for a moment, and Ryan's pulse beat faster, thinking of all of the possible outcomes, every one of them awful. Knowing Jen, Pebbles might be in the morgue.

"She was so slow I climbed over her before she could stop me. I was almost gone, but she grabbed my shirt and started yanking." Her hand went to her neck, unconsciously touching the welts. "She was yanking so hard, I thought I'd choke, but I wasn't gonna let her kill me. I fell back onto the bed so I could breathe, and she rolled on top of me." She held up her swollen, bruised wrist. "My arm got trapped. Every ounce of her loser ass fell on it."

Ryan tenderly manipulated the wrist. It was probably only sprained, but so swollen it had to hurt like hell. "Then what?"

"I slugged her right in the face." Ryan hated to see the pleasure that infused Jennie's expression when she said those words. "The blood gushing out of her nose finally got through her thick skull. She stood up and stared at me like she didn't know why she was covered in blood. The she stumbled downstairs and told Sandy some kinda bullshit. A minute later, I'm grounded for starting fights." Tears started to flow again, and she leaned against Ryan heavily. "Sandy always believes her. *Always*."

Ryan had a good idea why that was. Sandy seemed to believe that Pebbles was developmentally delayed and was picked on by the other girls because of her mental impairment. In fact, the kid abused inhalants and gasoline and her slowness was chemically enhanced. Jen had begged Ryan not to rat Pebbles out—and she'd stupidly agreed.

"No TV. No closing ceremonies." Her lower lip started to quiver, and Ryan's almost followed suit. "And I wasn't allowed to go to Ms. Smith's for a week." Her head dropped, and when she spoke again her voice was filled with rage. "I knew I'd kill Pebbles if I had to be stuck in that house for a week."

"So you ran away."

Jennie looked up and met Ryan's eyes. "You promised you'd fix it. *All* of you promised."

"And all of us screwed up. Every one of us has let you down." She wrapped her arms around the girl and started to cry when Jen snuggled up against her like a puppy, seeking the comfort that was much, much too little and much, much too late.

After leaving a note for Maria Los to explain the mess, Jamie guided the BMW over the Bay Bridge. Ryan sat at her side, with Jennie in the back seat. Neither speaking.

Jamie's hands tightly gripped the wheel, while her stomach cramped painfully. She should have called her mother. It was unconscionable not to. But she couldn't make herself. By the time they arrived, she *might* be able to be civil. Dark thoughts kept playing over and over in her head. How could she have left Jennie in that house one minute longer than necessary?

Marta answered the door, her face anxious and drawn. "Oh, Jamie." She put her arms around her then jerked up and stood tall. "Jennie!" Marta grabbed the girl in a hug, holding on so tightly Jen struggled. Then Catherine was on the landing, fighting to get her arms around Jen too.

Jamie looked up, and caught sight of a grim-faced Ryan, clearly struggling to keep her temper in check. Suddenly, Jamie felt protective rather than angry at her mom. There had to be a good reason for neglecting Jen. There *had* to be.

Minutes later, Jamie, Jen and Catherine sat at the kitchen table, with Jennie going over her story again. Ryan paced in the dining room, with the floorboards creaking when she walked over them again and again. Jamie wasn't sure who she was talking to, but she was on the phone as she rubbed the finish off the floor.

The only good news of the morning was that Jennie was talking more freely. Being in Catherine's presence must have had a calming effect on her.

Ryan came back into the room, speaking curtly. "The police have to come take a report." Her gaze landed on Catherine. "And a social worker's going to come by. They're...concerned." She turned and went back towards the dining room, saying, "I'm going to call Sandy now, then my family." They all watched her go, and when Jamie looked at her mother she noted how pale she was. Her hand shook noticeably when she picked up her tea and took a sip.

Too antsy to sit still, Jamie got up and went into the hall, hearing Ryan say, "I understand that, but I believe Jennie. Pebbles groped her, Sandy. For the sake of the other girls, you've got to report that to her case worker." Jamie made eye contact, but Ryan turned and moved further away. Clearly, she didn't want company. Jamie went back into the kitchen, where her mom was leaning over in her chair, her arms draped around Jennie's neck, both of them crying. Jamie'd never seen her mom look more guilty, more anguished. Her guts clenched in sympathy and she left the room to give them a little privacy. Since Ryan held the living room, Jamie decided to go upstairs to the new library. Maybe looking out at the bay would help calm her. If not, there was a full bar.

The water did have a calming effect, and Jamie quickly lost track of time. She started when her mother appeared, red-eyed and pale. "Marta's making lunch for Jennie and Ryan. I assume you're not hungry."

"Right you are," she said, unable to infuse her voice with even a hint of civility.

Catherine sat down, small and fragile in the large, upholstered chair. "I...I...there aren't words to express how much of a mess of things I've made. They were all right," she said, tears streaming down her cheeks. "I'm not the person to be Jennie's guardian. I don't have the capacity to care for a goldfish."

Once again, seeing her mother's fragility freed up her frozen empathy. Jamie slid off the chair and knelt to take her hand. "What happened? Why didn't you go pick her up as soon as you got home?"

"I...I was..." She bent from the waist, her head almost atop her knees. "I was afraid."

Moving closer, Jamie took her in her arms, always surprised to feel her body, as delicate and light as a bird's. "Afraid of what, Mom?"

"Of...starting. I was terrified of starting." She cried so hard she began to gasp for breath, but Jamie stayed with her, holding on and stroking her back.

"You were afraid of having Jen move in?"

"I was so jet-lagged, and so stressed by the whole thing. I thought...I thought I could wait until you and Ryan were here." She met Jamie's eyes, looking so deeply guilty that it was hard to hold her gaze. "I didn't think another day could possibly make a difference, but I was so, so wrong." Catherine sat up a little and wiped at her eyes roughly. "I'm so self-centered. So fearful... I'm the last person who should care for a defenseless child. Jennie would do as well with her mother."

"You're being ridiculous," Jamie insisted. "You're not self-centered, but you *did* let your imagination run wild. So...we move on." She got up and took her mother's hand. "Let's go downstairs and tell Jen that she never has to go back to the group home."

Catherine's eyes grew wide. "No! Martin and Maeve offered to take her. We'll get your father involved. He can talk to the judge."

"*You* are Jennie's guardian," Jamie said firmly. She tugged on her mom's hand, pulling her to her feet. "You love Jen and she's crazy about you. That's what matters. Yes, you screwed up, but you've got to get past that and dive in." She grasped Catherine by the shoulders and gave her a mild shake. "You've got a job to do."

Catherine fell into Jamie's embrace, her whole body shivering. "I'm not up to it. I've proven that."

"Wrong. You're just wrong. Jennie's hurt and angry right now, and she has every right to be. But she'll get over it. And so will you. Now, let's go." She started to walk, with Catherine resisting as forcefully as she could. But Jamie was taller and stronger and she easily pulled her along like a reluctant child.

"She'll never forgive me!"

"Of course she will." Jamie turned and put her hands on her mom's shoulders, forcing her to meet her gaze. "For God's sake, she forgave her mother for beating her and literally throwing her out of the house. This is nothing in the scheme of things."

Catherine pulled to a halt just short of the door. "I knew Pebbles was back." Her voice shook, with the words spilling out in a rush. "Marta called me on the day of my big meeting in Australia." Her voice dropped to a whisper as her eyes closed. "I *knew* it."

Jamie stood there, statue-like, staring. What in the holy hell had she been thinking? She'd insisted she desperately wanted Jennie, then let her stay in a dangerous place longer than necessary? What in god's name went on in her head? Jamie fought to focus, reminding herself that they had to move forward. Dwelling on mistakes wouldn't help. Jennie needed to get out of the group home—immediately—and Catherine was the one who had to make that happen. "That's...pretty awful. There's no way to sugar-coat that." She gave Catherine a shake. "But you still have to go downstairs and tell her that you're her guardian." Once again, she tugged her along. "Sometimes you can let your fears take over. Other times—like this—you've gotta gut it up."

When Catherine and Jamie got to the bottom of the stairs, Ryan was leading a police officer into the dining room. "She can handle it," Jamie said, her hand on the small of Catherine's back, herding her towards the kitchen.

Jennie was sitting in a chair, seeming like she was about to face the firing squad. "Are they gonna arrest me?"

With her heart beating hard, Catherine went to stand next to the girl's chair. "Of course not." Tentatively, she extended her hand and petted Jennie, tearing up again when the child leaned into her hand to soak up the comfort. "You were merely protecting yourself, honey. You didn't do anything wrong."

Jen looked up at her, blue eyes wide and frightened. "Don't let them take me back," she said, her voice trembling. "I'll kill her if she touches me again. I can't stop myself."

Catherine looked at Jamie, pleadingly. But Jamie merely gave her a stern look and turned to leave.

There was no escape. No one to rescue her. It was just the two of them, and she *had* to take control. She'd begged for this chance and had to seize it. "Let's go upstairs and sit on the deck for a while. I always feel better when I can see the ocean. Don't you?"

The girl gave her a puzzled look. *What a stupid comment!* Jennie had never lived near the ocean. When things got bad for her she had no outlet—no tranquilizing view to sooth her. She had to simply take whatever fell onto her narrow shoulders.

Once they'd reached the deck, Catherine turned on the heat lamps. Jennie was sitting directly under one, and she looked up at it curiously. "I didn't know you could make it warm."

"The lamps help a lot, don't they? Have you never been out here on a cool day?"

"I've never been out here by myself." She frowned as her gaze slipped right past Catherine. "I stay where you put me."

Good God, she could make you feel two inches tall with just a few words. "Do you like it here, Jennie?"

Big blue eyes blinked slowly. "Is that a trick question? You'd have to be a moron not to like it here."

"Would you like it if I could arrange…if I was allowed to…have you stay? Permanently?"

When her brow furrowed, the troubled gaze became very suspicious. There was a hard edge to her voice when she spoke. "What do you mean?"

"I mean, would you like to live here? With me."

Her head started to shake before Catherine finished the sentence. "They'd never let me. Sandy's gonna *kill* me for running away. And double kill me for being here after she told me to stay away. *And* I'll probably get thrown out of school for skipping today. I'm on my way to the Youth Authority." Jennie's eyes shifted to the doorway where Jamie stood.

"There's a social worker here. She wants to talk to both of you."

Jennie simply shrugged and got up. As Catherine followed her, Jamie whispered, "I told the social worker Jen didn't know about the custody arrangement yet. You haven't told her, have you?"

"No, we were just getting there."

Jamie took her hand, and they walked downstairs together, with Jennie leading the way.

A nice-looking woman was waiting in the living room, wearing a simple blue pantsuit, her short hair neatly styled. Catherine relaxed a bit when the woman's gaze met hers. There was kindness in those eyes.

"Mrs. Smith?"

"Catherine," she said, crossing to shake the woman's hand.

"I'm Terry Carmichael. With DCFS." She turned and nodded in Jen's direction. "And you're Jennie?"

"Uh-huh." Jennie hung back, as though she were afraid the woman would bodily drag her away.

Turning back to Catherine, Terry said, "Is this a good place for me to talk to Jennie?"

"Oh. Uhm…certainly. We'll be…" She pointed to the door. "In the kitchen."

"Great. We'll come get you when we're finished."

When they entered the kitchen, Catherine dropped into a chair, exhausted. "At some point, this day will end."

"I guess the good news is that this will probably be the worst day you two ever have. One day you'll look back on this and realize it's been all downhill from here."

Catherine looked at her daughter, briefly wondering if her thoughts were always so upbeat. "I can only hope you're right, but I have no idea what your optimism is based on."

After an interminable length of time, the social worker popped her head into the kitchen. "Can I talk to you alone, Catherine?"

Jamie jumped up and said, "I'll go sit with Jen."

"Thanks," Terry said, moving into the kitchen to take Jamie's seat. Terry let out a breath, shook her head and showed a wry smile. "She seems like a pretty good kid. Wary, distrustful, and angry, but that's to be expected with a kid who's been in as many placements as she has."

"Am I going to be allowed to keep her? I swear I'll do anything to make this work."

Terry cocked her head. "I'm not here to take her away. You're not the one who's damaged her." She looked down at her notes. "But it's going to take a while for Jennie to feel safe here." Meeting Catherine's gaze, she added, "The kid's very hurt. She feels like you and your daughter and her partner made some promises you didn't keep. She said her housemother has her faults, but she's never promised anything she didn't deliver."

"She's right. She's dead right." Catherine rubbed her temples; her headache was threatening to burst her head open. "I made a grievous mistake. I was in Australia when I got the call that I'd been awarded custody." She closed her eyes, shame filling her. "Instead of racing home, as I should have, I decided to stay and conduct my business. Then, when I got home on Friday, I chose to wait for my daughter to come home before I told Jennie about the custody decision. Jamie and Ryan have been very involved with her for a few years and I thought it would be best if we all discussed it together."

"I can see why you made those choices," she said, making a quick note.

"You can?" Catherine said, amazed.

"Sure. I'm an adult, and I know it's hard to juggle things. But a kid like Jennie needs structure, consistency and clear rules. It's better to keep her expectations low than to make a promise you're not one hundred percent sure you can keep."

"The child could hardly have lower expectations. I believe she's surprised when the sun rises."

"That's common. Almost every kid in the system has been let down."

"I'd give anything to have not done that to Jennie. Anything," Catherine fervently repeated.

"Well, hindsight's pretty perfect. Would you have come home if you'd known this Pebbles girl was going to act out on her?"

"Of course!"

"Then you're already a better parent than half of the ones I work with." Terry reached over and put her hand on top of Catherine's. "You'll make mistakes. Everyone does. Just try to learn from them."

"I will. I've learned a great deal today." She let out a soft chuckle. "More than I wanted to."

"Have you worked with at-risk kids before?"

"No. Never. This is all very, very new for me."

With ironic good cheer, she said, "Oh, you'll get to learn all sorts of new and exciting things." She made a few notes. "I'm going to have to put this in her file, of course. The judge will take notice of it. But you've got four months before he makes his final order to convince Jennie of what a great situation this is." She leaned forward and gave Catherine a pat on the shoulder. "I'm confident you can do it." Terry took a long look around the kitchen. "I'd move in at the drop of a hat."

After escorting Terry out, Catherine went to find her guests. As expected, they were upstairs on the deck. When she crossed the threshold, Ryan stood up and let her gaze glide right past, as if she couldn't bear to make eye contact. "We're going to take off."

Jamie jumped up and stood next to Ryan, smiling in a very artificial manner. "Ryan's certain she can fix the kitchen window if she has time to get to the glass shop. Ever since she's been working on the OFC she's certain she's a handy-woman."

Looking confused and wary, Jennie said, "Are you leaving me here? Sandy's gonna be madder by the minute."

Ryan squatted down next to her. "It's cool. I talked to Sandy. She knows you're staying."

Jen's gaze went from Ryan to Catherine, then back again. "And she said it's okay?"

"Yep." Ryan shot Catherine a pointed look, then met Jen's eyes again. "We've gotta go, but we'll be back later. Is that cool?"

"I guess so." Jennie looked at Catherine, clearly confused. "Is this what I'm supposed to be doing?"

"Yes, honey." She turned to Jamie. "Thank you both."

Jamie offered a quick kiss, but Ryan simply turned and walked away. Catherine watched, feeling like a puppy abandoned at the shelter. Shaking off the feeling, she took a seat next to Jennie and steeled her courage. "I got permission to have you stay here."

"But I'm grounded."

"Not any longer. You can stay with me from now on, Jennie. Permanently."

"Permanently?" Jennie's blue eyes half-closed as she peered at Catherine carefully. "What's that *really* mean?"

The poor child had been disappointed, abandoned, and lied to so many times she didn't trust the simplest words and concepts. Catherine spoke softly and clearly. "If you like it here, and want to stay, we can go to court in a few months and ask the judge to make me your permanent guardian."

A flicker of hope flashed across the girl's eyes. "I don't have to go back to the group home? Like…ever?"

"Not unless you want to."

Suspiciously, Jennie said, "You're kidding, right?"

"No. I'm very serious about this. I want you to live wherever you're happiest. I'm going to try very hard to make sure that's with me." Catherine reached out and put her hand on Jennie's knee. "I know how badly I let you down, and I have no excuse."

Once again, Jennie's lip started to quiver. "You lied to me," she said quietly.

Gripping her harder, Catherine spoke more confidently. She didn't *feel* confident, but Jennie needed to know someone was in charge. "That's not true. I didn't keep my promise to keep you safe, but I didn't lie when I made it. I just used bad judgment."

"Bad judgment?"

"Very bad judgment. Our first mistake was in not telling Sandy that Pebbles was harassing you."

Jennie's eyes opened wide. "You promised you wouldn't tell!"

"That was a mistake," Catherine said, now certain of that fact. "Sometimes you have to do things that have repercussions you don't like. If Pebbles had been removed from the home, it would have been safer for all of you."

"And they'd send her to the Youth Authority."

Catherine touched her chin, lifting it so their eyes met. "Pebbles is doing things that endanger the girls in the house, Jennie. It was a mistake to allow that to go on. I know you don't want me to do this, but I'm going to call Sandy and tell her about Pebbles keeping gasoline in the house."

Jennie sank back in the big chair, giving Catherine a long, sour look. "I don't want you to."

"I know that. And I wish I didn't have to. But I do." She stood up and gazed down at the child for a moment. "I'll be back in a few minutes."

Catherine crossed back into the house and went to her library. She nearly collapsed onto her desk chair, her head throbbing. There wasn't a single doubt in her mind that she had to make the call, and not a single cell in her body that wanted to do it.

Twenty minutes later, Catherine went back to the deck where she spotted Jennie, sullenly sitting right where she'd left her.

"Are the police there yet?"

"I don't think Sandy's going to call the police. We talked about alternatives, given that Pebbles has had such a tough year." She took in a breath, forcing herself to have some empathy for the other girl. "Being rejected by the last of her relatives had to be very, very difficult for her."

"She probably set their house on fire," Jennie grumbled.

Nothing about the situation was funny, but the dry way Jennie said that made Catherine smile. "We both know that's a real possibility.

Sandy's going to search the house to make sure there's nothing dangerous hidden in Pebbles room or the basement. Then we're going to see if we can find a private therapist for Pebbles. She clearly needs a lot of help."

Sharp blue eyes looked up. "Is Sandy mad at me?"

"Not at all, honey. She's at her wit's end with me, but she's very fond of you. If you'd like, I could drive you over there to say goodbye and get your things."

Jennie's head shook briefly. "I'll call her. That's good enough."

Catherine took the seat next to Jennie and nodded. "I can understand not wanting to go back. I'll trust your judgment."

Looking down, Jen said, "Ryan says I use bad judgment."

"Everyone does, sometimes. When we make mistakes we have to work harder to not make them again." She squeezed Jennie's leg. "I promise I will try to never let you down again."

"I'm really staying here?"

"You are... If you want to."

Jennie looked around, as if she were convinced someone was going to jump out from behind a chair to tell her it had all been a joke. "What happens when *you* get sick of me?"

Catherine had never been more certain that would not happen. If anything, her desire to parent Jennie was stronger than ever. Her confidence surged, and she looked directly into the girl's eyes. "That will *not* happen." She took Jennie's hand in hers and chafed it gently. "You will always have a home with me. *Always.* You know, I had to convince a lot of people that I was the right person to watch over you. I've been working on this for months."

"You have?"

"I have. And I'm very happy I did. We'll have our ups and downs, but no one will hurt you again. No one will touch you without your permission. I promise that on my life."

"Okay," she said, a small frown settling on her face. Not another word passed her lips. Like she didn't have a single question about how or why this massive change to her life had come about. She got up and went over to the edge of the deck and looked down at the cars that occasionally slid by. Watching her, Catherine had no idea what was going on in the girl's head. She wasn't even sure she was happy to be staying. It would take a very long time to know her better, to understand her cues. But even more important was gaining Jennie's trust. Jamie had been right. Sometimes you could let your fears run away with you. Other times you had to fight through them. Making sure Jennie was safe and secure and knew she could count on her was worth every bit of effort Catherine could expend.

The BMW was heavy with silence all the way back to Berkeley. Finally, Jamie couldn't stand it for another moment. "Am I getting the silent treatment too, or is that reserved for my mother?"

Ryan didn't answer immediately, but when she did, she sounded tired. "I'm just trying to get my thoughts together. Just because I'm quiet doesn't mean I'm quiet 'at' you."

"Don't even try to convince me you weren't being quiet 'at' my mother."

Several tense seconds passed before Ryan said, "Do you really think it would've been a good idea for me to say what was on my mind?" She turned her head, giving Jamie a perturbed look. "Sometimes, the smart thing is to keep your trap shut."

"Then you're the smartest woman in the world. You love nothing better than shutting me out."

"Oh, for god's sake, I do not!" Ryan yanked the car into the parking lane and turned it off. She sat there, frozen in the thrumming silence. For a full minute, she didn't move, didn't even blink. "Do you really want me to start venting about your mom? I'm more than happy to." Leaning over as far as her seatbelt would allow, she hissed, "I'd be damned giddy to get this off my chest!"

"She made a mistake! A fucking mistake!"

"She left Jennie in a dangerous situation. When. She. Didn't. Need. To. That's a *fuck* of a lot more than a mistake."

"How about you?" Jamie demanded. "Why didn't you keep track of Pebbles? If she's as dangerous as plutonium, I'd think you would have known what country she was in."

The only reaction Jamie could detect was a twitch around Ryan's left eye. What did it take to make this infuriating woman talk? "Did you ever check on her? Call her grandmother?"

Ryan finally turned and stared at her for what seemed like forever.

"That's the best you've got? Pebbles sneaking back into the country is the equivalent of your mom's not going to pick Jen up?"

"Yeah, it's close. Now go back in time and re-think your decision not to tell Sandy about Pebbles harassing Jen. If you'd reported her, she wouldn't have been in the house at all. She'd be in some kinda jail—which is where she belongs!"

Ryan shot her a look cold enough to shatter glass. Without another word, she started the car again and started to drive. "I'm going over to the group home to get Jen's things." She made very brief eye contact. "I'd rather go alone."

Now the silence was painful, as though it were on some kind of wavelength that could only be felt—not heard. As soon as Ryan pulled into the driveway, Jamie yanked on the door handle and got out. Just before slamming the door, she muttered, "You can be *such* a pain in the ass."

After a tense discussion with Sandy, Ryan stuffed all of Jen's things into grocery bags and made a few trips to load everything into the car. Her phone rang and she rolled her eyes when "Catherine" appeared on the screen.

"Hello," she said, trying to sound at least civil.

"It's me," Jennie said.

Ryan let out a breath, feeling like she'd dodged a bullet. "Hey, buddy. What's up?"

Quietly, like she was trying not to be heard, Jen said, "Ms. Smith says I'm staying here. Like for good."

"Yeah. That's true. Are you cool with that?"

Harshly, Jennie snapped, "Why's everybody fucking with me? Of course I wanna stay! Who wouldn't?"

"Right. Right. I'm sorry, buddy. I'm not thinking straight. I guess I'm jet-lagged."

"Ms. Smith said you're gonna bring my stuff for school. Are you?"

"I'm at your house right now. I've got your books and your uniforms."

"I didn't have time to get my computer before I took off. There's a big box kinda thing that covers the radiator in the kitchen. It's behind that."

"I'll go back and get it. I'll be over later tonight."

"Okay." Ryan could hear her take in a breath. "This is real, right?"

"Yeah, Jen. It's real."

After surprising and annoying Sandy by returning to root around in the kitchen, Ryan headed back towards Berkeley. But the thought of being in the car with Jamie for another forty-five minutes was too off-putting to consider. Once again, she pulled over to the side of the road, then texted her. "I need some alone time. I'll come get you after I take Jen's stuff to her."

It took just a minute for the reply to show on her screen. "Don't bother."

Furious, Ryan set off again, determined to get out of town before she did anything rash. Traffic wasn't bad, and it was only four when she found herself rolling down Chavez. She'd hardly been aware she was heading not for Pacific Heights, but Noe Valley, her unconscious mind leading her to where she needed to be. Her Aunt Maeve had a small driveway next to the house, and it was, blessedly, empty. Ryan knocked, perfunctorily, then entered the unlocked door. Ever since the carjacking, the family-wide practice of leaving doors unlocked had made her uneasy, but trying to get everyone to change was a battle she wasn't up to taking on. "Anybody home? Or are you trying to make things really easy for burglars?"

"The voice seems familiar," Maeve's melodic tone floated from the kitchen, "but it's been so long since I've heard it…" She emerged, a huge grin covering her face. "My darling girl. Come give me a hug." As she extended her arms, Ryan nearly leapt into them. Her feelings for her aunt could hardly have been stronger, and not having seen her for so long had been tougher than she'd bargained for.

"If Jamie hadn't kept my passport locked away, I would have been home in about three days."

"Listen to the lies tumbling from that mouth!" Maeve pulled away and pinched her on the cheek. "You know you had a divine time."

"Yeah, yeah, we did." Ryan stood tall and shook her head. "But our welcome home left an awful lot to be desired."

"Brendan called to tell us you'd found Jennie." She put her hands on Ryan's waist and looked into her eyes. "I was so relieved to learn she was all right, I've been floating around the house ever since. But you don't…

You certainly don't look happy."

"No. I'm definitely not happy." She started for the kitchen, always the locus of activity.

Maeve brushed by her to put the kettle on. "How about tea?"

"I'd love some."

"I can have scones ready in a half hour."

"Tea's enough, thanks. I need a little caffeine to be able to stay awake to fight with Jamie."

Maeve stopped what she was doing and gazed at Ryan for a few moments. "Oh, sweetheart, don't fight on your first day back. Can't you be happy Jennie's all right and leave it at that?"

Ryan sat down and considered the question. "Mmm, I'm not sure. I'm really ticked off, and Jamie's at least as angry as I am." She put her hands to her face and rubbed it. "I left her in Berkeley, and she told me not to bother coming back for her."

"Oh, my." Maeve sat down and put a hand on Ryan's knee. "What happened?"

Suddenly embarrassed about the fight, Ryan spent a minute trying to think if there was a way to omit any of the details. Regrettably, the situation wouldn't have made any sense without them. Taking a breath, she said, "I'm so furious with Catherine I couldn't even look at her when we took Jen over there. When we left, I kept my mouth shut to avoid saying anything harsh, but that's a guaranteed way to irritate Jamie." She extended her finger and gestured in a circle. "It went on from there."

Maeve grasped her shoulder and gave it a squeeze. "If the situation ever arises, feel free to keep your anger in check with me. I'm never in a rush to hear sharp words."

"Exactly!" Ryan slapped the table with the flat of her hand. "Trust me. Jamie doesn't want to hear me go ballistic, either. She wants me to be calm and talk everything out. But I can't do that!" She crossed her arms on the table and lay her head on top of them. "I hate it when we fight like this, especially when I'm jet-lagged and sleep-deprived. I didn't sleep at all last night, or this morning or whatever day it is."

"It's Monday, dear."

"It was Monday yesterday for me. And I truly don't want to have this day over again."

The kettle whistled, and Maeve got up to tend to it. "I'm sure you'll kiss and make up soon." After she poured the water into a tea pot, she scratched the back of Ryan's neck with her nails. Leaning over to kiss her cheek, she whispered, "You could apologize—sincerely. That might bring it to a close."

"I know, I know. I just…" She banged on the table with her fists. "How can she defend what Catherine did? She had Bren jumping through hoops to get custody, then waited five days after she got it to come home! Then, after she got home, she didn't rush right over there to get her. What the fuck?"

Maeve flashed a disapproving look, but Ryan didn't bother to apologize. She knew her aunt understood it was sometimes impossible to control your language—even though she clearly didn't appreciate vulgarity.

After pouring the tea, Maeve sat down and said, "I think you have to let this go, sweetheart. Catherine made a mistake."

"*A* mistake? Not calling to tell us Jen had run away? That alone is enough to make me blow a gasket!"

"Oh, sweetheart, I'm so sorry. I assumed you knew…"

"I knew nothing. Nothing." She dropped her head onto her arms again.

"That's simply dreadful. I wish I would have gone with my instinct."

"Which was?" Ryan lifted her head and gazed at her sharply.

She paused for a second, then spit it out. "I was…surprised you and Jamie didn't rush home. Your father and I talked about it at length, but we decided you must have had a hard time getting a flight or…" Shaking her head, she said, "It didn't make sense to either of us. I should know that when things don't make sense, they deserve further investigation."

"It's not your fault, Aunt Maeve. Catherine obviously wanted to handle this on her own, despite the fact that she clearly didn't know what the hell to do!"

Maeve continued to rub her shoulder. "If you'd been here this weekend to see the torment the poor woman went through, you wouldn't be so cross with her. I was afraid we were going to have to have her sedated."

Glumly, Ryan allowed, "I'm sure she was upset. I know she cares for Jen. I just…" She felt like growling, but stopped herself from being overly dramatic. "If it were up to me, I'd bring the kid over here tonight.

Catherine was a bad choice, and I'm angry with myself for not putting up a bigger fight."

"It's not up to you," Maeve said, her voice gentle and soft. "The decision has been made, and you need to support Catherine—not criticize her."

"I'm not!" Her voice took on the whining quality she hated to hear.

"I can't think of what you'd call this if it's not criticism. My advice is to make up with Jamie, then go over to Catherine's and have a celebratory dinner to welcome Jennie to her new home."

"I'm not hungry," she grumbled.

Maeve playfully tugged on her ponytail. "You're always hungry. Think of the prodigal son and try to recall the lesson."

"What's that? Screw up and spend all of your parents' money and you'll still be the favorite?"

"Yes, that's exactly right." This time the tug was a little sharper. "No wonder you found it so easy to leave the Church. You didn't understand a word of the gospel!"

"I know what you're saying. I do. I'm just…"

"You're angry and you're disappointed, and you worry that Catherine won't parent Jennie like you would." She patted her cheek, then cupped it lovingly. "I know you, sweetheart. But you're not in charge. You're going to have to sit on the sidelines and cheer them on. That's the loving thing to do."

"Sometimes I don't mind being a scold." A small smile peeked out.

"That will only make things worse. We all promised we'd support Catherine, and it's time to do just that."

"I'd rather stay here and wait for Jamie to come begging forgiveness."

"Then I'll call Catherine and ask her to bring Jennie over here for a welcome dinner." She leaned over and kissed Ryan's cheek. "Your good nature will reveal itself sooner or later, my dear girl. I simply think it should be sooner."

Catherine declined Maeve's invitation, saying Jennie had some schoolwork. But Ryan had all of Jen's stuff, so she had to appear at some point. Taking her aunt's advice, she went into the living room to text

Jamie. "My aunt says I'm being an asshole."

This time it took quite a while to get a return message. Knowing Jamie, she'd been asleep. For some odd reason, stress made her tired. "Your aunt's very perceptive." *Ouch.* Obviously, this wasn't going to blow over. Then another text came in. "Usually. But not today."

"I apologize for shutting you out."

"I apologize for poking you. Wasn't smart."

"Can I come get you?"

"I'm already at my mom's. Come over for dinner."

"Ok."

Ryan got up, went into the kitchen and gave her aunt a kiss on the cheek. "Thanks for the pep talk. We broke the ice with text messages." She tossed her phone into the air, as if it were scalding hot. "Seemed safer."

"I knew you two wouldn't stay angry for long."

"Luckily. I'm gonna take off. Wish me luck."

"You'll be fine. Just show Catherine the patience that I know you're filled with."

"I'm filled with something," Ryan teased. "I'm just not sure it's patience."

After having to park six blocks away, Ryan finally reached the house. In place of Marta, Jennie answered, an anxious look on her face as she looked at the bags in Ryan's hands. "Did you find my computer?"

"Sure did. Right where you said it would be." She placed one bag on the floor and put her arm around Jen's shoulders. "Why did you have to leave it in the kitchen? And why couldn't you tell Sandy you'd done that? She looked like she wanted to kick me in the butt when I was on my hands and knees digging around on the floor."

Jen shrugged her shoulders. "Couldn't trust her." Her eyes narrowed into slits. "She's on Pebbles' side…"

"You don't have to worry about that any more. Hell, you never have to go back to the East Bay if you don't want to."

"For now," she said, glumly. "I wonder where they'll put me next?" She looked up at Ryan, her doubts obvious. "There's no way this is gonna last."

Ryan gave it one hundred percent of her effort, and when they sat down to dinner things between her and Catherine seemed perfectly normal. Ryan watched her partner regale the group with stories of their last days in Sydney. Jamie was really performing—clearly trying to keep the mood light. As she watched, something clicked. Jamie wasn't able to admit to *herself* how badly Catherine had handled things. If she did that, she'd have to dredge up old memories of Catherine doing the exact same thing to her—abandoning her when she was stressed. It wasn't going to be easy, but Ryan decided right then that she'd do everything possible to keep her opinions about Catherine's parenting to herself. Her aunt was right. The decision had been made. Grousing about it wouldn't do a damn bit of good now.

After dinner, Ryan pulled the car up to the fire hydrant next to the house and waited for Jamie and Jennie to come down to help get all of the stuff Ryan hadn't been able to carry on her first trip. It took just a few minutes, and when they were finished, Ryan tugged on Jennie's shirt, keeping her close for a moment. "I know this is kinda freaking you out," she said, "but this didn't happen overnight. Everyone in the family got together and talked about where we thought you'd be happiest—and safest."

"Really?" Even in the dim light, Jennie's eyes shone with interest. "Your whole family?"

"Well, not the whole bunch. Just my father and aunt, my brother Brendan and his girlfriend, and Jamie's grandfather."

"*He* wanted to take me?" Her eyebrows shot up.

"No." Ryan chuckled. "He was just there when we were all talking. Catherine made the best case, but my father and aunt wanted you too. And if everyone didn't agree that I was too immature, I would have loved to have had you live with us."

Jennie gave her a look Ryan couldn't quite decipher. But its meaning became clear quickly. "Yeah. Everyone in town wants to take me home with them."

"Not everyone," Ryan said, smiling at the girl. "Just everyone who knows you well." She put her arm around Jen and gave her a long hug. "Catherine won, but we're all gonna try to be there when she's gotta go out of town and other things like that."

"She goes out of town a lot. A *whole* lot."

"I know. But it'll be okay. We'll make sure someone's here for you... every day."

Jennie gave her a lopsided grin. "Even if you don't, I should be okay. No one's gonna be huffing gas here."

Ryan laughed at the thought of Catherine or Marta sniffing gasoline fumes. She bumped Jen with her shoulder. "I know you're angry about what happened on Saturday, and you have every right to be. But we didn't screw up because we don't care, Jen. We all love you." She pulled her close and kissed the top of her head. "All of us."

Jamie walked up behind Jen and put a hand on her shoulder. "Put me in that crowd. I definitely love you." She added a kiss to Jen's cheek. "My mom's waiting for you."

Jennie looked up and nodded. Then she trudged up the stairs, nothing at all like a kid who'd finally gotten much more than she'd wished for.

Ryan walked around to her side of the car, got in and started the engine. Turning to Jamie, she said, "I think she'd feel more secure if she could go back to the group home—provided Pebbles was gone, of course."

"Yeah. Me too. Sandy made her mad, but she didn't lie to her. Like we did."

Ryan drove in silence for a few minutes. Then she made a few turns and pulled over at the top of the highest street in Pacific Heights. The car was pointed down towards the bay, with the twinkling lights of the East Bay and the bridge shining in the distance. After killing the engine, she eased her seat back and let out a sigh. "I had a super fun day. How about you?"

"It was stellar. Let's go find some other troubled kids tomorrow. Screwing up one isn't nearly enough."

Ryan took Jamie's hand, brought it to her mouth and kissed it. "I'm really sorry I made the day worse by making you angry. I hate to do that."

"I know, baby. And I'm sorry I need you to do something I know you're not capable of." She unbuckled her seat belt and kissed Ryan's cheek. "But it makes me crazy to have you clam up when I know you're mad. I assume you're really, really angry and are just waiting to lower the boom on me."

"That's never true," Ryan murmured. "I just get angry and know I'm going to say something I'll regret. I'm only trying to keep myself from hurting you."

"I don't know how to resolve this." Once again, Jamie kissed her. "But I promise to keep trying."

"Me too." Ryan leaned over and gave her partner a long, sweet kiss. "Can we finally go home and make love? We're like…" She checked her watch. "Nine hours overdue."

"Noe's closer. Let's head home. I'm ready to perform my wifely duties."

Ryan smiled at her as she started the car again. "I can't guarantee my stamina, but we need to connect."

"We need it bad. Hurry!"

After Jennie had been working on her homework for a few hours, Catherine cracked the door to her room, finding her sound asleep, her computer open and lying half on her leg. Stealthily, she entered the room and removed the computer, then closed it and put it on the chair by the bed. She fought the urge to kiss Jennie's head, not wanting to wake her. Instead, she took a soft throw from a chair and covered her with it. This wasn't the way she'd wanted to end their first day together, with Jennie lying on top of the bedspread, fully clothed. But there was no reason the end of the day would be ideal, given how things had gone earlier. Quietly, she exited and closed the door behind her, leaning against it for a moment to let out a satisfied sigh. This was all she'd wanted. Jennie lying safe and secure in her home—no troubled girls or harried housemothers in charge of her fate.

She checked her watch. Almost midnight. Giacomo would just be arriving at his office. With an embarrassing amount of pleasure, she dialed his cell phone.

"Tesoro? Tell me any news."

"Oh, Giacomo, it makes me feel so good to know you care."

"Of course I do! I've thought of nothing else! I spoke to the man who is in charge of security for my father's firm. He is going to make some calls today. He knows people who are skilled at tracking people who don't want to be found—"

"Giacomo," she interrupted. "You can relax. Jennie broke into Ryan and Jamie's house to get away from the girl who's been…" She wasn't sure how to characterize Pebble's actions. "Harassing her."

"Pardon? But why didn't she call you?"

She hadn't considered he'd ask that. There were some benefits from being so far away. Keeping humiliating gaffes from him was the one she most relished. "There were many layers of miscommunication. But she's asleep in her room now, and I'm finally breathing easier."

"You must be exhausted. I am, and I've only met the child once."

"I *am* exhausted. But I didn't want to go to bed until I'd spoken to you. I would have called you earlier, but I didn't want to disturb your sleep."

"That should never stop you, tesoro. When you need me, I want you to promise to call. Any hour of any day."

"I will," she said, tearing up at the sincerity in his voice.

"I'm so glad to know Jennie is well. You've made my whole day brighter."

"And hearing your voice makes me feel like I can sleep now. Not as well as I'd sleep with you here, but I feel much, much better."

"If you need me, I will come to you at once."

"No, that's not wise."

His voice turned soft and gentle. "When will we see each other? When you were here, you said early October might be possible."

"Oh, Giacomo, it's already October. I can't leave Jennie so soon. We're going to have to wait."

"I'm very sincere in my offer. I could come to San Francisco… tomorrow." She could just see the earnest look in his big, brown eyes.

"You know how much I'd love that, but I have to concentrate on Jennie for a while. If you were here, all I'd think of is…" It was silly to be embarrassed to admit how she longed for him, but it was somehow hard to express her inner feelings on the phone.

His voice dropped into a sexy growl. "That's what I would think of too. That's what I think of many hundreds of times each day. Your scent, the feel of your body when I hold you in my arms, your radiant smile." He sighed heavily. "You hold my attention, no matter how far away you are."

"And you hold mine. But I have to put Jennie first—at least for a while. Then we can meet in New York."

"I will make plans—tentative plans—for November. *Early* November. That is as long as I can wait."

"All right. A month should be long enough to have things settled here."

"That is far too long, but I will spend my days dreaming of waking to the most beautiful face I've ever seen."

Chapter Two

R yan growled at the alarm when it rang at six. Slapping at it with a fist, she grumbled, "Whose idea was it to keep this stupid therapy appointment?"

"Yours," Jamie said, clearly wanting to go back to sleep. She pulled the pillow from beneath Ryan's head and placed it over her own. "Bye."

That wasn't the warmest sendoff, but Ryan had only herself to blame. At the very least they should have gone back to Berkeley the night before. But after the tension-filled evening with Catherine and Jen, it had been all she could do to drive to Noe.

They'd both been intent on making love, but some evil force didn't want that to happen. Several cousins were at the house, watching a baseball game, and for some crazy reason, Jamie couldn't relax enough to enjoy herself when she could hear other people in the house. With the boyos gathered around a blaring TV, they could have been howling like monkeys and not be heard. But Jamie had been unbending, capping their crappy day with Ryan frustrated and grumpy.

Ryan's feet hit the floor the same moment Duffy started to snuffle under the door. He was uncanny. Resisting the urge to let him in so he could leap on Jamie and kiss her until she screamed, Ryan spoke softly. "No, Duffy. Wait." His whimper tugged at her heartstrings, but she was proud of her boy. He'd sit quietly—unless Conor or Kevin made a noise. Then he'd try for another victim.

After a very quick shower and an even quicker potty break for her boy, Ryan got into her car for the drive to Oakland. She truly hated to drive, but it would take her forever to get there going from MUNI to

BART to a bus. After a few minutes of self-assessment, she had to admit that driving was just nicer. And now that she had a car, she found lots of excuses to use it. That's how they sucked you in. Very few people resisted the luxuries they were able to afford.

Her mood was gloomy when she parked in a public lot not too far from her therapist's office. She hated therapy. Truly hated it. The concept of having to talk about emotional issues with strangers was anathema. She wished she was the kind of person who could open up and let other people into her inner circle, but that wasn't gonna happen. Some things were hardwired.

Barb jumped up when Ryan entered the waiting room to give her a rough hug. "I thought you'd never come back," she said as she added a lusty slap to Ryan's back.

"A week would have been plenty for me, but my partner would travel all the damn time." Ryan caught herself and decided that was enough grousing about privilege. "But it was great. How are you doing?"

"I'm okay." She smiled and Ryan realized that was a pretty rare thing for the normally taciturn police officer to do. "I'm getting close to making a decision about either going back on the force or starting something new."

"What would you do if you started something new?"

"Private security." She laughed and shook her head. "What am I supposed to do? All I know is police work."

"That's nice, in a way. You've worked hard at it and gotten really good at something." She was just about to complain about having too many interests, but wisely kept her mouth shut. Damn, she was a real pain today!

Ellen opened the door and beckoned them in. Ryan managed to smile, even though her stomach was always in knots when that big, dark door opened.

Catherine pulled up in a long line of cars to drop Jennie off at school. "Thanks," Jen said. "Should I…wait for you when I'm done?"

"You should." Catherine ruffled her hair, then gently patted her cheek. "I hope you have a lovely day."

"Okay." She started to get out of the car. "Uhm…you too. I guess I'll see you."

"Bye," Catherine said, before starting to pull away. She went just a block, then started searching for a place to park. She had to speak to the principal, and this time a phone call would not do. But with Jennie so anxious, she didn't want the girl to know about the visit. After scouring the neighborhood in vain, she drove back home, changed into walking shoes, and headed back on foot. It wasn't far, less than a mile, but it hadn't occurred to her to let Jennie walk. Now that she had her, she was skittish about letting her wander the neighborhood alone.

Sister Mary Magdalene was pacing back and forth behind her desk when Catherine knocked on the door frame. The sister smiled and signaled her to come in. There was usually a secretary in the outer office, but today the sister was on her own. "Yes, I agree. And we're more than willing to comply. But if the building department can't give us clear guidelines, we're simply guessing, and I'm sure that's not what you want." She held up a finger, indicating she'd be finished in a moment. "Yes, I think that's best. Thank you for your time. I look forward to hearing from you again."

When she hung up, she sat down and let her head lean back against her chair. "It's awfully early to have as many things go wrong as they have today." Sitting up straight, she placed her hands on her desk and gave Catherine an inquisitive look. "Shall we talk about Jennie?"

"I'm afraid we might be doing an awful lot of that." Catherine looked into the sister's warm, open face and felt like crying. "I'm in over my head."

Sister got up and moved to the front of the desk, leaning against it. She spoke softly, but there was a steely tone to her voice. "Nonsense. Yes, this is going to be a massive adjustment for you, but Jennie's a good kid at heart. She hasn't had nearly enough time to be a child, and I assume she'll have many fits and starts in her maturation process. But with your help, she'll get there."

"I *lost* her," Catherine said, feeling her cheeks flush. "I lost the child for three whole days. The first days I was her legal guardian."

"Technically, I suppose that's true, but in reality Jennie ran away. That's not the same as forgetting about her. She's a survivor, Catherine. When she feels like she has no other options, she makes her own decisions.

Granted, they're sometimes rash and immature, but I think it's a positive sign that she ran away rather than lose control with the other girl."

"I…suppose that's true."

"From the few flashes I've seen of her temper, I'm certain it was wise for her to get a handle on it before she did something she'd regret."

"She should have talked to her house mother."

"Of course she should have. But she obviously didn't trust her." She leaned over and gazed directly into Catherine's eyes. "You've got to earn and keep her trust. If you do that, I'm certain things will turn out fine."

"And if I don't?"

"I think we know the answer to that," she said gently. "You're going to have to work hard at this. Much harder than you did when your daughter was the same age. But she's reachable. I'm certain of that."

The words were simple. Easy, in fact. But they seemed completely out of reach. Like they were in a language she'd never been exposed to. "What do I do? Where do I start?"

"Talk with her. Ask her what she expects. How she'd like to structure her situation. Have a dialogue with her. Then I'd suggest finding a good therapist."

"I have a psychiatrist. He's down in the South Bay though…"

Sister waved her hand. "She doesn't need a psychiatrist. A child and family therapist or a social worker will do just fine. The girl's problems are simple. She just needs consistency and clear rules. Letting her build a relationship with a therapist will give her another adult who can step in and stop her before she gets off track."

"You really think she'll do well living with me?"

"I'm certain of it," Sister said, a big smile warming her face. "If I were a betting woman I'd wager a good amount of money on it."

The moment Catherine left the principal's office, she took out her phone and dialed a number from her "favorites" list. "Maeve?" she asked when the phone was answered.

"Hello, Catherine. Is our favorite teenager back in school today?"

"She is. But I need a pep talk before this afternoon when I have to pick her up. Are you available?"

"I am." A shriek echoed in the background. "I'm sorry for that. A certain toddler needs her morning nap. She's been up since five."

"Oh, I don't want to bother you. We can talk another time."

"No, no, give me twenty minutes and Caitlin should be down. But…" She paused for a few moments. "If she's not asleep when you get here, I'll never get her to cooperate. If the front door's closed, give me a few more minutes. If it's open, come right in…quietly."

Catherine allowed a half hour to pass, just to be safe. She knew from experience that Caitlin napped for an hour or even two, and she was afraid she'd need every moment of Maeve's time to stoke her courage.

Thankfully, the door was open as she walked up the stairs. Maeve was in the living room when Catherine entered, and she put her finger to her lips and tip-toed out to the back porch. Catherine followed her, and they each took seats on the mismatched lawn chairs, then Maeve took the baby monitor from her pocket and placed it on the table. "I should have offered you tea, but I was afraid of making a single extra noise." She let her head loll back while taking in a breath. "I might offer to trade one troubled teen for an overly exuberant toddler. Caitlin's a tiny hurricane today."

Catherine reached over and took her friend's hand. "If I'm asking for too much of your time…"

Maeve's free hand fluttered in front of her. "Don't be daft." She chuckled, her eyes twinkling with good humor. "Talking to adults during the day keeps me sane."

"I wish that could do the trick for me. As it is, I feel like I'm holding onto my sanity by a thread."

Clearly concerned, Maeve leaned close. She had the most empathetic eyes Catherine had ever seen. Like they simply weren't capable of a sharply judging look. Even when one was well deserved. "Tell me what's on your mind. Did Jennie not take the news about moving in with you well?"

"No, that's not it." She let out a wry laugh. "Although she certainly didn't seem very excited about it. More like she was resigned to do whatever she was told."

"I can imagine that's what's got her through life so far. Causing as little trouble as possible is probably her way of getting along."

"I'm sure that's true. God knows the child has more ways of coping than I do." She took a breath and let it out slowly to get her thoughts in order. "That's what I'm worried about. I know..." She was so embarrassed to be crying—again—in front of Maeve. She and Martin had been so supportive when Jennie was missing, never criticizing her, even though she deserved their censure. "I know what I did was unforgivable. I also know in my heart that Jennie and I should always be honest with each other. But I can't bear to tell her that I left her alone...in that house... with that girl..." She broke down in sobs for what seemed like the hundredth time in the last few days. "I will never, ever forgive myself for being so utterly frightened. Frightened of something so ridiculous." She met Maeve's understanding gaze. "How can an adult be afraid of taking a needy child into her home?"

Maeve clasped Catherine's hand between both of her own. Her hands were warm and soft, reassuring by their very touch. "One...it's not wise to tell her things that will only upset her more. There's no sin in having secrets from a child. She doesn't need to know anything more than that she's away from that troubled girl. Permanently."

"Are you sure?"

"I'm positive," she said, her tone so decisive Catherine didn't have the nerve to question her.

"And two, it's time to stop lambasting yourself. You can't dwell on the mistakes you've made. There isn't time!" She chuckled a little. "Children throw so many challenges at you that you don't have the luxury of lamenting your bad decisions. You try to snatch whatever you can learn from the situation and move on to the next one."

"Maeve," she said, her voice aching with pain. "I knowingly let that child stay in a home where she was being threatened. That's not something I can brush away."

"Can you go back in time and change things?"

"Of course not." Her eyes closed tightly, trying to stop the tears. "But I'd give so much to be able to." Sniffling, she added, "Ryan's not even able to look me in the eye. I think she'd slap me if she wasn't so well mannered."

Maeve gripped her hand once again and shook it. "Only one thing matters now. What have you learned from this experience?"

Catherine blinked slowly, thinking of the last few days. "I'm not sure I've learned anything. I *know* I should have never gone to Australia... But I'm not sure I won't do something like that again. When I'm anxious I tend to travel...anywhere. And I *know* I should have come home the moment I heard Pebbles was back in the house. But I convinced myself another day or two wouldn't hurt." She met Maeve's eyes, relieved to still see her open, accepting gaze. "I have a very well-developed ability to ignore the little voice in my head...I suppose it's my conscience...that tells me I'm being selfish or short-sighted."

"Then you *have* learned something. You've learned that you have to listen to that little voice—even when you're frightened." She leaned forward and wrapped an arm around Catherine's shoulders. "I know you were frightened to take Jennie into your home. Don't be shy about admitting that."

"I was terrified," Catherine sobbed, burrowing into Maeve's motherly embrace. "I needed Jamie and Ryan to help me figure things out...to step in and convince her if Jennie didn't want to come..." She sucked in a shaky breath. "I was worried about a hundred different things, yet ignored the one very real thing...the very real *threat* that Jennie had to deal with." Sitting up, Catherine reached into her purse and took out a handkerchief. She dabbed at her eyes and nose, deeply embarrassed to have once again lost control. "If I had to do it over, I'd have voted for you and Martin taking the girl. That would have let me be the friend who lends a hand, clearly a role I'm more suited for." A bitter laugh forced its way up. "That's what I was for Jamie through most of her youth."

"That's not true in the least! And, even though you don't believe it now, you're the right person to parent Jennie. I would have always been juggling her needs with Caitlin's, and Caitlin's would have had to take precedence. You can concentrate on Jennie, giving her the kind of undivided attention I don't think she's ever had." She leaned close and spoke softly. "And, even though I'd never say this to his face, my Marty can be awfully strict with children. It's one thing when they've been raised that way since birth, but quite another to try to lay down the law with a teenager." She sat up tall and added, "I know you'll reason with her and talk things out. In my opinion, that's what she needs."

"That's essentially what Sister Mary Magdalene thinks."

"Take her word for it, Catherine. That woman's watched more girls grow up than you can count. She'll give you good advice. I promise."

"But how do I get over the guilt?" Catherine asked, the weight of her sins feeling like they'd crush her.

Maeve's warm, caring gaze grew sober. "You ignore it. It won't help Jennie to have you beating your chest and saying mea culpas. And if it won't help Jennie, you don't have the time to devote to it." She got to her feet and pulled Catherine up. Placing her hands on her shoulders, she said, "Focus on the girl. Her problems are the ones that matter now. Move forward, Catherine. The past is a luxury you cannot afford to dwell on."

Forty-five minutes after their therapy session ended, Barb and Ryan stood in front of the building. "I think you made the right decision," Barb said. "You're doing great, and dragging yourself over here from the city doesn't make any sense."

"I'm really glad Ellen agreed. Jamie'd never let me quit if I didn't get the 'all clear.'"

Chuckling, Barb said, "There's no way Ellen gave you the all clear. She could just tell you were done and decided not to argue with you."

"Same thing," Ryan said, winking. "Jamie knows it's my modus operandi to wear people down until they get so sick of me they're glad to let me go."

"You'll be fine. We'll just do what Ellen suggested and be done with it."

Ryan shifted her weight from one foot to the other. Her eyes darted all around as they always did when she felt vulnerable. "Uhm…did you drive?"

"No. I live right on the 58 line. I took the bus. Why?"

"Uhm…" She not only couldn't stand still, she couldn't look Barb in the eye. Showing a stranger how frightened she was sucked in every way. "Will you drive my car?"

Barb clapped a hand on her shoulder and casually said, "Sure," making it seem like something they did all the time.

A few minutes later they were heading for the scene of the crime.

It had been over ten months, but Ryan hadn't been anywhere near any of the streets she'd been carried through on the night of the carjacking. Of course she was able to drive on the main ones—you couldn't get around town without doing so. But the smaller ones, the ones that just thinking about made her break out in a cold sweat—she'd avoided them consistently and purposefully.

It took a while to get to the Mission, but Ryan would have gratefully wasted another few days driving around aimlessly. Her stomach was a mess, and she was going to have to crack a window open if she kept sweating this much. Barb probably wouldn't have volunteered to go with her if she'd known what a wreck Ryan would be. But her years of police work allowed her to calmly chatter away like they were going out for an ice cream cone.

Finally, they reached the intersection. Ryan hadn't taken this shortcut to the Bay Bridge since that evening, even though it had always been her favorite. Jamie hadn't mentioned the change, but she had to know why Ryan stayed on the main thoroughfare even in heavy traffic. That seemed to be her way. She let Ryan broach difficult memories on her own, but maybe that wasn't the best idea, given Ryan's talent at avoiding things that troubled her. Sitting there, in the quiet car, only the ticking of Barb's watch breaking the silence, Ryan was astounded by the differences she saw.

The night of the carjacking had been foggy and gloomy with rain coming down in sheets. Every red light was a little lurid, every green one almost too bright. Garish, really. But today, a warm, sunny October morning, bore almost no resemblance to the streets that she still saw in an occasional nightmare.

"It's like a different place," she whispered.

"Huh? Didn't catch that."

"Oh. Sorry. I didn't realize I was speaking out loud." Ryan got out and did a slow turn, looking at every part of the intersection. Trucks, delivery vans and passenger cars slipped past her, all taking their wares over to the East Bay. Business as usual. Mundane. She got back into the car and found herself speaking. "It was raining that night. Foggy too. There was something…" She closed her eyes and tried to think. "Something kinda sinister about the scene—even before those two evil geniuses showed up. I think I'll try to replace that memory with this one."

"Good idea. It probably wouldn't hurt to come by at different times of the day to desensitize yourself." She put her hand on the shifter. "Ready to go?"

"Yeah." Ryan swallowed, then said, "Go straight for three or four blocks. I'll tell you where to turn." In silence, Barb inched along, giving Ryan plenty of time to take in every view. Ryan's voice caught when she said, "Take a right here." As they turned, she thought she might need to find a bathroom really, really quickly. As much as her stomach didn't want to take this trip, it was her guts that were thinking about vacating the premises. But she soldiered on, allowing the images to bombard her.

"You okay?" Barb asked gently.

"No. But keep going. Moscone Center," she managed, knowing Barb would know the way.

It was incredibly hard to keep her eyes open, but she forced herself to look at the intersections, the apartment buildings, the hospitals, churches, and schools she'd seen that night, knowing she'd never see them again. She'd had so much time to think, to reflect, to plan as they'd flown along that night. It had been like everything was in slow motion, the way a pitch sometimes seemed right before she hit it on the screws. One thought kept poking through her concentration during that horrible night. She was on her last ride through her city. The place she loved more than any other. A couple of small-time thugs were going to take everything that mattered and snuff it all out. And she was powerless to stop them.

When they reached the convention center Ryan tried to control her breathing. But as she thought of the prayers she'd offered up to her mother that night, she lost it. She thought of her parents, newly arrived immigrants, meeting and falling in love at Old St. Patrick's. The two people in the world who loved her with every bit of their hearts—and neither could help. Neither could rescue her, though she knew, without question, that each would give their lives for hers. She would die alone.

Her head dropped to the dash and she cried like a child. Not just because of the horrid memories. But because of all she'd lost that night. She'd been a different person ten months earlier. A braver, stronger, more resilient, more...faithful woman then. She'd lost her faith, and that had been a much, much more difficult trial than she'd admitted to anyone. As she sat there with a near stranger, crying like mad, the loss washed over her in waves.

"Hey," Barb soothed, stroking her back. "We don't have to do this. Maybe a little more therapy isn't a bad idea…"

Ryan sat up and sucked in a very shaky breath. "No. I can do it. I've *got* to." She wiped her eyes on her sleeves, then pointed. "Up to 7th Street."

Barb followed directions, and as they reached the street Ryan was hit with another memory. Of Jamie screaming and crying, begging her to hold on. It was sickening. Too sickening. "Wait!" As soon as the car stopped she fumbled with her seatbelt, threw open the door and vomited, splashing the contents of her stomach all over the front tire. She stood there, bent over, gasping for breath. After a minute, she spit in the street, then got back in, shaking and dripping with sweat. "Fuck me."

"Let's stop and get something to drink. Don't you wanna wash your mouth out?"

Ryan leaned her head against the window and took in a few deep breaths. If she stopped, she might not be able to continue. "Hang a left on Leavenworth. This is where the fun begins."

Barb didn't reply. She just put a hand on Ryan's thigh and gave it a good, hard squeeze.

Her voice was thin and weak when she said, "This is where the guy started shooting through the roof."

"You're alive," Barb reminded her. "They tried their best, but couldn't take you out."

"Just luck. I wish I believed there was a reason I made it, but it was just luck."

Barb looked at her for a few moments, then said, "I'd take some of that luck any time you want to share it."

"I know that. I really do." Her hands weren't shaking as badly, and when she really concentrated she could tell her fear was easing just a little. Barb was right. Ryan was alive because of a few lucky breaks. But no matter how it happened, she *was* alive. Something else would get her eventually. But she wasn't going to willingly give the assholes who tried to kill her another day of her life. "I got lucky. You didn't."

Barb shot her a look, and when she spoke her voice was cold and flat. "My luck was fine. My partner's sucked."

Ryan turned to look at her. As bad as her own trauma was, it was nothing like that guilt she would have felt if she'd killed someone she cared about. She wasn't at all sure she'd be able to go on. "Yours wasn't so hot either. Go up to Nob Hill."

The car climbed slowly, trailing behind a cable car. When they reached the top, Ryan felt like she did on a roller coaster right before a fall. Her stomach was in her throat, and she braced herself for a wild descent. But the car moved along slowly, cautiously. Just like every other time she'd crested the hill. It was a normal day, with cabs and limos and people standing out in front of the big hotels, just going about their business.

"Back over to Mission Street," Ryan said, her excitement growing. "Then head right down to the water."

This was the worst part. When Jamie was hanging out of the window, holding onto Ryan's leg with all of her strength, telling her a man was going to get out of the car and shoot her. She knew he had a bullet left. Just one. But at that range a five-year-old could have gotten it done.

A remarkable feeling of calm, thoughtful consideration had come over her that night. She would do what she had to do to save her own, Jamie's and Caitlin's life. But even though the world would have been a slightly better place with both of the brothers no longer in it, she'd consciously decided to wound, rather than kill, the driver. Even though they would have happily killed her, that didn't give her permission to do the same. Sinking to their level would have ruined her. The months of bitter recriminations she'd had over that decision vanished. She'd done the right thing. The only thing possible. She'd stayed true to herself.

"Where to?" Barb asked, yanking her from her thoughts.

They were cruising along the Embarcadero, the water blue and calm, dotted with ferry boats. Alcatraz popped out of the glimmering depths, seemingly just feet away from shore. Everything was normal. Blessedly, gloriously normal. The city was hers again. Every damn street of it. "Head back to Oakland," she said, brimming with confidence. "We've got another stop to make."

At two o'clock that afternoon, Jamie answered her cell phone. "Where *are* you?" she said, her patience at an end.

"Hadda get somethin' done."

"That's what you said at nine o'clock this morning. I've been sitting around all day, waiting for you."

"Done now. How 'bout pickin' me up?"

"Pick you up? You drove." Letting the tone of Ryan's voice and her sloppy enunciation reach her brain, Jamie yelped, "You're drunk!"

"Totally toasted. Whaddya say? Do I havta sit in this crummy bar 'til I'm sober? Gonna be a while."

"Where are you?"

"Hey," Ryan said to someone. "Where in the hell are we?"

Jamie could hear a woman's equally slurred mumblings. Then Ryan came back on the line. "The Last Chance. Oakland." She started to giggle. "I couldn't tell you how to get here if I had a map right in front of me."

"I'll find it. And Ryan?"

"Yeah?"

"Come up with a really good excuse for why you're in a bar, drunk, with another woman, in the middle of the day. While you're doing that, I'll go try to find a car to drive. I took mine in to have the oil changed, and had to leave it."

"Sorry," she said, snickering like a kid.

"I'll call when I'm close. In the meantime, stop drinking!"

"Maybe one more," she said. "It's my turn to buy. Can't be cheap."

"Keep working on that excuse, okay? You're really gonna need it."

"Roger that." She giggled again. "Sounds dumb when your name's not Roger."

"Goodbye, Ryan. Don't even think of leaving wherever you are. You'd fall off the curb."

"Roger. I mean Jamie." As she hung up, Jamie could hear her giggling again. *Good lord!*

It took quite a while to find a car, but Ryan's aunt Deirdre ultimately offered one up. Jamie only lied a little, telling her that Ryan was stuck in the East Bay with car trouble. Not being sober enough to drive was car trouble, wasn't it?

The bar was in a sketchy, nearly deserted neighborhood near the port. What in the hell was Ryan doing here? Looking for work as a stevedore?

Jamie pulled over near where a huge chain-link fence warned trespassers to stay out. The dogs that crashed into the fence, viciously growling and almost making her wet her pants were a less subtle warning. After dialing, she waited for Ryan to pick up.

"H'lo?" a strange woman's voice answered.

"Is...Ryan there?"

"Yeah. She's...Oh, there she is. Hold on." The woman started to chuckle. "She was dancing."

Flames were nearly sprouting from Jamie's ears.

"Yeah?"

"I'm in front. Stop dancing and get out here."

"'Kay. We'll be right there."

"We?" Jamie demanded to a connection that had been severed. A minute later, Ryan and another woman exited, both massively drunk. They formed an "A" as they leaned against each other at the shoulder, their legs working to hold them upright. They were just ten yards away, but Ryan stopped and looked around, like she had no idea where to go. Given that Jamie's car was the only one on the street, save for Ryan's nice, shiny BMW that would probably be stripped for parts in a matter of moments, it became clear how astoundingly drunk Ryan was.

She rolled down the window and called out, "Over here."

Ryan's head didn't snap right to it, but eventually she turned her gaze towards Jamie as a big, dumb-looking smile covered her face. She and her new friend approached the car. "We gotta take Barb home," she said as she fell into the front seat. "Is this..." She looked around, clearly puzzled. "Did you rent this?"

"Yeah. I found a place that rents fifteen-year-old Honda Civics." Pointing at the huge containers of laundry detergent and fabric softener in the back seat that Deirdre hadn't toted up to her house yet, Jamie added, "And they come with cleaning supplies."

"Weird," Ryan said, before resting her head against the window.

Jamie looked in the back seat, seeing their guest do the same thing. At top volume, she demanded, "One of you jokers has to tell me where to take Barb."

"Dunno," Ryan mumbled, eyes closed, head smashed into the window. "Oakland, I think."

Jamie turned around and grasped Barb's knee. "Wake up! Where do you live?"

"Lea me lone," she grumbled.

"God damn it!" Jamie got out, opened the back door, lifted the woman's purse and rifled through it until she found her wallet. "This better be a current address," she snapped before returning the wallet and hurling the purse at her sleeping passenger. "And put your seatbelt on." When she got no response, she half-straddled the woman and buckled her in, cursing under her breath. Ryan had better have a damned good excuse for this, but what that would be was anyone's guess.

Catherine sat in her car, anxiously waiting for Jennie to emerge from school. She scanned the ebullient faces of the first group of girls to emerge, all clearly relieved at having another day ticked off the school calendar. Group after group dashed out, most of them looking like they were fleeing a burning building. Then the more laid-back girls started to stream out. Many of them were alone, as was Jennie when she stood just outside the doorway and looked up and down the street.

Something about the poor child always made her look like she was being tested. If Catherine could effect any change, it was that Jennie would one day believe she was in charge of her own life.

Catherine had the top down, and she stuck her hand up in the air and waved. Jennie made eye contact, then started for the car, with Catherine watching her carefully. Jennie had seemed lighter, more playful when Catherine had first met her. Now, there was a hesitancy in her stride, a carefulness that made her seem much older than her age.

"Hi," she said, opening the door and sliding in.

"Hi there. How was school?" Oh, that was a silly question. No child ever had an answer for that.

"Fine. What's up?"

"Up? Nothing that I can think of. What would you like to do?"

"Huh?" Jennie regarded her with an expression full of confusion.

"Is there anything you'd like to do?"

"To do?" Completely blank. "Like what?"

"Oh, I don't know. We could go shopping, or out for a snack, or to the park. Or a museum."

"Museum? Just us?"

Catherine gazed at her, trying to guess what her question really meant. "Who would you like to take?"

"Huh?"

It would be so nice if Jennie could learn not to use that word so often. It truly made her seem much less bright than she was. But grammar and word choice were probably not the best places to start when forming a good relationship. "I'm not sure what you're asking, Jennie. Do you want to bring a friend?"

"No." She gave Catherine a narrow-eyed stare. "I thought you had to have a teacher take you." Frowning, she added, "You know. When your class goes."

"Oh! No, no, you don't need to go with your class." She tried to gauge Jen's interest. "You've been to the DeYoung, haven't you?"

"Uh-huh. My art class went last year."

"Let's go again. I haven't simply looked around in the longest time."

"Now? I've got homework," she warned.

"Is it in any area I can help you with?"

"I dunno. What do you know?"

Catherine laughed at her directness. "I'm reasonably skilled in English, French, Italian, history, social studies. Things that don't have formulas or numbers."

"Me too," Jen said, smiling for the first time. "Ryan wasn't here when I had to sign up for classes, so I didn't take any math. After the two classes I took in summer school, I'm done with the minimum."

"That's all I took, and it hasn't hurt me," Catherine said, adding a wink.

They'd been wandering around the museum for a while when a savory aroma wafted past them. Catherine caught sight of Jennie staring longingly towards the scent. "Would you like a snack, honey?"

"Really?"

"Oh course." She put her hand on her shoulder and spoke quietly. "Whenever you're hungry, just let me or Marta know."

She frowned. "We could only eat what they gave us when they gave it to us at the group home. Didn't matter if you were hungry or not."

Catherine had her doubts about that, but Jennie often had a unique take on events. She could have easily misconstrued a reasonable rule. "At our house, you can eat when you're hungry. Let's have a little something. We'll appreciate the collection much more if we don't want to nibble on the paintings."

Tuesday afternoon was a slow time, and they easily secured a table with a view of the sculpture garden. They settled into seats with a sandwich and soft drink for Jen and an espresso for Catherine.

Jennie took a big bite of her sandwich, then mumbled around it, "Real good."

When was the proper time to drop hints about table manners? Probably not the first week. "Are you having fun?"

"Yeah." A second passed where she looked uncertain. "That's okay, isn't it?"

What could that possibly mean? "Are you asking if it's all right to have fun?" *This was like communicating with an alien!*

"In a museum," Jennie clarified. "When we came before we had to be quiet and pay attention. They told us not to have fun."

It wasn't *possible* that anyone had told her that. Jennie extrapolated the mildest warnings into rules, yet took the clearest rules and broke them with impunity. She was a mass of contradictions and surprises. Many of them terrifying. "Yes, honey, of course it's okay to have fun. I always have fun when I'm looking at art."

"Why do you know so much about this stuff?"

"I was an art history major in college. And I read a lot of books about artists. Art is my passion."

"Mine too." She nodded, thoughtfully. "I'm not real good, but drawing's my favorite thing."

"That leads me to a question. I know you don't have a lot of free time, but I want to make sure you have the opportunity to do something that appeals to you. Would you like to take clarinet lessons or work with someone on your drawing?"

"Like...another class?"

"No, not at all. More like a tutor. For fun, Jennie, only for fun."

"Hmm." She took another bite and seemed distracted as she chewed. "Not sure. I promised Ryan I'd work on the clarinet she gave me, but I really, really love drawing. I might be able to take an art class next term, but I don't have any now."

"Let's see if you have time for both. And if you find you can't devote time to the clarinet, just tell Ryan. I'm sure she was only trying to help you do something you wanted."

"No, I think she wants me to do the stuff I say I'm gonna do. She'd rather I was responsible than happy."

Catherine had to bite her tongue not to laugh out loud. "That does sound a little like her. She's a very big fan of being responsible."

"That's okay." Jennie shrugged. "I'm a goof-off."

"No, you're not," Catherine insisted. "You've had a lot of stress in the last few years, honey. Now you're going to be in one place, with your own room, and the opportunity to pursue your interests. You're going to flourish. I'm certain of that."

Jennie shrugged again, dropped her head and concentrated on her sandwich.

"Are you... Is there anything on your mind? About living with me?"

"Mmm... Not sure. Should there be?"

Always trying to test to see if she was within guidelines. "Well, let's talk about us. What would you like to call me?"

Her eyes grew wide. "I don't think I..." She shook her head, still looking a little tentative. "Are you like my mom now? 'Cause I don't think I could..."

Catherine covered her hand with her own. "No! I'm not trying to take your mother's place. She will always be your mom. And one day, hopefully soon, you and she can see each other."

One shoulder rose and fell as Jennie looked away. "Yeah. I don't think that's gonna happen."

"If you want it to, I'll support you. And if you choose not to, that's fine too. As for us, I'd say that we're more like close friends."

"We're...roommates?"

"Mmm... A little more than that. Let's say I'm taking Sandy's place. Would you like to refer to me like you did to her?"

"I guess I could."

"It's fine if you want to keep going like we have been. But if you start to have friends over..."

"Friends over...to your house?"

"Your house," Catherine reminded her. "It's your house."

Frowning, Jen said, "I don't feel like that."

"You will. I'm certain. And one of the ways you'll feel like it's yours is if you have friends over when you want to."

"My friends don't know about you, or Ryan, or Jamie, or the group home, or my mom…" She shook her head briskly. "None of it."

"If you want to have close friends, you need to welcome them into your life, honey. What would you feel comfortable telling them?"

"Dunno." She crossed her arms over her chest and leaned back in her chair, the very image of a sullen teenager.

"How about this? Why not tell your friends about your father? That he's in the Navy and is being sent to… Where is he?"

"San Diego now, but he's gonna have to go back on a ship soon."

"Right. That he's in San Diego and unable to predict where he'll be next. So you're staying with me to finish high school."

"Who are you? My…what? My aunt?"

"Mmm… It's not wise to lie. Why not say I'm a close family friend?"

"I guess you are…" Her eyes darted around as she seemed to consider the situation. "I guess that could work." She gazed at Catherine for a moment. "Do I havta have friends over?"

"Of course not. It's your home, Jennie. To share or keep private. The decision is yours."

The girl looked even more confused. She clearly had little experience in making her own decisions, and that had to make each one seem bigger than it truly was.

They spent another bit of time talking about the Bay Area Figurative Art movement, and Catherine caught herself when Jennie started to look bored. "I'm so sorry," she said. "When I talk to someone who likes art, I can get carried away."

"I got a little lost. That's all. I don't know who any of those guys are. In school, they mostly talk about the really old guys, like Rembrandt and Van Gogh and Monet and stuff."

"Next time we can go to the Legion of Honor if you'd like. That collection focuses much more on European paintings."

"No, I like this stuff better. I like things that look like they're still around, know what I mean?"

"I think I do," Catherine said. "Maybe we should explore more contemporary art."

"This stuff's good," Jennie decided. She peered at the description. "1950. That's a long time ago, but stuff still looks like that. The European stuff's always about churches and Jesus and stuff that looks a million years old. I understand it's important…"

"There's no crime in finding what speaks to you, honey. Over time, your tastes will change, but I'm happy to admit to still liking a lot of things I was very interested in when I was your age."

"I don't think you were ever my age," Jennie said, a grin quirking up.

"I'm certain I was. If my mother were here, she could vouch for me." Catherine put her hand on Jennie's shoulder and led her towards the exit. "I know what I'd like if I were your age today."

"What?"

"I'd like a cell phone. If we rush, we can get to the store before they close."

"I don't need one…"

"I'd like for you to have one." She leaned over and placed a kiss on Jennie's head. "I always want you to be able to get in contact with me."

"Okay." She looked a little skittish. "But I might lose it. I lose stuff all the time."

"Then we'll get you another one." Catherine put her arm around Jen and guided her out. One day, with luck, the girl would be able to accept things with equanimity. But they were a long, long way from that.

Chapter Three

At six, Jamie went to check on Ryan, who was fully dressed, lying on her back on the sofa in the library, snoring loud enough to wake the neighbors. A remarkably loud snort/gurgle slapped her into consciousness, and she grabbed her head with both hands. "Kill me," she groaned. "Kill me now."

Jamie walked over and flung the window above her head open. "I don't know which part of your mysterious day caused this, but you're stinking up the whole room."

"My head," Ryan moaned, closing her eyes and burrowing her face against the leather.

"Are you still drunk?"

"Dunno. No. Well, maybe. I mean… I don't know. Jesus! Can you close the fucking window?"

Quietly, Jamie did, even though she thought some fresh air might help. "I have to take your aunt's car back. Are you sober enough for me to leave you alone?"

"Yes," Ryan groused, flipping onto her side. "I'm fine."

Jamie stood and looked at her for a minute. "Aw, screw it. I'll call my mom and have her take Deirdre to her bridge game. God knows what you'll do if I leave you alone."

"Shh!"

"I'll…" Jamie was about to snap off a reply, but Ryan's snores made it clear it would be a waste of her breath.

Jamie was upstairs in their bedroom at nine o'clock when a heavy tread sounded on the stairs. "Well, look what the cat dragged in," she said, surveying the mess of a woman who barely looked like her love.

Ryan shuffled over to the bed, sat, then dropped to lie across it. "As God is my witness, I'll never drink shots again."

"That's probably a good idea, if this is the result. Are you sober enough to go get your car? I guess it's no rush, since it's probably already been stripped."

Ryan turned her head slowly and gave Jamie a long look. "My car?"

"Yeah. Your car."

"What about it?"

She clearly had no memory of the entire afternoon. "It's in front of a bar on the Oakland waterfront," Jamie said, watching for a reaction.

Ryan's brows hiked up, but she didn't say a word.

"Should I take that nonresponse as a 'no?' Or maybe you're planning on taking your new girlfriend with you."

"New...what?" Her eyes were too swollen to open fully, but her mouth did.

"Who were you with all day? Why were you drunk off your ass at two in the afternoon?" It was cruel to shout at a hungover woman, but Jamie's imagination had been running wild all day, and her nerves were shot.

Ryan clapped her hands over her head, moaning. "Please, please show a little mercy. My head's gonna burst, I haven't had a thing to eat, and my stomach's so sour it feels like I've been chewing lemons all day."

The kind thing would be to get up and make something gentle for her stomach, like a nice, bland bowl of oatmeal. But Jamie couldn't manage nice. "I'm going to sleep. I'd suggest you eat something, then take a shower. If you're planning on sleeping here, that is. You might have made other plans during your travels."

With difficulty, Ryan managed to sit up and fix Jamie with a baleful look. "I slew a dragon today," she said, her chin beginning to quiver. "I thought you'd..." Sucking in a gulp of air she managed, "Be proud of me."

That got Jamie's attention. She had no idea what Ryan was talking about, but the look on her face said that something big had happened. Jamie scooted over and wrapped an arm around Ryan's shoulders, never able to refuse that sad, sweet face. Even when she smelled like a combination of beer, whiskey, body odor and…vomit? "Tell me what happened. Come on, talk to me."

"I've got to eat something. *Anything*," she moaned.

Jamie got up, then started to get dressed. "Since we've got nothing, I'll have to go to the store. But I'll bring you some acetaminophen before I go."

Ryan stood, tried to settle her hair, then yanked her shirt down to its normal position. "Let me get a shower, and we'll go together. We can hit up a coffee shop or something, then go get my car." She paused. "But you'd better know where it is."

An hour later, they sat in a grimy diner near where Ryan's car was parked. The place was filled with dockworkers and cops, and was bustling at ten o'clock at night, even though the neighborhood didn't have a single home anywhere near it.

"And then you convinced Barb she had to slay her own dragon," Jamie said, her eyes full of tears for the tenth time.

"Yeah. But she needed some liquid courage. We came over here at ten or ten thirty I guess, after we'd recreated the carjacking. Once we had a couple of shots in us, we went over to where her partner was killed." Ryan took a sip of tea, the pain in her eyes clear to even a passing stranger. "I've had some bad afternoons, but this was one of the worst. Seeing someone so strong, so courageous…" She stopped abruptly, wiped her eyes with her sleeve and finally continued. "I have a load of respect for her."

"I bet it's not as much as I have for you." Jamie threaded her fingers through Ryan's and held her hand tenderly. "I'm sorry I was so bitchy earlier. But you really had me guessing today, and none of my guesses were reassuring."

Ryan shrugged. "I should have told you what we were doing. But…" She looked down at the table. "Once I got up the nerve to do it, I just had to get it done. I didn't want to risk hearing you sound frightened or have you try to talk me out of it."

"I wouldn't have done that, but I understand the fear."

"Thanks," Ryan said, ducking her head again. Jamie looked at the dark curtain of hair that obscured her face. Such a brave woman. If she could only see herself as others saw her. Pausing for a few seconds, Jamie almost laughed. If Ryan could do that, she'd have such a swollen head she'd be insufferable!

It was late when they got back to the Berkeley house. The fog had come in late in the afternoon, dropping the temperature dramatically. Ryan went to the bedroom window and closed it, then went to her own room to get ready for bed.

Normally, she stripped off her clothes, then brushed her teeth. Tonight she made a turn and went to the bath first. She was sitting on the edge of the tub, still in her shirt and jeans, when Jamie poked her head in.

"Oh, sorry. I thought you were in your room."

"Changed my mind," she said around a mouthful of toothpaste. She got up and rinsed her mouth, then picked up her hairbrush and started to run it through her hair. "Tangles," she muttered. "I didn't take the time to brush it when I showered."

"Let me." Jamie urged her to sit, then started to slide the brush through her hair. The job was tougher than normal, and a few times tears came to her eyes when Jamie inadvertently caught and pulled some knotted strands. But Jamie seemed to really like brushing her hair, and Ryan didn't want to be churlish.

Ryan looked up, seeing the cat-like smile that often settled on Jamie's lips when she was feeling amorous. Surprisingly, that made her body tense up. Realizing she was dressed was suddenly soothing. *What in the hell?* They'd had some real struggles with being intimate, but they'd worked at it and gotten back to normal. Did just *driving* the carjacking route make all of the bad stuff come back?

The brush kept gliding through her hair, now tangle free. Jamie leaned over and Ryan could feel her warm breath on the back of her neck. She shivered, but not from pleasure. When Jamie's lips touched her skin, she had to force herself not to run. Taking steady, calming breaths, Ryan stood and edged out of the bathroom. "Be right in," she said, closing the door.

Once in her room, she paced around for a minute or two, finally going to sit on the window-seat and look out at the damp, foggy night. She opened the window to let herself feel the chill, and in seconds her skin was clammy. She just wasn't sure if it was from fear or the heavy air.

Softly, a knock echoed in the room. *Damn.* She really didn't want to talk. Her head was pounding, and her snack hadn't settled her stomach. "Give me a couple of minutes. I'll be in soon."

Surprisingly, Jamie didn't take the cue. Instead, she opened the door a few inches. "I'll be asleep in moments. Can I have a kiss goodnight?"

Ryan stopped herself from letting out an audible sigh. You couldn't let your partner know *every* time she annoyed you. You'd never reach your second anniversary if you did that. "Sure."

Jamie came in, wearing an interesting pair of pajamas. They were interesting in a way that would have had Ryan's engine running if it wasn't on the fritz, but it was definitely out-of-order tonight. "Those are cute," Ryan said, pointing at the peach-colored top and clingy bottoms.

"I did a little shopping while I waited for you to come home today."

Ryan looked up at her, noting the absence of any guilt. "I thought you were stuck at home all day."

"I was," she said, smiling. "And since I was stuck at home, I went shopping. There's a new lingerie store in North Berkeley." She put her hand on Ryan's shoulder, not commenting when Ryan flinched. "Do you need to be alone?"

"Yeah. I guess."

Soothingly, Jamie murmured, "That's fine, honey. Take as much time as you need." She drew closer, then wiggled onto Ryan's lap before draping her arms around her neck. It was impossible to shy away from her when Jamie was so insistent on being close. And it felt damned good too. "I just want to say goodnight."

"Goodnight," Ryan said, puckering up for a kiss.

Jamie placed a gentle one on her lips, but, as Ryan had expected, she didn't get up. "I'll get out of your hair in a minute. I just…" She dropped her head onto Ryan's shoulder and nuzzled into it. "I was really worried about you today. You've never disappeared like that."

"I'm sorry—"

Jamie cut her off with a brief kiss. "You don't need to apologize. But now that I have my arms around you, I don't want to let go." She lowered her head and touched Ryan's nose with her own. "Do you ever feel like that? Like you want to hold on until you feel safe again?"

"Yeah," Ryan said, her eyes starting to fill with tears. "I do."

"We don't have to talk. Let's just sit here and connect for a little while. Is that okay?"

What ogre would refuse such a sweet request? "Okay."

Jamie nestled her body into Ryan's, moving her hips and her shoulders to burrow as close as she could get. The weight of her body and the scent of her hair began to soothe Ryan's jangled psyche, slowly but decidedly. It was like holding something beyond precious—something irreplaceable, and very, very rare. Ryan soon found herself rubbing her face across Jamie's hair, then filling her lungs with her scent. It was as powerful as a sedative, completely tranquilizing. "I love you so much," she heard herself say.

"I love you too," Jamie whispered, her lips tickling Ryan's ear. She straightened up and pressed Ryan's head against her breast. "No talking. Just connecting."

Ryan sighed heavily as her own heart seemed to change its rhythm to keep time with the beating of Jamie's. Like they shared one strong, beating heart. A heart she wanted to nurture, to cherish. "I'm sorry I ran away today," she found herself saying, shocked by her choice of words.

"It's all right. I'm not angry with you, sweetheart." She moved back a few inches and Ryan almost gasped at her loveliness. When they were close like this, breathing the same air, she was often struck mute by Jamie's gorgeous face. There was something so pure, so innocent, so loving, so caring—that Ryan didn't have words for how it made her feel. Other than…wonderful.

Ryan leaned towards her and they kissed, their lips barely meeting. But the warmth of Jamie's skin penetrated the wall Ryan had put up, and she felt herself swept up into her lover's aura. They stayed just like that, kissing and holding each other tenderly for the longest time. Slowly, all of Ryan's barriers fell. Totally exposed, she revealed herself to Jamie's welcoming love. Finally, after God only knew how long they'd been there, Jamie said, "Can we go to bed now? I'm so tired I could weep."

Chuckling at the dramatic way she'd said that, Ryan patted her butt to get her to stand. Then she got up and stretched as she started to remove her clothes. When she began to unbutton her blouse, Jamie doggedly worked on her jeans, and soon Ryan was wearing her usual bed-clothes. Nothing. They went into the bedroom, hand in hand. Jamie got in and Ryan waited for her to scoot onto her usual side, then got in and snuggled up behind her.

"I can rally if you want…" Jamie said, a yawn making her mouth open to comic proportions.

"We've already made love," Ryan whispered. "It's time to sleep."

"Mmm…" Jamie turned onto her side and scooted back until her body was enveloped by Ryan's. "I love you."

"I love you, too. More every day."

Jamie took Ryan's hand and tucked it between her breasts, letting out a heavy sigh as she did. Then, in mere seconds, she was asleep. Ryan started to wonder how anyone could fall asleep so quickly, but her train of thought abandoned her as she nodded off with her face nuzzled up against the back of Jamie's neck.

When the sun woke her the next morning, Ryan's head was still throbbing, her stomach tender and sour. But it was time to get back to work. Jamie stirred, and Ryan cuddled up behind her, letting her warmth sooth some of the stress she still felt.

"Back to sleep?"

"Not me. But you can." She took her pillow and gently placed it over Jamie's head. "Bye."

Jamie pushed the pillow down and turned Ryan's way. "What's on your agenda?"

"Back to work. I have no idea what's going on with OFC, but I'm sure there's something I can do at the apartment building."

"You have to go now?" Jamie glanced at the clock. "It's only eight."

"Yeah." Ryan stood and stretched. "I don't deserve to sleep in. Gotta punish myself for getting drunk."

Jamie sat up and looked at her for a minute. Sometimes her cool, green eyes seemed like they could pierce your skin. "Why didn't you call me after you and Barb finished? Before you went to that second bar?"

Ryan sat on the edge of the bed and took her partner's hand. "I'm not sure. I guess…I guess I was really in the moment. We'd both done something important and we were…celebrating. Or maybe just trying to make the mental images stop."

"You didn't want me to offer to join you." Her level gaze was almost painful.

"Uhm...that was probably part of it." She took Jamie's hand and kissed it gently. "I'm sorry, babe. I needed to let things settle. I meant to have one beer, but that's the bar closest to Barb's precinct and there were people there she knew. It got out of hand pretty quickly."

Green eyes roamed over her face, assessing her like a science experiment. Ryan could feel a lecture coming. It didn't take long to arrive. "You tell me you worry about my getting drunk. But I do it to celebrate things. To have fun. You do it when you're upset or depressed or lonely. Might wanna think about that, bucko."

"Can I think about it after I punish myself by banging a hammer against a wall all day?"

Jamie extended her arms and Ryan fell into them for a long hug. "You can." She kissed her cheek. "And don't ever accuse me of not loving you." She set her feet onto the floor and started for the bathroom. "I'm giving up sleep to go with you today. Even though I don't have many skills, I can make sure you eat and don't go too wild on your first day back."

"But how can I punish myself if you're stopping me?"

"Just your bad luck to have a partner who tries to stop you from being stupid."

"Oh, that's a job much bigger than you'll ever be able to manage," Ryan decided, laughing until her head hurt too much to continue.

The boys had made huge strides in the month they'd been gone. Now the place was looking like a building you wouldn't be afraid to live in. The facade was a crisp beige stucco, with white trim on the exterior door and windowsills. As they entered, the newly painted hallway was positively cheery. All of the trim had been painted, but the carpet was missing, with the raw wood marred by paint and joint compound. Heading up to the third floor, Ryan opened the door to find the vast majority of the work done. The walls were square and painted, and all of the tile had been laid. "Looks like we just need appliances and carpet in here," she said. "The boyos have worked their butts off."

The second floor was in exactly the same shape. But the first floor, Tommy and Annie's place, was rough. Hearing some banging coming from down the hall, Ryan followed the noise to find Miguel and Fernando, the guys Catherine had hired. "Hey," she said. "You guys have really made some strides."

"Uh-huh," Miguel said. He was friendly enough, but he wasn't much for chatting.

Fernando was using a pry bar to yank molding off a doorframe.

"What's going on in here?"

"We're knocking out this door, then we're gonna patch it with drywall."

Ryan walked to the corner of the room and ran her hand down it. "But the outside walls are plaster."

"Yeah." Fernando got back to work.

Starting to prowl around the entire space, Ryan saw that they were planning on adding walls on either side of the new kitchen; one that would separate it from the mud room, and another that would create a dining room. The boys had carved out bedrooms, but those walls were drywall, along with cheap, hollow-core doors. Jamie was giving her a curious look, and when Ryan slapped at the door, she said, "If you're gonna have thick doors in only one place, wouldn't you want them on your kids' rooms?"

"Kids? Plural? Do you know something I don't know?"

Ryan grinned. "Nope. But Annie specifically wanted all three rooms set up as bedrooms. Conor suggested making one a home office, but Annie nixed that idea. I'm not gonna ask, but I foresee a sibling for the little dictator."

Jamie playfully slapped at her. "Caitlin's not a dictator. She's a little doll."

"She's a dictatorial doll." She put her hand on the drywall. "I want this done right, so I'm gonna push for real plaster walls. They'll probably be living here for the rest of their lives. Why not do it right?"

"You know I'm with you on that one," Jamie said, giving her a pat on the butt.

"But Fernando and Miguel aren't able to make those kinds of decisions. Let's go see what we can help with today."

They walked back to the pair and Miguel seemed a little surprised to see them again. "Are you here to work?" he asked.

"Yeah. What can I do?"

He squinted a bit, then took a quick look at Jamie. "Are both of you looking for something?"

"Yes," Jamie said, sounding a little exasperated. "I can clean up after you if nothing else."

"Cool." He nodded, looking pretty happy with the offer. "We need a lot of help. What's your specialty?" he asked Ryan.

"Don't really have one. I've been doing demo mostly. Strength rather than skill."

"How about the back yard?" Fernando said. "Nobody's touched it."

"Are there any plans?" Ryan asked.

"Probably. But you can't do anything until somebody cuts the weeds and breaks up the soil. There's patches out there that look like rock."

"Sounds fun," Ryan said. "Got any tools?"

"Not me," Miguel said, and Fernando also held his palms up.

"I'll call around and see if anyone's got more info." Ryan led the way to the front door. "Thanks, guys."

They went out the main entrance, with Jamie prattling on about making a nice, safe play area for Caitlin. But when they opened the rickety fence that led to the yard, she shut up quickly.

"This is tragic," Ryan said, shaking her head.

Jamie kicked at some of the long weeds. "There's brick under here."

"Oh, super." Ryan pulled out her phone and started making calls. No one was technically in charge, but Conor was darned good at filling the leadership vacuum. She reached him at his job site.

"If it was me, I'd rent a backhoe," he said after she'd posed the question. "You'll be done breaking everything up in a couple of hours."

"Am I supposed to drive a backhoe down the street to get it over here?"

"Ahh…good point. You're gonna have to buy a truck."

"No, thanks. But you're right about the backhoe. It's stupid to try to do this by hand. Got anything I can do inside until someone brings one over?"

"Got a deal for you. Come over to the house I'm working on and take up the floor. I'll go rent you a backhoe and deliver it."

"Deal," Ryan said, knowing her partner would not be accompanying her. "Hey, I wanna change out the cheap doors on Tommy's place. And I'd like to work with Kieran to put up plaster walls instead of that crappy wallboard."

"Well, well. Look who comes home after a month and wants to make changes."

"They're gonna be in that apartment forever, and you know it. It's not just a rental apartment, it's gonna be their home. Plaster walls are quieter."

"And more expensive."

"We can afford it," Ryan said. "I'll pay for the materials as a housewarming gift. If Kieran shows me the basics, I'll do it on my own."

"If Kieran could show you how to plaster in an afternoon…" She could hear him sigh. "If you wanna pay for the plaster job, it's fine with me. But remember, we're doing this to make a profit—not for our health."

"I'm doing this to provide my cousins with a nice home. And if I pay for the extras—we can all be happy."

On Tuesday morning, Mia forced her eyes open. They were in a motel, she were sure of that. She just wasn't sure where, exactly, the motel was. As she woke more fully, it came back to her. Gently laying her hand on Jordan's belly, she rubbed her until her eyes fluttered, then opened. "I hate to wake you, baby, but we're at least fourteen hours from Berkeley."

Jordan blinked slowly, then her head moved up and down a couple of times. "It's gonna take me a minute."

"You didn't sleep much, did you?"

"Not too much. I had to stay on my back, and that's not natural for me."

Mia's hand roamed all around Jordan's shoulder. "I wish there was some way I could make you better. It kills me to know you're in pain." She could tell from the look in her eyes that the pain was back. You had to be on your toes, because Jordan was constitutionally unable to complain.

"I'm okay. I got up at five and took a pill, but I should've done it closer to two. I was just too lazy."

"Then you should've woken me. That's why I'm here."

Jordan reached out with her uninjured arm and pulled Mia close.

"That's not why I thought you were here." She nuzzled her face into Mia's hair. "I thought you were here to slake my ravenous sexual hunger."

"No, that's why *you're* here." She turned onto her side and started placing delicate kisses along Jordan's jawline. "I hate to be in Salt Lake City and not make love. Jamie says the Mormons donated most of the money to make gay marriage illegal in California. I think we have to commit a few deviant acts in retribution."

"I'm always up for a few deviant acts. But they can't see that we're doing them."

Mia expanded her reach, and let her hand start to touch some of Jordan's more erogenous zones. "Let's just hope what they don't know *will* hurt them."

"I think I can rally. Probably wouldn't hurt to take another pill though."

Mia took a look at the clock. "It's a little early. You're not due for another hour." She climbed on top and scooted around until her right hip was directly over Jordan's left. "Look how cool," she said, craning her neck to see. "My 'Jordy' volleyball tattoo is right over your USA one. When we make love, they can kiss."

Jordan smiled at her, then gave her a gentle kiss. "Bring on the deviant acts. Making love kills the pain as much as one of those stupid pills."

Around three, Jamie cruised by a worn Victorian in the Hayes Valley. Ryan was sitting on the front porch, looking like she'd just run a marathon. Rolling down the window, Jamie called out, "Want a ride, good lookin'?"

"Sure do." Ryan loped down the sidewalk and got in, depositing a cloud of dust as she settled herself. "Kinda dirty," she said.

"Kinda dirty was what you were about five hours ago. I'm not sure what word to use for you now, but you need a better one."

"You know what I really need?" Ryan asked reflectively.

"A shower?"

"Yeah, that, but I also need a trade. If I'm gonna be working my butt off I want to learn a skill. It's gonna get old just doing scut work."

"I'm sure you'll pick something up. You're nothing if not determined."

"Yeah, but you need more than determination. Conor's right. I can't learn to plaster in a couple hours. Maybe I'll take some classes at a trade school."

Jamie reached over and tugged on a dusty ear. "I've never met a woman who's itching to get back to school as much as you are."

"That's me. Perpetual student."

An hour after they arrived home, Jamie went down to check on Ryan. She assumed she'd showered and had collapsed, but she was still filthy, sitting in front of her computer in just her underwear. "Why haven't you showered?" Jamie asked, exasperated.

"I wanna get moving on this. I made some calls, checked some websites, and did a little research." She put her hands behind her head and leaned back, looking like a businesswoman—in her undies. "Talked to Kieran. He said he'll work with me."

"No school?"

Ryan laughed. "If I want to be a union plasterer, I'll have to devote four years of my life to school and apprenticeship. Six thousand hours! That's more hours than a first-class degree from Cal."

"And no football team," Jamie teased.

Ryan got up and clapped her hands together. "At least I've made up my mind. Now I can shower."

Jamie watched her walk to the bath, marveling at her laser focus. Once that woman had a goal, woe to the person who tried to get in the way.

Ryan popped her head into the kitchen, hair wet, dressed in a nice shirt and jeans. "Need anything from the store?"

"No," Jamie said. "But you could chop onions for me."

Ryan still hadn't entered the room. The disappointed look on her face showed she hadn't been planning on that. "Uhm…do you *need* me to chop onions? Or were you just giving me something to keep me busy?"

"Agenda," Jamie said, wearily. "State it."

Her face morphed into a cute grin. "You're hard to fool."

"No, you're transparent."

"I wanted to run over to Brendan's to thank him for everything he did for Jen when we were gone."

"Oh, that's nice of you." Jamie walked over and stood in the doorway. She pulled Ryan's head down and gave her a kiss. "What are you taking?"

"Taking?" she asked blankly.

"If you're going to thank him, shouldn't you take a gift?"

"A gift?" She said it like the word was unfamiliar.

"Yes, honey. He really went out of his way. You should take him a nice bottle of wine or offer to take them to dinner or something."

Scowling, Ryan shook her head. "He doesn't like wine. And even if he did, we don't do thank you gifts."

"We could start," Jamie said, playfully nibbling on her ear.

"Mmm…I'll think about it. How about those onions? Need help?"

Jamie patted her on the butt. "Just giving you something to keep you off the streets. Go be nice." She started to go back to her work. "Take Duffy. I'm about to chop a bunch of carrots and you know how he loves them."

"Come on, Duff. I know you'd rather stay and beg, but maybe Brendan's an easier touch."

They reached Brendan's apartment as Maggie was struggling up the front steps with a heavy looking briefcase in one hand, a big paper sack in the other. "How about a hand?" Ryan said, grasping the bag.

"You're a lifesaver." She fumbled in her bag for her keys. "I'd give you a hug, but I'm about to drop this stuff." She got the key out and slid it into the lock. "Can you stay for dinner? I'm not sure I have enough, but I'll gladly order more."

"Ooo, I'm sorry. I didn't think you'd be eating yet."

"Neither one of us got lunch today, so we both knocked off a little early. How about it? Stay and eat?"

"No, Jamie's home making dinner. I just wanted to stop by for a minute."

Maggie got the door open, and Brendan called out, "Hurry up with the dinner, woman. We've gotta eat so I can make you see stars. It's been three days and I'm—"

Ryan couldn't help herself. She winked at Maggie and called back,

"Give the poor woman a break! It's bad enough she has to do all of the work around here."

"Great. Just what I wanted my little sister to hear." He appeared in the hallway, still in his tie and blazer. "Don't tell the cousins. Please?"

"Never." She walked down the hall and kissed his cheek, smiling when he wrapped her in a firm hug. "I'm just here to thank you for all you did for Jen, and Catherine. Uhm…Jamie and I want to take you guys out for dinner as a small thank you. Free any night this week?"

"Thursday works for me," Maggie said, her eyes dancing with pleasure. "If Jamie's taking us, it's gonna be nice."

"Thanks!" Ryan said, feigning outrage.

"You don't have to do that," Brendan said. "I didn't do much."

"Yeah, you did. And we'd like to do it. We never get to see each other alone. It'll be fun."

"All right." He walked into the kitchen and started to remove their takeout food from its containers. "Staying?" he said, looking at Ryan.

"No. Can't. Just came by to thank you."

He walked over to her and gave her another hug. "Missed you," he said, releasing her. "Sunday dinners were awfully bland without you two."

"They're gonna get more interesting," she predicted. "We'll be spending every Sunday trying to sort out whatever trouble Catherine's let Jen get into that week." She smiled weakly. "Sorry my cynicism's leaking out."

Maggie had taken off her jacket and was busy putting their dinner on plates. "It's going to work out great," she insisted. "I'm turning into the optimist of the family, but I'm certain Catherine's gonna be a great mom."

"Great?" Brendan said, one eyebrow raised. "I'd settle for competent."

"I'd settle for her not losing the kid," Ryan agreed.

"Oh, listen to you two!" Maggie grasped Brendan's tie and gave it a tug. "Once Catherine knows what to do, she'll do it. She's just inexperienced. Trust me."

"She *has* experience," Ryan said. "And she's repeating her past mistakes, one by one."

"I'm usually a realist," Maggie said, "so I'm not saying this out of naiveté. Every parent makes mistakes, but Catherine really wants to be a good mom to Jen. And that will go a long way towards getting the job done."

Ryan slung an arm around her shoulders. "I'm usually too realistic. I'll try to parrot your optimism—since we don't have much choice."

Ryan had only been gone a minute when Jamie's phone rang. The gods didn't want dinner to be ready on time tonight. She blew her hair from her eyes, the lengthening strands constantly annoying her, and grasped for the phone. "Hello?"

"Hi, cupcake. Did I catch you at a good time?"

"Sure, Daddy. I'm just starting dinner, but I suppose I'm in no rush. How are you?"

"Good. I'm good. Besides missing you, of course. It feels like years since we've spoken."

"It's been a while," she admitted, struck by a twinge of guilt for not calling while she was in Australia. "But we're home now, and if Ryan gets her way we'll never again leave the 415 area code."

He laughed for a few seconds. "I don't mean to make light of it, but, even more than your being a lesbian, your pairing up with a person who doesn't like to travel has shocked me more than anything you've ever done."

"Yeah," she agreed, chuckling a little herself. "It just shows how magnificent she is in every other way. I haven't had time to read the paper since we got back. Has the Jim Evans campaign apparatus been launched?"

"It has. I assume you'll say no, so don't feel pressure, but my campaign manager has really been pressing me to get you on board."

Her stomach flipped, and a sudden burst of anxiety made her heart flutter. "Me? What can I do?"

"According to Nate, just about everything. He wants you to speak at colleges, high schools, gay and lesbian groups, have teas with parents groups. You name it."

"And just what makes this Nate guy so sure I'd be any good at this? Does he know something I don't know?"

"Well, we talked about the opinion piece you wrote, and when I told him you'd written it yourself, he nearly wet himself." Jim cleared his throat. Something about the way he did it made Jamie tense up. "Uhm, I have to admit he thinks your notoriety would be a big help in getting my name out there. I hate, I *really* hate to try to make hay out of such a traumatic experience…"

"I bet old Nate won't lose any sleep over it." Jamie tried hard to keep her cynicism reined in, but it was tough.

"He's a decent guy. I don't know him very well, but what I've learned about him I like."

"What does Kayla think of him?"

"Kayla?" He was quiet for a minute. "I don't think I know. She hasn't really said…"

Typical. "No big deal. So… What's the bottom line? You know I've got plenty of time, so it wouldn't be hard for me to make some appearances, but I only want to get involved if you need me. I'm not looking forward to having people badger me about the carjacking—which will happen."

"You think so? It's almost been a year."

"People stare at us all the time, Dad. Lots of furtive whispers when we're out together in Berkeley."

"That's probably because you're both so attractive," he teased.

"Yeah, that's probably it. So? Do you need me?"

"It's a little hard to tell. We've only got a month until the election, and the polling numbers aren't very good. I've got a decent lead, but when they dig deeper, a lot of voters don't know Bob died. Nate's worried that my numbers aren't as solid as they seem."

She sighed. It was all on her. He wasn't going to be much help. "Have someone send me a list of things they'd like me to do. I'll take a look and see where I think I could help. I assume you don't need help in San Francisco."

Chuckling, he said, "If I don't get seventy-five percent of the vote in the city, I'll be amazed. No, as you'd think, it's the more rural areas that my numbers need the most help. But I don't expect you to spend the next month in the Central Valley or the High Desert."

"Good. My honey wouldn't be happy with that, nor would I."

After stopping for nothing more than bathroom and junk food

breaks, Mia and Jordan pulled into the Berkeley driveway at eleven that night. "I hope you have an extra pain pill," Mia grumbled, "'cause I'm stealing at least a half."

"I'll gladly share, but you have to take a whole one. It says so on the label."

Mia reached over and patted her cheek. "You're absolutely adorable. I'm sure the FDA is happy that at least one person pays attention to those warnings." She opened the door and stood in the drive, letting the familiar scents of Northern California fill her lungs. The scents were very different from Colorado, and the combination of sage, eucalyptus and rosemary hit her nervous system like a drug. "Ahh...we're home again, baby."

Jordan got out and stretched. "Let's not get back in a car for a few weeks, okay?"

Mia shot the car a harsh look. "We don't need to be anywhere near that beast. I'll even have Ryan come unpack the dreadful thing tomorrow. She loves to be useful."

"I feel horrible not being able to help. It killed me to watch you pack the car, and it'll kill me more to have to watch you unpack it."

"Honey, you can't even brush your teeth with your bad arm. It's gonna be a long, long time until you're back to normal." She walked around the car and took Jordan's hand. "But you'll get there. Now let's go inside and wash our pain pills down with something fun."

"The label says—"

"I was kidding." She couldn't help but grin at Jordan's suspicious look. "Mostly."

Jordan cursed softly, tried to turn over, then gave up. Her back ached from lying in one position, but every time she tried to turn onto her right side, it felt like someone had shoved an ice pick into her shoulder. The left side was better, but only because the right was so freakishly painful. Turning her head, she saw Mia, sound asleep, a tiny, satisfied smile on her face. They were home. Finally. There were dozens of things to do and nearly as many decisions to make, but being at home made everything better.

She raised her knees, and that helped take some of the pressure off her lower back. It wasn't dawn yet. Too early for another pill. Driving all day with so few breaks hadn't been wise, but Mia was so anxious to get back to Berkeley Jordan couldn't make herself ask for a more leisurely pace. It probably wouldn't have made any difference, anyway. Her shoulder was going to hurt no matter where she was or what she did. Chuckling to herself, Jordan decided that she'd be in a lot less pain if she acted more like Mia. She'd also be out of pills. But there wasn't much question that Mia would know where to get more. And if she couldn't get the exact same ones, she could load up on pot. Jordan had never had the slightest interest in illegal drugs, but if her shoulder kept feeling like it did at that moment, she might have Mia hook her up with the local opium den. God knows she'd have a contact.

"Why are you awake?" a sleepy voice asked.

"Go back to sleep." Jordan reached over and scratched Mia's back. "It's really early."

"Uh-huh. So why are you up?"

"The usual. I keep trying to turn onto my side, and the pain wakes me up."

Mia sat up and pushed her curls from her eyes. "Hmm…what can we do?"

"Don't worry about me, baby. You haven't had nearly enough sleep." She tried to pat Mia, but her hand was gripped firmly.

"How about your tummy?"

"I don't think so. I can't figure out how to get there without rolling over."

In a flash, Mia was up and padding over to Jordan's side of the bed. "We can figure this out. Stand up."

Even that took longer than it should have, but Jordan managed, waiting for further instructions.

In the dim pre-dawn light, Jordan could see the sharp intelligence flashing in those pretty brown eyes. "Okay. Stand at the foot of the bed."

"How's that gonna help?"

Mia knelt on the bed, facing the foot. "Get on your knees and shuffle up here. I've got it all figured out."

Once again, Jordan did as instructed.

"Okay. Lean forward, then I'll catch you and lower you down."

"Really? But I'll be stuck there."

"No, no." She shook her head. "As soon as you want to get up, I'll drag you down the bed until you can get your feet on the floor." She met Jordan's eyes and gave her a confident smile. "No problem."

"If you're sure. I hate to be a baby, but if I have to roll onto my side, I'm gonna cry like one."

Mia patted her chest as she braced herself. "I can handle you. At this point, I probably outweigh you—even though you're a yard taller."

"Not quite a yard." It took a surprising amount of trust to let Mia control her descent, but she did it without a hitch. Jordan shifted around and yanked at her pillow with her good arm. "Ahh…" She sighed. "My back thanks you…my shoulder thanks you."

"All better?" Mia tenderly ran her hand up and down Jordan's back.

"Much, much better. Just having you care helps loads."

"I want to do more than care. I want your back to stop hurting." She scooted over, then climbed over Jordan to straddle her. "I can't do as well as your trainers, but I can help get some of the kinks out."

"Don't have any trainers," Jordan said, her voice muffled by the pillow. "Gonna have to learn how to live without anyone watching me every minute."

"Ha! I'm gonna watch you ten times more carefully than your old coaches did. You're my star player."

"Best team I've ever been on. Team Mia."

On Thursday morning, Catherine was sitting in her office, looking at the latest statement from her financial advisor. Ryan's investing advice was continuing to pay off, and she idly considered how to thank the remarkably prescient woman. Cash was out, she didn't like to travel, she hated to receive gifts… A quiet throat-clearing caught her attention. "Hello, Marta. It can't be time for lunch, can it?"

"No, it's still early." She entered the room fully and stood next to the desk. "Do you have time to talk?"

"Of course. Sit down."

Marta did, but her change in position didn't relieve her face of its sober expression. "I hope I didn't make a mistake by waiting, but I wanted you to have a few days to get settled."

Alarmed, Catherine said, "What is it?"

"It's about Jennie." She bit at her lip as Catherine's pulse quickened. "She and her friend, Heather, had a…" Frowning, she said, "I don't know what to call it."

"Call it something!"

Marta reached out and grasped Catherine's hand. "Don't worry. It's not a horrible thing."

"Then just tell me. I can tell it's bad."

"Yes, it's…bad. I think." She took in a breath. "Heather and Jennie were up in Jennie's room. When I went up to give them a snack, I saw…" Her gaze slid to the floor. "I saw them kissing."

"What? Heather?" Her heartbeat was hammering away, but her anxiety started to ease. Of all of the things Jennie could do, kissing a girl seemed quite minor.

"Yes. I was shocked. So shocked I dropped the tray. Heather jumped up and ran from the house, Jennie was crying… It was all too much for me."

Catherine's stomach flipped. Marta deserved a nice, long vacation for all she'd had to put up with. "I'm so sorry you had to deal with all of this drama, Marta. I truly am. I hope things settle down quickly now that I'm home."

Marta blinked. "You don't seem upset."

"Well, Jennie has identified as gay for a while now. I suppose…" She shrugged. "Girls will be girls."

"She's a child!" Marta's cheeks turned pink as she stared into Catherine's eyes. "And Heather is an adult!"

"Oh, my! I didn't think of it that way. Heather seems so…young. As young as Jennie."

"But she's not. If she *had* been kissing her, it would have been against the law!"

"Wait…wait. What do you mean, if she *had* been kissing her."

"Jennie was kissing Heather. Heather wasn't kissing Jennie."

"Oh." Catherine sat up straighter, feeling increasingly confused. "How do you know that?"

"Heather came back to talk to me. She explained that she didn't feel that way for Jennie. And, later, Jennie agreed she'd been the one to act."

She gave Catherine a long look. "I don't think the social worker would like to know Jennie was trying to convince an adult to be sexual with her."

Catherine slapped her face with her open hand. "Good lord. I had no idea how easy I had it with Jamie!"

"Yes, I believe that's true," Marta said, standing to leave. The look she gave Catherine was a strange one. She didn't look angry, but there was something left unsaid. "We were also much younger."

Catherine's stomach continued to flip and dive when she found the age-of-consent law for California. Given Jennie's age, Heather could have been prosecuted for a felony. It was time for another heart-to-heart talk.

At eleven o'clock, Ryan stood on the front porch of their Berkeley house, impatiently waiting while Jamie rang the bell. "It's our house," she grumbled. "They called to let us know they were here. Why can't we just open the damn door?"

"Temper, temper," Jamie chided.

The door opened, and a puzzled Mia stared at them. "Did you lose your keys?"

"Our minds," Ryan said, sliding in past Mia. "Here's your coffee and donuts." She placed the carrier in Mia's hands, then kissed her. "Welcome home."

"You're grumpy today. What's that about?"

Jamie walked in and kissed Mia as well. "Grumpy-puss can't stand to let a few hours get past her. She was up at the crack of dawn, as usual, and she got antsy waiting for you to call."

"Did not," Ryan said, narrowing her eyes. "I'm in a perfectly good mood. But if you'd let me, I could have gotten the back yard broken up before we came over here."

"Conor told you he got the Bobcat for three days and only had to pay for one. You're not wasting a cent by doing it tomorrow."

"What's a Bobcat?" Mia asked. "And what backyard are you talking about?"

"You don't want to know," Jamie assured her.

Ryan started to walk towards the kitchen. "Where's the patient?"

"Still in bed. My poor puppy's in pain, even when she's taking the good stuff. Next I'm gonna try to get her to use medical marijuana."

"And that is…?"

"Marijuana you take when you're sick. Obviously."

Nodding, Ryan took one of the coffees and headed for the stairs. "About what I expected, given the prescribing physician."

Mia watched her go, quietly saying, "Good thing she's not grumpy."

Ryan poked her head into Mia's room. "Awake?" she said softly.

Jordan was lying on her belly, her face toward the window. When she spoke it was clear she was fully awake. "Regrettably."

Ryan walked in, went over to the window-side of the bed, bent and kissed Jordan's cheek. "Welcome home, buddy."

"Thanks. Can you help me get up? Mia convinced me to lie on my stomach, but I have to go through a complicated process to get up."

"Sure. Speaking of Mia, double-check your food if you don't want to get high."

"What?"

"Never mind. I'm cranky this morning. How can I help?"

"Not sure. It doesn't feel like I'm using my shoulder at all, but I must be."

Ryan saw some mottled skin, and she nudged Jordan's T-shirt away. "Oh, man, have you looked at this? It looks like someone banged on you with a hammer."

"Feels like it too."

"Is the pain all in your rotator cuff? Or up in your neck too?"

"Neck, now that you mention it. That's what hurts when I try to get up."

"You're probably still in spasm. Relax completely and let me pick you up." She knelt on the side of the bed and got her hands under both of Jordan's shoulders. "Stay loose. You'll be on your knees in a second."

Jordan was as light as a feather, and she rose with surprisingly little effort. "Much better," she sighed. "Now I've gotta pee!" With that, she ran for the bathroom, leaving Ryan chuckling in her wake.

Mia sat with her back up against the arm of the sofa, feet in Jamie's lap. "Doesn't the whole house seem brighter?" she asked, kneading Jamie's thigh like a cat.

"It does. It really does." She grasped both feet and squeezed them. "I'm so glad you're home."

"But this isn't your home any more, is it? You're living in San Francisco."

"Yeah, I guess we are. We come over once a week to check the mail."

"Gonna sell it?"

"No, I don't think so. It's a great house, and if Ryan goes to grad school in Berkeley we'll want to have it. You guys can just keep it warm for us until we know what we're doing."

"No, no, we'll get an apartment. We can't sponge off you like that."

"Oh, please. You're hardly sponging. Why would you want a place like this to sit empty? It won't cost me any more to have you two here."

Mia poked her with a foot. "Of course it will. You know I've always got something running. Your electric bill will skyrocket."

"Fine. You can pay the utilities. Then we're truly even."

"I don't know, James." Mia looked around, a slight frown on her face. "This is a pretty big house for just the two of us."

"It's really not. I kinda thought we'd be rambling around in here, but we didn't. You'll settle right in." She snatched Mia's feet into an embrace and acted like she was going to kiss them. "Say 'yes'. Please, please, say yes."

"Oh, all right. But I'll pay for everything but the property taxes."

"No way. I'm gonna keep paying Maria Los."

"I should! I'm the one getting the benefit of her work."

"I'm just keeping her busy. No sane person would have her come three times a week."

"Three?"

"Yup. And don't give me a hard time about it. Or about Estaban or Raimundo or Zaragoza. They're all part of the manor."

After breakfast, Mia and Jamie set off for a spa day, while Ryan and Jordan sat in the backyard, planning.

"I'm gonna lose my mind," Jordan predicted. "Can't run, can't lift weights, can't start school 'til January and I don't have a job. All this year I craved time off, but now that I've got it—I don't want it."

"I'll be lucky if the authorities will let me take classes in January. Ideally, in her world, Jamie and I would lie around and read books all day." Just talking about it made her lip curl up.

"Mia's about the same, but she's not much for reading," Jordan said, chuckling.

Ryan turned to look at Jordan. "Do you read?"

"For fun? Like novels and stuff?"

"Yeah."

"Nope."

Ryan slapped her on the knee. "That a girl! Jamie makes me feel like a dunce for not reading, but it's not natural. She can sit inside on a beautiful day, curled up in a chair, doing nothing!"

"Not for me," Jordan agreed. "But I'm gonna have to find something to do to kill time until I can move around again. Any ideas?"

"If it were me, I'd find someplace that had classes starting now. Wouldn't even care what I was learning."

"Mmm, I guess I could do that, but I'm not all that fond of school for school's sake." She shook her head mournfully. "Mia's gonna turn me in for a new model if I don't find something to keep me busy." Making a face, she added, "That's a joke. I'm a model."

"That's one thing you could do. You don't need two shoulders to model."

"I'd rather slam my shoulder against a wall. But…you're right. I've gotta bring in some money, and that's all I know how to do."

She let her head dip back, and as the sun lit her face Ryan gazed at her for a few seconds. It was nice to have a friend who was wired like she was, but that just made her feel worse for her predicament. "I can keep you busy for the afternoon."

Jordan's eyes opened slowly as she turned her head and regarded Ryan. "A whole afternoon?"

"Yeah. The whole damned thing."

"You're on. Where do we start?"

"Gotta head down to the South Bay."

"The South Bay? Why?"

"'Cause that's where the Evans women keep their stock of top-notch doctors. One of them's gonna take a look at your wing."

"You really know how to show a woman a good time, Boomer. I can see why you were such a player." Jordan got up and tugged on Ryan's ponytail. "Let's get going."

"The appointment's not for two hours."

"Good. We can get some serious food. The drugs I'm taking trash my stomach, so I need to eat every three hours."

"I need the same thing—because of gluttony."

At four o'clock that afternoon, Jordan and Ryan sat on the first row of benches in their old gym, watching their former team get ready for practice. The orthopedist had mostly agreed with the team doctor, and thought it was worth a try to avoid surgery. Thankfully, he fitted Jordan with a serious neoprene sling that held her arm tightly against her body, which reduced her pain almost immediately. She'd been a little grumpy since they'd left the office, and Ryan hadn't been sure visiting Cal would be a good idea, but she'd been proven wrong.

They'd spoken to every player they knew, with all of their buddies fawning over Jordan for a while, which lifted her mood like a veil being snatched away. Having an Olympian in their midst was a big deal for the players, and Ryan had to banish the tendril of jealousy that sometimes popped up when she considered how much she would have loved to have been on the team with Jordan. But that was a silly fantasy that she rarely let herself dwell on.

"I'll risk sanctions by the NCAA to sneak you two back on the team."

Ryan turned to see Coach Placer grinning at them.

Jordan jumped up and gave him a hug, then Ryan did the same. "I've got another year of eligibility," Ryan teased. "But Jamie won't let me enroll in school, so it's no-go for me."

"Don't torture me!" he playfully begged. Suddenly serious, he put a hand on Jordan's shoulder. "How's the arm?"

"Bad. But Boomer dragged me to an orthopedist today who agreed that it's not totally stupid to try PT over surgery."

"Great news. Really great. You don't want to let them cut you unless you've got no choice."

"That's exactly how I feel. He said it wouldn't hold up to the kind of abuse I've subjected my shoulders to in the last year, but it might be fine for civilian use. I'm gonna immobilize it until the swelling goes down, then start the fun stuff."

"So…" His eyebrows hiked up. "No Athens, huh?"

"I've got to get on with my life. I'm hoping to be a practicing architect by the time the next games roll around."

"If I could afford to have a house built…you'd be the woman I'd hire."

Jordan graced him with her best smile. The one that Ryan had seen weaken knees. "Thanks, Coach. I'd give you the friends and family discount."

A buzzer went off and he shot it a grumpy look. "Gotta get started. Any chance you two could drop by on a regular basis? I could use some help—especially with the freshmen."

"I've got nothing but time," Jordan said. "But Ryan's turned into a construction worker."

As the coach moved towards his team, he turned and gave her a very puzzled look. "Construction?"

"Don't ask," Jordan called after him. "It makes no sense at all."

Jamie lay on her back on the treatment table, her skin tingling from whatever mixture had been applied to it. Mia lay on the table next to her, softly purring as she stretched her body out. "Does it make me a bad person to admit I'd rather lie here and be pampered than do just about anything else?"

"If you're bad, I'm worse. My excuse is that it's in my genes. You can't pull that one. Your mom isn't the spa type."

"Nope. I'm starting the Christopher pampering lineage. I can only hope that my children will one day model my slothful behavior."

"Speaking of sloth, have you given any thought to what you're going to do for a job?"

"I was hoping to be the test subject at a massage school, but I haven't seen any ads for those high-paying jobs. Got any ideas? I want something where I put out the least amount of effort for the most money."

"Sadly, for women, that's prostitution."

"That's not my style," she said, dismissively. "I'd never do something I loved so much with strangers. Besides, even though Jordan isn't very jealous, I don't think she'd dig it."

"Yeah, that would be a hard sell. No slightly more viable ideas?"

"Not really. I haven't spent a lot of time thinking about it, but I'd better start. Jordy still has a pretty hefty savings account, even after wasting thousands of it on those vultures who keep trying to pass as her family, but I hate to dig into it. Graduate school is going to cost a lot, and I don't want her to have to work while she's in school."

"I know you don't like to take money from me, but I hope you know I'm always willing."

"I know, James. And I appreciate it. But we can't be your permanent dependents."

"Well, you could…»

"You could talk me into it without too much trouble, but not Jordy. She's got that Scandinavian independent streak."

"I'm familiar with the Irish version of that streak," Jamie said drolly. "If Ryan were any more independent, she'd have her own apartment. Luckily, she's my sex slave, and that gives me some control."

"I know I should be concerned about not having any job prospects. But I'm so goddamn giddy about having Jordy to myself that I can't think of anything bad enough to bring me down. The USOC doesn't own her body anymore. Now, I do. And I'm going to spend this fall staking my claim."

"I feel the same. This is the first time since I've met her that Ryan doesn't have anything competing for her attention. No classes, no teams, no job. It's driving her nuts, but I can live with that." She let out an evil-sounding laugh. "If I let her, she'd over-schedule again, which would drive *me* nuts. It's her turn."

Jennie had a little spring in her step when she exited her school and ran across the street, without checking for cars. She slid into the passenger seat of Catherine's car, a perky smile on her face. "Hi! What are we gonna do today?"

"What would you like to do?" Catherine had to smile at the little scamp. When Jennie was comfortable, and let her real personality shine through, she was absolutely adorable. "We were out too late yesterday. You can't afford to stay up until eleven doing your homework."

"Okay." She slumped down a little. It was awfully easy to take the starch from her sails.

"But we can do something for an hour or two. What strikes your fancy?"

"I dunno. What is there to do?"

She looked so puzzled. Like there were only a few things to even consider, and she didn't know what any of them were. "Let's go gallery hopping."

"What-whatting?"

"Trust me," Catherine said, smiling at her naïveté. "We'll have fun."

A little while later, they were parked in SOMA, heading for one of Catherine's favorite galleries. When they entered, a young man jumped up from an ultra-modern desk and nearly sprinted for them. "Ms. Smith! It's so good to see you again!"

Catherine flinched. She was used to having people fawn over her, but she was a little uncomfortable having Jennie witness it. "Hello there," she said, forgetting the man's name. "I assume you're showing the same works you were when I was here for the opening, but I wanted my young friend here to see Jun Lee's work."

"Of course. Of course. Would you like a glass of champagne?"

"No, thank you," Catherine said, as Jennie's head snapped up. She probably would have accepted anything the man offered. "We'll just saunter around, if you don't mind."

"I don't mind a bit. Arthur isn't in today, but I'll tell him you came by."

"Do that. Although we've been seeing each other at so many things, he's probably tired of me."

"Oh, that will never happen, Ms. Smith. I can assure you of that."

Catherine decided that was probably true. As long as she had money, no one who sold art would tire of her.

She led Jennie to the far side of the gallery, then found herself prattling on about the young artist. "Jun Lee is a local girl. She learned to draw in high school, then just kept on refining her technique. Surprisingly, she's had no art school training."

Jen looked at her blankly. "Art school? You can go to school just for art?"

"Of course. Maybe you can go one day."

"Why aren't I going now? Art's the only thing I like, and it's the only thing I'm good at!"

"Oh, honey, I wasn't clear. You study art after you graduate from high school. You still have a way to go."

Shoulders slumped again, Jennie stood very close to one of the pieces, staring at it intently. Catherine backed away to let her take as much time as she wished. Surprisingly, the girl stood there for a good ten minutes, finally saying, "I can't tell how she did this." Her fingers hovered just above the surface, but she knew enough to resist the urge to touch. "Did she put fabric down first?"

"No." Catherine moved to stand next to her. "She uses a tiny brush, then carefully builds layers, making it look more like fabric than paint. It's interesting, isn't it?"

Jennie looked a little stunned. "The colors, the way they blend…it's *amazing*."

"I'm so glad you like it. The path to being a good artist is studying others. Given that I have a huge appetite for art, we can hit up every gallery in the city."

Excitedly, Jennie looked up, meeting Catherine's gaze full-on. "Really? We can do stuff like this all the time?"

"All the time. But we have a lot to see here. Jun Lee is very prolific."

Jen turned and narrowed her eyes. "Is that… I don't know what that means."

"Oh. Just that she creates a lot of pieces."

"Hmm…okay." The look she gave Catherine indicated she wasn't sure she believed her. But who would lie to a child about the meaning of a word? Right then, Catherine decided they weren't going to talk about Heather yet. They had to build some trust first. As quickly as possible.

On the way home, Catherine said, "I know that you're happy to be away from Pebbles, but changing everything about your life has to be challenging."

"It's not hard being in a really, really nice place."

"No, but it's very different. And when things are different, they can be challenging. I think it might be good to talk to a professional while we're getting settled."

"What kinda professional? Another social worker?"

"I was thinking about a psychologist. Would you be willing to do that?"

Jennie started to study the scenery as they moved along. Finally, Catherine could see her shoulder move up and down. "If I havta."

"I won't force you to go, but I'd really like for you to. I think it will help."

With a quick look that turned into a slight smile, Jennie said, "That means I havta."

Catherine laughed. "Okay. You havta. I'll make the appointment."

Chapter Four

On Friday morning, Ryan arrived at the OFC worksite when Miguel and Fernando were still taking their tools from their truck. "See you got some muscle," Miguel said, twitching his head towards the Bobcat in the back yard.

"Yeah. Conor rented it for me. But…" She hated to admit it, but she was wary of starting the job. She'd used Bobcats before, when helping one of her uncles out, but that had been years earlier, and under close supervision. Even though she was very tempted to just give it a whirl, she didn't want to go down in family history as the one who drove the excavator through the foundation of the building. "Are you guys…do you have much experience with Bobcats? It's been a while since I've operated one."

"Yeah," Miguel said, "but we've got some stuff to finish before tomorrow when the whole gang shows up. "Mmm…" He stuck his hands in his back pockets and rocked back on his heels for a moment. "Don't you have any extra cousins who could teach you?"

"Don't worry about it." She stood there, tossing the keys in her hand, thinking. "I've got some other options." Miguel and Fernando grabbed their gear and beat a hasty retreat. A guy never moved faster than when he was trying to avoid a job he didn't want to do.

Taking out her phone, Ryan dialed her Aunt Maeve's house. She smiled when her father answered. "Hey, Da. Are you at home today?"

"That I am. What is my lovely girl up to?"

"How about a trade? I've got the use of a Bobcat with a backhoe attachment on it. If you'll help me stop myself from destroying the whole apartment building, I'll help you load it into your truck and take it to your house to break up your concrete-like backyard."

He didn't pause a moment to think it over. "Have yourself a cup of coffee. By the time you're finished, I'll be there."

As promised, Martin arrived before Ryan finished her coffee. To her dismay, he was accompanied by a child shrieking with joy. Ryan approached the passenger side and spoke through the slightly open window. "Was this a good idea?"

"I had no choice. Your aunt is otherwise engaged, and Tommy didn't get home until seven this morning. He's too tired to be of much use."

"Uhm, not to put too fine a point on it, but you could have told me to figure it out for myself."

"I haven't seen hide nor hair of you for a solid month. Get over here and give your father a kiss."

Leaving Caitlin to shriek, Ryan ran around the back of the truck and let herself be enfolded in a long, robust hug. "I thought of you a hundred times each day," Martin said, his voice catching as he spoke.

"Me too," she said, even though that was a bit of an exaggeration. She and Jamie had been so busy, she'd barely had time to think. "I'd better get the wee one, or she'll break your windows.

Ryan ran back around, reached inside the truck, and extracted Caitlin from her carseat. She held the baby up, letting her legs dangle. "She's grown a foot!"

"Not quite," Martin said, smiling at the pair. "But I'll agree she's sprouting like a weed."

Now having to raise her voice to be heard over the baby's chatter, Ryan said, "I might as well take her to the park. God knows she can't be left alone for a second."

Martin started to roll up the sleeves of his chambray shirt. "I assumed Jamie would be here, and could mind the baby while we worked."

Caitlin kicked and fussed, wanting to get down. Ryan let her go, prepared to snatch her back up if she tumbled on the uneven surface. "My beloved doesn't see the point in rising before eight."

"Well," Martin said, approaching the Bobcat, "you must admit she doesn't have many faults. It seems unkind to complain about the few she's acquired." He held his hand out. "Let me get her started and see how she handles."

Ryan reached into her pocket, but found the keys didn't want to leave her hand. "I was kinda hoping you could help me figure out how to use it."

His hand was still extended, fingers twitching. "I will. Once I'm comfortable."

Rolling her eyes, Ryan handed the keys over. There was no doubt whom she'd acquired her need to be in control from. "I guess we'll just wait for you to get comfortable."

"From a distance," Martin warned. "You never know what will fly up from one of these things."

Grouchily, Ryan took Caitlin and went into the building, then walked all the way through the apartment on the second floor. From the small landing, they could watch while being protected from flying objects. The apartment had been cleared of all construction materials, providing a pretty safe play space for the rambunctious child. Ryan fished her car keys out of her pocket and gave them to Caitlin to play with. Immediately, they went into her mouth, and she began to gnaw on the plastic/metal key for the car. Not ideal, but Ryan figured she couldn't hurt herself permanently.

Martin started the machine, and in seconds a satisfied smile covered his face. Enviously, Ryan watched him slowly maneuver it around until he had a good grasp of its speed, power and reaction time. When the backhoe crashed into the edge of the bricked-in portion of the yard, Caitlin came running from wherever she'd wandered off to. "Up!" she demanded, even though she was a little indistinct on the "p" in the word.

Her motor skills were good, and she seemed as sharp as a tack, but Cait had far fewer words than many of the other kids her age. Neither Tommy nor Annie ever said a thing about it, though, which Ryan appreciated. For first time parents, they were very laid-back, making them stand out among the high-achievers the local park was filled with. Ryan picked Caitlin up and they watched as the claw thrummed against the ground another time, shattered brick and dirt and a fine dust making a cloud where it struck.

"Bow," Caitlin said, imitating the percussive sound. She looked up at

Ryan for confirmation.

"Yeah, that's a bow," Ryan said. "Big bow."

The little blonde head nodded. "Big bow."

Ryan nuzzled her face against the baby's sweet-smelling hair. "Who's in that truck, huh? Is that your grandpa?"

Cait looked at her for a second, then nodded. "Gampa." That was a new one, and Ryan nearly cried when she tried to imagine the look on her father's face when he'd heard that for the first time. Then Cait's voice grew in force as she rattled off a few words. "Gampa! Tuck! Bam!"

"Does it hurt your ears?" Ryan asked, giving the closest one a tickle.

Cait raised her hand and examined the spot Ryan had just touched. "Eeya," she said, making Ryan chuckle. Sometimes the kid had an accent that was just too cute.

They went through the parts of the body, with Caitlin able to name most of them, having made huge progress in the month Ryan had been gone. After zooming through nose and eye and mouth and face and hair, Ryan pointed to herself. "Ryan," she said. "Can you say Ryan?"

Cait's eyes narrowed slightly, then she let her face fall into Ryan's chest. She wanted to say it, you could tell she was trying. But she lifted her head, looked directly into Ryan's eyes and said, "Funny," just as plain as day.

"Funny? That's my name?"

"Funny," she said again, laughing that goofy, fake-sounding laugh that kids often pulled out.

"I guess I'll take it, but keep working on Ryan, okay? And don't listen to your grandpa when he tells you my name's Siobhán. He's silly."

"Silly," Cait said, then patted Ryan on the shoulder, before turning her attention to the yard when the Bobcat cracked into a section of brick.

The two of them stood there, both fascinated, as Martin worked his way around the small yard, prying every brick from beneath its tangle of weeds. "I think my chances of getting to do any work are about the same as yours," Ryan grumbled, but Caitlin didn't seem to mind. She watched as carefully as she did a colorful commercial on TV, barely moving as she sat on Ryan's hip, watching her gampa rip the place apart.

The backhoe did a great job of ripping the place asunder, but it didn't have a bucket attachment. That meant Ryan could either go try to rent one, or she could do the dirty work of gathering the bricks by hand. She and Caitlin went back outside to the yard, while Martin surveyed his handiwork. "It all comes back to you after just a few minutes," he said, clearly proud of his work.

"When do I get my lesson?" Ryan asked, fixing him with a pointed look.

"Will you look at the time!" He checked his watch in an exaggerated fashion. "My bride will be home by now, and she can mind the baby while I work on my yard. Will you come with me, or should you get to work on picking up this mess?"

Ryan stood there, hands on her hips, thinking. Kieran was going to work with her tomorrow, so she wouldn't have the time to do it then. With regret, she handed the baby back to Martin. "Thanks for doing the work. Maybe next time I'll learn something."

"You've learned something today," Martin reminded her as he kissed her cheek. "Never give an O'Flaherty the key to a new machine. You'll never reclaim it."

After putting the baby, who was crying bloody murder, in her carseat, Martin and Ryan got the Bobcat into the truck, using the ramps Conor had rented. Now winded and dirty, Ryan found a wheelbarrow and started to make two piles: one neatly stacked pile of intact brick, another of broken ones that she tossed into the wheelbarrow. Then it was simply a matter of pushing it out to the dumpster, and shoving it up the ramps the guys had made. The ramps wouldn't pass safety inspection, just being concrete blocks with a sheet of plywood over them, but the inspectors weren't looking for things like that—thankfully.

Two hours of back-breaking work had the yard cleared of brick. Now it was an unholy mess of massive clods of dirt, ankle-breaking holes and rock-hard edges that Martin hadn't been able to reach.

Ryan went over to the porch to sit for a minute. It wasn't very warm out, probably around sixty-five, but she'd been working hard enough to build up a sweat. Her phone rang, and she felt around in her many pockets to find it. "Hello?"

"Not very friendly," Jamie chided her.

"I didn't check the display, so I didn't know it was you. Wanna come over here and help me break up the yard? I figure we could get it done in two hours—if we both work like dogs."

Chuckling, Jamie said, "Yeah, that's just what I was going to offer. Right after I checked myself into an asylum."

"Nice. It's very rewarding to know my one true love won't help me in a simple task."

"Your one true love would happily go by one of the home improvement stores, interview the guys standing around looking for work, load three of them in the car, and have your job done in two hours. And, I might add, since I can speak Spanish, they'd know exactly what I expected of them."

"If you're going to try to trip me up with logic…" Ryan laughed at herself, knowing she was being irrational. Working as hard as she was for no money was just nuts, but she couldn't stop.

"Do you want me to bring you a snack, baby? I'm more than happy to."

"What are you up to?"

"I'm at my mom's. Jen just got home. She's got a history quiz on Monday and I said I'd help her go over the stuff they covered this week. But I could afford to take a quick break to bring my best girl a treat."

Ryan thought for a moment, her mouth watering at the image of some ice cream or candy. "No, as much as I'd love a chocolate malt, you should stay and help Jen. I'll go grab a shovel and work my fingers to the bone."

"That's my girl. Always rational. See you later, snookums. I'll make you a special dinner."

"Anything edible would be special right now. I'm faint with the hunger."

"Don't keep begging or I'll make Jen wait. And I know you don't want that."

"No, I don't. I'm just whining. Ignore me."

"Consider it done. Bye."

Ryan decided to start on the edges of the yard, the spots where the Bobcat hadn't made a dent. The ground wasn't quite as hard as rock, but it was close. She guessed a mattock would be the right tool, given the extra weight in the head and the sharp cutting edge, but there wasn't one on the job site and she couldn't countenance buying one for a single day's use. So she went with the second best option, an old flat-faced shovel someone had left out. The handle was wood, and rough from being exposed to the elements, but it was good enough.

She needed gloves, but the nice deerskin ones she had for interior work would be ruined in short order, so she did without. Luckily, she had on her steel-shanked work-boots, and they let her jump onto the shovel to force it into the unyielding soil without breaking any bones in her foot.

It was very tough work. Stupid tough when she thought about it. It would've made sense to at least water the worst parts of the yard, but that would have taken an hour and wasted a precious resource. As she worked, she got progressively more angry with herself. This was true scut-work, the kind of work none of her cousins would do. Jamie had been right. Hiring a few guys with the proper tools would have been the smart thing to do—but she'd been too cheap and unreasonable to do it.

"You look like you need this."

Ryan whirled around to see Catherine just a few feet away, extending an insulated foam cup. She looked like she was trying to find a way to stand where her dark slacks and suede loafers wouldn't be ruined. But besides looking uncomfortable with the terrain, she seemed tentative.

Feeling just as tentative after their last tension-filled meeting, Ryan slammed the shovel into the ground and moved forward. "If that's a malt, you're a saint."

Catherine held the cup out. "Only half of that's true."

"Let's go someplace a little cleaner than this." Ryan smiled at her, trying to show with just her expression that she was over her anger.

"I think that would be just about anywhere."

There truly wasn't any spot in the building where dust and dirt hadn't penetrated. Given there was also no furniture, the options were even more limited. They wound up at the curb, with Catherine sitting in the passenger seat of her convertible, and Ryan sitting on the sidewalk.

"I truly don't mind if you get my car dirty," Catherine said for the fourth time. "I have it washed every week."

"I'm good." Ryan took a lusty sip of her malt. "I'm better than good, thanks to this. I don't know what it is about ice cream, but it's the one thing that always cheers me up." She smiled up at Catherine. "Besides your daughter, of course."

"That goes without saying." Catherine's smile faded a little as she nervously cleared her throat. "In addition to wanting to save you from starvation, I needed some time alone with you."

"Yeah." Ryan nodded, but found herself unable to look directly into Catherine's eyes. "I've wanted to talk to you too, but…" She shrugged. "I wasn't sure how to approach you."

"Ryan," Catherine said, her voice taking on some of the strength that had begun to inflect it in the last year, "you don't need an excuse. You're always welcome to tell me exactly what's on your mind."

"No, no, that's not going to happen." She took a breath and considered how to order her thoughts. "I…uhm…I sometimes think of you as a friend—"

A look of shock passed across Catherine's face, pulling Ryan up short.

"No! I meant I think of you as a friend *and* as a mother-figure, and I've been taught that you don't criticize your parents."

"Oh, dear," she said gently. "I'd be honored to have you think of me in a maternal way. But that doesn't mean you can't tell me when you think I've made a mess of things—as I know you do." The car door was open, letting her reach down and grasp one of Ryan's dirty knees. She shook it gently, saying, "Even though you didn't criticize me with words, the look on your face the day you found Jennie was harsh enough to knock me down." She smiled when she added, "I would much rather have had you tell me how you felt than assume you wanted to strangle me."

Ryan couldn't help it. She just hoped Catherine knew her teasing wasn't mean-spirited. "If I'd said what was on my mind, you might have wished I'd only given you a murderous look." She looked down at the sidewalk as she collected her thoughts. "I was irrationally angry, Catherine. And when that happens, I say things I regret. I've worked hard to keep those outbursts to myself, and I honestly think it's for the best."

"Fine," Catherine said, giving her another pat. "You know what works for you. Given that you don't seem irrationally angry now, we need to clear the air."

"I think it's pretty clear. Jen doesn't seem to have any lasting scars from what happened with Pebbles, and Jamie's told me she's got a therapist now." Shrugging again, she said, "I think we should forget about what happened and move on."

"I'm not sure that's wise." She gazed into Ryan's eyes when she looked up. "I agree about moving on, of course, but we need to remember our mistakes to avoid making them again." Her eyes closed briefly and she looked like she might cry. "I let Jennie down in five distinct ways. In each of them I knew I was making a mistake, but I convinced myself, or let other people convince me—that it was okay."

"Other people...?"

"Yes." Catherine locked her gaze on Ryan, making her squirm. "The first mistake was a collective one. Not telling Sandy about the things Pebbles was doing was a very bad choice. Many of the other things that have happened flowed from that first decision."

Ryan had to bite her tongue to not say what was on her mind— that if Catherine wanted to slough this all off on a decision they'd made months ago—she was going to have a fight on her hands. "We didn't make that decision lightly," she said, keeping her response brief.

"No, of course we didn't. But we all knew Jennie was crying for help, yet we allowed her to limit our response. That wasn't wise."

Ryan thought back to the first time Jen had revealed she was being harassed by the kid. She'd begged them not to rat her out and they'd agreed—mostly because they, like Jennie, didn't want the girl to be sent to the Youth Authority. But some kids didn't have the skills to live in a group home, where the supervision was much lighter than in a Youth Authority facility. Pebbles was clearly, in retrospect, one of those kids. "Okay. I see your point."

"Also, if I'd told Sandy about Pebbles' behavior, Brendan would have been able to get Jennie out of the house much faster. That would have helped prevent this last incident."

"Yeah, yeah, you're right," Ryan said, her head dropping down as she thought of how she'd let a fourteen-year-old kid decide how to stop another kid from messing with her.

"Not telling Sandy about Pebbles' inhaling things was incredibly naive." She paused a second. "I finally got up the nerve to tell Sandy about that."

"You did?"

"I did. To say she's sick of me and my intermittent meddling is an understatement." She showed a sad smile. "I can't very well defend myself.

Everything she said was true."

"Don't be hard on yourself. This is a big change for you. I know you're doing your best."

"Nonsense," Catherine said sharply. "I went to Australia when my custody application was pending." Her lips disappeared as she bit on them tightly. "When Jamie insisted I come with you, I leapt at the chance. I had permission to run away—my favorite long-term coping mechanism." She rolled her eyes. "It's gotten more acute since I'm not drinking myself calm."

"That was a bad choice," Ryan agreed. She felt emboldened by talking so frankly and decided it was all right to unload. "But the worst one—"

Catherine cut her off. "Was knowing Pebbles was back in the house and not going home immediately."

Nodding, Ryan said, "That's almost a tie with knowing you could get custody immediately and not going home."

"I realize that," Catherine said, her voice quiet but determined. "That was *all* my fault. My only defense is that we'd let Jennie stay for so long…knowing that Pebbles was harassing her. Knowing that Pebbles kept gasoline in the basement." She looked very irritated with herself. "It was childish and foolish and remarkably immature on my part. My only excuse…and it's a bad one…is that I was afraid to start."

"To start? What do you mean 'start'?"

Catherine took in a long breath. "This is another of my issues. I'm usually fine once I've begun something. But starting…making that first step all on my own…" She shook her head again. "I get so frightened that I can't take that first step."

"The first step was…what?"

"Talking to Jennie. Telling her I was going to be her guardian." Her hand fluttered in front of her face. "It was all too much for me. I had to wait until you and Jamie were here. Then, if Jennie balked, you'd have been here to convince her."

Ryan's mouth dropped open. "You thought she wouldn't want to live with you?"

"Yes. That's exactly what I thought. I needed back-up, and you two were the only ones I trusted to both convince Jennie and support my faltering courage." Her gaze slid to the sidewalk. "I was too ashamed to admit to your brother or your aunt how much support I need."

"Aww, Catherine." Ryan knew she'd get her dirty, but she had to at least hold her hands. She grasped them, and met Catherine's timid gaze for a few long moments. "We all need support. I've been afraid to drive through half of my damn home town for a whole year. I feel like a ten-year-old when I get behind the wheel and find my hands shaking."

"But you still do it," Catherine said. "That's the difference between us. You face your fears and I run from mine."

"Not true," Ryan said decisively. "If Jamie hadn't forced me to go to therapy and stick with it when I wanted to quit, I might never have gone near the Embarcadero in a car again. I *hate* being weak."

"I *hate* being rejected," Catherine said softly. "I thought Jennie would see how weak I was and decide it was best to stay with Sandy. I honestly thought," she said, now starting to cry, "that she was safer with Sandy than me alone. Even when a girl was openly harassing her. I couldn't do it alone." She gulped in a breath. "I still don't think I can do it, but I'm better now." She met Ryan's eyes, her frailty so apparent it was shocking. "You and Jamie are the only people I can be completely honest with." Her head dropped and she added, "I drank myself into a stupor each night Jennie was missing." Their eyes met again. "I'm ashamed to admit that, but I have to be honest—with someone." She cleared her throat as she dabbed at her eyes with a handkerchief. "Please don't tell Jamie about my drinking, if you can avoid it. I know she worries."

"So do I," Ryan said, grasping Catherine's hand again. "But I know you're working to control it. And I'm confident you will."

"I don't want to lose your respect, Ryan. It means so much to me."

"You won't." She scrambled to her knees, leaned in and kissed Catherine's cheek. "Jamie said something to me—in anger—the day we got back. She said that if I'd told Sandy about Pebbles when I first learned about it, none of the other things would have happened. I brushed her off, but she was right. Dead right. We've both made mistakes, Catherine, but Jennie's resilient. We'll work to make her feel safe, and secure and wanted. *All* of us will do that. Together."

After Catherine left, Ryan picked up her shovel again, then stared out across the yard. She'd finished about ten percent of the total. No longer able to convince herself this made any sense, she snapped out of it, got into her car and drove home. After walking over to her aunt's, she found her father happily tearing his own yard apart. She approached him after making sure he saw her. "I called the rental place. They've got an attachment we can use to break up all of this dirt and rake it smooth. Can I borrow your truck to go get it?"

"Of course. But that's an awfully big waste of money, darlin'. We can do the same thing with shovels and pitchforks."

"All true," she said, as she turned and headed for his truck, knowing the keys would be on the floor. She wasn't much for going against the O'Flaherty dogma of doing everything possible by hand, but she'd had quite enough of breaking her back for one day. The rest of the project was going to be accomplished with machine-muscle.

Jamie sauntered over to the worksite around five. She wasn't sure what she'd find, but knew it would be dirty. Following the loud noise coming from the yard, she found Ryan, grinning like a fool, as she maneuvered the Bobcat around the yard, using a kind of massive rake to smooth the lumpy soil out. Martin was standing awfully close to the cab, shouting instructions and making movements with his hands that mimicked what he wanted his daughter to do.

He caught sight of Jamie and waved her off. "Too dangerous!"

But Ryan shut off the machine and got out. "Cool, huh?" she said, still grinning.

"Very. I wanna watch you work, but I don't want to lose any body parts."

Martin walked over and hugged her. "I can't believe you've been here since Monday and we haven't seen you!"

"Lots of things going on. But we're back for the indefinite future."

"I couldn't be happier about that. You can stay, but you have to wear safety goggles. Hearing protection isn't a bad idea, either."

Jamie turned her head and looked up at the small porches on each of the floors. "I think I'll head upstairs and watch from a safe distance. It's a little dusty down here." She pointedly looked at her partner's dirt and grime-coated T-shirt and carpenter's pants.

"Enjoy the view," Ryan called as she walked away.

"How can I do that when you're sitting down?" She turned and laughed at the wide-eyed look Martin was giving her. "Sorry," she added. "Couldn't help myself."

They'd been home for two days, and Mia couldn't delay any longer. She picked up her cell and called her mother, after making sure Jordan was nowhere near. It wasn't a good idea to let Jordan hear too many family fights—which could never be predicted.

"Hi, Mom. We're back in town."

"My baby's home!"

"Yep. I'd hop in the car and come see you, but I need a few days without driving. Jordy couldn't help, so I had to do it all."

"What? Her shoulder's so bad she can't even drive?"

"I suppose she could have, but she's taking pain meds, and I don't trust her reflexes."

"Well, well, well. Aren't we the prudent adult?"

"Trying, Mom. Really trying."

"When can you manage to get back into your car? We'll have a special family dinner to welcome you home."

"Welcome *us* home. I'm ready, willing and able to tell the entire family about Jordan."

There was a lengthy pause, which Mia took as a positive sign. Having her mom take a second before snapping at her was progress. "I'll just bet you are," she said, with a surprising amount of lightness to her voice. "But you know how I feel about that, Mia. Now's not the time."

"Fine," Mia said, deciding to let this one go for the moment. "Just make sure no one's at my welcome home party who can't bear to hear the truth. Gonna be a small party."

"Less to cook," Anna Lisa said, not taking the bait. "So…what are your plans?"

"My first thing is to get a job. Jordan will get one too, of course, but physical therapy's got to be her priority. In January, she'll be back at Cal, finishing up her degree."

"Then you'll both start graduate school in September. Stanford

Law's waiting for you, Mia, and you made a solemn promise you'd follow through."

"I know, Mom. But I can't sit around watching grass grow. I need some dough coming in. Got any ideas?"

"Not off the top of my head. What are your skills?"

That was a dig. Mia was two seconds away from stating what she was best at, but decided to play nice. "Anything an unskilled, but willing person can do. I'll probably wind up pulling espresso or selling T-shirts."

"Under which freeway will your cardboard box be located?" She let out a laugh that reeked of derision. "You have absolutely no concept of money."

"I have a concept of how much rent is, Mom. That's why we're staying at Jamie's." She could feel herself tense up, knowing this wouldn't go down well.

"Nonsense. What we paid for your share of the rent is twice what you could earn making espresso."

Taking a breath, Mia told the truth. "Jamie doesn't want to sell, and she's not living here. So she only wants me to pay for utilities. I can handle that."

"That's freeloading, and you know it." An aggrieved sigh, one Mia had heard hundreds of times, came through the phone. "Don't worry about the money. We'll pay your rent until you're out of law school. Unless you want to move back home so you can be closer to Stanford."

"That won't work," Mia said. "We need our own space, and you need your sanity. And I don't need for you to pay rent. Jamie doesn't want it."

"You don't realize this, but the best way to ruin a friendship is by taking advantage of your friends. Please don't let that happen, Mia. It's not worth it."

"I appreciate the advice, Mom, but we've got this worked out." She caught sight of Jordan entering the room. "Gotta go. Let me know when that big rockin' welcome home party is. I'll bring a bottle of wine. One ought to do it. Bye!"

Jordan walked over and slid an arm around Mia's shoulders. "Mom?"

"Yep. How can you tell?"

"Just the tone of your voice. Are we having a party?"

"We are." Mia turned and slid her arms around Jordan's waist. "With everyone who knows about our relationship. That leaves…four of us.

Woo hoo!"

"Small is beautiful," Jordan said, grinning.

"How about you? Do you want to…uhm…contact your family to let them know you're back?"

"No, thanks." Her grin faded, then she gently disentangled and slipped away.

Mia gamely followed her upstairs. When she stood in the doorway to their room, Jordan was sitting on the bed, looking out the window. "You okay?" Mia asked. She put her hand on Jordan's back and scratched it lightly.

"Yeah. I guess. Uhm…I've gotta get back into therapy." She looked up and met Mia's eyes. "I know it's expensive…" Her big blue eyes blinked slowly. "But I've gotta."

Mia snuggled next to her and started to place tiny kisses along her jawline. "Your mental health is worth as much as your physical health, baby. We'll spend the next couple of months fixing both your head and your shoulder. Don't give it another thought."

"It's expensive…" She looked away, clearly troubled.

"So? We'll use savings until I get a decent job. Let's not forget that every dollar in the bank came from you, so don't even think about arguing about spending it."

"I'm gonna need everything I have for grad school. It…" She sucked her lower lip into her mouth and worked it over her teeth. "We're gonna be stretched to the limit."

"No, we're not. I'm gonna get a good job. Promise." Mia had no idea what kind of job would pay for utilities and Jordan's therapy, but the therapy wasn't optional. She didn't want to do it, but she'd hit Jamie up if she had to. Jordan's mental health was worth breaching a barrier she'd sworn she'd never even consider.

Jamie was already in bed when Ryan came out of the bathroom that night. She always looked so pretty right before bed. Hair brushed, face washed, teeth sparkling clean. The fact that she was usually naked didn't hurt the look one bit.

Tossing the covers aside, Jamie patted the mattress. "Jump in here, you gorgeous thing."

Ryan took her literally, leaping for the bed, which slammed into the wall and creaked like the springs would snap. Jamie sincerely hoped they would, but knew her only real chance of getting a new bed was to move into their own house. If Ryan insisted on having the family heirloom accompany them, they could make the O'Flaherty bed a conversation piece.

Ryan giggled when Duffy came running down the stairs and started to sniff loudly, his black nose visible under the door. "It's okay, boy," Ryan called out. "No one was hurt. We're just playing."

It wasn't possible that he understood her, but they could hear him quietly climb the stairs to head back to Conor's room—where he was allowed to sleep on the bed. "That's either a very well-trained dog, or he's got a very short attention span," Jamie observed.

"He takes after me. The attention span part, that is. God knows I'm not well-trained." She flopped down and let out a massive sigh. "I feel like I had a fifty-pound weight attached to my back today. Every muscle I have is crying."

Jamie didn't comment, knowing she had nothing supportive to say. Ryan working the way she did was silly. But she'd reminded her of that so many times she was teetering on the line of being a scold, and she truly didn't want that to be the way they interacted.

Ryan turned and searched Jamie's eyes, clearly waiting for a response. To avoid giving one, Jamie pulled her close and kissed her. "I love you," she murmured.

"Love you too." Ryan obviously didn't want to let the topic drop, which was odd for her. "At least I had a good break. Thanks for sending your mom over."

Jamie sat up and stared at her. "My mom? I didn't send her anywhere. What are you talking about?"

Ryan's eyes opened wider. "You didn't? How'd she know to bring me a malt?"

Rolling her eyes, Jamie lay back down. "You act like a person would have to have some extraordinary ability to know you're always up for a malt. It's not like she knew you needed a..." She cocked her head. "What's a unique tool you might need for your project?"

"A pick mattock?"

"Fine. It's not like she brought you a pick mattock. Whatever that is." Jamie started to relax, then sat up again. "I wonder why she didn't mention she stopped by to see you."

"Uhm…" Ryan had that deer-in-the-headlights look. The one that made it clear she had info she wasn't handing over. "Maybe you'd left by then."

"No way. I was at her house when she said she had to run an errand, and I was still there when she returned. I didn't ask where she'd gone but…" She tried her most intimidating stare, hoping to get Ryan to open up. It never worked, but there was a first time for everything. Surprisingly, Ryan started talking.

"I don't know why she didn't tell you she came to see me, but I'm really, really happy she did."

"Yeah, yeah, I know you love ice cream—"

Ryan put her fingers to Jamie's lips, cutting her off. "That's not it. I'm glad she came because she wanted to clear a few things up." Her smile was so full of pleasure, Jamie found herself copying it. "I know it's hard for her to initiate a chat about a loaded topic, given she hates those kinds of talks as much as I do." Ryan slipped her arm around Jamie's shoulders and pulled her close. "So I'm just really happy she feels secure enough with our relationship to put herself out there."

"That's really nice. So…what did you talk about?"

Ryan kissed her cheek, then nuzzled her face into Jamie's neck until she giggled. "Ask your mother."

Ryan emerged from her bedroom the next morning to the delightful smell of soda bread baking in the oven. A big grin lit up her face as she dashed up the stairs. "What a nice way to wake up," she said, going to her aunt to kiss her cheek.

"I could hardly stop your father from coming over here two hours ago. He was up with the dawn!"

"I'm desperate to spend time with my girl," he said, smiling at Ryan. "Time that doesn't involve operating dangerous machinery, that is. I came by each night this week, I'll have you know, but you've been otherwise engaged."

"Lots of irons in the fire," Ryan agreed. "And the one night I was home, you were at work. But now that we're back, you'll see me so much you'll be sick of me."

"Not humanly possible. And don't act like you won't be taking off again soon. You two are always off to one place or another."

"Not if it was up to me—"

"It's not," Jamie's voice and then her lips tickled Ryan's ear.

"Is that my most beloved girlfriend sneaking up on me?"

Swatting her on the seat, Jamie said, "It certainly is. And if you don't watch it, I'll book tickets to go somewhere. Somewhere far away." She moved across the room to hug both Martin and Maeve. "Luckily for you, Ms. O'Flaherty, I share the instinct to stay very close to this extraordinary family."

"You look wonderful," Maeve enthused. "Your skin positively glows! That's what tromping around Australia for a month will do for you."

"That's what hours at the spa will do for you," Ryan corrected, sotto voce.

That earned her another swat to the seat. "Keep it up and you'll have to sit on a pillow," Jamie threatened.

Ryan tucked an arm around her waist, then carefully grasped her dominant hand and held it tightly. "No matter what it cost, your skin does glow. I was complimenting you, sweetheart."

Maeve patted Ryan's cheek before dashing into the kitchen to check on breakfast. "It's been a while since you've kissed the Blarney Stone, but its effects are still holding."

They all sat down to breakfast, with Ryan giving a speedy version of the highlights of their trip. "Now that we're home, we've got to concentrate on pulling Jennie into the family."

"True. Very true," Martin said. "Having her at Sunday dinner will help."

"Oh, her birthday is next week," Jamie said. "Mom's got all sorts of plans."

Martin raised an eyebrow. "Far be it from me to tell your mother how to treat the child, but if she wants to fit in, she'll have the usual celebration with the whole clan."

Ryan watched, fascinated, as Jamie processed this. Jennie was going to be a member of the Evans...or Smith clan, and that branch of the group wasn't satisfied with a cake and good wishes. "I'll talk to my mom," Jamie said, reaching for another piece of soda bread as she deftly changed the subject. "Oh, Maeve, the priest I was telling you about is starting a class. Every Wednesday night for ten weeks. Are you in?"

Martin gave his daughter a pointed look. "I think we've been shut out without a fare thee well."

"You and Ryan are more than welcome to come, Martin. I just know you won't want to," Jamie added, smiling.

"What's the class?" Ryan asked. "You know I love to go to school."

"Poetry in the psalms," Jamie said, not blinking as she stared at Ryan for a moment.

The O'Flahertys exchanged looks. "I'm busy for the next ten Wednesdays," Ryan said.

"I don't have my book in front of me, but I seem to recall something pressing on Wednesday nights as well," Martin agreed. "I'm afraid we'll have to wait for the next class."

"Maeve?" Jamie asked, giving narrow-eyed glances at her partner and father-in-law.

"I am perfectly free and very interested. I don't know much about poetry, but I love the psalms. Consider it a date."

"Maybe we should have dinner beforehand," Jamie said. "That will give us a little time to chat."

"Oh, that would be lovely. I can't tell you how much I enjoy dining out."

Martin rolled his eyes. "I'll make a lovely meatloaf for Wednesday. What do you say, darlin?"

"If you'll add some colcannon, you've got a date. Just promise we won't have to read poetry first."

After Ryan left to spend her Saturday with Kieran, learning the rudiments of the plaster trade, Jamie walked over to her mother's home. The weather was lovely, the kind of October day that makes tourists mistakenly believe San Francisco was generally as warm and temperate as Los Angeles. Wearing one of her Sydney Olympics T-shirts and a pair of jeans, she set off, forgetting that she had to cover over three miles.

Spending most of the last month doing nothing more energetic than screaming and jumping up every time Jordan or one of her teammates did something fantastic hadn't done much to keep her in shape, and by the time she reached Pacific Heights, she'd already decided she was taking a cab on the return trip.

As always, she rang the bell, pleased when Jennie flung it open. "Hi!" she said, smiling brightly.

"Hi, yourself. How'd you beat Marta to the door?" Jamie stepped in and gave Jen a quick hug.

"She's at the grocery store." Lowering her voice, Jen added, "Your mom never answers. I think she'd let people stand out here forever."

"This is true," Jamie agreed. She was fairly sure her mother knew *how* to open a door, but she had to admit she had very little practice. Probably another rule her very strict, very proper mother had imposed upon her. "Is my mom home?"

"Yeah." Jen just stood there, obviously not having been instructed on the proper way to greet guests. That would happen eventually. Jamie was sure of that. She took a quick look at the younger woman, surprised to see her wearing a pretty, blue crew-neck sweater and chinos. "Are you guys going out?"

Jen narrowed her eyes, as she often did when she was trying to guess at the hidden meaning behind an innocuous question. "I don't think so. Are we?"

Blinking, Jamie shook her head. "I have no idea. I just noticed that you looked nice...very put together."

"Oh!" Now Jennie nodded, seemingly assured of her response. "Yeah. Your mom thinks it's important to look good—even when you don't havta."

"Yeah," Jamie agreed, trying to hide a chuckle that was determined to break free. "That's definitely my mom's belief." She plucked at her shirt. "I don't usually wear a T-shirt when I'm coming to see her, but I'm going over to help out on the OFC project later and I don't want to ruin anything good. That's one messy place."

"Can I go with you?"

"Uhm…" Jamie almost agreed. Then she thought better of it. "Let's go see what the Smith/Willis agenda is for the day."

Crestfallen, Jen shrugged her shoulders. "I know what it is. I've got homework. Then somebody's gonna come by and talk to me about clarinet lessons."

Jamie mentally rolled her eyes. Jen's memory was very poor when it came to recalling obligations she wasn't fond of.

Jennie went back to the dining room, where she'd spread her books out, while Jamie climbed the stairs, finding her mother in the library. "I thought I heard voices," Catherine said, looking up from her computer. She stood and extended her arms, waiting for Jamie to walk over for a hug. "I hope you've come by just to spend the day."

"No, I've got to get over to the OFC. Colm and I are going to plan the tile layout for Tommy's place."

Catherine regarded her fondly. "You're the first Dunlop or Smith to do an honest day's work in generations. I love that you help out—even though you could afford to have everything done without lifting a hand."

Jamie sat down on one of the cushy upholstered chairs. She was tempted to sit sideways and drape her legs over the arm, but she didn't feel comfortable doing that in her mother's home. "That's not the O'Flaherty way—as you well know."

Catherine sat back down and rested her chin on her braced hand. "If you're not here to while away the day, you must have an agenda."

"Always," Jamie agreed. "Today my agenda is Jen's birthday. Martin wants to have a party for her tomorrow—the *usual* party," she stressed. "One barbecue, one cake, no presents. I didn't rat you out, but I had a pretty good idea you were planning more than that."

Catherine made a face. "I was definitely planning something special, and presents are not optional. I thought we'd drive down to Hearst Castle. Jennie is fascinated by art and she might enjoy seeing how you can do anything to excess."

"And you're doing that when?"

"Wednesday. And yes, that's a school day." Catherine shifted her eyes to her computer, then made a few keystrokes. "You'll recall spending all of *your* birthdays doing something fun—no matter when they fell. Jennie deserves the same kind of treatment."

"I wasn't in Jen's situation, Mom." Jamie got up and moved over to the desk, where she perched. "Jen's a long way from the honor roll, and Sister Mary Magdalene frowns on her taking many days off."

"I know, I know," Catherine said blithely. "But the poor child has never had anyone make her feel special on her birthday. Isn't that more important than a single school day?" She was gazing up at Jamie with a wistful look in her eyes.

"Probably. So do both. Have the party at Martin's, letting Jen feel like one of the gang. Then do whatever you want on Wednesday. She can have a foot in both worlds."

Catherine put her hand on Jamie's knee and gave it a gentle squeeze. "Fabulous idea. What time should we be there?"

"Three? Or earlier, of course. What about church? I'm going to start going even though my recently paganized girlfriend isn't into it. Are you going to make Jen go?"

Catherine put her hand over her mouth. "I have no idea if the child's even been baptized! This round of parenting is certainly different from the last. I wasn't old enough to be a good mother then, and now I barely know my teenager's name!"

Late on Saturday afternoon, Catherine was on the deck enjoying the gorgeous day while reading a book. A subtle throat-clearing made her look up. "Hello, Marta."

"The clarinet teacher is here. Would you like me to bring her up?"

"Oh, yes. That would be great. Tell Jennie to come up too, won't you?"

"Of course."

Catherine stood and stretched her back out. She'd been sitting in one place for hours, always finding it hard to stop in the middle of a good book. She smiled, thinking of her mother's insistence that the maid dust her when she cleaned the spacious library Catherine used to spend long hours in.

Marta reappeared, along with a perky-looking young woman and a less perky-looking teenager. Catherine walked over and extended a hand, "Catherine Smith," she said. "Have you met Jennie Willis?"

"I have. Sophia Romano. It's good to meet you, Ms. Smith."

"Catherine, please. Have a seat."

Both Sophia and Jennie sat on striped, springy, upholstered chairs, with Jennie moving hers so she could face the bay in the distance. "Jennie's interested in learning to play the clarinet, as I told you on the phone. She's learned the basics, and has gotten fairly competent at reading music, but I think she'd agree that she's still a beginner."

Sophia tried to get Jennie's attention, finally snapping her fingers. Jen's head swiveled quickly and she looked a little startled. "Sorry. I didn't think anybody was gonna talk to me."

Catherine mentally rolled her eyes. The girl seemed to assume she was little more than decorative when adults were around.

Luckily, Sophia handled it perfectly. "We're here to talk about you taking clarinet lessons. You're integral to the conversation."

Jennie's eyes narrowed a little and Catherine bit her tongue to stop herself from telling her what "integral" meant. They were going to have to have dictionaries close at hand to improve her vocabulary. But that was a discussion for another day.

"Okay," Jennie said. "Did you ask me something?"

"Not yet. But I will." Sophia was a determined-looking woman who couldn't have been much older than Jamie. Catherine guessed she was of Italian descent, both from her name and her dark curly hair and soulful eyes. Catching sight of her hand, Catherine noted her long, elegant fingers—perfect for a clarinetist. "Why do you want to play the clarinet?"

"Uhm…" Jennie shot a look at Catherine, as if this were a test she hadn't studied for. "I dunno."

"Sure you do," Sophia said, leaning closer. "It doesn't matter if it's a dumb reason, but you've gotta have a reason."

"Uhm…my friend at school plays in the band, and I like to hang out with her."

"Good! She plays the clarinet?"

"The flute. She said clarinet's easier."

Laughing, Sophia said, "Not if you do it right. But a clarinet has more flexibility than a flute, in my opinion. You don't see many flutes in jazz bands."

"Were you in a jazz band?" Catherine asked.

"I've played in every kind of ensemble you can imagine. Right now I'm in a trio, playing gigs all around the Bay Area."

"Really? We'll have to come hear you. What's your group called?"

Chuckling, Sophia said, "Benny Goodwoman. Benny Goodman had a trio, and we're doing the same, but all women."

"That's wonderful," Catherine said. "Do you book enough work to stay busy?"

She shrugged. "We're busy, but I'm trying to get on with a chamber ensemble in San Jose, since the work would be steady."

"And you teach, obviously."

"I do. To be honest, I'll work anywhere." She let out a laugh, flashing a charming smile. "I'd do birthday parties and bar mitzvahs if I could find a way in."

"But you graduated from Juilliard!"

"I sure did. But I'm back home in San Bruno, living in my old room and thinking about playing on BART platforms."

She seemed so cherry delivering such grim news. "Are there so few jobs?"

"Very, very few. I could have worked more in New York, but I hated it there. I'm a Bay Area girl and couldn't wait to get back home." Chuckling again, she added, "I kinda thought I'd have my own apartment, but at least I'm not trudging through the snow."

"Are things that tough for your classmates?"

"For a lot of them. It takes years to develop a following if you're going out on your own. I'd love to play in an orchestra, of course, but those jobs are few and far between—especially since I want to stay close to home. Luckily, I love jazz and my bandmates are a lot of fun. We're all Juilliard girls."

Jennie jumped in, showing a little light in her eyes. "Am I too old to start? I'm almost fifteen."

Sophia gave her a long, assessing look. "I think you've got a few good years left." She smiled warmly, probably trying to make sure Jennie knew she was joking. "You're the perfect age. I started out on sax and switched to clarinet when I was about your age."

"Why'd you switch?"

"My band teacher talked me into it. She thought I could be first-chair at clarinet, and we were pretty weak there. Then I got into it and really liked having a smaller case to drag around. It's the little things that count."

"I don't think I wanna do this when I grow up," Jennie warned. "I'd just like to get into the band like by…next year."

"You're a sophomore?"

"Uh-huh."

Sophia nodded thoughtfully. "I'll come listen to your band. Check out the competition for you."

"Really?" Jennie seemed perfectly charmed by the young woman and Catherine was right behind her.

"Of course. I'll talk to the music teacher, too. If your goal is to be in band you might have a better chance if you play trumpet or drums or sax. It all depends on the mix he or she has to work with."

Catherine held her breath for a second, sincerely hoping the band did not need an additional trumpet.

Chapter Five

On Sunday morning, Martin, Maeve, Catherine, Jamie, Jennie and Caitlin sat in a cafe near Charles's church. Jennie and Caitlin sat sporadically, with the older of the two chasing the younger while the adults watched. They hadn't planned on having tea before the service, but Martin had insisted on leaving so early that the prior service was still going on.

"How did the little one take the news that she's going to be a church-goer again?" Martin asked when Jennie was out of ear shot.

"Like she takes everything," Catherine said. "With resigned acceptance. I'll consider myself a success when the child argues with me. All of the fight has been drained from her."

"I never fought with you," Jamie said. Catherine didn't mention their one big fight—over her participation in the AIDS Ride and Jamie's turning herself into a body-builder. Catherine found it funny now, but it was far from that at the time. Now that she looked at the confident, fit young woman sitting next to her, she once again acknowledged how little attention she'd paid to Jamie's desires and goals. She wouldn't make that same mistake with Jennie.

That morning, Ryan had gone running with Duffy, worked on a problem with someone on a math message board she monitored, vacuumed and dusted the whole house, written long letters to her grandparents and her aunt, sent a chatty email to Aisling, then gone to the store to buy bread and cold cuts for everyone to have for lunch. Conor and Kevin had both gone over to the OFC project to get a few hours work in, so she had the place to herself. She was going to do her best not to acknowledge to Jamie how great it felt to be alone. "Kinda like the old days, huh, Duff?" she asked her companion who looked up at her with what seemed like adoration. "It's like back when I was at USF, with Da and Conor and Rory all off at work, just the two of us and a quiet house. If everyone gets into this Episcopal thing, we're gonna have that again—every Sunday morning." She leaned over to hug him as he whipped his big body around at the sound of feet on the stairs. Ryan found herself on the floor, then being licked wildly by Duffy who was so excited by the arrival of anyone that he couldn't stop himself from running to the door and back to her three times in the moments it took for the group to climb the stairs.

Martin stood in the doorway, shaking his head. "So that's what the princess gets into while we're worshiping the Lord? Lying on the floor, playing with the pooch?"

Jamie's head squeezed in under Martin's outstretched arm. "She's probably been there for hours, missing us desperately."

Ryan got up and dusted herself off. "Exactly true." She went towards Jamie, then turned and headed for the kitchen sink. "I'm going to wash my face," she said wearily. "I know the drill."

"I thought there'd be a big, hot breakfast waiting for us," Martin teased.

"There's a big cold lunch waiting for you." Ryan emerged with a platter displaying neatly laid-out meats and cheeses. "And I bought everything for the party this afternoon." She looked up and met Jennie's eyes. "And I even know what kind of birthday cake to make." Chuckling, she added, "Jamie's gonna make it, but I told her what kind you like."

"I like every kind of cake," Jennie insisted.

"Then you're in luck, since we're gonna make three."

"Three?" Jen squeaked.

"Big crowd," Ryan advised. "We've got a few who only like chocolate, a few who prefer white cake, and one special one who likes coconut."

"That's me," Jen said, smiling.

"That's me!" Jamie added almost simultaneously. They slapped hands, with Jamie adding, "Coconut rules!"

Jen seemed a little overwhelmed by the size of the crowd, as well as being the rather muted center of attention. Catherine sidled up next to Martin and said, "Your idea to have Jennie's party here was a very good one. She's not used to having the focus placed on her, and these parties always seem…" She stopped, unsure of how to finish the sentence without it sounding like an insult. "More like a regular family get-together than a big, ornate fête."

Martin gave her a smile. "We're not fête people. I hope every member of this family knows how glad we all are that they were born. There's no need to embarrass any of them with too much fuss."

Catherine nodded, thinking it wise not to tell him of her plan to take Jennie to Hearst Castle on Wednesday. There was no way he'd approve.

Nearly every member of the extended family stopped by at some point during the afternoon. It was almost six o'clock when Heather and Ashley arrived. A little breathless, the pair gave Ryan a hug when she opened the door. "Sorry we're so late," Heather said. "Coach kept us for hours. He said he's gonna make us stay until one of us can consistently block that freshman you guys saw the other day."

"You might be there awhile," Ryan teased. "The kid's got game."

"I know. I know." Heather looked up at the short flight of stairs that led to the living room. "Sounds like a big party."

"The usual." Ryan clapped her on the back, thinking she'd start up the stairs. But Heather hesitated.

"Uhm…we're both really busy now that volleyball season's cranking. I don't think we'll be able to tutor Jen anymore."

"No worries," Ryan said, giving her a gentle push. "Catherine's got everything under control. For all I know, she's hired a bunch of retired professors to parse every word Jen hears."

Ashley laughed, but Heather kept staring at the door at the top of the stairs, almost like she was afraid.

"Everything okay?" Ryan asked.

Surprisingly, Ashley started up the stairs, leaving them behind. "Talk to her," she said when she got to the top, glaring at Heather.

"What's up?" Ryan asked.

"You didn't hear anything?" The young woman looked like she wanted to bolt.

"I hear a lot of things. What specific thing are you talking about?"

Relief flooded her face. "Uhm, nothing. Everything's fine." She started up the stairs, only to be stopped by Ryan's hand gripping her arm.

"Spill it. You look like you're about to walk into a pit of vipers."

She stood stock still, eyes darting nervously. "Something…happened when you guys were gone. But it's not a big deal and if you don't know about it, it's not as big a deal as I thought it was—"

"My room," Ryan ordered. "Now." She still had her hand around Heather's bicep and she effortlessly turned her and marched her downstairs.

"It's no big deal…really," she squeaked. "I probably made it sound worse than it was…" Ryan gave her a gentle push and Heather dropped to the bed.

"Tell me about this not very big deal." She hated to intimidate the shy kid, but something big was going on. She could feel it in her bones.

Heather's eyes shifted around the room, as if she were looking for another place—any place—to focus on. She obviously couldn't find one, because she slowly lifted her head and looked right into Ryan's penetrating gaze. "When you guys were gone, I went over to see Jennie more than usual. School had just started, and I wasn't that busy yet. Plus, I could tell she felt…»

"Abandoned," Ryan supplied for her.

Heather visibly swallowed. Nodding, she said, "Yeah."

Ryan moved over to the love-seat and sat down, thinking for a minute. "Jen's had a tough year. We really shouldn't have been gone as long as we were. I'm sure she did feel abandoned, and I'm really glad you stepped in to take up some of the slack." Smiling at the girl, she added, "You're a good person, Heather. Jen's lucky you've taken an interest in her."

"That's the problem," Heather said, her voice rising in pitch. "She's taken an interest in me. An *interest*," she stressed, her eyes wide.

"A sexual interest?" Ryan asked, her heart starting to race.

Heather dropped her head, clearly embarrassed. "Yeah, I guess so.

She…uhm…she kissed me. And right when she did Marta came upstairs and saw the whole thing. She thought I'd…" Poor Heather's cheeks were so pink she looked like she'd been slapped.

"Oh, fuck." Ryan slumped down in the love-seat, a little sick to her stomach. "What happened?"

"I freaked out and ran out of there before either of them could say a word. But I gutted it up and went back to explain to Marta what had happened. She called your friend Sara, and she talked to Jen about the whole thing."

"Sara? Why in the world…"

Heather held her hands up. "I don't know what happened. I just know that Sara came over and took charge."

"You haven't talked to Jen since?"

"No. Chicken," she admitted, her color rising again. "I sent her an email, telling her it was no big deal, but that's all I could handle…"

Ryan got up and went over to stand by the bed. She put her hand on Heather's shoulder and gave it a firm squeeze. "I'm really sorry that happened."

"It was bad." Her voice grew softer as she added, "But Sara got me calmed down pretty quickly." She swallowed, her gaze shifting to the floor. "And she talked to me—about me and gave me some good advice. I'm…thinking about taking it."

Chuckling, Ryan said, "The advice must not have been too good if you're only thinking about taking it."

"It's…it's about being gay." She looked up and met Ryan's eyes. "Me, that is. I'm probably…"

Ryan sat next to her and put an arm around her shoulders. "Hey, there's nothing to be embarrassed about. In case you haven't noticed, you're among friends."

"Yeah," she said, smiling shyly. "I didn't think it'd shock you."

"I don't know how you feel about it, but I'd choose to be gay if I had the option. It's all been good for me, Heather. Really."

"I don't think I'd choose it," she said softly. "But I'm gonna try to figure this out. Sara suggested I go to the group they have on campus."

"Damned good idea," Ryan agreed. "This is the best time in your life to be around other people exploring all sorts of aspects of themselves. Does…Ashley know?"

Heather's head shook swiftly. "No. Well, she knows about Jen kissing me, but I didn't say more than I had to. I think she'll be cool with it, but…you never know."

"No, you can never be a hundred percent sure of how people will react, but if you don't talk to her soon I can guarantee she'll be hurt."

Heather's head snapped up. "Huh? Why?"

"Because you talk to her about other things that bother you or that you're working through. If you won't talk to her about this, she'll think it's because you don't think she's open-minded enough to deal with it." She paused. "Which is probably true, right?"

Heather made a sour face. "Yeah, I guess. But she's my best friend!"

"Then treat her like one. Tell her you're struggling with this, or tell her you're just starting to work on it. But tell her something." She bumped the younger woman with her shoulder. "She might already have an inkling."

"Did she say anything to you?"

"Hell, no! But she's pretty perceptive. Have you ever hung out with a guy? Had a crush on one?"

"No. Not really."

Once again, Ryan put her arm around Heather and hugged her. "You're cute as heck, Heather. If you were into guys, you'd have one by now. Ashley's probably figured that out."

Putting her hands over her face, Heather mumbled, "This sucks."

"Yeah, it kinda does. But once you tell a few people it'll get easier. Promise."

"Couldn't get much harder, so I guess you're right."

Ryan smiled to herself, thinking of how she'd felt at Heather's age. It hadn't been much fun, but getting through it had led her to where she was today, and today was very, very sweet.

An hour later, Ryan stood on the back porch and looked down at the people gathered around the picnic table. Jennie was yammering away as she always did when Heather and Ashley were around. That was good news. At least the kid didn't feel awkward after making an unwanted pass. An arm slid around her waist and she turned to catch a soft kiss on her cheek. "Thinking deep thoughts?" Jamie asked.

For a moment, Ryan considered whether to tell Jamie about the Heather situation, then decided against it. She'd probably hear about it eventually, but Ryan hated to talk about people without a solid reason. And Jamie knowing this wouldn't help anyone. "Nope. Pretty shallow. Having fun?"

"Sure. I'm glad your father convinced my mom to have the party here. This is good for Jen. She's kind of the star, but in a muted way."

"Yep. He made the right call on this one."

"Jen came up to me a while ago and said, 'Why are we having the party here? There's a pool at your mom's house, and it's lots bigger.'" Jamie rolled her eyes. "I think she's getting used to having money."

"Never takes long." Ryan turned and took Jamie in her arms, then whispered in her ear, "I wonder where the boatload of presents are?"

"I don't know," Jamie said, laughing softly. "But I'd be the most surprised person in the world if all Jen gets is a cake. That's not the Evans... I mean, Smith, way."

Leaning back, Ryan asked, "What did you get for your fifteenth birthday?"

"Mmm, I don't remember. But we spent it in Fiji." She looked up and wrinkled her nose. "It's in February you know, and I wanted to be warm."

"My little princess had some pretty phenomenal birthdays, didn't she," Ryan teased. "Luckily she had twenty-one great ones, 'cause from now on she has to be happy with a cake and the usual suspects gathered around the barbecue, arguing about the proper way to cook chicken."

Jamie put her lips right next to Ryan's ear. As always when those sweet lips caressed her, goosebumps started at her neck and raced up into her scalp. "Luckily for you, I'm perfectly content with your rustic ways, O'Flaherty." They were the only two on the porch, and with the darkening skies they weren't very visible to the people in the yard. Still, Ryan was amazed and pleased when Jamie slid a hand between them and gave her nipple a serious tweak.

"Right out in public?" she gasped. "Really?"

"That'll teach you to tease me about my spartan birthdays. This will help, too." The sharp spank that made half of the backyard guests look up had Jamie in stitches. "You all know she deserved it!" she called out.

Being on a long vacation had freed up a part of Jamie that had always been hidden. Ryan sincerely hoped it stayed around.

On Wednesday morning, Catherine got up extra early. Once she was ready, she went downstairs and arranged the cards, balloons and a few small gifts on the kitchen table. Marta was already at work, preparing Jennie's favorite pancakes for her birthday breakfast.

The door to the kitchen swung open and a delighted teenager stood there, open–mouthed. "Is this for me?"

Catherine felt a surge of pleasure at seeing how such a small gesture made a big impact on the girl. Jennie honestly didn't seem certain that the little celebration was for her. "Happy birthday!" Catherine said, echoed by Marta.

Tentatively, Jennie approached the table. "I've never had balloons before. They're kinda cool." She gripped the string of one and tugged on it. "How do they stay up?"

"They're filled with helium," Catherine explained. When she didn't see recognition lighting up Jennie's pale blue eyes, she added, "They fill them with gas that's lighter than air." Obviously they haven't covered much in chemistry class yet.

"Oh. I get it. You get them at a store or something, right?"

"Yes, we're pretty well equipped, but neither Marta nor I have a helium tank."

Marta was chuckling as she piled Jennie's plate up with pancakes. "Cumpleaños feliz a ti, Jennie," she said as she delivered them.

Still looking a little amazed, Jennie mumbled her thanks, then sat down and dug into her breakfast. Catherine had been disappointed when the therapist she wanted Jennie to try only had that afternoon available for their first session. It had seemed perfectly reasonable to whisk Jennie away from school for the day to take her down to Hearst Castle. But seeing how just this tiny celebration seemed to disorient her, Catherine was glad her plans had been disrupted. She simply couldn't treat Jennie the same way she'd treated Jamie. It would be too much of a shock to the poor girl's system. They were going to have to take things slowly, and she sincerely hoped the therapist would be able to help them do just that.

Dr. Fernandez was exactly the type of person Catherine had been hoping for. She was young, seemed streetwise, engaging, open, and not easily ruffled. The three of them spoke for about a half-hour, with Catherine urging Jennie to answer most of the questions. For the next fifteen minutes, Jennie and the doctor spoke in private. At the end of the session, Dr. Fernandez called Catherine back in.

The doctor regarded Jennie with a warm smile. "If you're willing to continue to see me, I think we can form a good working relationship, Jennie. What do you think?"

"Working relationship?" Her startled gaze when to Catherine. "What does that mean?"

"Just that you can learn to trust Dr. Fernandez enough to share things with her," Catherine said. "Therapy *is* work, but not in the traditional sense."

"Okay," Jennie said, turning back to the doctor.

That wasn't a huge vote of confidence, but the doctor was undoubtedly used to working with kids who were even less enthusiastic than Jennie was.

"If possible, I'd like to meet twice a week. It usually takes a while to get comfortable with each other, and I'm sure you'd both like to start making progress."

Catherine wasn't crazy about the idea, given how much schoolwork Jennie had, but she decided to put her reservations aside and trust this young woman. But she thought it best to make it clear this was going to be a stretch. "We'll do whatever you think best. But Jennie needs a few hours every night to complete her schoolwork. I want to make sure she has some time to herself."

"I understand," the doctor said. "And I agree. We'll meet twice a week for as long as we need to, then we'll switch to just once." She gave Jennie a knowing smile. "I remember what it was like to be in high school. Do you do anything outside of class? Play sports or anything?"

"No. I'm a klutz," she said, as if this were an intrinsic element of herself that was unchangeable. "But I'm gonna start taking clarinet lessons."

"Oh, that'll be great. I played trombone in my school band. I bet you'll love it."

"I hope so," Jennie said. "But I don't know when I'll have time to practice."

"Don't worry about that," Catherine said. "We'll work out a good schedule."

"How about Tuesdays and Thursdays?" Dr. Fernandez said. "I can do…" She looked at her laptop, squinting at the small screen. "Six?"

"That's fine," Catherine agreed. "That will let Jennie have a few hours after school to get a head-start on her homework."

"Great. Let's start on Tuesday." She extended her hand and shook Jennie's, then Catherine's. "You understand that from now on, Jennie and I will speak in private, right?"

"Oh, certainly. That only makes sense."

"It does," the doctor said. "If Jennie ever wants you to join us, that's her choice. If she doesn't, everything that we talk about will be between just the two of us." She let her brown eyes settle on Jen's. "You understand that, right?"

"Yeah. Okay," she said, not looking thoroughly convinced. "See you next week."

As they walked out of the office, Catherine said, "I don't know about you, but talking to a therapist always leaves me feeling drained. Why don't we do something fun to recharge our batteries? Marta's making your birthday dinner, but she won't be ready for us until seven."

"Okay." Jennie's eyes lit up, making her look even younger than she already did. "What do you wanna do?"

They were close to Union Square, and Catherine recalled there was a big art supply store not too far away. "I'd like some ice cream, then I'd like to go shopping."

Jennie still seemed excited, but her eyes had dimmed a bit. Catherine was certain the spark would be back when the girl saw they weren't shopping for clothes—for a change.

After Jennie's favorite dinner of tacos, refrijoles and Spanish rice, she took Ryan up to her room to show her all of the new art supplies she'd gotten that afternoon. Jamie stayed behind after insisting she was going to help Marta clean up. Of course, Marta would allow no such thing, and she politely but firmly suggested Jamie and Catherine go outside to enjoy the evening.

Catherine led the way, and when they got to the deck she closed the doors for privacy. "You should have seen me at the art store," she said, laughing. "It's so much harder to buy just a few things than it is to take ten of everything the child lays her eyes on!"

"I think that's the right decision, Mom. She needs to know she can have whatever she needs, but not whatever she wants. That's a lesson I remember Poppa very clearly giving me when I was really young."

"I never learned that," Catherine said, reflecting. "But I wish I had. I was so spoiled it took years for me to be happy living on your father's salary."

"I think I'm pretty moderate, but you see how Ryan struggles with money. And god knows she's a lot more mature than Jen—usually," she added, laughing. "Jen was just above public assistance when she was with her mom, so living with you is a massive change."

"I don't think I knew that," Catherine said. "But she acts like nearly everything we do is an epic adventure."

"It is to her. She's remarkably innocent in so many ways."

Catherine took a look at the door, not seeing any sign of Jennie. She got up and moved to sit next to Jamie on a love-seat. "In some ways. In others…she's less so."

"What happened?"

Taking another quick look, Catherine said, "When we were gone, Heather came over to help Jen get settled with her new courses. Somehow, Jennie decided that not only was Heather a lesbian, she would welcome an overture."

"An overture?" Jamie said, her voice rising.

"Marta was taking a snack upstairs, and she interrupted Jennie as she was kissing Heather."

"Oh, shit!" Jamie slapped a hand over her mouth. "What did Heather do?"

"Ran like a criminal," Catherine said, chuckling at the image of the lanky young woman dashing from the house as if it were on fire. "But she came back later to explain to Marta that she hadn't encouraged Jennie."

"Jesus," Jamie said, dropping her head into her hand. "It's always something with Jen."

"I wasn't too upset when Marta told me," Catherine admitted. "Until she reminded me that Heather could have been prosecuted for a sex crime if she'd been the aggressor. *That* got my attention."

"What does Jen have to say?"

"We haven't spoken about it yet. I was going to bring it up in therapy, but we had so little time…"

"You've gotta talk to her, Mom. She can't just go around hitting on college-aged women." She blinked. "She also can't just kiss people who she isn't sure are into her!"

"I know. I know. I'm not sure how to approach it, but I've got to do it." She put her arm around Jamie and gave her a hug. "Have I told you lately how much I appreciate how well-behaved you were at fifteen?"

"Yeah, you've told me," Jamie said, leaning over to place a kiss on Catherine's cheek. "But I have an unlimited need for praise. Feel free to continue."

🐾

The house was rocking when Jamie and Ryan got home. Kevin, Brian, Liam and Conor had their long bodies squished into small places in Conor's room, watching the baseball playoffs. Jamie found herself less interested in baseball when the Giants weren't involved, and they'd been eliminated in the divisional playoffs by the Mets the week before. That fact didn't seem to diminish the enthusiasm of the O'Flaherty boys though. Taking a quick look, Jamie saw a lot of empty beer bottles, figuring they played a part in the noise level.

Ryan was edging further and further into the room, but Jamie snagged the back pocket of her jeans and pulled her back out. "You're not going to stay up late and watch baseball, then get up at the crack of dawn to go work on the house. Come on now. You didn't even know the game was on two minutes ago."

Conor had the ability to make a sound just like that of a whip being cracked, and when he made it everyone but Jamie laughed. "You're just jealous because your sister has someone who cares about her and looks out for her welfare," she said, after sticking her tongue out at him.

"Nah. He's just jealous his sister has someone who wants to give her a pop," Brian said, snorting.

Jamie wasn't sure why, but Brian's teasing sometimes got under her skin. "G'night boys," she said, refusing to rise to the bait.

When they got to the room, there was a note of annoyance in her voice when Ryan said, "Why didn't you want me to watch the game?"

"If you want to watch the Mets and the Cardinals, go right ahead. But since you were cursing the ground the Mets walked on just last week, I didn't think you were a fan."

"I just don't like them when they're beating the Giants. Other than that, I like them as well as any other team. You know I like to watch with the boyos."

"My bad. I just wanted to talk to you about something, and I guess I'm anxious to get it out."

Immediately, Ryan took her hand and led her over to the love-seat, one hundred percent of her attention focused on Jamie. It was awfully nice to have a partner who knew what was important. "It's nothing horrible, but it is…*concerning.*»

With her expression full of interest, Ryan said, "Concerning…you talking to your mom alone… I have a feeling Jennie's involved."

Jamie touched the tip of Ryan's nose with a finger. "You're a very good guesser." She took a breath as she collected her thoughts. "Here's the deal. While we were gone, Jennie got it into her head that Heather would be up for little playing around."

Ryan's face lost all expression. When that happened, she was covering something up. *Always.* In seconds, Jamie's blood pressure started to rise. "You rat! You knew!"

Shrugging, Ryan said, "You know I don't like to be a snitch."

"This is being a snitch? Telling Jennie's legal guardian that she's doing something inappropriate with an adult is snitching?" Gripping the shoulder of Ryan's shirt, Jamie gave her a shake. "We're not talking about something that happened at recess!"

"I assumed your mom knew, since Marta found them."

"But you didn't *know* that."

Eyes shifting to the ground, Ryan's head tilted lower. "I screwed up."

Jamie gripped her chin and forced her head up so their eyes met. "Do you mean that, or are you saying that so I stop bitching at you?"

A bit of her devilish charm showed when Ryan said, "Will I get in trouble if I say it's a little of both?"

Jamie got up and pointedly ignored the last question. "I'm going to take a long bath. Why don't you go watch the baseball game. I need a timeout."

Ryan got up and started to approach her, then veered off and stood in front of the stairs. "I'm going to take you at your word. But if you didn't mean that, I'll stay here and let you yell at me."

Making a whooshing motion with her hands, Jamie said, "I meant every word. Pray that the game goes into extra innings. Maybe then I'll be able to remind myself you're almost a perfect partner. Right now it's the 'almost' part I've got to stew about."

Chapter Six

The weather had changed from warm, dry, blue-skied and summery to a cold gray dreariness. But that didn't stop Catherine from going ahead with her plans. She'd learned from Jamie that the best time to get information out of a teenager was during a car trip or while walking. Since Jennie's first clarinet lesson was at six o'clock, an extended car trip was out. So she put on a warm sweater, added a stylish lightweight wool scarf around her neck, and set off to meet Jennie after school.

The girl emerged from her building and Catherine watched her eyes dart from car to car, looking for the Mercedes. After Catherine waved energetically, Jennie finally turned in her direction and gave her a quizzical smile as she approached. "Where's the car?"

"I thought it would be fun to walk home."

"Okay." Catherine knew it wasn't wise to wish that her teenage charge would put up more of a struggle, but it wasn't good for Jennie to always so benignly agree with almost anything an adult suggested.

It was a short walk home, so to give them extra time Catherine started to lead Jennie towards Alta Vista Park, one of her favorite spots in the neighborhood. As was often the case, Jennie didn't question why they weren't going directly home. After spending a few minutes asking very open ended questions, designed to encourage the girl to open up about her school day, Catherine brought up the delicate topic. "I spoke with Marta about that little incident between you and Heather."

Jennie's eyebrows shot up, and she mumbled, "I figured that would happen."

"Do you want to talk about it, honey?"

Warily, Jennie said, "Am I in trouble?"

"Of course not! Why would you be in trouble?"

They'd reached the park, a relatively small one right at the top of Pacific Heights. On a clear day it seemed as though you could see forever. Today, however, you had to guess which direction the Marina was in. Jennie trudged up the stairs to reach the top of the park, where she sat down on a bench to watch a couple of dogs playing roughly. Jennie gave Catherine a sidelong look. "Everybody acted like I was a huge jerk. Like I made Heather do something she didn't wanna do." A fire burned in her eyes. "She's like a foot taller than me, and lots stronger. She could've just pushed me away or punched me." Her chin stuck out a little, making her look strangely defiant. "She didn't."

Catherine put an arm around her shoulders and hugged her, her heart hurting for the incredibly small arsenal of tools Jennie had at her disposal when it came to figuring out normal human interaction. "Honey, Heather isn't the kind of girl who would punch you for kissing her."

"Why not? They're always telling us you don't have to let people touch you if you don't want them to."

"That's true. But there are much subtler ways of communicating with people you care for. And I'm sure Heather cares for you."

"No she doesn't. She just thinks I'm a kid."

She looked so crestfallen. Like all of her normal confidence had abandoned her. "She probably does think of you as much younger than she. It's a very different experience to be in college than high school, and four years is a much bigger gap now than it will be when you're older."

"I'm not great at math, but four years is four years no matter when they happen."

"That's simply not true, honey. An infant and a four-year-old are worlds apart. But Jamie and Ryan are three years apart and they seem exactly the same age."

Snickering, Jennie said, "Jamie seems older most of the time."

"Right." Catherine laughed along with her. "That's true. But the difference between being fourteen and eighteen is pretty steep."

"I'm fifteen," she said. "And Heather's not like a normal eighteen-year-old. You can't say that's not true. I've got lots more experience than she has in a bunch of things."

Patting her gently, Catherine said, "I'm sure that's true, but that's not the critical thing here." She took a breath and made herself be brutally honest. "Heather's not interested in you in that way. And even if she were, it would be wrong for her to act on it. She's an adult in the eyes of the law, and you're a child." Jennie's cheeks reddened and she seemed about to argue. Catherine held up a hand. "Those are facts, Jennie. Not feelings. Trying to be sexual with an adult is a very bad idea for you—and an even worse idea for the adult. San Francisco is a very open-minded place, but Heather could go to jail for being sexually involved with you."

"Even though we're girls?" Now her brows were almost at her hairline.

"Yes, even lesbians have to obey the law. The law isn't about intercourse. It's about inappropriate sexual touch—no matter the sex of the people involved."

"So you think she's just afraid of going to jail?" There was a hopeful tone to her question.

"No, I don't think that's it. I think Heather considers you a friend—not a romantic partner."

"Yeah, you're right," she said, slumping down on the bench. "I'm too young for anything fun."

"That's not true. You're simply at a tough age. Not quite old enough to do things on your own, but old enough to want to."

Her look was now more of a glare. "I've done plenty of things on my own. Things you don't know about."

"I know about some of the things," Catherine reminded her. "Like hitchhiking down to Ryan's softball game." Even though Jennie looked angry, Catherine scooted closer and put her arm around her shoulders. "I still have nightmares about that. And your running away, of course. My therapist had to work hard to keep me from drinking a case of vodka that weekend."

Jennie pulled away and looked up curiously. "You have a therapist?"

"I do. I called her at least thirty times the weekend you went missing."

"Why? I know how to take care of myself."

"No, you don't, honey. You have some good instincts, but you're still young, and you don't always think things through. When I couldn't find you…I was overwhelmed with fear. It was one of the worst times of my life."

"Really?" She squinted, then cocked her head. "Over me?"

"Yes," Catherine assured her. "Over you. I care for you deeply, Jennie, and it would destroy me if anything happened to you."

"Why'd you want to drink vodka? Does that make you feel better?"

"No." She paused, unsure of how much to reveal. Then she decided to just be honest. "Well, yes. When I'm drunk I don't feel pain. But the next day I feel much worse in every way, so it's a bad idea."

In a quiet voice, Jennie said, "My mom used to drink—a lot. That's why my dad left."

"I'm sorry to hear that. It's tough to have to deal with that when you're a child." Being honest was good, but Catherine decided not to tell Jennie of her own parents' drinking. She didn't need to know things that didn't directly affect her.

"Yeah, it was. Then she met that pastor who got her to stop." She shrugged. "I liked her better when she drank. That religion stuff really sucked."

"But you don't mind going to Charles' church, do you?"

"Nah. That was fine. He didn't talk about how we were all going to hell even once."

Catherine laughed. "No, mentions of hell and damnation are pretty few and far between. And the church is very welcoming to gay men and lesbians. I think you'll like it if you give it a chance."

"I will." She looked around for a second, then started to briskly rub her arms. "I don't know about you, but I'm gonna freeze up here. Can we go home now?"

"We definitely can. I'm going to call Marta and ask her to have two mugs of hot cocoa ready for us when we reach the door."

They got up and started to walk. "I'm sorry you were worried about me when I ran away," Jennie said quietly. "I don't think of other people when I do things like that."

"You'll learn to," Catherine assured her. "Over time, you'll realize how much we all love you and you'll remember that when you're tempted to do something dangerous."

"I hope you're right. But Ryan can tell you I don't learn things very fast."

"I'm persistent," Catherine assured her, hoping that she truly was.

Jamie called her mother's home at 5:30. "Hey, Mom. I'm going over to pick up Pigpen at the OFC house. Do you two want to go with me to see her progress? She's really excited about this wall she's plastered."

"That does sound enticing," Catherine teased, "but Sophia's here for Jennie's first clarinet lesson, and I shouldn't go have fun without her. She's…well, we talked about Heather today and she's feeling young and left out."

"How'd it go?"

"Better than I thought it would in some ways, worse in others. The girl has so few social skills. She honestly thought Heather should have punched her if she didn't want to be kissed. Violence seems like a perfectly natural instinct for her."

"She's had a tough life, Mom. It's gonna take all of the combined Smith/Dunlop social skills to make a dent. But you're going to do it. I just know you are."

"I certainly hope you're right. You'll have to come by some Monday afternoon to meet Sophia. I think you'd really like her."

"We will. How long is the lesson?"

"Just an hour. But I could probably convince her to stay for dinner. Maybe next week?"

"My calendar is clear next week. Let's plan on it."

"I'll put you on the schedule. Oh, I meant to ask how you feel about having your name on bumper stickers and plastered to telephone polls."

"Not great," Jamie admitted. "But I've got a big Evans sign in my front yard in Berkeley. I should probably put one on the front deck here in the city, but I don't want to irritate Martin every time he walks up the stairs."

"He'll never be a fan," Catherine agreed.

"No, he won't. Sadly, I've gotta step it up and do a little campaigning. One of dad's minions called today and asked me to go to the Central Valley to speak at a couple of junior colleges on Tuesday."

"How I envy you!"

"Sarcasm doesn't sound right coming from you, Mom," Jamie teased. "You might have divorced dad just over this. I can't see you putting on the plastic smile as you go from one banquet to the next all over the great state of California."

"That wouldn't be my idea of fun, but I suppose I would have done my part if circumstances had been different."

"You're a trouper. Now I've got to go collect my little mudder."

"Mudder?"

"I've learned that's a term for a plasterer. The stuff they use is called mud."

"We learn all sorts of fascinating things from Ryan, don't we?"

"We do. And most of them are things we would have been perfectly happy not to know. I just can't admit that to my sweetie."

Jamie drove over to The Mission, finding a serviceable parking space only two blocks away. As she walked down the street, she saw Ryan sitting on the front steps of the apartment building, chugging what looked like a liter of water. "Did somebody work too hard today?"

"This somebody sure did." She tilted the bottle into her mouth, swallowing a quarter of the liquid. When she let it drop down to dangle near her leg, a hand rose and dramatically wiped her brow. "If I'd had any idea how hard it was to plaster a wall, I never would've suggested it."

"My poor little lamb." Jamie stood close and rubbed Ryan's shoulders when her head dropped to rest on a hip. "Want me to take you out for a nice dinner tonight?"

Looking up, Ryan gave her a wry smile. "You know there's nothing I like better at the end of a long day than to get dressed up and sit in uncomfortable chairs with a bunch of strangers. But if you want to go, I'll be your date."

"That's right neighborly of you. But I'll give you a pass." She ruffled her hand through Ryan's dusty hair. "You look like you need a date with a long bath and a cold beer."

"That's my *perfect* date," Ryan agreed, showing a slow, sexy smile. "I just need a bigger tub so I can have my beautiful girlfriend in there with me."

"That'll come in our new home—if we ever get one. Count on it." She extended a hand and pulled Ryan to her feet. "I can take you away from all this for a couple of days next week. Wanna go to the Central Valley with me?"

"For fun?"

Jamie gazed at her for a moment. "Think about that for a minute and let me know what the Central Valley has that I can't find a bit closer to home."

Ryan tapped her chin with a finger, acting like she was thinking hard. "Maybe the almond harvest is something you've always wanted to see? If this is when they harvest almonds, that is. My knowledge of… horticulture? Agriculture? Is kinda weak."

"No such luck. I'm going to two junior colleges to give a stump speech for the Honorable Senator Evans."

Ryan's expression was one of near horror. "You don't really want me to go with you, do you?"

Slightly annoyed, Jamie said, "Good thing we haven't taken our marriage vows yet, 'cause you're not doing very good on the 'in good times and bad' part."

Ryan stood up tall, took Jamie's hands in her own and looked into her eyes. "If you need me, I'm there. It's just the thought of people staring at me…"

Jamie could see the storm clouds dim those pretty blue eyes. She stood on her tiptoes, then pulled Ryan down to kiss a cheek covered in white, powdery dust. "I'm sorry, sweetheart. I forget that you're still…"

"Weird," Ryan supplied. "The carjacking hardly crosses my mind on most days. But having a bunch of kids staring at us reminds me of the media frenzy. You know that part was as bad as almost being killed."

"I know that, and I'm sorry for even asking. My bad."

"No bigs. Let's go inside where I will amaze you with my trowel work."

"Sentences I never thought I'd hear," Jamie teased as she followed her partner into the building.

They walked through the long apartment, bypassing the living room, three bedrooms, two full baths and the rough outline of a half bath next to the new kitchen. That space was nothing but plywood floors and markings made with orange spray paint, but at the back of the room a sturdy-looking, brownish-gray wall stood. It didn't look very nice; all lumpy and bumpy, but Jamie kept that opinion to herself. "Wow!" she said, amping up the enthusiasm. "Did you do this all by yourself?"

"Of course not. Kieran came by and spent a couple of hours with me. He did most of the work of putting up the lath and mixing the mud. But I did the scratch coat."

Jamie put her hand out to touch it, but Ryan gripped and held it. "Still wet."

"Scratch coat, huh? Is it scratchy?"

"Uhm, no. As you put it up, you angle your trowel to scratch those horizontal grooves in it. That lets the next coat have a good base to adhere to."

"It's super cool," Jamie said, staring up at Ryan with a smile she tried to make adulatory.

"Kieran will probably think it looks like crap, but he's being very, very patient with me. He's gonna let me do the scratch coats on the other walls, too."

"Just that?"

"Uh-huh. I'm gonna be his dogsbody for the finish coats. He doesn't want me to screw them up."

"Is it really that hard?" Jamie looked at the very rough, very grainy wall, having a hard time imagining how two more coats would make it smooth.

"A hell of a lot harder than I thought. I've seen Kieran plaster before, but never paid much attention. It's all in the wrist," she added. "And my wrist isn't very good."

Jamie took her hand and kissed the dusty wrist. "I think it's perfect." Ryan smiled down on her and for the first time in days Jamie got a tingle in a good place.

"You're really sexy today," Jamie said, tilting her head and squinting a little to get a better look. A snug, royal blue T-shirt, probably snug from repeated washings and being procured when she was ten years younger, covered Ryan's torso. The sleeves were tight, making her biceps look like they were going to break through. The shirt was short, too, just covering the waistband of her wheat-colored carpenter's pants. These were recent vintage, but they were already well broken in and settled low on her hips. That might have been because of the tools she had hanging from loops on the backs of both rear pockets.

Most people would have looked at her and wanted to stick her in a shower, but Jamie unaccountably loved to see her dirty—especially when it was dusty dirt, not grimy dirt.

"You're giving me 'the look,'" Ryan teased.

"That's 'cause you look good enough to eat."

"Really?" Ryan moved over to a window where the reflection let her take a good look at herself. "I'm a mess! I should have worn a hat or put my hair back. I thought I had some bands in my tool bag…"

Jamie walked up behind her and pressed her face between Ryan's shoulder blades. "I like it down." She put her hands on Ryan's breasts and gave them a gentle squeeze. "I like these up." In seconds, the nipples started to harden. "You're so compliant," Jamie murmured as she rubbed her face against Ryan's back.

"Autonomic response. Are we… Do you really want to start this here? We can be home in five minutes."

"Here." Jamie squeezed her again. "Right here."

"Let me lock the door at least." She dashed for the front door, snapping the lock hard enough that Jamie heard it. Ryan's booted feet echoed down the hallway, and when she arrived, one of her cocky smiles was in place. "It's either standing up or squished in a bathtub. Your choice."

Jamie approached and stood a foot away, just taking her in. When Ryan knew they were going to have sex she often wore a smile that was beyond adorable. Confident, sexy, anticipatory. The cool thing was that she never smiled that way unless they were getting ready to get down. That made it cooler.

"Upright and fast. Every guy's dream," Jamie chuckled. Delicately, she used her fingers to flick the white dust off the almost microscopic hairs on Ryan's arms. Then she peeled the T-shirt from her, turned it inside out and cleaned her face.

"Thought you liked me dirty."

"I do. But god knows what that dust is. I don't wanna eat it."

"Gypsum."

"Still don't wanna eat it," Jamie decided. Then she linked her hands around Ryan's neck and pulled her down for a kiss. "Just like I like you. Dusty and a little sweaty."

"I'll never understand it—"

"Stop thinking. Start reacting," Jamie said as she pushed her against one of the intact walls.

"Yes, *ma'am*."

Ryan's nipples got harder in a flash. There was no surer way to turn her on than to be a little dominant. Unfortunately, Jamie generally liked being chased. But once in a while, she liked to take over. When Ryan was a little dirty, and they were somewhere vaguely semi-public, she couldn't help herself. She teased Ryan for being into the possibility of being caught—but she liked it too. In her case, it was best if the possibility was more theoretical than real. Like today.

Jamie's hands went to her breasts as their mouths met. Warm, lush lips and pliable, willing flesh was a great combo and Jamie took full advantage, palming her breasts as her tongue slipped into Ryan's mouth.

"I like this," Ryan purred.

"I know." Jamie placed a hand on the back of her neck and pulled her down a little, making her sweet mouth more accessible.

But Ryan pulled away after just a minute, moved across the room and dragged over two big, white plastic tubs of something. She grasped Jamie by the waist and effortlessly placed her on them, one foot on each. Now Jamie was half a foot taller than Ryan, making her feel like the larger, more powerful partner. She'd ignore the fact that she probably couldn't have picked up the tubs and knew she couldn't pick up the partner. But reality and sex didn't have to match. It was better if they didn't, in her experience.

Towering over Ryan made her clit throb and she went at her with even more enthusiasm. Soon they were grappling with each other as Jamie kissed her with a ferocity that left them both panting. "I love you," she whispered into an ear that still bore a little white dust along the pink shell-like edge.

"I know you do," Ryan said, looking up with a vacant gaze. "But sometimes you just wanna fuck me. This is one of those days." She puckered up for a long kiss, then added, "I love these days."

Smirking, Jamie whipped Ryan's sports bra off, then let her hands take over. The first time she touched that firm skin always made her arousal skyrocket, and today was no exception. Ryan's breasts were astoundingly luscious, and she thought she loved them more than usual from her new vantage point. Her hands pressed against them in different places, feeling Ryan's pulse beat at a slightly different angle.

Thankfully, Ryan wasn't just taking pleasure—she was giving it. Her hands were perfectly placed to grab and squeeze Jamie's ass, and she was so enthusiastic that she kept drawing squeals of pain from her. But it was such good pain…the kind you only got from sex.

Jamie let her nose sniff all around Ryan's head, neck, and shoulders. "I absolutely *love* the way you smell." Her eyes shifted down to meet Ryan's loving gaze. "You don't look so bad either." She lifted Ryan's breasts in her hands, then dipped her head and laved each hard nipple. "You could make a fortune with these. People would give up an entire paycheck for photos." Their eyes met again. "But I'm really happy I'm the only one who gets to play with them. I'm *really* possessive." This time, she sucked hard when the tender nipple entered her mouth. Ryan's hand went to Jamie's head and rested there, as though it was getting into position if it had to defend sensitive skin from a too ardent attack.

Hopping off the tubs, Jamie said, "I can't get to the good parts when I'm that tall."

"Hey! I'm that tall and I don't have any trouble."

Jamie held her close and nibbled all across her chest and shoulders. "Everybody knows you're super-talented. I'm not a demigod like you are."

Chuckling, Ryan said, "We've already established I'm not a demigod. A semi-god—maybe."

"Gorgeous and clever. A very good combo." With a sultry look, Jamie held Ryan's waistband taut, then slid the zipper down. Her hand snuggled inside Ryan's panties, heading for her prize. "Mmm," she purred. "Gorgeous, clever and very responsive. I think I'm gonna keep you."

"Like you could get rid of me." Ryan let out a heavy sigh as Jamie's fingers slid into her wetness. "A woman with fingers that talented is worth her weight in gold." A soft chuckle followed. "Come to think of it, you might literally be worth your weight in gold. Double win!"

"Pay attention," Jamie instructed as her fingers started to move. "I'm trying to get somewhere here."

Ryan draped her arms around Jamie's shoulders, then spread her feet further apart. Her head tilted back as her eyes fluttered closed. *Now* she had her. As the seconds ticked away, Ryan's skin got slicker and her body shivered roughly. "That's my girl," Jamie cooed. "Just relax and feel my fingers."

A soft noise escaped from between Ryan's open lips. Jamie looked up to see nipples so hard they'd turned dark pink, her tongue barely peeking out from her lips. *Such* a sexy woman. As Jamie's fingers slid inside, Ryan bore down on her hand, then started to push forward. The gentle hands on Jamie's shoulders now gripped her tightly. Then a hand slid down and nestled up against Jamie's. "Gotta come," Ryan panted. Jamie continued to swirl her fingers into her slickness while Ryan delicately let her fingers glide over her clit. In moments, Jamie's fingers were gripped by Ryan's spasming flesh. A chill raced down her spine at the soft moan that caressed her ears. Hearing Ryan experience pleasure was one of the sweetest sounds Jamie had ever heard. To know, without question, that her touch, and their connection created that pleasure made it all so much better. "I love you," Jamie whispered as Ryan leaned heavily against her.

"And I love you. I'm already missing you and you aren't gonna leave for days."

"But I'll come home soon." She kissed her cheek, then her salty eyelids, then her mouth. "You're too alluring to stay away for long."

They had no regular soap, and no towels at all, so Ryan couldn't do much to freshen up. "What's this stuff?" Jamie asked, holding up a can of something that might have been a cleaning product.

"Some petroleum-based solvent so strong it'll take your fingerprints off. I think I'll stick with water." Ryan looked remarkably clean after she'd run water over her face and arms. Jamie always carried a hairbrush, especially now that she was growing her hair out. Lovingly, she brushed Ryan's hair, making it smooth and glossy.

"You don't look at all like a woman who's just had her bell rung in a grungy construction site."

"Thank you," Ryan said. "That's a lovely compliment. Hey, when are you and Annie going shopping for fixtures? We'll be ready for them within a week or two at the most. You girls have to get shakin'."

"Girls," Jamie scoffed, taking her cell phone from her pocket. "If Annie and I are girls, what does that make you?"

"I'm not sure, but you and Annie seem different from me. And that's not just because I'm a semi-god."

Chapter Seven

Slowly, Mia opened her eyes on Saturday morning. She was on her side, facing Jordan who was peacefully sleeping. That was a relief. Her partner needed her sleep to bounce back from the months of anxiety and overwork she'd put into being on the Olympic team, but her injured rotator cuff had ruined her sleep for nearly two weeks now. Luckily, the neoprene brace that the orthopedist had given her allowed her to sleep much, much better. She was now down to taking only a long-acting ibuprofen pill.

Turning over, Mia started to inch out of bed, but a hand landed on her hip, effectively stopping her. "Where are you going?"

"I was going to go make you a cappuccino. I don't think I can use the espresso machine as well as Jamie does, but I thought my sweetheart deserved breakfast in bed."

"Are you ready to get up? I could sleep another hour, but I don't want to if you're up."

Flopping back down, Mia rested her hand on Jordan's leg. "I've got nowhere to be, and nothing to do." She turned her head and gave Jordan a luminous smile. "That's my favorite state of being, by the way. If not for being worried about your shoulder, this would be the absolute best time of my life."

Jordan turned and faced her. She didn't even wince, which was a very good sign. With a curious grin, Jordan said, "What's the best time in your life before you met me?"

"Mmm…" Mia gave the question the consideration it deserved, then said, "any of the summers during college. They all kinda run together, but it was fantastic to have weeks of nothing to do and lots of friends to do it with." She gently poked Jordan on the chest. "How about you?"

Jordan had clearly been anticipating the return question, speaking quickly and decisively. "The year before my dad left. My parents got along well enough, my dad got home at a decent hour, I was doing great in school, could read French pretty well, and was just starting to fall in love with volleyball. Everything seemed stable, and I was safe."

"My goal in life is to make you feel that way again," Mia whispered. "I'd do anything in my power to take care of you."

"I know that," Jordan said, her smile showing the tenderness she felt. "There's not a doubt in my mind that's true. But I think I have to make myself feel safe, and that takes therapy."

Tentatively, Mia said, "You seem... You seem a little more down ever since your session yesterday. Isn't therapy supposed to make you feel better?"

With a gentle smile, Jordan nodded. "It does, but only over time. Apparently, it has to make you feel much worse for a while."

"You've been going how long?"

"This will be my twelfth year, but only my fourth with this therapist." Her eyes widened, and she spoke quickly. "I really do think it's helping. I know it's not going as quickly as you'd like—"

Mia put a gentle hand upon her lips, silencing her. "I have no expectations about timing. I'm just glad you have someone to talk to who you trust."

"Mi mrff mruu."

Chuckling, Mia took her hand away.

"I trust you too," Jordan said. "I hope you know that. But it's different in therapy. She knows how to pull things out of me that I'd rather not have pulled, and that's not a safe thing for a girlfriend to do."

Snuggling closer, Mia put her lips right at Jordan's ear. "Some goofy part of you seems to think I want to be your therapist, or I want you to stop therapy, or something else crazy. None of that is true. I want you to go for as many visits a week as you need. If that's five, that's okay." She was gently rubbing Jordan's hip the whole time she spoke, and the rigid posture slowly loosened.

"I'm worried about money. It kills me to spend my savings when I know I'll need them for graduate school."

"Tell the truth," Mia said. "Are you getting pleasure out of lying around the house with me?"

It took Jordan a long time to answer. Her eyes locked on Mia's, then danced away. "You know how much I love spending time with you. If this was a regular vacation, or I was waiting to start a job, this would be heavenly."

"But it's not, and you're not."

"No, I'm not. I want to be having fun, to just relax and enjoy the hell out of you, but I'm having a tough time getting it done." Her eyes closed briefly. "I feel like crap about that."

Mia tenderly ran her hand through Jordan's silky hair. "Shh…don't be so hard on yourself, baby. No one expects as much from you as you expect from yourself."

Jordan gave her a small smile. "I've heard that before. Doesn't seem to sink in."

"That's one more thing you can work on in therapy." Mia licked a wet stripe up the side of Jordan's face, making her giggle and try to push her away. "Here I am, perfectly enjoying hours and hours of doing nothing— my favorite state of being—and my otherwise fantastic girlfriend doesn't like being a slug. We might be incompatible."

"Then I'll learn to be a slug," Jordan said immediately.

"Good answer. But I don't think it works that way." She rolled over, let her feet fall to the floor, then got up. "I'm gonna make a call. Don't go away." As she got to the door, she added, "While I'm gone you can decide if you want to make love before or after breakfast." She held up two fingers. "Those are the only two choices in play."

Mia went into the den to ensure her privacy, then pressed a button on her phone. "Dad?"

"Hi, honey. You're not calling to cancel tonight, are you? Your mom's already cooking."

"Nope. I just wanted to talk to you for a few minutes—alone."

"Oh, boy." His voice changed, making him sound drained. "What's your mother done now?"

"Nada. I'm calling for a favor."

"A favor? Okay. Let me hear it."

"Who do you know who wants to hire a charming, engaging, hard-working, very attractive woman?"

Adam laughed for a few seconds. "Everyone wants to hire that woman. Is she a lawyer? Send her right over."

"It's me! You should have realized that from the description."

"I'm teasing," her father said. "Your mom told me you're looking for work."

"Well, why haven't you come up with anything? Jim Evans is gonna be my next call, and I know you don't want him to find out you can't hook your own flesh and blood up."

"I'm thinking…"

"Think harder. I need a *good* job, preferably one that has domestic partner benefits."

"Not asking too much," he mumbled. "Uhm, do you know anything about public relations?"

"Of course. I love to relate to people in public."

"Focus, Mia. Can you give me a serious answer?"

"I don't know a thing, Dad, but I can research the hell out of it."

"Great. One of the senior associates here at the firm was telling me about his wife's new crisis management firm." He let out a laugh. "I think you'd be a natural. I'll see if she's looking for someone who can learn from the ground up."

"I was kinda thinking about learning from the top down. I need some money coming in, dad."

He laughed again. "One thing you've got is nerve. That's an asset in PR. I'll ask the guy on Monday."

"You don't have his home phone number?"

She could hear his defeated sigh, one he'd developed years earlier from dealing with her mother's demands. "No, I don't, honey. But I'll make a point of it on Monday."

"Great. Thanks, dad. We're looking forward to tonight."

After a shared mug of decently prepared cappuccino, a long, foreplay-filled shower, and an even longer bout of lovemaking, Mia lay mostly atop Jordan's body, marveling at the heat she gave off. "For a skinny woman, you throw off a lot of BTUs."

Jordan's head swiveled and their eyes met. "BTUs? You know what BTUs are?"

"Of course not. But when my dad used to complain about how much heat I was letting out of the house by leaving my window open, he always talked about BTUs. I figured they had something to do with heat loss."

"They do," Jordan said. "I'm sure he'd be glad his warnings finally had an impact."

Mia slid her hand down Jordan's body, letting it rest on a protuberant hip bone. "Rumor had it that you were going to start trying to put some pounds back on. But ever since you threw up after eating ice cream in Sydney you haven't really amped your calories up. What gives?"

Smiling fondly, Jordan said, "I like how direct you are. You wanna know something, you just ask." She placed a soft kiss on her lips. "That's cool."

"Then answer instead of delaying." Mia put her hands on either side of Jordan's shoulders and pressed herself into a push-up. "Is your stomach funny from the drugs you were taking?"

"No, not anymore." With a twitch of her head, Jordan indicated she wanted Mia to lie next to her, which she did. "It's...more complicated than that." Her head tilted forward and she looked at her bare body. "This is the first time in a long while that I don't feel fat. I'm not—"

"Fat? Baby, you're skin and bones!"

After clearing her throat, Jordan continued. "I'm talking about how I feel. How I look to you isn't the same as how I look to me."

A sick feeling settled in Mia's gut. In Colorado, she'd seen snippets of what was probably an eating disorder, but she'd convinced herself Jordan was just following orders from the team dietician. If this was the weight Jordan preferred...

"I know I'm too skinny," Jordan continued. "But when I get down this low I get a lot of positive feedback from my modeling agent and photographers and...my mom."

"But you don't want to model any more—"

"I don't," she interrupted. "I really don't. But the pay's *so* good. I could easily make more in a few months than I'd make in a full year as an architect. Given that I'm exactly what Ralph Lauren's agency loves, I could be busy doing print work for...ten years if I age well." She had an anguished expression on her face and Mia's heart clutched in sympathy at the pain she could see there. "It's so hard to turn down great money for doing something so easy."

Mia sat up and stuck a couple of pillows behind her back. After raising her knees, she pressed her hands against them and thought for a few minutes. "Tell me what you like about modeling."

"The money." Her eyes narrowed for a flash, and she added, "And sometimes I get to keep the clothes."

"Nothing else?"

"Nothing." Her head shook firmly.

"Tell me what you don't like about it."

"Really?" Jordan tilted her head to gaze up. "You can't guess?"

Mia ran a hand along her arm, trying to soothe her with her touch. "I'm not like you, baby. I'd love to have people telling me I looked good. I'd love to go to exotic locations…hang out in clubs…make a lot of money. I'd like to have people recognize me." She chuckled evilly. "I also wouldn't have minded hanging around a bunch of really pretty women. Before you, of course."

"Of course," Jordan agreed, showing a very weak smile.

"I'm teasing." Mia hovered over her again, then dipped down for a long kiss. She had to fight to retain Jordan's gaze, but she managed. "I'm totally teasing."

Jordan stroked her flank. "I know." Wrapping her good arm around Mia, she tumbled her onto her back. "I totally know that. But talking about modeling upsets me. I feel like you don't…get it."

"Then give it to me. Tell me what upsets you, 'cause the kinds of jobs we're going to get aren't very glamorous. And they pay crap."

With a burst of anger, Jordan spat, "I'd rather spend every dime of my savings and have to skip grad school than go back to modeling. I. Hate. It."

"I've gotta have more," Mia said. "I understand you hate it, but I'm trying to understand why."

Jordan got up, grabbed her sling and sat on the edge of the bed next to Mia. "Help me."

For the next minute or two they worked together to get her arm immobilized. Then Jordan started to get dressed, only to plop back on the bed. "I have to put my bra and shirt on first. Fuck me!"

"Hey…" Mia took her in her arms and gently stroked her back, then her hair, whispering soothing sounds the whole time. "Just talk to me. Tell me what's got you so riled up. We can get dressed when we're done talking."

"Fine." She got up and started to pace. "I despise being judged for how I look. It reminds me too much of how I felt when I was young."

"Because you were judged…by your mom?" They'd never talked about this. Mia was sure of that.

"Yes. By my mom." She stopped and gave Mia a long look. "From as far back as I can remember, whenever I was in a new class, or a new volleyball club or even going to someone's birthday party, I'd get home and she'd say, 'Who was the prettiest girl there?'"

Mia gawped at her. "What the fuck?"

"Yeah. What the fuck. We'd be at the playground near our house, and she'd tell me what was wrong with the other girls. 'Too fat, weak chin, hair too curly, bushy eyebrows, short-waisted.' The list goes on and on and on." Her eyes narrowed. "These were children—elementary school kids. Six and seven and eight-year-olds."

"And you were supposed to what…rank yourself?"

"Right. And if I didn't declare myself the winner, she'd want to see the other girl. Then she'd tell me if I was right or not."

Mia's eyes were about to pop from her head. "Then what?"

Jordan's expression turned into a sneer. "Then she'd tear the other girl down every chance she got. To her face, if she could." She took in a breath. "I made the mistake of telling her Carolina Gianinni was the prettiest girl in my volleyball club."

Struggling to contort her expression into a smile, Mia said, "Carolina sounds Italian."

"She was." Jordan's face slowly took on a weak smile. "I guess I've always had a weakness for pretty Italian women—even before I knew I liked women." She started to pace again. "Every time she saw Carolina, she'd make a comment that sounded innocuous enough, but was really cutting when you thought about it."

Mia didn't mention the times Daniella had done the same thing to her.

"So I had to keep insisting I was the prettiest girl in every situation, or my mom would track a girl down and try to destroy her confidence!"

Looking exhausted, Jordan sat on the edge of the bed. "I got so tired of it. So tired of trying to be thin while still having enough energy to play my sport."

"And you were just a little girl," Mia soothed, while wrapping her arms around Jordan's rigid body.

"It's not that bad," she said, pulling away. "I wasn't abused or anything. Most people wouldn't mind being the prettiest girl in the class. But I hated it. Hated it in ways I can't even explain." She took Mia in her arms and whispered, "I like that you think I'm pretty, but sometimes I wish you liked me for my brain or my work ethic or something I had something to do with."

A flock of thoughts flew around in Mia's head. She was crazy about how Jordan looked. But her sexual desire for her had ebbed a bit since she'd gotten so skinny. This was probably not a good day to admit she was as shallow as Daniella, but it was a great day to make a few things clear.

"I *do* love how you look, but that's mostly because of how sexy you are," she soothed. "And being sexy is mostly about attitude. You control *all* of that, baby. Every bit of it."

"Really?" Jordan looked at her with an achingly fragile expression.

"Definitely. You're super sexy, and that's from your confidence and your playfulness and your…self. You'd be just as sexy if you had mousy brown hair and crooked teeth."

"My mom wouldn't think so…"

"Not to be rude, but *fuck* your mom. Fuck her and her stupid ideas and her cruelty to you and the other girls she screwed with. She's a very good example of pretty people whose ugliness shines through." Mia wrapped her in a tight embrace and held on for a long time. "Your mom sucks, baby. How she managed to raise such a sweet girl is something I'll never understand—but I'm very, very glad she did."

For the first time in a while, Mia was glad they were going to spend the evening with her parents. Compared to Jordan's, they were iconic role models of sound parenting practices.

Jamie was at Maeve's house, playing in the backyard with Caitlin when her phone rang. "Hang on a second, Punkin," she said to the child.

"Your cousin's calling." After pressing a button, she said, "Go. My time is limited."

"Geez! What kinda welcome is that?"

"There's a toddler coming for me with a watering can. Make it snappy." Caitlin laughed riotously as Jamie danced away from her. She didn't have much water in her can, but it was enough to ruin Jamie's suede driving shoes. Why she'd dressed nicely to visit was a question asked too late.

"Wanna go to Berkeley and take the children out to dinner?"

"I don't have time for crank calls, Ryan." She shrieked when Caitlin made a lunge for her, watering can flying, just missing Jamie's shoes.

"Not a joke! Really! I want to spend some time together and don't want you to have to go over there and cook."

Jamie's eyebrow lifted and she looked at the phone curiously. "You're serious. You want to treat our friends to a nice dinner."

The pause told a lot. "Uhm, did I say nice? I don't remember saying nice."

"Ha! Well it's gonna be nice. You call the children and tell them we'll pick them up at 7:15. I'll make the reservations. Get home in time to spruce up, hot stuff. I'm making the most of a seldom-experienced phenomenon."

At 7:15 Jordan exited the Berkeley house, looking terrific. Her hair was loose around her shoulders, but she kept it from falling into her face with a thin scarf she'd turned into a headband. A hunter green tweed jacket showed off her broad shoulders, but the sumptuous-looking off-white cashmere turtleneck sweater softened the more sober jacket. Jamie couldn't tell what fabric her black slacks were made from, but they fit perfectly. As Jordan often did when she dressed carefully, she'd added a heavy gold-colored necklace and bracelets on each arm. Jamie knew they were all inexpensive, costume stuff, but Jordan looked so wealthy and cultured that no one would ever guess.

As Jordan strolled down the sidewalk, Jamie couldn't help but murmur, "Jesus, that's one fantastic-looking woman. Who taught her to walk like that?"

"Dunno," Ryan said. "But she looses her athlete walk when she dresses up. I can't turn mine off."

Jamie turned and smiled at her partner. Ryan was right. Unless she wore heels, which she'd done twice in two years, her walk always identified her as a jock. But Jordan could walk like a model whenever she wanted, then switch it off and look like she just came off the volleyball court.

The back door opened and Jordan slid in. "Sorry Mia's running late. You know how she is."

"Yeah, we know," Jamie said, chuckling. "I know better than most. We almost didn't get to take the SATs because I stupidly rode with her. Last time," she added. "I haven't been in her car to go anywhere important since we were sixteen."

"I don't have that option," Jordan said. Jamie looked in the rearview mirror and saw her charming grin. "But she's worth waiting for."

Ryan reached between the seats and clapped Jordan on the knee. "You look great, buddy, and since I didn't hear any moaning when you got in the car, your shoulder must be better."

"Better than it was at first, that's for sure. I usually wear the sling, but it's okay if I don't move it much."

A door slammed and they all looked to see Mia fumbling with her keys. Then she came flying down the sidewalk, curls bouncing. The door opened and she slid in. "Made it!"

"Nice dress," Jamie observed. "I've got one just like it."

Mia smoothed the skirt of the tailored, black crepe dress. "You've got shoes just like these too. I looked for jewelry just like yours, but couldn't find any. I had to wear Ryan's massive platinum necklace." She leaned forward and playfully slapped at Ryan's arm. "You should have this thing in a safe, not lying out."

"I took all of my jewelry to the city," Jamie said. "You should have told me what you were wearing. I would have brought something."

"I didn't realize that having my necklace in its case in my desk drawer was 'lying out,'" Ryan said.

"That's the first place a thief would look. Or the tenth. Took me a while." Mia reached up and put both of her hands on Jamie's shoulders. "Both of you should try to be more considerate about my jewelry needs."

"Noted." Jamie started the car and headed for Oakland. "I still can't believe this was my intended's idea, but I'm really glad we're going out together."

"I hate to have you treat us, but we're trying to keep our expenses low," Jordan said, a note of concern in her voice.

"I *love* to go out to dinner," Jamie said. "And going with four lets me taste three times as many dishes." She shot a look at Ryan. "Given that I live with a recluse, I need to maximize my opportunities. You're honestly doing me a favor by going with us."

"I hate to accept meals and spa days from you, but I do it out of love," Mia giggled. "I can't help that I'm so other-directed."

Ryan put her hand between the seats again, this time pinching Mia on the leg. "I told your girlfriend how pretty she looked, but I was too distracted by seeing you wearing my one piece of nice jewelry to compliment you. As always, you look fabulous."

"Thank you, Ryan. You look very nice in your uniform."

"Newish shirt," Ryan said, pulling her shirtsleeve down to reveal the wide blue stripe.

"You look good," Jordan said. "Not as good as Jamie, but that's to be expected."

"Maybe I'd look better with a nice *necklace*," Ryan said, turning to give Mia a playful glare.

"Not with that shirt!" She laughed. "You can't wear a cool necklace like this with a tailored shirt. Jeez!"

"I don't have the 'dress up like a girl' gene. Hence, the uniform," she said, sliding a hand down her body. "You three are going to have to carry the style banner for the whole company."

They were shown to a table by a jeans and T-shirt-clad man. Then another came over, dressed the same, asking, "Bottled or tap?"

"Sparkling," Jamie said. As he walked away she said, "The service in Oakland isn't as obsequious as it is in the city." A quick look at their fellow diners had her whisper, "And we're ten times more dressed up than anyone else."

"I like being overdressed," Mia said. "They'll all wonder if we're super famous—but under the radar."

Jamie hadn't checked out the crowd when they'd walked in. She'd intentionally stopped that practice when they'd reached the zenith of their unwanted fame the year before. Now she usually kept her eyes glued to the back of the person leading them to a table.

Her curiosity got the better of her, and she took a few furtive looks, noting that some of their fellow patrons were checking them out. It didn't bother her—at least now. They were, in fact, dressed more carefully than the rest of the diners, plus two of them were over six feet tall and gorgeous. Given that she was a senator's daughter, and Jordan had just gotten a ton of media for being an Olympian from the Bay Area, Mia was the only one most people on the street wouldn't recognize.

Reaching under the table, Jamie took Ryan's hand, noting it was dry and relaxed. *Thank god.*

"I like it here," Ryan said. "I'd go out to dinner more often if I could wear jeans."

"It's a deal," Jamie jumped in before Ryan could renege. "I'll find good places where you can wear your plastering clothes." She took Ryan's hand and playfully gnawed on it. "Just go with me."

"Gotta admit," Mia said, squinting at Ryan, "I'm surprised you don't hop to it and take James out. You're usually really compliant…when given proper marching orders." Reaching across the table, she patted Ryan's hand. "You're not usually rude like that."

"Rude?" Ryan's eyebrows shot up. "I'm being rude?"

"Yeah. Kinda." Mia took a quick look at Jamie, who held up her hands, opting out of the discussion. "You know James loves to go out, and she's got plenty of dough to handle it. And…when you don't go out she cooks for you. Kinda rude. Your not going out makes her do a ton of work."

Now Jamie jumped in. "I like to cook. Usually. But I *love* to go out."

Ryan looked at her with wide eyes. "Do *you* think I'm being rude?"

Put up or shut up time. "Uhm, no, not rude. Not at all." She squeezed Ryan's hand, watching her tense up. "But you do know how much I love to go out, and you tend to…"

"Refuse," Ryan finished for her. "Okay. I've said it a dozen times, but I'm gonna do it this time." She closed her eyes for a moment. "Let's make Thursday night our restaurant night. Feel free to book us for the indefinite future." Giving Mia a wan smile, she added, "You can make it for four any time you like."

Feeling like she was getting an early birthday present, Jamie bubbled, "I'll do my best to pick places as casual as possible. And we don't have to do it every week…"

"It's okay," Ryan soothed, her eyes full of love. "Any place you want. I don't mind wearing my uniform once a week. If I'd joined the fire department, I'd have to wear one every day."

"You're welcome," Mia said, poking Ryan in the side.

A dark brow rose dramatically. "For…?"

"Keeping you out of trouble. James lets things slide, then gets mad when you don't pay attention to what she needs."

Jamie gripped her arm and squeezed. "Don't tell her things I've told you!"

"Personal observation," Mia assured her. "You've been mad at me over things I spaced on." She gave Ryan a superior smile. "I'm more aware than some people around here."

Grinning in defeat, Ryan said, "Wish I could say you were wrong, but I truly can't. Thank you, Mia," she said, dipping her head.

Their server returned, bearing sparkling water and menus. "We've got a ton of specials. I can tell you about them or bring over a board. Or both."

"The board," Ryan said quickly. As he walked away she said, "When I read the specials I can have Jamie interpret and not look like a dunce."

"You're no dunce," Jordan said. She reached into her big bag and pulled out a large-format booklet. "As promised."

Jamie saw the familiar blue and gold colors splashed across the booklet, then spied a photo of Sproul Plaza. "The winter course catalog?"

"Yeah," Ryan said, obviously itching to page through it. "It's online, but I like reading the real thing."

"When did you learn it was out?" Jamie asked.

"Uhm…today." Ryan swallowed.

"Like a few minutes before you arranged for this lovely dinner party?"

"Uhm…" Squirming in her seat, Ryan nodded.

"So you won't go to dinner to make me happy, but you *will* go to get your hands on the new course calendar." She took the booklet, rolled it up and bopped Ryan on the head with it. Rolling her eyes, she said, "I bet everybody in the whole restaurant just saw me do that."

"Yep," Mia agreed. "Looks like every one of 'em."

Chuckling, Jamie said, "Screw it," then leaned over and kissed Ryan lightly. "You're in trouble, but I'll suspend your punishment until we get home."

They'd all eaten too much, and Mia and Jamie had both had one or two more glasses of wine than they should have, but Ryan was going to be the designated driver as part of her punishment. While they waited for the check, Jamie gazed at Ryan, who was getting better looking by the minute. "I think I'm done with being your minder. If you want to take sixty credit hours, have at it."

"I can't," she said, shaking her head, "Even if you were serious, which I know you're not. There's too much to do on the OFC project."

"Then why even consider Cal? If time's an issue, USF or SFSU are so much closer."

"Because I love Cal," she said, her eyes so filled with feeling that Jamie's heart skipped a beat. "I wasn't anywhere near ready to graduate. And, if I go to Berkeley, I'll be able to hang out with Jordan a little bit."

"Hey! I'm in Berkeley too," Mia said.

"Yeah, but you'll be working."

"Yuck. I wish I was the gorgeous one. I'd gladly sell my looks for cash. I hate the thought of having a real job."

"Much sympathy," Jamie said. "God knows I don't want a job either."

"I'd love one," Ryan said, with Jordan immediately echoing her.

"Do you ever wonder we're just one off on the partner thing?" Mia asked. "You and I would be awesome together, James. And Jordan and Ryan are practically identical."

"Opposites attract," Jamie decided, "and my sweetie and I could hardly be more different. We just agree on one thing." She lowered her voice, but had a feeling she was still being a little loud. "We both dig chicks."

Ryan pulled up to the Berkeley house at eleven. "Are we staying or going?" she asked, cocking her head at Jamie.

"If Mia will come with me to Fresno tomorrow, we're staying. Come on," she begged. "It'll be fun!"

"The Central Valley isn't fun. Do we have to stay overnight? I have to put Jordy's sling on her."

"I can do it myself," Jordan said. "Go if you want to. I don't mind a bit."

"I'll come to Berkeley tomorrow night and get Goldilocks tucked in," Ryan said. "So…we're staying?"

"We are," Jamie said. "You can drop Mia and me off at SFO on your way home in the morning. There's an eight a.m. to Fresno that has plenty of seats available."

"Woo-hoo! Fresno!" Mia said, holding her hands up while she danced in her seat. "You know how to show a girl a good time!"

Jamie hadn't mentioned they had to go from San Francisco to Los Angeles before changing planes for Fresno. But since Mia was asleep on her shoulder for most of the trip, she didn't feel too bad about her omission.

As they started to descend, Mia groggily sat up and ran her hands through her hair. "Where are we?"

"Almost in Fresno."

"Right," she said slowly. "Then where are we going?"

"To the College of the Sequoias in Visalia."

"Why do sequoias need to go to college?" she grumbled before leaning her head back and quickly falling asleep again.

Maybe I should have come alone!

Mia rallied, and by the time they got to the banked-seating classroom where Jamie was supposed to speak, she was her normal, garrulous self. "God, it seems like years since I was in college," she said as she watched students file in. "They seem so young!"

"Most of them are freshmen," Jamie said quietly. "They're in some intro to poly sci course. Their professor wants them to debate the election."

"Mmm, cutie at eleven o'clock," Mia said.

Jamie took a look, seeing only a tall guy with broad shoulders. "The guy?"

"Uh-huh. You know men are my fantasy now that I can't have them. Same reason I crave ecstasy. If it's forbidden, it's compelling."

Jamie gave her a gentle push. "And you're confounding. Go take a seat. We're about to start."

"I have to stay?" She looked more than shocked.

Hurt, Jamie shook her head. "No, of course not. Meet me back at the car in an hour and a half."

"Screwing with you," Mia teased, giggling as she dashed up the aisle to sit in the very last row.

Jamie had spent a good amount of time working on her stump speech. Her father had been completely hands off, not even asking to vet her comments. His minion, however, wasn't so tactful. He and Jamie had e-mailed back and forth for the past few days, with him wanting her to focus on policy issues that might affect college students. She thought that was a waste of time, and having just been a college student herself, she thought she had a better perspective. She thought it was important to make it clear that her father was open-minded enough to change his mind when presented with new facts. Humanizing him seemed the right way to go. But she had made a few concessions, and had kept more policy points in than she thought anyone would listen to.

Afterwards, Mia came down and gave her a big hug. "You did great! I didn't nod off until you started talking about that bill about giving people better loans or…whatever in the hell that was."

Jamie chuckled. "I kept telling the policy guy that most students aren't interested in details about pending legislation. Maybe I'll cut that out before I do the next one in Hanford."

"Wow! Visalia and Hanford, all in one day!"

On the way to Hanford, they stopped for lunch, finding a Mexican place that served tamales good enough to make you cry. Mia insisted that Mexican beer was mandatory to wash tamales down, but Jamie thought it best to give her stump speech sober.

"When we were driving here, I saw a sign for Corcoran," Jamie said, knowing her voice betrayed her discomfort.

"Corcoran…?"

"Where the guy who tried to kill us is gonna be locked up—hopefully forever."

"Ooo…I haven't wanted to ask about that, but isn't there gonna be a trial?"

Jamie reached over, grasped Mia's beer and took a hearty slug. "Nope. I didn't tell you about this, 'cause it happened right before the Olympics and you had your hands full trying to keep Jordan calm."

"Hey," Mia said, locking her eyes on Jamie's. "I've got two hands. One of them is yours—always."

"Thanks." Jamie cleared her throat. "I'm not sure why, but I didn't talk to anyone but my dad about this. Not even Ryan," she added softly.

"Uhm…she was kinda involved…"

"I know. But she was in a bad place when my dad called to say the jerk was pleading guilty."

"Well, that's a relief! You would've had to testify and I know you didn't wanna do that."

"No kidding. But, knowing Ryan, she would have wanted to go to the sentencing hearing. I just didn't want her to be exposed to that cretin again. The thought of having my sweet baby in the same room with him gave me the willies."

Mia reached over and squeezed her hand. "Then you did the right thing. How'd your dad…" She nodded. "Sometimes I forget he's a big deal. Someone would call him about stuff before it made the news."

"Thank goodness no one in the family except for Martin and Maeve reads the paper. Martin called me after he read the blurb, and he agreed it was best not to get the princess involved." Chuckling, she added, "I was glad Martin didn't know about it beforehand. He would've gone to the courtroom and jumped over the railing to strangle the guy." She gazed at Mia for a moment. "I don't think I'm kidding."

"So…is the guy in this prison? How long did he get?"

"Yes, and not long enough. He got fifteen, which will have him up for parole in seven, I think."

"Seven years! For trying—hard—to kill three people!"

"Yep. The prosecutor was surprised he got that much time. But I'm glad he's off the streets for at least a few years. Maybe he'll have a come to Jesus moment and realize the error of his ways." Jamie lay her head down on the table and let out a sigh. "I'm so glad Ryan didn't come with me today. When I saw that sign I know I would have said something, and she's feeling so good I don't wanna bring it up. She'll ask at some point—when she's ready."

Given Ryan's limited knowledge of the plastering trade, she wasn't able to be much help on the OFC project at this point. Her skills were demolition, rough framing, and any of the carpentry that required math. She wasn't skilled in finish carpentry, but she could work out the angles on a mitre saw as quickly as Conor could. But all of that work was finished, leaving her to do the scut work for Miguel and Fernando. Today that meant ripping out the old carpet in the master bedroom, then prying off the strips that had held it down, searching for any elusive tacks, then taking everything down to the dumpster in what seemed like endless trips.

She was relieved when the guys knocked off at three. They, like her brother, liked to start early and stop early—letting them get back to San Jose before traffic got horrible.

Knowing she was too dirty to go to Catherine's, Ryan went anyway—having to acknowledge she wouldn't have the energy to return if she went home to shower first. She'd used the Shop-Vac to suck all the loose dirt off her clothes, then turned the hose around and used the blower to clean her hair as well as could be expected, but she was still a grimy mess.

Luckily, Catherine wasn't home to see her. Marta answered the door and welcomed her in. "Jennie will be glad to see you," she said after giving Ryan a gentle hug. "What can I make you to eat?" She playfully patted Ryan's belly. "I can hear echoes in there."

"Oh, I don't need anything," Ryan demurred.

"If I were to make a turkey sandwich and put it in front of you, would you push it away?"

Ryan smiled at her tenacity. "Well, I'd hate to be rude…"

"Go on up," she said as she went into the kitchen. "Jennie is in her room. I will bring your snack up in a few minutes."

"I can come back down…" But Marta was already in the other room, acting like she hadn't heard Ryan's offer.

She usually took the stairs two at a time, but today one seemed quite enough. Jennie's door was open, and she was sitting on the window ledge, resting against the attractive ironwork Catherine had installed upon the social worker's insistence. "Good thing Catherine put those bars in," Ryan said, making Jen's head snap up. "Or you'd be rolling down Divisadero."

"Nah." Jennie got up and walked over to Ryan to give her a hug. "I wouldn't do it if the bars weren't there. You gotta admit they're cool to lean on, though. I can see all the way down the street."

"Got a balcony for that," Ryan reminded her.

"This is cooler," Jennie said, unrepentant. "What's up? Are we gonna go somewhere?"

"Yeah, I thought we would. Let's go to 'Math world.' My favorite place."

"Uhm…what are we gonna do there?"

Ryan gave her a playful push. "We're gonna do your math homework. What's been going on so far this term?"

"Nothing," Jennie said. She walked over to her books and picked up a chemistry text. "Can you help me with this?"

"Sure." Ryan hefted the book in her hand. "But I thought you might need a hand with trig."

"Not taking it," Jennie said, looking right into her eyes.

"What? Why not? That's when math gets really fun."

"I finished everything I *had* to take this summer. I'm done," she said with finality.

Ryan sat on the bed and started to idly thumb through the chemistry book. "The more math you have, the easier college will be, buddy. You know that."

Jennie walked back to the window and pressed herself against the curved wrought iron. "No, I don't. And even if I did, I'm not going to college."

Ryan's head snapped up. "What? Catherine could get you into Stanford with one phone call. Don't be a dope, Jen!"

"I'd drop out of high school if I could. I hate it," she said, her anger clearly showing. "I'm not as smart as the other kids. *Everything's* hard for me."

"You're plenty smart," Ryan insisted, even though she knew Jen wasn't at the top of the food chain when it came to formal education. "You've got all sorts of skills."

"None of 'em are worth anything at school. I don't have any art classes, and can't take another one until next year. That's the only thing I'm good at. The *only* thing."

"But college is so much more than just learning math and science and the other stuff. It's a great time to learn more about yourself and what you like."

"I know what I like. I like art. Only art."

"Does Catherine know this? That you're not planning on college?"

Jennie turned her head, acting like she hadn't even heard the question.

"Come on," Ryan said, getting up and going over to stand by her. "Talk to me."

"She knows I don't like school," she finally said.

"You'd better tell her you're not even going to try to go. She'll be disappointed, but there's no sense in letting her make plans you're not gonna keep."

"I'll tell her," she grumbled. Jen looked up at the attractive clock above her desk. "Are you gonna help with my chemistry? I've only got forty-five minutes."

"Why? What's on your agenda?"

Sighing, Jennie said, "I promised to practice my clarinet for forty-five minutes, from five 'til five forty-five every weekday."

Ryan smiled encouragingly. "That's great. I can help you with that, too."

"Let's stick to chemistry." Jennie took the book and paged along until she got to a fairly early chapter. "Do you know anything about covalent bonds?"

"Yeah," Ryan said, turning the book around. "I know a thing or two about covalent bonds." She scanned the book, re-familiarizing herself with the high school level of the topic. "Why don't you want help with your clarinet? Jamie's out of town and I've got the whole night free."

As Ryan looked up, she saw a flash of anger pass across Jen's features. "You said you'd teach me. You didn't. Ms. Smith...Catherine found someone who'll show up if she pays her. I'm doing things *her* way."

"Aw, shit," Ryan mumbled. "I've apologized a dozen times, buddy."

She tried to put her arm around Jen, but she backed away, still glaring at her.

"I *know* you were busy. I *know* you didn't have a lot of time for me. But why do you make promises you don't keep?" She grasped her chemistry book and shoved it into Ryan's belly. "*Now* you're gonna help me with chemistry? It's the middle of October, and this is the first time you've come. You don't even know I'm not taking math. If I *was* taking trig, I'd have flunked out by now!"

Feeling like Jen had kicked her in the gut, Ryan moved over to a chair next to the bed. "I'm sorry," she said, hanging her head. "I make promises I can't keep." Looking up, she met and held Jen's gaze. "But it's not because I don't want to, or because you're not worth it. I promise Jamie stuff I don't follow through on all the time. Hell, I do the same to my father, my brothers. I say 'yes' to everything. And that's not fair to you…or them."

"I don't want to talk any more," Jen snapped. "Tell me about this stuff so I can practice." She took a breath, then her shoulders squared. "I said I'd practice every day, and I'm keeping my word. Even when I don't want to."

Ryan sat in her car for a few minutes, after having basically been thrown out of Catherine's house. She felt like crap, but had to admit she'd been in this exact situation several dozen times. It was childish to agree to do more than she was capable of. She had to make a vow—and stick to it—to only take on projects she could comfortably fit into her schedule. To try and do more only hurt the people she loved—and that sucked.

After starting the car, she headed for Berkeley. For a change, she was on autopilot, not considering her route. Ten minutes later, she found herself at the spot. The spot they'd been carjacked. Immediately, she felt like she'd vomit or scream or…something. But the feeling only lasted a minute. It was a long minute, but it eventually ended. Now, shaking and slightly sick to her stomach, she decided to do what Barb had suggested. Carefully and slowly, she started down the route again, noting everything.

It was not yet dusk, on a day that had been warm and sunny. The fog was starting to come in, with the temperature dropping ten or fifteen degrees in what seemed like minutes. But it still felt nothing like it had that rainy, black night. Today there were plenty of cars zipping around the city, and lots of people walking along the streets, most of them probably coming home from work.

A group of high school kids were running up a hill, chasing each other while laughing. Her expression, which had been frozen, started to thaw as she watched them play.

Her car dipped and jerked as it traveled over the cable car line, then it started to climb Nob Hill. The knot in her belly eased as she glided over the hill, just able to see the fog creeping in like a fox into the henhouse. This was *her* city. A couple of assholes weren't gonna take it from her.

The car eased through traffic to finally draw near the bay. There weren't many places to park in the neighborhood, but she managed to jam the BMW into a sliver of a spot. She'd be back before it could be towed.

Ryan jogged to the water, then stood there and watched the sun set. A peaceful feeling settled over her as the sun disappeared into the gray water. This *wasn't* the place they drove into the water. That place had only existed on that dreadful day in December. It was gone forever. This was a new day, her day. She was alive and well and blessed with family and friends and…Jamie. No one on earth was luckier than she was at that moment.

Taking her phone from her pocket, she dialed the familiar number, waiting just a second for Jamie to answer.

"Jealous?" Jamie's warm voice came through the line. "We're at the motel we all stayed in during your tournament in Fresno."

"No, I'm not jealous," Ryan said, wiping the tears from her eyes. "I just wanted to tell you how very much I love you."

Jamie didn't answer right away. Then her voice got quieter and the acoustics changed. She'd probably gone into the bathroom so Mia couldn't hear her. "Are you okay, honey?"

"I'm good. Actually, I'm great. I'm also kind of a screw-up, but that's just the way things are. But most of what I am…most of the good parts… are because of you. I needed to tell you that."

"I love you too, Ryan. More and more all of the time."

"Kinda cool, isn't it?" Ryan watched the last of the sun's rays dim. "It's like there's an inexhaustible amount of love to go around, and we're just starting to tap into it."

"Are you…drinking?" Jamie asked delicately.

"Not a drop."

"You're kinda poetic tonight."

"Maybe a little lovesick. You can cure me tomorrow."

"You've got a date, baby."

"Call me before you go to sleep. I'm heading over to Berkeley now."

"Will do. Big kiss. Feel it?"

"I do." She wiped at her eyes again, so grateful for what they shared. "I really do."

Jamie exited the dive-bar bathroom, squinting to find Mia. The room was dark, with just a couple of lamps illuminating a pool table. A smallish window in the door let in the last exceedingly bright rays of the sun, briefly blinding her.

"Over here," Mia called out.

Following her voice, Jamie nearly ran into her at the jukebox. "I know it's early, but I'm famished. Why don't we go find some dinner?"

"Got to finish my drink first." Mia hoisted her watery margarita. "What's up with Ryan? You looked kind of freaked out when you disappeared."

"She's fine. Actually, she sounded really good. I just wanted to be able to hear her."

"Jukebox sucks." Mia raised her glass to her lips and downed her drink in two big sips. "Now I need Mexican food again. Nothing else tastes good to me after I've had a margarita."

Jamie studied her friend for a minute, thinking of alternatives. Finally, she had one. "I can't take Mexican twice in one day, so we'll go where you want, them go by this sushi place I heard about. I'll get something to take back to the room."

Mia reached out and tickled under her chin. "You don't have to do that. You know I love sushi. Besides, you're the one who said she was hungry."

"Really? You don't mind?"

Mia put her arm around Jamie's shoulders as they walked through the door and into the dusk. "If you know of a place, it's because you did some research. So we're probably going to the best sushi place within a couple of hundred miles. I can suffer."

The sushi wasn't the best in the state, but it wasn't bad. Not being anywhere near water had to hurt when it came to super-fresh fish. But being with Mia made even average food first rate. Their server, probably a kid from Fresno State, was very, very friendly. So friendly that when the check came and Jamie turned it over, she wasn't surprised to see written there, "If either/both of you wants to get a drink later, call me. Alex 559-325-0001." Chuckling, Jamie turned the bill around. "Wanna save this?"

Mia looked at it, then laughed. "Good one. I like a guy who goes right for the 'who wants a three-way?'" She caught Alex' eye and gave him a thumbs up.

"Mia!" Jamie whispered. "He'll think you're gonna call him."

"Nah." She took the pen that Jamie had signed the charge slip with and wrote, "If I wasn't in a monogamous relationship with a smoking hot woman, I'd definitely be calling you later." "There," she said, smiling. "His ego gets a boost and so does mine."

Shaking her head, Jamie stood and went for the door. Mia came up next to her and planted a noisy kiss on her cheek, then grabbed a handful of her butt. "In case Alex is watching, I want to make him think you're the smoking hot woman."

"I'd tell you that you were incorrigible, but you'd take that as a compliment!"

"Damn straight." Mia took Jamie's hand and they laughed all the way to the car.

"Ready to go back to the motel?" Jamie asked when they were buckled in. "Or are there more local guys you want to taunt?"

"I'm still kinda hungry. I need something…just not sure what."

"Dessert?"

"Oh, yeah. Definitely something sweet."

"I'll drive around and you can call out if you spot something."

"Nah. Head to 7-11. They've always got something I like."

Jamie followed orders, and a short time later they were back in their room. Mia was in a T-shirt and her underwear, lying on the bed, eating ice cream with a fork, the only implement that particular store wasn't out of. Jamie wore traditional pajamas, something she always did when staying in a motel. Ever since she'd seen something on TV about bodily fluids on motel furniture, she couldn't bear to have any uncovered skin touch anything.

"Don't take this the wrong way," Mia said thoughtfully. "But it's nice to go out with someone closer to my hotness number. Tonight was the first time a guy's noticed me since Jordy and I got together."

Jamie batted her eyes. "How could I take that the wrong way? You're happy I'm less attractive than your normal traveling companion. Who could take offense at that?"

"You know what I mean." Mia scooted around and held a forkful of ice cream up to Jamie's lips. "Jordy's hardly a regular human woman. She's more like some kinda Nordic goddess."

"True," Jamie said. "But I think Ryan's orders of magnitude hotter than I am, and I still get noticed by guys. Not that I care," she stressed as she climbed onto the bed and shook Mia like a rag doll. "Since I'm in a monogamous relationship. *And* I'm a lesbian."

"I'm only half of that," Mia reminded her. "Or maybe three quarters. But the straight part of me misses being checked out." She sighed heavily. "I guess I'm just jealous. I'd *love* to be as pretty as Jordy. It's totally wasted on her."

"Oh, I'm sure she appreciates having people look at her. You don't get into modeling if you don't have a healthy ego."

"Ha! She hates modeling like you hate…." She seemed to think for a moment. "I can't think of anything you hate this much."

"Really? I knew she wasn't crazy about it, but I thought she must have liked it when she started."

"Nope. Never. And she barely notices when people check her out. And they do it *all* of the time," she said dramatically, throwing herself onto the bed face-first, almost dropping her pint of ice cream. Now she flung herself into a sitting position, showing more energy than Jamie had seen from her all day. "And that's just the tip of the iceberg. I guess I didn't see this much in Colorado, since we were rarely outside in the real world together, but guys kiss her ass like you wouldn't believe."

"Well, she's really pretty—"

"No, no, no, no." Mia held up a hand. "You're not getting it. People give her stuff for free. All. Of. The. Time. If she's anywhere near the front of a line, a guy will wait on her before the other people. Guys jump off their stools to offer them to her at the coffee shop. She's treated like the friggin' queen!"

"People *give* her stuff?"

Mia's eyes narrowed for a moment. "Perfect example. We were at Mitchell's, that bar on Ashby. We're trying to be frugal, so we ate at home and went over there for a drink, just to get out of the house."

"Yeah, I know the place. It's nice."

"Right. So the bartender comes over to her and puts down some delicious concoction and says, 'I'm trying to work on a different take on a Cosmo. See what you think.'"

"That's not that odd. Maybe he was really—"

Mia cut her off. "When she said she wasn't crazy about it, he asked what she'd rather have. Then he went and made that—and *gave* it to her. No charge."

"Now *that's* odd."

"You think? After she told him what she liked, he delivered two. Then I had to *pay* for mine. Only hers was free. He was gazing at her like he wanted to genuflect when he said to me, 'Eight bucks, miss.'"

"Ooo... That was a massive slap in the face."

"Then the guy at Ray's Burgers made her a chocolate malt and just stuck it in with our order—no charge. He made a big deal about how hungry she looked. Like I can't afford to feed my woman!"

She was fuming now, and Jamie couldn't help but laugh. "I'm sorry, but that's hilarious!"

"Oh, yeah, it's hilarious until your dad does it."

"Your dad?" Jamie's mouth was hanging open as she waited for the punchline.

"Uh-huh. Remember when they had our big welcome home party for just the four of us?"

"Yeah. That was just the other day."

"Right. So my dad was being super nice all through the meal. That's not uncommon, so I didn't really notice anything different until I went into the kitchen after he'd offered to get more wine. He was in the powder room, with the door open, using a tissue to clean his teeth."

"Weird, but maybe he's got a hangup about food in his teeth."

"Sure, it all sounds normal." Her eyebrow rose and her voice took on a dramatic edge. "Then I saw him take a comb out of his back pocket and neaten up his hair."

Jamie slapped a hand over her face, slowly opening two fingers to peek out at Mia. "Please tell me that's all he did."

"Nope. He straightened his tie, then smiled. Like he was fucking practicing!"

"Like a fourteen-year-old boy on his first date!" Jamie said, her mind reeling with images of Mr. Christopher behaving like a dope.

"Exactly. If my mother had seen him…" She trailed off, the list of things she might have done too long to mention.

"Damn, that would freak me the fuck out. I think my dad gets that Ryan's attractive, but I'm sure he's not hot for her." She closed her eyes and told the truth. "He's hot for Jordan."

"Fuck me hard!" Mia yelped.

Jamie grasped her shoulder and gave it a shake. "You can't fight this. She's objectively gorgeous, so you've either got to suffer with it, or use her to your advantage. I know you. You can figure out ways to get discounts normal people would never qualify for."

"Hmm…" Mia nodded sagely. "Good point. I'll make sure she's with me when I buy anything. Anything at all." She gave Jamie a playful push. "You act like this is all new to you. The same thing must happen with Ryan."

"Nope. Never."

"What? Why? She's just as exotic, just as unique."

"Don't know. But she's told me guys have almost never approached her. They've gotta be kinda ancient to notice her, to be honest. Ninety year old men are nuts about her."

"Hmm…we need a sociologist to study this. It makes no sense."

"Given that I think she's the prettiest woman in the world, it definitely makes no sense. But I'm glad for it. I'm so possessive I'd be starting fights over her—and, given that I'm a total wimp, she'd have to finish them for me."

Chapter Eight

Jamie returned to San Francisco with just enough time to take a quick shower and head over to Maeve's for their dinner and spirituality date. She felt guilty about leaving a sad-eyed Ryan to fend for herself, but she'd come to realize that dealing with a little guilt was better than dealing with a lot of resentment. And if she couldn't go out and participate in the things she enjoyed—resentment was right around the corner.

When she pulled up in front of the house, Maeve dashed out, looking pretty darned excited. She was dressed very nicely; wearing a print dress Jamie hadn't seen before, with heels a little higher than she normally wore. Maeve got in and started to buckle her seatbelt. "I always feel like I'm sneaking off from school when I go out on my own," she said, giggling like a girl.

"You know, I'm not too far from that. As much as I love Ryan, there are a lot of things I like to do that she'll never, ever want to do with me. But I can't let that stop me."

Maeve patted her lightly on the leg. "I never, ever went out on my own during my first marriage." Whenever she talked about her late husband, she always seemed sad. Jamie had the feeling her sorrow had little to do with mourning, and much more with regret. "I won't make that mistake with Marty. If we both pursue our interests, we'll have more to talk about when we're together."

"What does Martin like to do?" Jamie asked, having never seen him go anywhere but work and church.

"Nothing," Maeve said, smiling. "He loves to tinker around in the yard, have an early dinner, then read the paper while he talks back to the TV. I like a little more variety."

"He sounds like his daughter, but she doesn't read the paper or watch TV! She's perfectly happy to have dinner, then sit on the deck and watch cars go by. I swear she'd be content to never go more than a mile from her home."

"Consider yourself lucky. Marty would be happy to knock that down to a quarter mile, and that's only because his favorite bakery is almost in the Mission."

"We've got a real pair of explorers on our hands, Maeve. A regular Lewis and Clark."

Jamie got in a little after nine, finding Ryan, Conor, Padraig, Seamus and Duffy jammed into Conor's smallish room, watching baseball. "Hey," the humans called when she poked her head in. Duffy had the good manners to get up and come over to sniff and lick her knees.

"Hey." She entered and saw Seattle and the Yankees on the screen. "Uhm…didn't this happen yesterday?"

"Shh!" Several voices rose as one. "We don't know what happened. It's on tape."

"I know what happened," she teased. "I read the paper."

"My father would slay me to even think this, but I'll deck you if you tell," Seamus threatened.

"Then I'd have to kick your ass and it'd get ugly," Ryan said, turning to wink at Jamie. "Go put some comfy clothes on and join us."

There was about six inches of available space on the bed. "Nah. I'm gonna read for a while. Anyone want to hear about the poetry in the psalms?"

Ryan tentatively lifted a hand, to the guffaws of her brother and cousins. "I do. But after the game."

"No rush. You have made known to me the path of life. You will fill me with joy in your presence."

Four sets of eyes stared at her, with Ryan's mouth slack.

"That was written about God, not you, honey. Don't be so full of yourself."

A few minutes later, Ryan came downstairs. "The game's not over, but I think the Yanks are gonna win." She tilted her head thoughtfully. "If I'm wrong, tell me to go back upstairs."

"You're not wrong." Jamie crooked a finger, beckoning Ryan to join her on the love-seat. "Subway series. Mets and Yankees. How you missed that on the news, I'll never know."

"I miss a lot." Ryan snuggled up next to her and purred like a kitten. "Missed you. Both today and yesterday."

"Missed you too, but I'm glad I went. I had fun with Mia, as always. I should have assumed this, but I learned that people in the Central Valley have different concerns than we do in the Bay Area."

"Yeah, I guess they would."

"Lastly, I really enjoyed hanging out with your aunt tonight. I'm gonna love our Wednesday dates."

"Don't forget our Thursday night date. I'll eat a light lunch to make sure I'm hungry tomorrow."

"Ha." Jamie poked her in the belly. "A light lunch for you is a heavy dinner for me." She bent and kissed Ryan on the ear. "I'll go easy on you and choose someplace close and casual."

"Don't have to," Ryan insisted. "A deal's a deal. I'll eat anything from Asia to…" Jamie could see her trying to picture the globe. "The farthest place from Asia."

"Hmm…if you went straight through the world from, let's say, China, you'd probably wind up around South America."

"Really?" Ryan gave her a very suspicious look.

"I think so, but I'm just guessing."

"Well, feel free to find an Argentine restaurant. The choice is yours."

"Got it. Now, do you really want to hear about the psalms?"

"Sure. Tell me all about 'em." She yawned lustily.

"Go brush your teeth and get into bed. Then I'll tell you what I learned."

A few minutes later Ryan was lying on her side, looking up at Jamie, who had a couple of pillows propped up behind her back.

"I'm all ears," Ryan said before leaning in and taking a nibble of Jamie's.

"I really like this priest. Her name's Caroline and she's super-smart."

"Doesn't sound right to have a priest named Caroline, but go on."

Jamie cleared her throat. "Well, she pointed out that in all of the psalms, no one ever talks about issues or current events or politics, even though they must have had more issues than we do.

"Makes sense. Why does she think that's true?"

"She thinks the Psalmists wanted to go beyond, beneath, and through the issues to talk about principles. The big ideas that pervade time. So they used elusive language. Language that makes you dig for meaning. I *love* that," she said, feeling a little jolt of pleasure at the concept. Then she felt a stream of warm breath on her chest. *Sound asleep.* Jamie bent to kiss Ryan's forehead, then she shifted down to press against her warm body. She knew in her heart that if Ryan was still watching the game she'd be as alert as a cat watching a mouse. But she had to give her credit for at least *acting* interested. That was enough.

Catherine was lingering over a cup of coffee on Saturday morning when Jennie came into the kitchen. "Good morning," Catherine said. "Did you sleep well?"

The girl gave her a lopsided smile. "I always sleep well here. Nobody gets up in the middle of the night to fight or cry or try to sneak out. You don't know how nice that is."

Catherine had to admit that was one hundred percent true. "Well, since you're rested, let's do something energetic today."

"I don't have to stay inside and do homework?"

"Of course not. You work hard during the week, honey. You need your weekends to relax and enjoy yourself."

"But I've got a report I've gotta turn in on Monday, and it's gonna take me hours to do."

"Topic?"

Jennie sat down and her shoulders slumped slightly. "History. I hate history."

Catherine reached over and put a hand on her shoulder. "Luckily, I like it a lot. We'll devote two hours to working on it this weekend."

"I'm really bad at writing, so it always takes me a long time to get stuff to make sense. There's no way I can do it in two hours."

"Two hours is enough," Catherine said firmly. "We'll get it done—together."

Jennie brightened immediately. "Cool. So what are we gonna do?"

"We're going to get some breakfast into you, then we'll go down to Hillsborough. I'm sure we can find something down there to get our blood moving."

Jennie looked up with a big grin as Marta put her breakfast down in front of her. "Do you think it's warm enough to go swimming?"

With a decisive head nod, Catherine said, "I'm certain of it."

They reached Hillsborough by ten, where they were welcomed by Helena, who'd been alone in the house for nearly a month. Catherine led Jennie through the house, and as they reached the back, Jennie said quietly, "Is that lady here all the time?"

Chuckling, Catherine said, "She is. Helena's my housekeeper."

"I thought Marta was your housekeeper."

"No, Marta's my cook. I would prefer that she only cook, but when I moved to the city she put up such a fight that I gave in and allowed her to also clean the house."

Jennie tilted her chin in the manner that Catherine now recognized reflected confusion. "Why would somebody fight to do more work?"

"Exactly!" Catherine said, thinking that maybe she and Jennie did have a few things in common.

They walked past the pool, eventually winding up next to a small building that abutted the tennis court. "I am seriously out of practice, but I thought we might have fun playing tennis."

The girl frowned and replied with a flat, "I don't know how."

Catherine hated that was always Jennie's first response. She had so little confidence in herself, and was always worried about doing something improperly. Yet another attribute for her wish list for Jennie—a bigger ego.

"No one knows how until they learn. Let's try and see if we have fun."

"Okay," she said, clearly reluctant. "But I'm really clumsy and slow."

Catherine patted her on the back. "Youth makes up for a lot."

After unlocking the door to the tennis equipment room, Catherine went through her old rackets, looking for the one that Jamie had used when she was young. It had an oversized head, and was light—perfect for a beginner. Racquet technology had changed greatly in the last fifteen years, but Jennie merely needed to learn the basics. A top-notch racquet was overkill.

They went out to the court, where Catherine spent a long time showing her how to hold the racket, how to follow through to avoid strain on her elbow, how to position her feet, and all of the other basics. "Okay, I think we're ready to get a little exercise. You stay right here, and I'll go to the other side."

Catherine prudently supplied an entire basket of balls for each of them, not wanting to spend the day chasing errant shots.

In just a few minutes, she could tell that Jennie would be able to play tennis if she wanted to, since she was surprisingly mobile and had strong arms. In fact, a few times Jennie walloped a return that made Catherine flick her racket up to avoid being hit right in the face. Jennie was right, however, when she said that she was clumsy. After watching her stumble around, Catherine called a halt. They met at the net, where she said, "First we go out for lunch. Then we buy you proper tennis shoes."

Looking down, Jennie said, "These are tennis shoes."

"No, they're not. I think those are for skateboarding. Tennis shoes are never slip ons, honey. You have to be able to plant your foot to play."

"But I like this kind."

"I'm not supervising your normal choice of footwear, but you'll break your neck wearing those when we play. And given how you slammed the ball a few times, I think you're going to be good at this. Proper shoes are a wise investment."

The luminous smile that the girl gave made Catherine feel better than she had in a long time. Such small things had such a large impact.

On Saturday morning, Ryan pulled a nearly comatose Jamie from their bed and guided her to the bathroom. "You made me promise to get you up," she soothed into her ear. "You have only yourself to blame."

"What time is it? Four a.m?"

"Exactly," Ryan agreed. "Plus three."

Jamie stopped in front of the mirror, braced her hands on the sink and glared balefully at herself. "You can't start working at seven. There's a city noise ordinance."

"We won't all be there until eight. If the noise police come, I'll create a diversion so you can run away."

"Ha-ha. You're awfully damn chipper for the crack of dawn."

"You're chipper too." Ryan kissed the top of her head. "It just takes a while for your chipperness to reveal itself."

Every single cousin was present by 8:30. The boys had given Fernando and Miguel the weekend off, so there were only fifteen people tripping over each other. Sean and Seamus were on the roof, putting a fresh coat of tar on just to be safe, and Jamie almost envied them. At least they were outside with a little room to move. Although the smell of hot tar was nothing to envy…

Liam, Declan and Dermot worked in trades not needed at the moment, so they'd taken on the task of sanding the wooden floors that covered the long hallway, the living and dining rooms, as well as each bedroom. They started off in the master bedroom, but even with the door closed the air quickly turned dusty and so gritty it made Jamie's eyes water.

Ryan and Kieran were covered in gray mud, along with both gray and white dust, but they were making good progress in patching the walls where doors had been removed.

Jamie mostly tried to stay out of the way and keep things neat. That wasn't a big contribution, but she felt she had to do something when every other member of the clan was working so hard.

Around eleven, Annie, Tommy and Caitlin arrived, bearing trays full of Mexican food. In seconds, every machine stilled, then the entire crew went to stand outside in the backyard to eat. A couple of sawhorses and a old door made a serviceable table, and everyone dug in—with their hands. Their *dirty, filthy, grimy* hands. When no one was looking, she snuck back into the house and washed hers, unable to act like a true O'Flaherty, totally impervious to dirt.

When she returned, she chuckled at the sight of many of the big men lying on their sides in the recently broken-up dirt, eating like ancient Romans. Ryan was sitting cross-legged on the ground and she looked up and smiled when she spotted Jamie. "Am I clean enough to sit next to?"

"You're a lot better than Sean and Seamus," Jamie said quietly. "What would compel those two to become roofers? That's gotta be the worst job in all of constructionland."

"They're not good in math or geometry or spacial relationships," Ryan said quietly. "They couldn't even figure out how much paint a house would take. Square footage screwed them up every time."

"Math? Why do you have to be good at math to paint?"

Ryan's brows hiked up. "You need math for almost everything, especially carpentry and framing. But even carpet layers have to be able to calculate square footage."

"How about plasterers? Does Kieran have to know math?"

Ryan thought for a minute. "I guess not. Not much, that is. You've gotta know ratios and proportions for your mix but that's a visual thing as much as a math thing." She leaned over and said even more quietly, "Besides not knowing math, the twins aren't very patient or detail-oriented. When each of the cousins graduated from high school, all of the uncles got together and decided what trade they thought each kid could master. I'm not sure they thought the boys could even be roofers, but they figured their screw-ups wouldn't be as visible."

"Except to the people who live on the top floor!"

Chuckling, Ryan nodded. "There's that, I suppose. But I haven't heard of them being sued, so they must be doing all right."

"Who do they work for?"

"The city." Ryan rolled her eyes. "What can I say? It keeps them off the streets."

Conor finished his lunch, then stood and stretched his long arms out. "Hey," he said to the group. "Anybody have a problem with me using Miguel and Fernando on jobs when we're done here?"

"Why would we mind?" Frank asked.

"Dunno. I'm not sure I can find anything for them, but I wanna keep them connected. When we get the next place, I'd like to hire them full-time. They're good, and someone will snatch them up if they see their work."

"I'm good with that," Frank said. He turned to Jamie. "But that means you've gotta get the next house lined up. Quick."

"And it's gotta be a house," Niall said. "We've gotta start flipping houses or this isn't gonna work."

"We've decided I'm in charge of buying the next house?" Jamie asked, stunned at this development.

"Yep," Frank decided, with lots of heads nodding.

"Since when am I good at buying real estate?" Jamie asked quietly.

"You're the best we have," Ryan replied just as quietly. "You're kinda like Sean and Seamus. We've gotta put you to work, and you can't break your neck just *looking* at houses." She jumped up and ran away well before Jamie was able to pinch her.

Mid-afternoon, Ryan went looking for her partner. It didn't take long, since there weren't many hiding places. The smallest bathroom was more than filled, with Annie, Colm and Jamie standing shoulder to shoulder. "Secret meeting?" Ryan asked, poking her head in.

"Picking tile and deciding how to lay it out," Colm said. Ryan looked at the edge of the tub where a bunch of different tiles were lined up. "Jamie's gonna help again," he added. "Ten or fifteen more jobs and she'll be good at this."

"Oh, I'm sure she could be good," Ryan agreed. "I'm just not sure she's motivated."

"I'm plenty motivated. If you can be a plasterer, I can be a tile setter."

"I'm going to put an ad in the paper for tenants as soon as the units are carpeted," Annie said. "Will you let me in to show the units? You're one of the few with keys."

"Happy to," Ryan agreed.

"I'd like to have the tile set by the end of next weekend," Colm said. He looked at Jamie. "Are you available to work at night this week?"

"Sure am. Maybe I can get my girlfriend to do the second shift with me."

Ryan waved as she left. "That's a definite possibility."

At six p.m., Ryan floated on the surface of a huge hot tub at a spa in Japantown. "I don't know how you found this place, but I'd like to be a regular," she said. Holding up a hand, she added, "Don't tell me how much it cost to get this room to ourselves. You know my enjoyment of things bears an inverse relationship to how much they cost."

"It wasn't bad," Jamie assured her. She wrapped her arms around Ryan and pulled her onto her lap. "I like holding you this way. It'd be fun to be able to do this on land."

"Not gonna happen, so we'll have to come here more often. Of course, we could always go down to Hillsborough. You can play with me in the pool for free down there."

"But I can't do this," Jamie said as she grasped Ryan's breasts and started to squeeze them gently.

"True. I guess some things are worth paying for. Privacy's a big one."

After Sunday services with her mother, Jennie, and Maeve, Jamie went over to the OFC to stand around and watch people work. She did everything she could think of, but it wasn't a cleaning up kind of day. After being kicked out of every room for some important task, she finally went out and sat on the front step, figuring she'd go back in and sweep up when the boys started to leave.

A horn honked, and she looked up to see Martin, clearly on his way home from work. "Will we have a full house for dinner tonight?" he called out.

Jamie got up and walked over to his truck. "We're going to be there, and I know Mom and Jen are. Want me to check with Conor and Kevin when I see them?"

"That would be lovely. I'm off to take a nap. Dinner will be served at six—at your home."

"Sounds great. I've always wanted to have dinner on the table when I get home from work." She laughed. "That was a total lie, but it sounded good."

The whole group was cleaned up and ready for dinner at six on the dot. Brendan, Maggie, Conor, Kevin, and Catherine joined Martin and Maeve at the dining table, while Jamie, Ryan and Jennie sat at a card table placed almost at the entrance to the kitchen. "Not only do I have to sit at the kids table," Ryan said, clearly teasing, "but I bet I'm gonna have to get up every time somebody needs something from the kitchen."

"We all have to use the gifts God gave us," Martin said, smiling at her. "You've always been good at hopping to it."

As always, Catherine had brought wine, and this time Martin had carefully put a glass in front of each member of the family. Ryan watched him as he poured a small measure of wine into each glass, knowing that something was up. Her father was *not* a wine drinker. The mystery was solved as soon as he finished saying grace. He held up his glass and said, "I have an announcement to make." Every head turned to stare at him. "It's nothing awful! You look at me like I've set the place on fire." That cut the tension a little, and he continued, "My last day of work will be December the thirty-first." Ryan was the first, but not the only one to let out an audible gasp. Martin continued. "It's time for me to start my second career." He turned slightly and locked eyes with his wife. "Being a better husband to my bride, and sharpening my skills as a carpenter."

"You are going to find another job?" Catherine asked, clearly flustered.

"No, I'm going to work less. Significantly less. My new employer will be the O'Flaherty cousins."

"Do the O'Flaherty cousins know this?" Ryan asked, eyes wide.

"No, I'd say they don't. But I'm a good worker and I think they'll take me on—since I won't ask for pay. I also plan on getting more involved in my new church." He met Jamie's gaze, adding, "I invited your grandfather for dinner, but he had another engagement. I wanted to let him know why Maeve and I are drawn to join his flock." He looked up, blinked a few times, then said, "St. Patrick drove the snakes out of Ireland they say, and right now we need someone to drive them out of the Catholic Church. I will no longer support an organization that spends its energies on preventing prudent people from having more children than they can afford, and blatantly trying to shame people for loving someone of their same sex." His voice grew rough and his eyes narrowed menacingly. "All the while they ignore their own grievous sins.

"I'm sure the Episcopal church has its problems and some bad apples as well, but they haven't paid hundreds of millions of dollars to cover up their sex crimes. Nor have they gone to great lengths to shield their priests from prosecution." Maeve reached over and patted him on the hip. He met her gaze, then visibly forced himself to change his tone. "Anyway, I wanted you all to know our two pieces of news. You'll be seeing me around more than you might want, and I'll never darken the door of St. Philip's parish again." He held up his glass a little higher. "Sláinte!"

Much later that evening, Jamie and Ryan lay in bed together. "This is really going to take some time to sink in," Ryan said. "I'm glad Da's retiring, of course. He hit his twenty-five years when I was still in high school. But it's going to be weird to not have him at the station."

"It'll be weird for him too," Jamie predicted. "He's not crazy about change." She trailed her hand up Ryan's side and tickled her ribs. "Kinda like someone else I know."

"I like change…in some things. Just not in big stuff…like having my da leave his job."

Jamie looked at her glum expression and realized this was going to be another change Ryan would have to adapt to. She was just glad her partner was pretty much back to normal, and briefly wondered if Martin had held off until he was sure Ryan was more solid. That's just the kind of thing he'd think of. He was a hell of a da.

Chapter Nine

Bright and early on Monday morning, Mia drove Jordan to North Berkeley for her first physical therapy appointment. Jordan looked at her lover's profile, noting the half-closed eyes and hair pointing in all directions. "I could have easily taken a bus, honey," she said. "I know this isn't your favorite time of day."

Mia turned and showed a wan smile. "There isn't a bus that'd take you anywhere near the place. And you can't drive." Her gaze lit on Jordan's sling. "Yet. Soon though."

"I hope so." She'd been tapping her feet, and slowly realized she was nervous. But she didn't like to talk about things like that, believing that bringing them up made them more real.

"It's gonna be fine," Mia said, giving her another quick look. "It'll hurt at first, but it'll feel so much better once you get the other muscles strengthened."

Reaching across the car, Jordan put her hand on Mia's leg and gave it a squeeze. "Is it obvious I'm nervous?"

"Little bit. Want me to be in the room with you? I'll pop him if he hurts you."

"Nah. They'll just find another therapist to torture me and you'll be in jail. Net loss." She jiggled Mia's leg. "But I appreciate your offer. Why don't you just drop me off? I'll call when I'm done."

"I think I'll stick around." She slapped one fist into the other palm. "You might need backup."

Jordan exited into the waiting room, finding it filled with older people, all of whom looked up when she opened the door. They went back to their magazines immediately, and Jordan left the building. A short walk led her to the car, where Mia was lying in the back seat, sound asleep. Smiling at how cute she looked, scrunched up with her knees raised, Jordan lightly tapped at the window. That didn't rouse her, so she went to the driver's door and got in.

"Jordy?"

"Luckily, yes," she said, chuckling. "I can drive home."

Struggling for a moment, Mia pulled herself up by grabbing Jordan's headrest. "Really? You don't have to wear the sling?"

"Nope. Nick says I should only wear it when it's really bugging me."

"So it feels better?"

She had such a hopeful tone to her voice that Jordan hated to be honest. Being evasive was the better choice. "It's pretty numb right now. I've had ice on it for a while."

"How will it feel when it's not numb?" Mia's gentle hand rested atop the shoulder. If only her concern could mend flesh.

"I guess we'll have to see." Jordan flashed a smile in the rearview mirror. If it felt like it had when she and Nick were doing a series of stretching exercises, she was going to consider a liquid lunch.

They drove for a while through the increasing traffic, finally winding up near campus. "Want coffee?" Jordan asked.

"Yeah. How about that new place on Telegraph? It's supposed to be good."

"If I can find a place to park..." Jordan focused on the subtle signs people gave off when they approached a car. "That guy's gonna leave," she predicted. "Not bad. We're only two blocks away."

Once they'd gotten the car parked, they walked down the street, holding hands. Mia used to walk on her right side, but since the injury she'd switched to the left. The woman should consider being a spy. No one paid closer attention to detail while appearing to be thinking of absolutely nothing.

Mia opened the door, but Jordan stopped and read a sign on the big window. When she entered, she said, "They need help. I'm gonna check it out."

"Making coffee?" Mia made a face. "You can do so much more."

"Better than nothing, baby. And working in a coffee shop is something I could keep doing when school starts." Without waiting for Mia to agree, Jordan caught the attention of a woman who looked like she might be in charge and said, "Hi. Can I talk to someone about the job you have available?"

The woman looked her up and down, clearly assessing her. "What hours are you looking for?"

"I can work any time until winter term starts. After that—I'd take classes that wouldn't interfere."

"Hmm… Any experience?"

Flashing a grin, Jordan said, "I like coffee, I'm not particular about my schedule, and I'm used to working hard."

"Good enough." The woman pulled a piece of paper from her apron pocket. "I've got six to two available. Minimum wage. Twenty percent discount on beans. As much coffee as you want. No more than one food item per shift."

Mia broke in. "She doesn't eat anything you have. How about a twenty-five percent discount on beans?"

The woman gave her a puzzled glance. "Your agent?"

"Partner," Jordan said. "And protector."

"Must be nice." The woman held a hand out. "Amy. I'm one of the co-owners. Can you start tomorrow?" Her gaze slid to Mia. "With a twenty percent discount on beans?"

"Definitely. I'll be here at quarter 'til. I'm Jordan and this is Mia."

Mia smiled and shook the woman's hand. "Jordy doesn't drink much coffee. Can I have the one she'll get tomorrow today?"

"Must be nice to have an agent. Yes, you can both have a free drink—today. After tomorrow you've got to pay for yours, Mia."

"I wouldn't dream of asking for special favors," she said, giving her most ingratiating grin. There was no way Amy believed her, but no human could resist Mia when she was really putting on the charm. Jordan assumed a pretty pair of brown eyes would be watching her work, while cadging free coffee whenever she wanted it. And that was just fine with her.

Late on Monday afternoon, Jamie and Ryan stopped by their real estate agent's office for a meeting. As they went in, Ryan said, "Old Ray didn't get to see you very often during the last deal. Think he'll remember what you look like?"

"Funny," Jamie said, tweaking Ryan's nose. "He saw me plenty. He just didn't see me after we had a deal. But now that we're in the city, I'll be more flexible about going to his office to sign things. He's stuck in the last decade, and I don't think I can drag him out of it."

They announced themselves to the receptionist, and Ray came out a few minutes later to lead them to a conference room. "Can I get you girls some coffee?" he asked. Ryan looked at Jamie, who was regarding the man with a very cool look. "I mean ladies," he said quietly.

"Let's all agree we're women, then we can put that away," Jamie said, surprising the heck out of Ryan. She wasn't usually very sensitive to things like that.

"I know you're women, but I have to call you something," he muttered. "It sounds stupid to say, 'Can I get you *women* some coffee.'"

Now Jamie's prickliness made sense. Ray had more than one condescending bone in his beefy body, and Jamie didn't have a lick of patience for that.

"That does sound stupid," Jamie said crisply. "Let's drop the pronouns and get to the point. 'Can I get you some coffee' works perfectly, and you don't have to worry about offending anyone." His expression was partly blank, partly confused. "It's not a big deal, Ray. Let's talk about real estate."

"Got it," he said, obviously relieved. He slid a folder over to her, which she opened and paged through. "I've got three apartment buildings and two single families," he said. "The singles are priced higher than I think they should be, and they both need a load of work. That one," he added when Jamie landed on the listing, "is an estate sale. The guy who died in there hadn't cleaned the place since Eisenhower was president."

"Mmm. I don't want to look at the apartment buildings. The cousins have decided they don't want any more rental units, and doing a condo conversion is a big headache. We want a single family with potential. Obviously, we'd love to get a bargain."

He pulled the folder back and looked at the two homes. "Neither of these is great. This one has to go through the probate court, and that's a pain. The other one is my listing, so I know the people. They have a crazy view of how much their place is worth."

"Okay." Jamie stood and Ryan followed her lead. "Keep looking. I think we should buy two or even three homes. The boys all have different trades, and they'll be better off if they don't have to all be in one place at a time."

He blinked up at her. "Three homes? You can get mortgages on three homes at once?"

"Nope," she said as she started to leave the office. "I'll pay cash."

They left him sitting, slackjawed, in the room. When they reached the sidewalk, Ryan said, "Why were you busting his chops? And since when do you object to being called a lady?"

"I don't," she said, showing an impish grin. "He just rubs me the wrong way. I don't think we've ever spoken that I haven't given him a hard time about something."

"But you don't mind working with him?"

"Not a bit. Now that I've trained him, he doesn't waste my time. That means a lot to me."

Chuckling, Ryan said, "Sounds like you're training him in many areas. If he didn't want your business, he'd tell you to beat it."

"That's true in most business relationships. Luckily, we don't have to like each other."

As they walked towards their car, Ryan said, "I couldn't do that. If I don't like a person, I don't want to do business with them."

Jamie took her hand and kissed it. "That's why you're the brawn and I'm the brains in this operation. I'm not emotionally invested. I won't let myself fall in love with a property, or get too close to an agent. It's all business to me."

Ryan sat on the edge of the bed, watching Jamie linger in front of the closet, carefully choosing her outfit for the day. "It really wouldn't be any trouble to take you to the airport," Ryan said. There was just enough of a begging tone to make her reframe the comment, hopefully sounding less like a child. "I don't have to start work at eight on the dot."

Jamie turned and gave her a sweet smile. "I know you love to drive through rush-hour traffic to take me to the airport, but I'm putting my foot down this time. If I take a cab, I'll be able to sit in the back of the car and read. And you'll be able to go to work."

"There's not much for me to do," Ryan said, still trying to take the grumpiness from her voice. "I'm not good enough at anything to work on my own."

Jamie walked over holding a dress in her hand. "Then do something fun today. I know this is a tough concept for you to understand, but you're not an indentured servant to the OFC." She put her fist up to Ryan's temple and tapped it a few times. "You aren't going to share in the profits, honey. You're not invested like your family is."

"I know. I know." She shoved her hands into her back pockets, feeling awfully childish. "But there's a lot of work to be done and I don't have anything else I need to do…"

Standing on her tip-toes, Jamie placed a quick kiss to Ryan's lips. "I know I'm wasting my words, but you promised you'd take it easy this fall. You said you wanted time to think and work on math problems, and I'm pretty sure you haven't done that once."

Sheepishly, Ryan said, "I helped a kid with her homework when you guys were at church."

"That's not what I mean and you know it." Jamie slipped the dress over her head, then turned and waited for Ryan to zip it. As she walked back to the closet, Ryan watched how the dark-colored dress moved with her body. "You could make yourself think deep thoughts today."

"Huh?"

Jamie turned quickly. "Were you staring at my ass?"

"Uhm…yeah. But you were wiggling it at me. I couldn't help myself."

After slipping into a pair of low heels, Jamie walked back and slid her hands around Ryan's waist. "I'll wiggle any way you want when I get home tonight."

"You're sure you'll come home? No chance of them sending you someplace else?"

"Honey, I don't think there are a lot of colleges around Eureka. Humboldt State's about it." She pulled Ryan down for a kiss. "I'll be home tonight. My speech is at noon, I'll be finished by one or one-thirty, then I'll zip back to the airport. I should be home by dinner."

"We'll go out."

Jamie raised an eyebrow.

"We will! I'll find someplace nice and make reservations. If I dangle a good restaurant in front of you, I know you'll make sure to get to your plane in time."

"I don't need any additional incentives. You're all I need to be happy."

"And an occasional four-star restaurant."

Smiling warmly, Jamie said, "That's optional. Only you're required."

Ryan and Duffy stood on the deck, waving as Jamie's cab zipped down the street. "Do I go to work or do something a little different?"

Duffy looked up at her, as if he wanted to answer. But he didn't carry his end of the conversation, leaving Ryan to decide for herself. "I'm going to do something different." After going inside to grab a few net bags, the pair headed for the grocery store. On the walk, she called Marta. "Hi there, Smith residence. It's Ryan."

"Hello, Ryan. Let me get Catherine for you."

"No, I want to talk to you. I've got about ten hours, and I want to make one of Jamie's favorite dinners. Can you help me?"

"I could make her favorite dinner and have you both come here. Wouldn't that be easier?"

"It would. But I hate to take the easy way out."

Ryan and Duffy were back at the house, organizing all of the ingredients for a red mole. Without warning, a stab of anxiety caught her right in the gut, doubling her over. Stunned, Ryan stumbled toward a straight-backed chair in the dining room and dropped into it. Duffy sensed something was wrong, for he trotted over and bumped against her leg, staring up with his head cocked.

"I don't know what's wrong," Ryan said as she petted his head. "But something is." She checked her watch. 9:15. Exactly when Jamie's plane was supposed to take off.

Ryan had *never* experienced this kind of unfocused fear that perfectly coordinated with a specific event. Numb, she stood and dashed down to her room, turning on her computer. She didn't know of any way to check on a particular flight, but she started scrolling through every news service she could think of. If anything had happened, it would be reported. Sick with worry, she stayed right where she was for almost an hour. Nothing.

Now Duffy seemed anxious, flinching and barking at the smallest noise. She grabbed his leash and her keys and went for a run around the neighborhood, determined to keep going until she felt calmer.

She wasn't sure how much time had passed, but she was in Bernal Heights when her phone rang. *Jamie!*

"Hi," Ryan said, trying to keep the panic from her voice. "Everything okay?"

"Sure. No problems. I'm just about to get into my rental car. Are you okay? You sound funny."

"That's me. Always funny."

"Yeah, that's you all right."

She wasn't buying it. Clearly. "Duff and I are out running. I decided not to go to work today."

"Wow! No work and an offer to take me out."

"Scratch that last part. But I'll have a reason for you to come home. Promise."

Jamie's voice warmed her as easily as a hug. "There's nowhere I'd rather be than with you. Promise."

"Got it. Hurry home."

"I will. I'll call you before I catch my plane."

"Love you," Ryan said as she clicked off. She reached down and roughly ran her hand through Duffy's coat. "Sorry I dragged you all the way over here, boy. But we can go home at a slower pace. Everything's fine."

After stopping at a convenience store to buy a bottle of water that they shared, they started off again. About half-way home, Ryan started to obsess about all of the things that could happen to Jamie while driving a car in an area she'd never been.

Angry with herself, she spoke to the dog once again. "Something's going on in my head, Duff, but I'll be damned if I know what it is. But I'm not going to run your legs off again. I obviously can't outrun whatever it is."

After returning home, she called around, finally finding Annie at home with Cait. "Hey. I've got the day off and thought you might like a little alone time."

Immediately, Annie said, "I'll put her in a cab. Give me ten minutes."

"I'll come get her," Ryan said, finally able to laugh a little. "And don't leave her on the front porch. I'll be there soon."

"Not soon enough!"

Duffy leapt from the loveseat in the living room, bounding across the floor to fly down the few steps that led to the front door. Ryan got up and tried to put some order to her hair. She'd been asleep just long enough to be thoroughly disoriented, but she made it to the door by the time Jamie opened it. Her arms enfolded Jamie in a hug and she hung on, not even letting her enter the room.

"I smell something…" Jamie kissed Ryan and took her hand as they fought with Duffy for space on the stairs. "Are you cooking?"

Ryan led her to the door of the kitchen, where a dozen ingredients lay scattered across the counter, along with pots and pans, knives and spatulas. "I tried to cook. With Caitlin. After I took her home, I called and got reservations at a nice restaurant. When we get back I'll clean up."

Jamie looked up, her eyes narrowed. "What's going on? You've been funny all day."

"I haven't felt funny. I've felt really bad. Over dinner, you can tell me why."

They shared a small table at a crowded restaurant in Chinatown. Ryan stared at her salt and pepper Dungeness crab, trying to decide how to begin to attack it. The whole crab had obviously been cooked, but given that it was still intact, it looked like it might skitter across the table and bite her.

Jamie poked at it with a chopstick. "I warned you. You can't say I didn't."

"I eat crab all the time. But this one seems…kinda lifelike."

"That's a good way to describe it. I stick with the black cod. Much less threatening."

Ryan scoped out the other diners, seeing most people ripping the crab apart with their bare hands. It was gonna be messy, but she would have gladly eaten every meal with her hands. Jamie was watching her like she was trying not to laugh, but Ryan didn't mind. It was *so* good to have her home.

"Want a taste of my cod?" Jamie held up a bite, perfectly balanced on her chopsticks. The woman acted like she'd been born in Beijing.

Taking the morsel in her mouth, Ryan chewed thoughtfully. "It's good. But mine is a whole sensory experience. I get to eat it, play with it, wrestle it, probably wear it…"

"Use the crab cracker and your tiny fork. Want me to help?" She was pulling the dish in front of her as she made the offer. "Simple. See?" Jamie expertly pried the shell off, snapped the legs, then broke it in half. "Just use your fork now." She picked up a bit of snowy white meat and popped it into her mouth. "Delicious."

Ryan used the tiny fork to pry the meat from the shell. "I don't know why this seems tough. I really do eat crab all the time." She gave Jamie a wry look. "The whole day's been bolloxed up."

Jamie's hand cupped her knee, then slid up her leg to settle, comfortably, on her thigh. "Were you worried about me?"

"Uh-huh. All day." Ryan kept her focus on her crab. She hated to admit how unsettled she'd been, especially since there was no earthly reason for it. It was easier to talk if she didn't look directly into those empathic eyes. "I was sure your plane had…" She shrugged. "Spent an hour hitting the refresh button on my computer, looking at every place I could think of to tell me if there had been an accident."

"Oh, sweetheart. I'm sorry you're still having trouble."

Unable to resist, Ryan looked right into Jamie's eyes. "You think this is…from the carjacking?"

"Of course. What else could it be? You have post traumatic shock, baby. It hasn't even been a year yet. This is all perfectly normal."

"Says you." She went back to her work, occasionally pulling out a bite big enough to bother with. Next time she'd order something that provided more calories for less work.

"Yeah. Says me." Jamie held up another good-sized bite of her cod, which Ryan gratefully accepted.

"Thanks. I'm gonna have to order something else. I don't think there were three ounces of meat in this thing."

Jamie signaled their waiter, who cruised over and paused. Quickly, she said, "Spicy chicken with XO sauce, please." He nodded, made a quick note and took off again.

"Is that what I wanted?"

"I know what you like, sweetheart. Let me take care of you."

Ryan dropped her little fork and sighed. "I used to be so friggin' independent. Now I can't get through a day if you're not in the same area code."

"Not true. You did fine when Mia and I were in Fresno. It comes and goes, Ryan. You've just got to acknowledge what it is and ride it out. Don't try to fight it."

"That's hard for me. I was sure…" She looked up and met Jamie's eyes. "I've never had such a sense of panic. I felt like I'd been hit in the gut with a sledgehammer. Since it was exactly the time your flight was supposed to take off, it freaked me the fuck out."

"I bet it did." Jamie took her hand and placed a gentle kiss on it. "But here's what probably happened. You were anxious about my going, and you knew when the plane was supposed to take off. Then, when you saw the time, the two connected and you panicked. It was your subconscious mind that tripped you up."

"I wasn't looking at a clock."

"I know how those big baby blues take everything in. You probably caught a glimpse of a clock and didn't even register it."

"Mmm…I guess that's possible."

The server raced to the table, placing a steaming dish right in front of Ryan. She looked up to thank him, but he was long gone. She used her normal-sized fork, too hungry to bother trying to finesse her chopsticks. As soon as she had a bite of the spicy chicken in her mouth, she nodded and smiled. "You know what I like."

"I do. And one thing you like is routine. It's tough for you when I'm gone. Your subconscious mind thinks about it all day and keeps nagging you."

"Yeah. That's it. It gnaws at me. All day."

"I've only got one more visit planned, and I'm taking you with me."

"Someplace cool?"

"Yeah. I think you'll like it. I'll surprise you. How's that?"

"If the surprise is as good as this chicken—you've got a deal."

Mia stood in front of Jamie's closet on Tuesday evening, idly pushing dresses along the rod. "I'm going for professional but a little offbeat. Most of Jamie's stuff is too safe or too dressy."

Jordan was sprawled across Jamie and Ryan's bed, watching carefully. "She should be more thoughtful. You're gonna have to speak to her about that."

"Ha. Ha." She pulled out a dress that had a little more edge to it. "How about this one?"

"It's nice," Jordan agreed. "But it needs the right shade of shoe to highlight that stripe."

"Like Jamie would have a dress that didn't have the perfect shoe." She dropped to the floor to scan the neatly labeled boxes. "I love how organized she is. Makes stealing her clothes so much easier." She whipped out a box labeled, "Grass Green Slingbacks." "Check this out," she said, turning the box around for Jordan to read. "Perfect, right?"

Jordan took a look at the contents of the box when Mia opened it. "Perfect. Now model for me."

Mia got into the dress, then slipped the shoes on. She did a slow turn, asking, "Good?"

"Excellent." Jordan got up and gave her a hug. She was still using only one arm, but her hugs remained awesome. "You don't have a thing to worry about. You're gonna do great tomorrow."

Mia pulled away and looked up into her face. "That's a funny comment."

"It is?"

"Yeah. Why would I have anything to worry about?" She started to undress, sliding the garment down her arms.

"You're going on a job interview. It's your first, right?"

"Yeah, but it's not like I don't know how to talk. If this chick likes me, we're good. If she doesn't, we're not. Not much I can do about it either way, right?"

"Uhm, I hate to tell you this, but most people are super nervous when they go on a job interview. Especially for one they really want."

Mia hung the dress back up, making sure to put it in its proper space. "I'm not like that. This is exactly like a first date. Nothing to get excited about."

Jordan poked at her playfully. "Not to burst your bubble, but most people are nervous about dates, too."

Staring up at her, Mia said, "Why?"

"Because they want the person to like them."

"Huh." She took Jordan by the hand to lead her to their bedroom. "That seems dumb. Just be yourself and see if anything's cookin'. That's the Mia way."

"I love the Mia way." Jordan laughed softly. "Maybe because you felt something was cookin' with us."

"Waaaaay before you did, buddy. Count your lucky stars."

"I count them every night," Jordan agreed before bending down to place a very hot kiss on Mia's lips.

"I have a feeling I'm gonna get lucky before my big interview." Mia looked into Jordan's eyes, seeing a hearty supply of interest.

"You're gonna have all the luck you can handle."

At 9:30, Mia strolled into the coffee shop, catching Jordan's eye. A huge smile greeted her, making her confident her extra time in front of the mirror had been worth it.

"One large skinny latte," Jordan called to the guy at the machine, bypassing the four people already in line. She winked, then got back to serving people in order.

When Mia got to the front of the line she leaned over the counter and puckered up. Jordan hesitated, then drew close and placed a gentle kiss on her lips. "The guy at the machine just burned himself," Mia whispered as a man rushed to the sink to run cold water over his hand.

"I hadn't planned on coming out to the whole store," Jordan said, her cheeks a little flushed.

"That makes one of us. I'm staking my claim. Hands off," she said a little louder.

"Shh!"

The woman behind Mia chuckled as she watched.

"Can you take a break? You've been here for hours and hours."

Jordan checked the clock. "Mmm, not until ten. We're kinda busy, honey."

"Some of us have to get to work," the woman behind Mia spoke up.

"Haters gonna hate," Mia muttered before giving Jordan another quick kiss. "Thanks for the coffee, babe. See you this afternoon."

"Good luck!" Jordan waved as Mia moved over to the pick-up area.

"Get a room!" the next customer grumbled. Mia was going to lob something back, but she didn't want to spoil her zen-like mood. She looked great, she'd gotten a kiss from her girlfriend, and she had a big latte in her hand. All was going according to plan.

The PR firm was located in the Embarcadero, not far from Mia's father's office. The elevator zipped her up to the twenty-second floor, and when she got off she regarded the outer door carefully. "CIA" was printed in red letters on a pearl gray square that seemed to float on the door. The font was nice—bold, yet slightly feminine. She opened the door to find a receptionist sitting at a glass desk, the surface in front of her completely clear.

"Hi. I'm Mia Christopher. I've got an appointment with—"

"Carly," the woman said. "She's waiting for you. You can go right through that door."

"Great. Thanks." Mia opened the door, finding herself in a large office with views of the bay. A thirtyish woman was on the phone, and she indicated that Mia should sit. That was good. She had time to scope things out while Carly was busy.

The room was very modern, very clean, very spare. They *had* to generate paper, but there was almost none of it on display. Modern, color-saturated pictures hung on the walls, and the carpet was short-napped and dark gray. Probably industrial.

Carly was cute, or maybe interesting was the right word. She had that super-smart look about her, with attractive, very current glasses that covered dark eyes that were constantly scanning the computer screen in front of her. She was dressed about like Mia was, in a simple but well-fitted dress, with little adornment. That made Mia smile in satisfaction. She'd gotten it right.

Mia turned her chair around, looking out at the Bay Bridge and her East Bay home. She would have rather been lying on her bed, watching TV, but you had to get off your butt at some point. Might as well be now.

Carly hung up and said, "Hi, there. Carly Adams."

Mia swung around and shook her extended hand. "Mia Christopher. Good to meet you."

"Same here. Let's cut to the chase. Tell me what you know about crisis and risk management." Her eyes showed that she was teasing, but only a little.

"Hmm. I like to use analogies to explain things." She thought for a second, then said, "The client's like your kid. The one you desperately want to get into an Ivy-league school. You want to build him up and make him sound like the smartest, coolest kid in the country. But," she added dramatically, "given that he's a kid, he's inadvertently screwing up right and left. You've got to make sure everyone knows his best traits, while doing your best to minimize or hide his screw-ups. Bad news travels fast, and no one wants to give anyone a second chance." Mia took a breath. "But even if he murders kittens with his bare hands, he's still your kid and you've got to stop him from going down the drain. That's when you pull out all the stops and fly into damage control. That part's really tough…" She let a smile show through. "But fun." Now when she took a breath, she straightened up and pointedly looked at the firm logo, located right behind Carly's desk. "I love the name of your firm, by the way. When you've got great initials, you've gotta use them."

Carly took off her glasses, leaned back in her ergonomic chair and smirked at Mia. "I wouldn't describe my business the way you just did to a client, but you get it. It's all about jumping in front of bad news and pushing good news in any direction you can."

"I can do both," Mia said, absolutely confident of her ability to do just that. "I'm not afraid to call anyone in the world. And I'm persistent. *Damned* persistent," she emphasized. "To a fault."

"You're a little young, and a lot inexperienced," Carly said, squinting as she regarded her, "but I can teach you the details. I *can't* make someone gutsy."

"People have been trying to make me less gutsy since I was born. It's time I started to exploit my natural talents."

Jordan was sitting on the front porch when Mia pulled up, and by the time she got the door open, Jordan was inches away. "How'd it go?"

With a haughty smile, Mia said, "It went super. I'd be the most surprised woman in the world if I didn't get an offer. We even talked about salary." She chuckled. "Actually, we negotiated."

"Fantastic! I'm so proud of you!" Jordan put an arm around her and hugged her as well as her limited reach would allow.

"I'm proud of me too. I wheedled another twenty thousand bucks out of her."

"*Another* twenty thousand?"

"Yeah. She told me what she was thinking about paying, and I said that wasn't enough for me to even consider." They started to walk into the house together, with Jordan giving her a stunned look. "I insisted my potential was worth a lot more than she was willing to pay, even though I acknowledged she might be worried she'd be stuck with a dummy."

Jordan gave her a warm smile, so filled with pride that Mia almost misted up. "No one who talked to you for more than a minute would think you were a dummy."

"Well, you never know. So I proposed she pay me minimum wage for ninety days. If she likes me as much as I know she will, I'll get four times that. If she doesn't—I'll quit."

"That's…" Jordan stood in the doorway, staring. "How'd you know to do that?"

"Dunno. Just seemed smart. I didn't want to get stuck making a low salary, and I wouldn't go all the way to the city for minimum wage, so it seemed like a way for both of us to win."

"You are soooo smart," Jordan said, her eyes filled with pleasure. "I'm so lucky to have such a smart girlfriend."

"If this works out—and it will—you can quit making coffee ninety days after I start, baby."

"Nah. I like it. It's making me more social."

"Well," Mia linked her hands behind Jordan's neck and pulled her down for a kiss. "You can do whatever you like. But I'm going to be able to support us. Stick with me kid. I'm gonna give you the kind of lifestyle you grew up with. We're gonna be luppies, baby."

Jordan kissed her, lingering for long seconds. When she spoke, she was just inches away. "How can we be lesbian urban professionals if you're not a lesbian?"

"I'm in love with a lesbian, and we're going to be together until time stops. So I'm a putative lesbian. Since my interest in the other sex will never be on display, I might as well go with what everyone assumes."

"I like it. You're a lesbian by default."

"No, I'm a lesbian by choice. I choose you." She stood on her tiptoes and gave Jordan a tender kiss. "Every day for the rest of my life."

With Jennie's Monday clarinet lesson, and her therapy sessions on Tuesday and Thursday, Wednesday was the only day the girl didn't have to rush to an appointment. To reward her for sticking to the schedule, Catherine made sure they did something fun every week. It seemed that nothing clicked with Jennie more than art, so that Wednesday afternoon found them at another contemporary art gallery.

Jennie had taken to gallery hopping like a duck to water, much to Catherine's surprise. She seemed more sure of herself, or maybe it was simply that she was interested enough to ask the gallerist questions—perceptive questions—about technique.

"I like this guy a lot," Jennie said, after staring at a still-life for an amazingly long time. "Most of the time, everything in a still-life looks pretty." She pointed at a pomegranate, clearly rotted through. "This is more like real stuff."

"I agree. He sees the darker side of beauty, and how transient it is." Jennie looked up at her sharply. When Jamie was a girl, Catherine had insisted she look up every word she didn't know. With Jen, adopting that practice would have made her feel like a scold, given how many holes Jennie had in her vocabulary. "It doesn't last very long."

"Right." She nodded, looking sage. "I guess it doesn't."

They moved to another painting, this one of a mother and child. But instead of a peaceful picture of maternal love, the mother looked worn-out, and the look she gave her screaming infant was far from loving. "I bet this is what my mom looked like when I was a baby," Jen said, staring at it critically. "The mom looks like she wants to throw the kid in the trash."

Catherine slipped an arm around Jennie's shoulders. They weren't often very physical with each other, but she was slowly getting more comfortable showing her affection. "Every mother has moments like that. But it's usually just moments. I bet the same was true with you."

"Doubt it," Jennie said as she moved on.

After thinking about it for just a second, Catherine decided to broach the topic of Jen's mother. "Do you have any interest in seeing your mom?"

Jen turned and looked at her for a few seconds. Catherine couldn't begin to guess what was on her mind, so she simply waited. "Yeah. Of course. But she doesn't wanna see me."

She said this with such finality that Catherine decided not to follow up. "How about your father?"

"Mmm…I'd like to see him, but he's shipping out soon."

"Then we'll wait until he's back home and go see him. He lives in San Diego, right?"

"Yeah." Jen had her arms crossed over her chest and was gazing at another painting. "He's gonna be gone a long time. Like six months."

"Oh. Well, we could go this weekend and catch him before he leaves."

Jennie seemed to grow even more sullen. "I don't like my stepmother. She thinks my dad only has one kid—the one he has with her."

This was getting nowhere quickly. Time to change the subject. "What about your friends? Have you given any more thought to inviting them over?"

"Not really. But…" She shot Catherine a hopeful glance. "They wanna go to the Castro for Halloween. Sandy never would've let me go, but I'd really like to."

"Then you should go." She checked her watch for the date. "That's only a week from now. Have you given any thought to your costume?"

"Uhm…no. I didn't think you'd let me go."

"Jennie." Catherine put her hands on her shoulders and made eye contact. "When you want to do something, ask me. I might not allow it, but we can always have a discussion about it. Don't assume I won't let you do things."

"Okay," she said, clearly anxious to move away. Catherine let her go, then followed her to the next painting. "Why don't you have your friends come to the house before you go? Marta would love to make spooky snacks for you."

"What are spooky snacks?"

"Oh, she carves little bones out of jicama, and makes eyeballs out of radishes. They looked so real they scared Jamie half to death when she was small."

"So we could just have a snack and then take off?"

"Yes, honey. You don't have to stay all night. I know the fun of going is being unsupervised." She ruffled Jennie's short hair as the girl looked up and smiled.

"I've been unsupervised a lot, but my friends haven't. They've gotta be home by nine, so we don't have a lot of time to waste…"

"Have them come over at six. That will give you time to have some food, then I'll drive you over to the Castro. We'll arrange where to meet, and I'll pick you all up at 8:45 so we make sure we get them home in time. They live in the city, don't they?"

"Yeah. They live pretty close." She gazed at Catherine somewhat dubiously. "You'd really do that?"

"I really would." She took out her appointment calendar and made a note. "And I'll call your therapist to see if we can switch your time. If we can't, you may skip therapy to go to the party. Halloween's but once a year."

Once again, Ryan enjoyed a Sunday morning to herself. She thought it best not to reveal how much she loved her two or three hours of alone time, but she wasn't actually ashamed of it. It was good to have time alone—especially away from your partner. Being apart gave you something to talk about.

As she had the week before, Ryan had made lunch for the crew, but today only Jamie returned.

"I've got enough food to make sandwiches for six," she said as she stared at the doorway which had been graced by Jamie only.

"Nice to know how special I am." Jamie walked over and kissed her, then tickled under her chin. "Your father's working today, Jennie's got homework to conquer, and your aunt is meeting some women from St. Philip's to go on some kind of afternoon retreat. So I'm all you've got, blue eyes. Disappointed?"

"Not too badly." Ryan bent and kissed her on the forehead. "I'll go wrap everything up. Remind me I've got plenty of food for lunch this week."

"Will do." Jamie followed her into the kitchen. "But you're not going to need lunch tomorrow or Tuesday…or Wednesday."

"I'm not?" She stopped and gazed at Jamie, waiting for the punchline.

"Nope." Jamie draped her arms along Ryan's shoulders and pulled her down. "We're taking tomorrow off to do something fun. Something *really* fun," she added. "And your actual birthday's on Tuesday, so we have to play then too. And on Wednesday, I'm taking you to Marin. You and Duffy, that is." She reached down and grasped a handful of Duffy's curly black hair, tugging on it a little.

"Really?" In her mind, Ryan went through what was happening at the OFC project. "I promised Miguel and Fernando I'd help them get everything prepped for painting."

Jamie held her tighter and playfully nibbled on her nose. "They're getting paid. You're not. You can take time off from the job you don't officially have any time you want, goofball. And you want to take Monday, Tuesday and Wednesday off."

Smirking, Ryan said, "I didn't know I wanted that. My memory…"

"You do. We're going to have a lovely day in Marin. At some point in the day we're going to have really fresh oysters and cheese and all sorts of good things."

"I guess I can't argue with that." She started to put the food she'd bought into containers. "Not that it would do me any good anyway."

After dinner that night, Jamie went downstairs to pack up a few things. She returned, toting a small bag. "We've gotta get going," she said, nudging Ryan in the back.

Ryan, who was still sitting at the dining room table, turned and looked at her, clearly puzzled. "Where are we going?"

"To Berkeley. That's where we're gonna have fun tomorrow."

Resigned, Ryan stood and started for the kitchen. "Then we'd better start cleaning up."

"We'll do it," Conor said, elbowing Kevin, who was seated next to him. "Early birthday present."

"Don't you mean 'only' birthday present?" Ryan smirked.

"Yeah, I guess that's more accurate." He got up and put his arm around Ryan's neck and kissed her on the top of the head. "Have a great day, Sis. Which I'm sure you will, given Jamie's in charge."

"It's gonna be memorable," Jamie agreed, practically bubbling with excitement.

It took another ten minutes to say goodbye to everyone, but they were finally on the road by eight. "Why'd we have to leave so early?" Ryan asked. "Is something happening tonight?"

"Not really. But I want to get to bed early. I've got big, big plans for the morning."

"Hey, were we supposed to bring Duffy? You said he was going with us to Marin."

"He wouldn't like what we're doing tomorrow." She reached over and pinched Ryan's cheek. "Guaranteed."

Chapter Ten

The next morning, after having coffee and muffins at Jordan's new coffee shop, Jamie got in the driver's seat.

"Secret location?" Ryan asked.

"Not very. You've been where we're going." She looked so smug. So adorable.

"I like letting you be in charge." Ryan relaxed her seat and stretched out. "Are we going far?"

"Not very far at all, almost birthday girl. Jordan looked cute in her beret, didn't she?"

"She'd look cute in a gunny sack."

"What's a gunny sack?"

Ryan considered the origins of the term, coming up with nothing. "I suppose that's where you kept your gunny."

"I think the owner of Jordan's shop is a little precious, trying to have the servers look like French stereotypes, but… I guess she wants to be different."

"I predict it won't last long. You know how people are. They'll start wearing them in weird ways. Actually," she said, thinking about it. "Jordan was the only one who wore hers in the traditional way." She chuckled. "She's not much of a rule-breaker."

"Look who's talking. No one loves rules as much as you do."

"Hey! It's not like you're not a… Who's a person who breaks all the rules?"

"That's a Mia," Jamie said, turning to offer a wink.

They drove on in the heavy rush-hour traffic, heading for San Francisco. But Jamie took one of the last turnoffs in Berkeley, with Ryan saying, "Oh. We're going to the marina. Cool. You know how much I love being on your big boat."

"I do." Jamie turned again, giving Ryan a smile filled with love. "I want you to only do things you enjoy on your birthday."

"You can tic off that checkmark already, snooks. Being with you today fulfills all my wishes."

"Then we're set."

She parked in the mostly empty lot, and Ryan got out to survey the scene. "On such a lovely day, why isn't anyone here?"

"I'll never understand it. Everyone knows October is usually our best month. But the place is jammed all summer, with people going sailing when it's fifty degrees, misty and foggy. I suppose we think summer is the time for sailing, even if fall is better." She went to the trunk and pulled out a big tote bag.

"What's in there?" Ryan asked, trying to sneak a peek.

"Things." Jamie held the bag close to her chest. "Presents for my baby."

"Cool. I love presents."

"Hope that's true." Jamie took her by the hand and led her down one of the docks.

"Your boat's over there," Ryan said, pointing at Jim's forty-five foot Swan.

"I know. But yours is right here." Grinning, she pointed at an emerald green sailboat. It was much, much smaller than Jim's. Actually, it looked a little like a row boat, with just enough room for two. But a long mast lay down the center of the boat, making it clear this was no rowboat.

"Mine?" Ryan asked, stunned.

"Yep." Jamie slid her arm around Ryan, pulled her close and murmured, "Happy birthday, my sweet sailor."

"I'm not..." Ryan bit her tongue. She *had* to be gracious! "I'm not a very good sailor, baby. Are you sure this is a good idea?"

As though someone had dimmed the lights, some of the fire left Jamie's eyes. "Of course I do. I guarantee you're going to love sailing. Especially in the right sized boat."

"And this is the right size?"

"This is the perfect size. It's made for two, and best when one is bigger than the other. The larger one usually hikes out while the smaller one steers." She slapped herself on the chest. "Since I'm a pretty good tactician, and you're very good at being…ballast…this will be perfect for us."

Ryan couldn't avoid being swept up in her lover's excitement. "Thank you, honey. I can't imagine how much a boat cost, so I'm not going to even ask."

"Less than you think." Jamie stepped into the boat, then sat down. "This little baby is ten years old. I had new gelcoat put on her, and that cost more than the hull." She smiled up at Ryan. "I knew you wouldn't enjoy it if it cost thousands and thousands."

She couldn't help but fish for details. "So it was only thousands?"

"Barely." Jamie met her eyes. "Seriously, honey. The hull was super cheap. The guy who owned it had it sitting out, uncovered, for eight years. It was a mess." She patted the non-skid part she sat on. "I had to replace a bunch of stuff, but the boat could easily last for another thirty years. It'll be a fun hobby for us to enjoy together."

"Okay," Ryan said, nodding. "Sounds like you've given this a lot of thought."

"I have." Jamie chuckled. "While you've been working on the OFC, I've been working on this. The guys at the boatyard are so sick of me it's not even funny. But I've finally got it just like I want it."

Ryan forced herself to let go of her worry about spending money on frivolous things and took in the sleek, green hull. "I love the color."

"Everybody leaves theirs white. I wanted yours to be cooler than that."

"It's very, very cool." Ryan moved around the hull, stopping in her tracks when she saw the name Jamie'd had stenciled, in a lovely gold script, on the back…stern. "Who told you about Gráinne O'Malley?"

"Everybody knows about her. She's probably the most famous Irish woman pirate."

Nodding, Ryan said, "I forget you know a lot of stuff you have no need to know." Meeting Jamie's eyes, she said, "Really good job. On the boat, and the color, and especially the name."

She started to get in, but Jamie said, "Don't you want to take her for a spin?"

"Sure. That's why I was going to get in."

"You might want to dress a little better. You'll freeze your butt off."

"Okay. I'll go get those rain suits from your dad's boat."

"No need. I've got us all hooked up." She jumped out of the boat, nimbly landing on the dock. "Let's hit the locker room."

"We can't get dressed right here?"

"We could…but you've gotta take off your jeans. Do you want to show off your birthday suit? It's a really nice one…"

"To the lockers," Ryan agreed, taking Jamie's hand.

It took a while to stuff themselves into neoprene, skintight suits. "These are as bad as wetsuits," Ryan said, checking herself out in the mirror.

"Almost the same, but these have more padding in the knees." She stood back and whistled. "You look fan-frigging-tastic in that."

Frowning, Ryan looked at her image. "I usually buy black. This silver color shows everything."

"Exactly." Jamie wrapped her arms around her and hugged her tightly. "Every part would have a little spotlight if I were in charge."

Looking down on her, Ryan said, "You are."

"Right-o, matey!"

They went back to the boat, adding heavy waterproof jackets, Ryan's in blue, Jamie's in yellow.

"Now all we have to do is set the mast, raise the sails and hit it."

"Sounds easier than I bet it is," Ryan said.

"Nah. This will be a snap."

They worked together, with Jamie doing all of the directing. She was a natural at running the show and giving clear orders. If she ever went broke, she could run a complex assembly line with little problem. Once the sails were set, Jamie said, "Get in and I'll cast us off."

Ryan looked around. "No motor."

"No need." Jamie pushed the boat away from the dock, jumped in at the last second and started to steer.

"See that line?"

"Yeah."

"Move it so the centerboard drops."

Ryan raised her eyebrows, but followed orders. As she moved the rope out of its fitting, the boat seemed like it had put on running shoes. They zoomed out of the harbor, spray hitting them both in the face. "What's that called?" Ryan asked, pointing at the stick in Jamie's hand. A gust of wind hit her, blowing her hair around her head.

"The tiller. It moves the rudder, which is at the stern, and the centerboard, which is just a piece of metal or wood, keeps us from sliding across to Japan."

"Does your dad's boat have a centerboard?"

"Nope. His has a keel filled with lead. That's why his doesn't do *this* as well."

She got a demonic gleam in her eye and steered the boat so Ryan's side went up into the air—making her stomach lurch. Then the boat slid back down onto a mostly horizontal attitude.

"Holy crap!"

Jamie pointed to the tote bag, and instructed, "Take out the last two things in there. We're gonna need 'em."

The bag was secured with a bungy cord, and Ryan got it unfastened. Inside, she found two complicated looking things…almost like life preservers, but with all sorts of straps.

"I should have had you put that on when we were on shore, but I wanted to give you a thrill," Jamie said, grinning unrepentantly. "That's both a life preserver and a hiking harness." She grabbed at it and held it right-side up. "You can leave those fastened and step into it. I promise I'll keep the boat level."

With a warning scowl, Ryan stood, shakily, in the skimming boat. It took her a few tries, but she got into the harness, then adjusted the straps so the circulation to her legs wasn't cut off. "Want me to hold the…tiller so you can get into yours?"

"I won't need mine. You're going to do all of the work." She put the harness on over her head, adjusting it so it was merely a life vest. "But I might fall out, so I'll be careful."

"If you fall out, what am I supposed to do?"

Jamie laughed. "If I fall out, you'll already be gone. If we both go, just hold on to anything you can grab, and try to keep your head above water."

"Uhm…I think that part's instinctive."

"But sometimes hard to do. It works best if you turn so the water's not hitting you in the face. Did I mention you're tethered to the boat?" She unhooked one of a dizzying series of ropes and snapped a metal clip to a sturdy stainless hook that sat right at Ryan's pelvis. "If you fall out, I can pull you back in pretty easily. If I fall out…" She smiled. "I'll try not to fall out."

"Jesus, Jamie," Ryan said, her heart starting to beat quicker. "I don't know how to sail to turn around and pick you up!"

"I know. But you'll be being dragged through the water until the sail looses its wind, so there's not much you can do anyway. Just hold on. If I fall out, I can swim to you."

"This is crazy dangerous!"

Jamie slapped Ryan's neoprene-clad leg. "I know! Isn't that the best part?"

Slowly nodding, Ryan found herself agreeing. "I guess it is."

Jamie handed her a line. "Put your gloves on and get ready for some fun."

Ryan did, then gripped the line.

"I'm going to tack over there," Jamie said, pointing. "When I do, the port side's gonna fly out of the water. Hold onto the line, put your feet on the non-skid part you're sitting on, and lean out. You'll get the feel for it."

Wide-eyed, Ryan got ready, and when the port side started to rise, so did she. The line she held was on a pulley-system and she could pull herself closer in or let her body stretch all the way out. Jamie was obviously going slowly, letting her get used to the sensation.

"I think I'm catching on," Ryan called out. "This is hell on your thighs."

"And your back and your abs. Kinda tough on the shoulders too. Good thing you've been swinging a hammer since June."

"Yeah, I think I'm in...Yeow!"

With that demonic look in her eyes again, Jamie let the boat really take off. Ryan's stomach was in her throat as the little boat dove and pitched in the three-foot swells. She was stretched out, holding onto the lines with all of her might, while also trying to center and balance herself.

"You don't have to hold on so tightly," Jamie called. "The harness will do a lot of the work."

Ryan lightened up on her hold, which helped a lot, then concentrated on keeping her knees bent while anticipating the bumps. It was a little like surfing, but you had more control. And you could do it while looking at a gorgeous blonde who was grinning like she'd never been happier. "Sailing rocks!" Ryan yelled as a wave hit her right in the face.

When they got home, Ryan raced for the shower, Jamie right behind her. They stripped out of their dry clothes, the racing suits having been removed at the marina, and jumped into the shower together, trying to warm up.

The door opened and Mia walked in and leaned on the sink. "What's going on?"

"Rhetorical question?" Ryan called out, having to raise her voice to be heard.

"I can see you're huddling in the shower. I just can't understand why."

"We're freezing," Jamie said, her teeth chattering. "We got *so* drenched, mainly because I forgot to buy hoods for our racing suits. Coming back, the wind was blowing right into our faces and the sun was hiding behind the clouds. I thought we'd turn into blocks of ice."

"Oh! How's the new boat?" Mia pointed at Ryan. "You have no idea how much time your girlfriend put into getting that thing fitted out."

"It's really, really cool," Ryan said. She turned so her back was to the spray, bent her head and kissed Jamie soundly. "Thank you."

"I'll let you thaw out in peace." Mia started to close the door, then whipped it back open. "I got the job! I start Wednesday!"

"That's so cool!" Jamie said, with Ryan echoing her praise.

"I'm gonna need clothes…"

"All of my dresses and skirts are here, all at your disposal."

"I'll buy my own, but I've gotta wait until I start to earn some serious bucks."

"We're really happy for you, Mia," Ryan said. "Now get out!"

"Don't have to be so touchy." She started to leave again. "You'd think someone who just got a boat for her birthday would be in a better mood."

Ryan looked down at Jamie, who was smirking. "Does she do that when you travel with her? Just walk in on you?"

"Yep. Unless I lock the door, which I do most of the time."

"Are you certain her parents weren't wolves?"

"Pretty sure. She just doesn't do well with barriers. Of any kind."

After they'd dried off and were both wrapped in terrycloth robes, they sat together on the loveseat. After just a moment, Ryan jumped up and locked both the door to the hall and the one to the bathroom. "I want to be alone for a while." She stood with her hands on her hips, assessing the window. "Think she can climb in that?"

"Probably," Jamie said, chuckling. "But it's too much trouble."

Ryan sat back down and Jamie cuddled up against her. "Who had a great day?"

"I sure did. I can't tell you how much I enjoyed sailing. And today was *sailing*. There was such a huge difference between going out on the little boat and your dad's. It's a whole different thing, and I enjoyed the hell out of it."

Grinning, Jamie said, "I knew you would. It's wet and wild, just like you."

"That's me." Ryan hadn't taken the time to dry her hair. After grabbing a pen from the table, she twisted it around a couple of times and stuck the pen into it to keep it from getting Jamie wet. "After we're warm, I'll let you dry my hair. I know you love to."

"I do. And if I can stand to let mine grow all the way out, you can return the favor."

"I'm not sure that's something the pirate queen would do, but I'll make an exception for you."

Jamie looked up at her, grinning with such pleasure Ryan was nearly moved to tears. "You'll probably never understand this, but I get so much joy from buying you something you enjoy. When we were out there, and you were whooping it up, with that huge smile on your face…" She pulled Ryan down and planted a long, leisurely kiss to her lips. "I'm sure I enjoy your birthdays as much as you do."

"My present was epic," Ryan said. "Every part of it. But I'm still surprised you knew about Gráinne O'Malley. Is she really universally famous?"

"Mmm… I'm not sure. I don't recall when I first heard about her, but I *clearly* recall Elizabeth telling me that pirates were not something little girls should be interested in."

"Oh, she would have loved me," Ryan said, chuckling. "We played pirates for years. I was always Gráinne, ordering all of the other kids around. My brothers and cousins wouldn't have it of course, but I could pressgang a few boys from the neighborhood into following me."

"You played pirates? Like playing house?"

"Uh-huh. For years. My aunt made me a costume." She laughed. "It wasn't much, just a sash and a belt for my sword. I didn't have the kind of boots I wanted, so I wore Rory's rain boots. I must have looked like a lunatic."

"I…I have a vague memory of playing pirates with an older girl." She waved a hand in front of herself. "That must have been a fantasy. Elizabeth would never have let me do that, and God knows she was with me every hour of the day."

"Hmm… I roamed all over town, but I'm pretty sure my lands didn't extend down to Hillsborough."

"No, that would have been a little extreme—even for you." She tickled under Ryan's chin. "Did you wear your costume all the time?"

"Whenever I could get away with it. I was a strange kid. More in a fantasy world than the real one most of the time. I loved Halloween, not just because it was my birthday, but because everyone was dressed up. Not that I had any shame at being in my pirate outfit, of course. I just thought other kids were missing out on being somebody else most of the time."

"My little pirate," Jamie said, cuddling closer.

"The pirate *queen*," Ryan corrected. "The queen of the Connaught. When I take you to Ireland, I'll show you her lands. She was a very powerful woman in Mayo… In the whole region, for that matter."

Jamie snuggled her face against Ryan's neck. "She wasn't as powerful as you are. Powerfully cool, powerfully smart, powerfully sexy. I'd gladly bow to your reign."

"If you'd ever gotten to San Francisco when you were a kid, I would have happily taken you into my band."

"I was in San Francisco all the time." Jamie made a face. "For church, museums, the symphony…" She let out a sigh. "Even though I was barely allowed to get my hands dirty down in Hillsborough, I got to wear casual clothes. In the city I was always in a dress."

"That would have changed if you'd been in Gráinne O'Malley's band. Elizabeth would have had a fit!"

Ryan wasn't totally into it, but Jamie convinced her they should go to a costume shop and rent adult-sized pirate costumes for Halloween. Most of the things the shop had to offer were clearly meant for a woman who was trying to audition for a pirate-themed strip club. But by cobbling men's and women's costumes together, they finally had something Ryan would wear.

The outfit was a stunner: a purple brocade vest, very ornate, with gold braid, and billowy black pants, tucked into high black boots. A crimson sash across her chest and a scabbard for an impressive sword mostly finished the costume, but to add to the rakish look Jamie was going to tie a scarf around the crown of her head.

It was easier for Jamie to find an outfit she liked, since she didn't mind looking like a pirate wench. Her choice made her breasts stick out a little more than she was comfortable with, but that was obviously the name of the game. Ryan certainly seemed to like the display, and that was the point of dressing up. Making Ryan happy.

They went back to San Francisco, and spent a long time getting ready. Ryan could be strangely perfectionistic when she was in a certain mood, and she fussed over her clothing for much longer than normal. "When I was a kid I didn't care if I looked like a ragamuffin," she said, shaking her head. "Now I hate to look silly. It's gotta be right or I can't do it."

Jamie came up behind her and held her in a loose embrace, looking into the mirror along with her. "You look wonderful, sweetheart. I should be the one worrying. The girls are falling out of this thing."

Grinning, Ryan turned and nuzzled her face into the inches of exposed flesh. "I'm glad only a few people are coming over for dinner. If my cousins were here, I might have to run a few of them through with my sword." She backed up and whisked the silver-colored piece from her scabbard. "I think I would have liked living in an age where you carried a sword." She whipped it around, slicing the air with the heavy piece.

"You'd be super hot with a sword. Correction. Since you're already super hot, I guess you'd be super-super hot."

Ryan put the sword away and wrapped Jamie in a hug. "And I'd be using it all the damn time, trying to defend your honor. It'd get old, I suppose. It's best to live now."

"You seem a little down today. Are you?"

"No." Ryan always denied even a hint of a negative mood. Jamie was going to have to figure out a way to get a straight answer out of her that didn't require being direct.

"Anything on your mind?"

"Nope. It's empty—as always." She turned and looked at her image in the mirror, making minor adjustments to the scarf that allowed her hair to lie across her shoulders, while keeping it from her eyes. "It's just my family, your grandfather, Mia and Jordan tonight, right?"

"Yeah. My mom's gonna come by, but she can't make dinner." Ah-ha! That was it. "Are you a little…just a tiny bit bummed that Jen and my mom aren't coming for your birthday dinner?"

"Of course not. Jennie's got a chance to hang out with her friends, and she should jump at it." She squinted at her image, then roughly tightened the scarf. Thank God she didn't know how much it had cost. Even though it looked perfect, she'd never wear it if she knew it was real Italian silk. "Remember Jennie made it clear we're not to even acknowledge her if we see her and her friends. Make sure to drum that into Mia's head."

"I will honey, but I think you might be imagining things that Jen didn't mean."

Ryan turned and stared at her. "She acted like I suggested she and her friends join us for an orgy! All I said was that we might see them and they could join us if they wanted."

She had the most adorable pout on her face. One Jamie couldn't avoid kissing. "She hurt your feelings."

"No, no, I can't take things fifteen-year-olds say too seriously. I know she doesn't want her friends to know she's gay. Or that she knows gay people. Or that she's my little sister. Or that your mom's her guardian." She sighed. "The kid's in so many closets it's not even funny. I wish she felt more grounded…in any area."

"She'll get there. For tonight, we'll turn and run the other way if we see her. No problem."

A few hours later, Jamie sat on the arm of the chair her grandfather occupied. "Wait… You're telling me you actually took me out once—alone—on Halloween?"

"I did," he insisted. "I wanted you to have a day where you could play like a normal child, so I brought you over to the city to make sure Elizabeth wouldn't track us down."

"Do you remember what we did?"

"I just wanted you to be able to get dirty. We went to the park, Golden Gate, I think. I even bought play clothes so you wouldn't ruin your costume. I knew if that happened, we'd never be allowed to have another day out."

"I'm amazed. I wish mom was here so I could hear her take on this. She must have had to wrestle with Elizabeth to set me free."

"You had a ball," Charles said. "My memory of that is as clear as day. It took you a while to figure out how to play without supervision, but you got out there and made a friend."

"It must have been like taking a puppy to the dog park for the first time," she said, laughing ruefully.

"It wasn't too far from that." He narrowed his eyes, a look he often adopted when he was testing his memory. "I remember your playing with an odd little girl. She might have been semi-homeless or something. Definitely unsupervised. Hungry too. I felt so bad for her, I found myself offering her a ride home…" He slapped himself on the cheek. "I must've been off my rocker! A priest trying to lure a little girl into his car! I thought about that for weeks." He rolled his eyes. "That's probably why I remember the whole day so well."

Jamie felt a strange chill climb up her spine as a memory fought to enter her consciousness. "Did I have a princess dress?"

"Exactly! We took rolls of film. I'm sure you have photos somewhere in Hillsborough. But you won't have any photos of the play clothes I bought for you. I kept them at my house, and you destroyed them over the next year. I never saw you as happy as when you were running around that small park by my church, chasing the other kids."

"I know this is off-the-wall, but do you remember if any of the kids that day were dressed as a pirate?"

His eyes opened wide. "Yes! The little girl I tried to kidnap was dressed as a pirate." He laughed, clearly imagining the scene. "I bought you both lunch, and she was very careful to put her sword on the table so she didn't hurt herself. Her sword was wood, but she seemed to think it was sharp enough to take off a leg. The child ate like she hadn't eaten in three days." He sighed. "There are so many kids in the city who don't get regular meals."

"Poppa," Jamie said, her excitement growing. "I think that was Ryan!"

"Ryan?" His eyebrows rose. "But…how could… No. That's not possible, honey. What are the odds?"

"Not good. But she told me she ran around in a rag-tag pirate outfit. And God knows she eats like she's been starved." Jamie looked up and waved her hand. "Ryan!"

"Yes?" As always, she was there in a flash.

Snaking an arm around Ryan's waist, Jamie said, "I might be projecting, or be locked in some kind of fit of fancy, but Poppa says he took me to San Francisco once when I was a kid and that I played with an older girl." Ryan blinked, clearly interested. "I played *pirates* with her."

Ryan's alert gaze went to Charles when he said, "I just remembered another thing, Jamie. You were very interested in pirates after that. You wanted to learn about some woman pirate, but Elizabeth said books like that weren't proper for little girls." He chuckled slyly. "I bought you a book anyway, but as I recall you didn't care for it because there were no women in it. You were dead set on knowing more about this particular pirate but I couldn't find a single book about her." He looked up at Ryan. "Do you think…?"

Slowly, Ryan turned and looked at Jamie. "I think it was us." Her voice was barely a whisper. "I remember being in the park and playing with a little girl on my birthday." She shifted her gaze back to Charles. "You bought me lunch."

"I did," he agreed, nodding. "This is…"

"Amazing," Jamie said. Turning to her grandfather, she said, "Excuse us?"

"Sure, honey. I'm…I've got to sit here for a minute and let this settle. This is…"

"Amazing," Jamie said again as she got up and took Ryan's hand. They passed through the small crowd, automatically heading for their room. When they got downstairs, Jamie closed the door behind them. She put her hands on Ryan's shoulders and stared into her eyes for a long time. "I…I can't decide whether I believe this or not. Could it be true?"

"It can," Ryan said, her eyes glowing with a warmth that made tears come to Jamie's eyes. "I wish this part wasn't true, but I remember your grandfather more than I do you. I guess it's because you were three years younger... I just remember a really nice guy who bought me a big lunch on my birthday." She closed her eyes, thinking. "He asked me to do something with you...play a game or listen to a story or something. Then..." Her eyes grew bright. "I got into a fight with a kid who stole your crown!"

"Oh, my God. It was you!" She threw her arms around Ryan and gripped her in a crushing hug. "We played together!"

"Fate?" Ryan asked, gazing deeply into Jamie's eyes.

"I hope so." She rubbed her face into Ryan's neck, overcome with feeling. She wasn't even sure what the feeling was, but it was intense. "Poppa says we have pictures. Maybe you'll remember me better if you see a picture."

"We might have some too. My father was always taking pictures when we were kids. Especially on birthdays and at Christmas. Let's go look." She grabbed Jamie by the hand and started for Conor's room, where the bulk of the family albums still resided.

"We've got company, honey. And they're here for your birthday."

"Can't wait," she said, not even slowing down. They went into the room and Ryan got down on the floor, reading off the dates, "1980, 1981, 1982. Maybe then?"

"Give it a try."

Ryan grabbed the book and started to page through it. She'd only gone a few pages when she slammed it shut. "Too early."

Jamie had seen the first photo, of Ryan's mother surrounded by the kids at a Christmas tree. It had obviously been their last together. She had to bite her lip to not cry, but knew Ryan wouldn't want that. This was a good memory and she wanted to keep it pure.

"Let's try 1984," Ryan said. She paged through quickly, revealing photos of the boys at each of their birthdays. Jamie smiled to herself, seeing that the celebrations hadn't changed a bit. A big cake, a bunch of relatives, and no gifts. Then Ryan slowed and slapped her hand onto a photo near the back. Jamie leaned over and saw her. Messy dark hair, oversized white shirt streaked with dirt, a red sash across her chest and a wooden sword held up by a leather belt. She looked proud, haughty even, and her left hand was resting on the hilt of her sword—just in case she had to whip it out. She stood in front of a birthday cake with nine candles lit, the glow from them highlighting her glittering eyes.

"The prettiest little girl I've ever seen." Jamie hugged her with all her might, kissing every part of her head and cheeks she could reach. "You were my pirate." She finally let Ryan stand and they hugged tenderly. "I dreamt about you. About running away with you on your pirate ship. Your life seemed so exotic. You seemed so…free."

"I wish I'd had a ship. I would have carried you to it and made you my…assistant queen? How would that work?"

"You have a ship now. You're the queen of…Berkeley Marina."

"I feel weird about this whole thing," Ryan admitted. "It's spooky."

"It is. But it's also way, way, way cool! Let's go show everyone!"

Ryan grasped her and held her close. "No. Let's keep this between us. For tonight at least. It's…more special when it's our secret."

Jamie nodded. "Your wish is my command." She knelt, holding Ryan's hand, then gave it a small kiss. "My pirate queen."

Late that night, Jamie and Ryan and Mia and Jordan sat with one of Jamie's albums open in front of them. Ryan smirked as her partner yammered on and on about the magic of this early meeting. In fact, Ryan didn't find it all that odd. San Francisco was big, but there weren't many big parks with things for kids to do. Golden Gate was the spot to go, and she was there all of the damn time, especially when there was something going on. On every holiday, they had organized games for kids, and that was plenty to get her and keep her over there. By the time she was nine, she'd take off the moment breakfast was over and stay out until the last straggler was being dragged away by a parent. That made the chance of her running into half of the kids in the Bay Area pretty good.

Besides being in the park all of the time, she was very prone to finding stray kids for her little band. Kids who didn't seem to fit in with others were her weak spot. And Jamie had to give off that "only child, underdeveloped playing skills" vibe. So if they ran into each other, she could see herself gamely agreeing to play with her. But it was still special. *Really* special.

She looked at the photos of Princess Jamie, all dolled up in a dress that had to cost more than Ryan's entire wardrobe, shoes included. Maybe even sporting goods included. But she looked like she could have easily been a real little princess. There was something about the imperial way she stood—so mature and self-possessed for a little kid. She wasn't even seven years old and she had presence. That was the only word Ryan could think of for the aura she gave off. The kid, her Jamie, had presence even as a six-year-old. And she had a whole hell of a lot more of it now. Ryan tucked an arm around her waist and lay her head on her shoulder. It had been a fantastic birthday. One of the best in memory. Maybe *the* best. She'd received the best present of her whole life—knowing that, even at six, Jamie had been too compelling to resist. That was a such gift. Oh! And the boat! That was beyond cool. She closed her eyes as she listened to Jamie's melodic, excited voice tell their friends every detail of the story. She could listen to her talk all night long, and given the way Jamie was wound up…there was every chance that she'd get to.

By the time they got to bed, Ryan assumed they'd go right to sleep. They were driving up through Marin County in the morning, and they'd have to leave by seven to beat traffic. Ryan lay in bed, already a little disappointed they weren't going to make love. Ever since they'd returned from Australia they'd been slightly out-of-sync. It wasn't that they weren't having sex at all, but it wasn't as frequent as it had been, and they didn't seem to be on exactly the same page. When Ryan was ready to go, Jamie was too tired to show much enthusiasm. Actually, Jamie's libido had been tamped down ever since they'd returned. Her one burst of interest had been that afternoon at Tommy's apartment. While quickies like that were fun, they didn't make up for a long, really intimate evening. That's what Ryan missed. Being intimate.

Jamie came out of the bathroom and Ryan forgot what she'd been musing about. Her nose started to twitch to catch a whiff of some recently applied perfume. But her eyes were so filled with the image of a smoking-hot Jamie, freshly showered and clad in a mint green silky camisole and multi-hued green striped bikinis that she could feel them widen.

"I've got a present for you," Jamie said, sliding into bed on her knees, hands behind her back.

"Don't need a thing," Ryan said, closing her eyes to breathe in.

Sometimes, when Jamie looked particularly sexy, she had to close her eyes to force any of her other senses to work. Tonight, the perfume was so alluring she really wanted to enjoy it for a second.

"Okay." She moved her hand quickly as she leaned over and placed whatever she'd been holding on the floor. Ryan hoped whatever it was could be returned. The last thing she needed was another present. Wasn't a boat enough?

Flushing the thoughts of presents from her mind, Ryan sat up enough to be able to tumble Jamie into her embrace. They lay face-to-face, with Jamie grinning down at her. "I know we'll be tired tomorrow, but I can't let your birthday pass without showing you how much I love you."

"You showed me lots and lots in the past couple of days," Ryan murmured. "I know how much you love me."

Her grin was very playful. "Fine. Then I want to show you how much I desire you."

"That's very nice to know. Now that I know you've had a crush on me since you were six…" She chuckled at the thought. "Wouldn't it be cool if that was the day you discovered you were drawn to women?"

"Girls," Jamie said, giggling. "Pirate girls."

Ryan moved her onto her side, but kept her close. Close enough to share a pillow. "I wish I remembered you more from the day in the park. But…" She took a breath, trying not to cry. "Given that it was October, I'd only been back from Ireland for a few weeks. It always took me a while to get used to being in America again. You know that was just my second year…without Mama."

Jamie snuggled against her, gently stroking her back. "I know, honey."

"I felt closer to her in Ireland. Being with her mother and father and sister made it seem like she was just in another room or something."

"I understand. Really, I do."

"Running into an older guy who showed an interest in me would have reminded me of my grandfather—and how much I missed him."

"I don't mind that Poppa was your favorite Evans…that day," Jamie said, smiling sexily. She was so good at pulling Ryan away from the brink of being maudlin. Just one of her many, many charms. Soft, tender lips settled atop Ryan's, banishing thoughts of Ireland, grandfathers, birthdays and everything else. When Jamie's lips touched hers it was like a chemical reaction. And once it began, Ryan was powerless to stop it.

"Mmm," she heard herself moan softly. "You have the most wonderful lips."

"The better to kiss you with, my dear." They lay together, slowly turning up the heat as they traded kisses at a very leisurely pace. This had been what Ryan craved. Touching, caressing, breathing in a full measure of Jamie. Letting her senses revel in the experience of loving someone with all her heart.

Jamie's hands slid down and slowly pulled her camisole over her head. She paused right before it slid off and shook her breasts in front of Ryan's face. *Damn* she was so sexy it should have been illegal. Ryan craned her neck to capture a pink nipple and explore it with her tongue. Jamie shifted so she was now on top of Ryan, with her breast poised right over Ryan's open mouth. "They're yours, baby. Whatever you want to do…"

Ryan wrapped her arms around Jamie's back, pulling her down so her breast filled her mouth to overflowing. She suckled it lustily, making Jamie squirm against her. Why didn't they do this three or four times a day? There was *nothing* more fun than just starting to make love to the woman who made her pulse race out of control.

They rolled around on the big bed, with Jamie pulling back and impotently trying to get away from Ryan's voracious mouth. She clearly loved being chased, and when Ryan was in this mood she would have chased her to China. Gladly.

They played for a long time, never escalating things very far. It felt so good, and connected them so completely that Ryan could have stayed right at that level until morning. But one small part of her body wanted to keep going, and it demanded satisfaction. She slipped her thigh between Jamie's legs and slid up and down a few times, leaving a trace of her wetness as she moved. Her body was covered in a faint sheen of perspiration, and when Jamie's fingers trailed down her back, goosebumps also covered her. "Don't be in such a rush," Jamie chided. "I've got that little present for you and I really think you'll like it."

Present. Now? Had to be sex related. "Great," Ryan said, unable to form longer sentences.

Jamie pushed her onto her side, then reached down to pick up whatever she'd dropped earlier. "On your belly."

Ryan's eyes popped open. This was getting interesting. She complied in milliseconds, then waited for instructions.

Jamie's hands gripped her hips, pulling her to her knees. Then slick fingers slid between Ryan's cheeks and she purred like a tiger. "Happy birthday to me," she growled.

Suddenly, Jamie's lips were caressing her ass, kissing all across it, then down to the tops of her thighs. Ryan was shaking—the way she always shivered when Jamie got anywhere near her most erogenous zone. Then her cheeks were spread open and Jamie's face nuzzled at her.

Ryan almost fainted. Of all the things she'd ever hoped for, this hadn't even been on the list. But her body wasn't afraid to ask for more. She pushed back and felt a tongue slip right into her. The sensation was as powerful as electricity and wired directly to her clit. All she could do was moan and ask for more.

Jamie had her by the hips, moving them in a circle as she probed her, thrilling Ryan to the limit of her capacity for pleasure. But there was just enough of her rational brain functioning to have a tendril of guilt clog her mind. She'd made it so clear that she wanted Jamie to play with her ass—but she *knew* that wasn't something Jamie craved. She started to feel worse and worse even though Jamie was going at her like she was enjoying the hell out of the experience.

Ryan reached around to give her a gentle nudge, feeling…rubber or latex or something. As her fingers moved along, she realized Jamie was using a barrier. Her guilt vanished. A barrier would let her do exactly what Ryan wanted, but wouldn't be too down and dirty for her somewhat skittish lover.

Holding herself up with one arm, Ryan used the other to grip Jamie's shoulder, trying to pull her in even closer. Jamie responded immediately, gripping both of Ryan's hips hard as her tongue danced. It was so freakishly exciting Ryan could barely breathe. She pounded the pillow with her fist, her pussy tingling so hard she was afraid she couldn't hold off… "Unh!" she cried as a sweeping orgasm shot through her body, weakening her legs until she started to collapse.

Jamie barely got out of the way as Ryan's body fell hard. "God!" she gasped, starving for air.

Then Jamie lay on top of her, grinding against her as Ryan tried to get her breathing under control. "I need to…" Jamie whispered into her ear. Then she propped herself up on her hands and pressed her vulva against Ryan's thigh. She rode her for a minute or two, with Ryan able to do nothing more than grip her leg, urging her on.

Quickly, Jamie's body shuddered and she collapsed atop Ryan once again, sweat gluing them together. "God damn," Jamie moaned. "That was crazy." She rolled off and lay on her back, taking in deep breaths. Ryan was still on her belly, too enervated to move. "Hey, I didn't give you a birthday spanking," Jamie said, chuckling weakly. She got in one sharp slap, then Ryan gripped her hand.

"I've just got one heart. Let's keep it pumping for a while longer, okay? I wanna see my next birthday."

🐉

Jamie's body tingled with her favorite sensation—the aftermath of a handful of orgasms. Her breathing was still elevated, her body so overheated she couldn't take even a sheet covering her. Turning her head, she gazed at the cat-who-ate-the-canary look that covered Ryan's beautiful face. "Proud of yourself?" Jamie asked, her voice slow and lazy.

"Uh-huh." She leaned over and placed yet another kiss upon Jamie's lips. If they'd been counting, that had to have been one of hundreds they'd shared that night. No one liked to kiss more than Ryan. "Got you good." Her grin grew even broader. "But not as well as you got me."

"Count on getting a little surprise for every birthday." Jamie stuck an arm around Ryan's neck and pulled her down so she could speak into her ear. "If we're having a bad year, you might stick with me until your birthday just to see what I've got in store for you."

Ryan straightened out and pulled Jamie up against her chest. "You'll never catch me doubting your skills... But you're quickly running out of real estate. By my fiftieth birthday you're going to have to use a scalpel to find new territory."

"Nah. I'm creative. I'll think of new ways to do it."

Ryan gently kissed Jamie's temple. "I only want you to keep exploring if you really want to. I don't need tons of variety."

Jamie took her hand and pressed it to her chest. "Baby, we're still in our honeymoon period. We've got decades ahead of us. We'll need variety to keep things fresh."

"I guess," she agreed. But Jamie saw the little worry line between her brows and thought she knew what had caused it.

She put her fingers on Ryan's chin and turned her head until their eyes met. "I like variety too. I promise I won't ever do anything I'm not into."

"You were into…?" She raised an eyebrow, then let her gaze drift down.

"Have you ever asked me to do that?"

"No!"

Something about the way she said that made Jamie ask, "You *have* done that before, right?"

"Uhm…" Her eyes closed and after a second the tip of her tongue peeked out. That was her "I'm really wracking my brain" look. "Yeah… kind of."

"Details?" Jamie gave her a long look. "I'm interested."

"Someone I liked tried to do it once, but I could tell she wasn't into it so I stopped her."

"Ahh…you thought she was only trying to please you."

"Yeah, yeah." Ryan's head nodded decisively. "I don't think it's a surprise to anyone who's been with me more than once that I'm kind of into…" She waggled her brow, making Jamie laugh.

"Yes, honey. Anyone paying attention would know you're into the back as well as the front." She patted Ryan's butt playfully. "No strangers?"

"Mmm…" Her eyes closed again.

What was she hiding? Something—for sure.

"A few have tried, but I didn't let them."

"What?" Jamie sat up and leaned on an elbow. "Why not?"

Ryan looked like she was being pinched. "Well, if a complete stranger wanted to stick her tongue there…" She took in a breath and continued, "I worried about where else that tongue had been."

"Double standard!" Jamie slapped at her until Ryan grabbed her hands, both of them laughing.

"I know, I know. But I was always thinking about being safe. Realistically, in that situation, the chances of her catching something from me were higher than me catching something from her, but it still squicked me out."

"Interesting." Now she sat up even taller. "Did I squick you out?"

"God, no!" Ryan laughed loud enough to make her belly jiggle. "First off, I know where your tongue has been." She tried to catch Jamie's tongue but missed by a mile. "Second, you used a dental dam. That let me relax and enjoy it. And I *did* enjoy it. We haven't been…" Her lips pursed briefly. "We haven't been very intimate for the last couple of weeks. Not that I need kinky things to feel intimate, but having you do something that's past your comfort zone just to please me…" She tucked her arm around Jamie and hugged her tightly. "It felt very intimate."

"It was intimate. But I didn't do it just to please you." She leaned in and placed another long kiss on Ryan's slightly swollen lips. "I wanted to do something different, but I did it because I thought it would be hot. It *was*," she added. "Super hot."

Ryan rolled over and got very, very close, eyes glittering. "You seriously enjoyed it?"

"I did. Granted, I wouldn't think of doing it without a barrier, but once the woman at the sex toy store suggested—"

Ryan cut her off. "You went to the sex toy store?"

"Sure. I've got time to do all sorts of things when you're slaving away on the OFC project. I talked with a really cool woman."

Ryan slapped her face with the flat of her hand. "I would have loved to have been there to hear that conversation."

"No way! She gave me a few more ideas that I'm gonna use on you. What you don't know *will* excite you."

Ryan lay back and Jamie could feel some of the muscular tension leave her body. "I don't know how you're going to top this birthday, babe. You're setting the bar really, really high."

Jamie snuggled up against her, then reached down and pulled the sheet up to cover them. "This is true. Just remember where the bar is— 'cause you've gotta match it in February."

Chapter Eleven

Six a.m. came awfully early the next morning, with Ryan unable to jump from bed with her usual enthusiasm. She watched Jamie shuffle into the bathroom, half asleep. Maybe they should have gotten to sleep earlier, but there was no way she would have given up their lovemaking for sleep—so there was no sense in moaning about it. After allowing Jamie a few minutes of privacy, Ryan went into the bathroom when she heard the shower start. "Are we really going to go all the way to the house to pick up Duffy?"

"He's a vital part of my plan." Jamie stepped into the warm water, extended her hand and pulled Ryan in with her. "If I had ten minutes to blow," she purred while running her hands all over Ryan's back. "I'd spend them on you."

"You're pretty wound up for a woman who can't open her eyes."

"Don't need eyes for what I want to do." She stood on her tiptoes and puckered up for a kiss. "I guess I'll have to catch you tonight."

"I'm yours for the taking. Obviously."

Shortly after seven, the trio was settled in the BMW, heading for the Golden Gate. Jamie was driving, now awake from her triple espresso, with Ryan placidly listening to her gab away. There was something calming about her voice that sometimes made it hard to keep her eyelids open…

A sharp pain made Ryan straighten out her neck. She blinked when she saw green fields, rolling terrain and an occasional cow. "Damn! How long have I been asleep?"

"Not all that long." Jamie turned and smiled at her. "Duffy's been listening to me. Aren't you glad we brought him?"

"Sure am." Ryan stuck her hand between the front seats and reached through to give him a pat. "He's a good boy."

"Are you feeling okay today? You seem a little..." Jamie turned and narrowed her eyes for a moment. "Off."

"No, I'm on." She relaxed the angle of her seat, trying to stretch out a little more. "I was in that half-awake/half-asleep state, and I kept thinking of stuff."

"Thinking...what?"

Trying not to sound too ponderous, Ryan said, "Just that I'm falling behind on my schedule. I was pretty sure I'd have a baby by the time I was twenty-five, and even more sure I'd be finished with the majority of my grad school work." She shrugged. "I don't even know what field I want to work in."

"You and me both, baby. Since I'm not going to grad school I'm running out of delaying tactics." Her smile was both sweet and reassuring. "You're much further along than I am. You have too many interests. I have too few."

Ryan reached over and rested her hand on Jamie's thigh. "You don't need to work, so there's no rush. You'll find something that appeals to you and get right to it. Everything I want to do takes years and years of schooling. That means I've got to make some decisions. Soon."

"How about the GRE? Not that you need to take it. I'm sure every school in the Bay Area will—"

Ryan clapped her hand over Jamie's still-moving mouth. "I'm going to take it next week. One small decision will then be off my list."

"Are you doing the math test or the bio test?"

"I thought I'd do both. Couldn't hurt."

"And you're preparing... How?"

Shrugging, Ryan said, "I don't think those test prep things help very much."

"Of course you don't." Smirking, Jamie shot her a quick look. "I'd need a full-time tutor if I was going to take it, but given how well you did on the Putnam..."

"I'll do okay," Ryan agreed, ready to get off the topic. "I'm going to apply to Berkeley and UCSF. But Berkeley's my preference."

"In what subject, baby? Even for you I think they'll want to know which department name to put on the Ph.D. they hand you on the first day."

"You're a very funny woman." She turned and looked at their companion, happily panting away. "Right, Duff?"

"Wroff," he replied, giving his usual response when he was directly addressed.

"Seriously, Ryan. I know I haven't convinced you, but I think you should focus your prodigious brain on making money, and you don't need a graduate degree to do that."

"That's a great idea. I'd be so happy I might burst." It wasn't hard to make sure even a smidgen of a smile didn't peek out.

"I know you're not into money for its own sake. But you say you want to help people, and the best way to do that is with money."

"I'm not at all sure I agree with that. I might luck into doing something really important in science or math. You honestly can't know."

Jamie turned briefly and smiled at her. "You'll do something important. I'm sure of that. But the truth is that there isn't anything you can do individually that can't be done better by a group. And if we have enough money, we could do all sorts of things."

"You have plenty of money. *Plenty.*"

"Really? How much would it cost to develop a continent-wide program to convince people in Africa not to circumcise their daughters?"

"Whew. That would take a lot. And I don't think money's the issue. Religion, culture, tradition… And don't forget the subjugation of women and their sexual desire. That's a biggie."

"But you see my point. Most of the world needs cleaner water, stoves that burn renewable resources, electricity, indoor plumbing, the internet. Trying to make a dent in any of those issues would take a hell of a lot more money than I have."

"True," Ryan agreed. "But I think your ideas are too ambitious. You could easily fund local programs that would make a big impact on a few people, and you've got plenty of money to do that."

Jamie kept taking her focus from the road, giving Ryan repeated glances. "Where's my real girlfriend? What kind of fantastic robot are you?"

Ryan let out a quick laugh. "I know this will surprise you, but I'm getting more realistic in my goals."

Jamie grasped her heart while taking in a gasping breath.

"Yeah, I know it's not like me, but it's true. Robin Berkowitz's suggestion has really stuck with me. Tech is the kind of environment that fosters ideas that can improve lives—quickly."

"But you've always talked about working in bio research."

"Yep, and that's what I'd love to do. But only if I was certain I could make a discovery that would turn out to be meaningful. That's not possible." She moved her hand up and down Jamie's leg, finding it settled her brain to have more contact. "You know I have a grandiose streak, and it was in full flower when I was certain I wanted to work in a lab. I'd give *anything* to find a cure for breast cancer. But, realistically, they're decades away from that. Right now the field needs people who are committed to basic science. People who don't have to achieve great results to keep them motivated." She squeezed Jamie's thigh. "I'm not one of them. It's taken me a long time to realize this, but I can't be stuck in a lab doing research on mice for the next fifty years. It takes a certain kind of person to do that, and even though I wish I was wired like that—I'm not. I need more feedback, more results, more excitement."

"Especially since you no longer have the thrill of sexual conquest," Jamie said, wrinkling up her nose. "You've given up a lot of excitement to be in a monogamous relationship, so you'll need to get your thrills from your work."

"Uh-huh. You almost made my heart stop last night!"

"Yeah, but as you pointed out, I can't do that on a daily basis. You've only got so many nerve endings."

"And they all belong to you."

They rode along in silence for a while, with just Duffy's open-mouthed breathing providing background noise.

"Oh, I forgot to tell you about your last birthday present," Jamie said, snapping Ryan to attention.

"No more presents! A boat is really, really enough!"

Jamie smiled at her. "For your final present, I give you guilt-free permission to sign up for as many classes as you want for winter term. I know I said something like that the other night when Jordan gave you the catalog, but I want to make it clear that I meant it. You've proven you don't know how to relax, so you might as well get calluses on your brain as your hands."

"Super, super, super!" Ryan bubbled, already thinking of how the classes she'd lusted after would fit into a schedule that would let her get home by dinner.

The sun was shining brightly when Jamie pulled into a parking lot not too far from the beach. Duffy had been wagging his tail ever since they'd started to slow down, and when Ryan opened his door he hurled himself onto the ground and started to run in circles, yapping with glee. "I'm as happy as you are," Ryan said, starting to chase him, both of them circling each other as Jamie laughed.

"The dog's supposed to chase his tail. You do it volitionally."

Ryan stopped and started to play with Duffy, rubbing his head and roughly wrestling him when he jumped up and put his paws on her shoulders. "This is true. But I'm convinced I'm at least half dog. When the cost of sequencing a human genome drops, I'm gonna do mine just to prove my point."

"Wouldn't surprise me a bit," Jamie said as she grasped Ryan's hand to lead her to a path. They were very close to the ocean and her nose started to twitch as the fresh, salty scent hit her. Duffy was on his leash, even though he was well-behaved enough to stop when ordered. But you never knew when something too alluring would make the best-behaved dogs act like…dogs.

They reached the beach, and since there wasn't another person around Ryan let him off his leash. He bounded up and down the shore like he was rocket-powered, going out a few hundred feet then coming back just as quickly. After a few of those sprints, he settled down and stayed close as they walked. "I see someone in the distance," Ryan said. "Duffy!" He stopped and turned his head to look over his shoulder balefully. "I know you don't want to have your leash on, but it's the law."

They walked further, finally seeing two women and two dogs, all of whom Duffy wanted to meet. As they got closer, Jamie spent a moment looking at the owners. "Possible members of the tribe?"

"Always a possibility," Ryan said, turning to smile. "Want me to ask?"

"No!" Jamie slapped her on the shoulder as they got near enough to speak. "Hi," Jamie called out. "Beautiful dogs." They were real beauties. Australian shepherds, one blue merl and one black with a good amount of both copper and white. They were a little shorter than Duffy, and weighed less, but they were well matched. Duff had a tendency to overpower small dogs, but these two could hold their own. Ryan obviously thought so too, because she dropped his leash so the dogs could socialize.

"Thanks," one of the women said. "Jodie's mine. Starly's Phyllis'."

"This is Duffy," Jamie said. "I suppose he's Ryan's, but I'm his step-mother."

Ryan got down into a squat and both of the Aussies approached her, sniffing and giving her an occasional lick. Duffy, of course, couldn't stand to let anyone take too much of Ryan's time, so he forced his way into the group and blocked either of the newcomers from monopolizing her.

"He's very rude," Jamie said, as she bent over to play with the Aussies. Duffy quickly abandoned Ryan to get to Jamie, knocking her onto her seat in the wet sand. "Great!" She got up with Ryan's help, then tried to dust off her slacks. "I've got to give a speech in two hours. My pants had better be dry," she said, grabbing a handful of Duffy's hair and giving it a shake.

"You're giving a speech?" Ryan asked.

"Yeah. You're staying to play. You've got about five hours of freedom." She turned to the women. "I'm Jamie, by the way."

They all shook hands and learned that Jodie's mom was Nancy. Jamie was pretty sure her guess was accurate, but the fact that Nancy had said each of them owned a dog had thrown her off. "Are you locals?" she asked.

"No, we're camping. We've got our RV over at the Olema campground."

Ahh. Two women, two dogs and an RV. They *had* to be lesbians.

"I wish we camped," Ryan said wistfully.

Jamie thought of how freaked out Ryan had been by the dog-like coyotes in Hillsborough. What would she do if she saw something a little less tame? An RV would probably be a necessity for her city-girl. "Maybe we should get an RV one day. Maybe another dog, too."

"Another dog?" Ryan grasped Duffy by the ears, shielding him from Jamie's suggestion. "I barely have time for this one!"

"Having two can be really nice," Phyllis said. "They keep each other company."

"I suppose," Ryan agreed. "But this guy needs a lot of exercise, and my beloved partner isn't much for getting up early to go for a run."

Jamie pinched her on the waist. "You can get a leash with two leads. Problem solved." She checked her watch. "I'm going to let you play. I'm going to run over to Roehnert Park and give a talk to the Gay/Straight Alliance at Sonoma State. I'll be back by four. Meet you at the trail head?"

"Great," Ryan said. She gave Jamie a kiss, then both Phyllis and Nancy said goodbye. As Jamie headed back she turned and watched Duffy romp with the other dogs. Jodie had the cutest walk, prancing with her head held high. Very regal. And Starly was a ball of energy. Just what Duffy needed to tire him out. As for Ryan, five hours should pretty much deplete her excess energy as well. Hopefully.

Ryan and Duffy were waiting as planned when Jamie returned. She could have made it back a bit earlier, but she knew that was a waste of time. Ryan would be off somewhere until the last possible minute. When Jamie rolled down her window, she saw that her guess had been right. Ryan's face was wet and her shirt clung to her body, and Duffy was panting when he wasn't lapping at the collapsible water dish Ryan always carried when they went very far. "What feats of strength and endurance did you two get up to?"

"We chatted with Phyllis and Nancy for a long time, then I decided I wanted to see the tip of Tomales Point. It said it was a three hour hike, but I only had two hours to play with. Had to run for a lot of it," she said, still slightly out of breath.

"You could have cut it short, baby. I could drive you to Tomales Point."

Ryan looked at Duffy and said with an accusing tone, "Why didn't you tell me that?"

"Get in you two. We're stopping for the freshest oysters you've ever had."

"Duff doesn't like oysters, but I bet he'd like to sniff at the shells." They both got in and Ryan buckled herself in. "Missed you," she said, leaning over for a kiss.

"That's a lie, but one I appreciate."

On Monday, Catherine reached for her ringing phone and smiled when she heard Maeve's voice. The lilt of her melodic tone always felt like a breath of spring air. "How would you like to come by for a cup of tea? I have the day to myself and would love to spend some of it with you."

"That's a fantastic idea," Catherine agreed. "I just need to leave my house by 2:15 to pick Jennie up." She looked at her watch. Already noon. "Why don't you come over here? Marta would truly love to make us some tea cakes."

"Is parking a problem? I don't want to spend all of our time driving around the block."

"How about a walk instead? If we both start off now we can meet in the middle and come back here. Then I'll drive you home after I pick Jennie up."

Laughing, Maeve said, "It's hard to believe we live less than three miles from each other, given the machinations we have to go through to spend an hour together."

"Put your walking shoes on and get going! We don't have time to waste."

A half hour later, they met at the edge of Alamo Square. Maeve smiled broadly and gave Catherine a hug. "I know I saw you just yesterday, but we don't get a chance to really talk at parties. It's all very topical."

"I couldn't agree more." She slid her arm through Maeve's, then turned to head back toward home. "How did you manage to have the whole day to yourself?"

"Caitlin's with her mother, and my delightful husband is working the day shift. I went to mass, cleaned my house, and was just about to start thinking about dinner when I decided I needed to have a little fun." Smiling, she leaned close, hugging Catherine's arm as she did. "You're the first person I thought of."

"You can't imagine how happy that makes me. I've said it before, but I must say it again. Ryan's a gem, but I think I won a prize equal to Jamie's. Having you as a friend has been fantastic for me."

"For me too. And now that no one's around to hear, tell me how things really are with Jennie."

Catherine let thoughts of the last weeks sail through her memory. "We've had a very calm few weeks. As I've told you, she follows orders like a soldier—so long as she agrees with them. And she's not the type to complain about a thing. She's practicing her clarinet, studying at the proper time, going to bed when I remind her to. No problems at all."

"That certainly doesn't sound like the children I hear about from my friends at church. It sounds like each of them are glued to the television?"

"Not Jennie. They had a television in the group home, but they all had to agree on what to watch—"

"Oh, my," Maeve interrupted, "How could you get a group of girls to agree on anything? Much less what program to watch?"

"Exactly," Catherine agreed. "Because of that, she hasn't developed much interest. She seems to prefer to spend her free time drawing."

"You've struck it lucky there. Kevin would have the television turned to some sporting event twenty-four hours a day, and Tommy's not much better."

"I'm sure Jennie could find some shows that she'd be interested in, but she hasn't expressed any desire. I'm *not* complaining."

"You haven't complained about anything. And I'm very glad that things are going along so smoothly."

"They are," Catherine said. "But I'm afraid a few bumps might be in front of us." When Maeve turned to look at her she added, "I spoke with Giacomo a few days ago. He has to come to New York next week and he's pressuring me to join him."

"Pressuring you? You don't want to…?"

Catherine could feel her cheeks begin to flush. "If I admitted how much I want to see him, you'd think *I* was fifteen. No, it's not lack of desire. I'm worried about leaving Jennie. It's just been a month…"

"Ahh, yes. I can see why you're hesitant." She squeezed Catherine's arm again. "But you need support, too. You can't give up the things that make you happy—especially when you have people who can take over for you."

"But I hate to impose—"

"Nonsense. We'd love to have the girl stay with us for a few days."

"A week," Catherine said, cringing when she uttered the word. "I was going to go for a week."

Maeve waved a hand in the air. "A week is nothing. I'm sure my Marty wouldn't mind a bit. He's very fond of the child."

"I truly appreciate the offer, but I'm going to see if Jamie and Ryan wouldn't mind stepping in. Ideally, Jen would be able to stay at home and stick with her routines, and I know Martin wouldn't want to move to my house."

Maeve laughed. "You know him well. He'd do it, of course, but it would be a production." She rolled her eyes. "It would literally be a production once we moved all of Caitlin's things over. Not to mention how worried I'd be that some of your knick-knacks would not remain intact."

"*Very* good point. I'm glad Jennie's past the stage of grabbing things and throwing them to the floor. A child-proof home would be difficult for me to arrange at this point of my life. I do love my little baubles."

"I've never had baubles," Maeve said, smiling. "Maybe I'll get one or two when Caitlin's past the throwing things stage."

"I'd love to be able to buy you some pretty little objects d'art for your birthday. We'll shop for the next few years. Then I'll be ready to go when Caitlin can go through a room without practicing her overhand toss."

Maeve winked at her. "Don't be in a rush. We're a *long* way from that."

After stopping for oysters, Jamie insisted she also had to stop for some cheese. Ryan didn't complain, and they headed for home with an extra dozen oysters and three kinds of cheese. By the time they reached the 101 Ryan was asleep. Jamie looked in the rearview mirror, catching sight of Duffy also conked out. What a delightful pair of driving companions they were!

Since her mother loved oysters as much as Jamie did, they stopped by the house to share. As soon as they greeted each other Catherine said, "Ryan, would you mind checking Jennie's chemistry homework? She's worried about it, and I'm no help at all."

"Sure." She started for the stairs, but paused to say, "I'm always willing to help. Call me when things like this happen."

"I will."

Ryan was barely at the second floor when Catherine said, "How about a cookie. Marta made some fabulous ones for Jennie and I asked her to put a few aside for you and Ryan."

They got up and went into the kitchen, sitting at the table while Jamie ate one of the treats. "These are really good, Mom. Thanks for letting me have first crack, since I wouldn't get a bite if Ryan beat me to it."

Catherine turned and eyed the closed door. Something was making her nervous or anxious, and Jamie couldn't tell which.

"Do you and Ryan have any plans for the rest of the month? Any trips you're considering?"

Chuckling, Jamie said, "Ryan isn't considering any trips at all. Ever. And I'm not in the mood to torture her. We're here for the indefinite future. Why?"

"Well..." Catherine gave the door another check. "Giacomo has to go to New York for business, and I'd like to meet him there." Her lips were pursed and she seemed...embarrassed. "I know it's awfully soon for me to leave Jennie, but I promised Giacomo we'd me able to meet in October at the latest and it's already November..."

Jamie focused, trying to make herself ignore her gut instinct—which was always negative towards Giacomo. Instead, she thought of how she'd feel if she couldn't see Ryan for months at a time. She had a tough time with that too, given that she couldn't imagine anything that could prevent them from being together. But just the concept helped her summon some empathy. "Ideally," she said, taking her mom's hand and holding it, "you'd stay close to Jen until she was fully comfortable here." Catherine opened her mouth to speak, but Jamie finished up. "We all know that's not practical. You need time with Giacomo, and having that time will make you happier. A happier parent is a better parent."

Catherine looked so relieved Jamie's heart ached for her. She was *really* trying to be a good guardian, but she'd never, ever had to curtail her travel. Years of taking off whenever she felt like it had to be a hard habit to break.

"Do you really think so?" Catherine asked, her dark eyes filled with hope.

"Yes, I do. You'd go mad if you had to stay home for the next two years. Jen can roll with this. I'm sure of it."

"I spoke with her therapist, and she said it would be all right—and much better if Jennie could stay at home and keep her schedule intact."

Jamie smiled and nodded. "We'd be happy to stay here and watch her. How long will you be gone? A long weekend?"

Catherine flinched noticeably. "A little longer than that. I'd like to go for a week." She cast another look at the still-closed door. "I think we're doing very well, but this is a massive adjustment for me. To spend my evenings and weekends with Jennie I've cut back on so many things that give me sustenance. I truly need some time to relax—with Giacomo. He…" Her cheeks colored slightly. "He helps center me."

"You need to figure out how to balance your needs with Jen's, Mom. Giving up the things you love isn't a great idea."

"I know. But it's hard to justify going to the symphony and leaving Jennie home alone. We come from such different situations, Jamie. She was surrounded by people every minute and I've been mostly alone, able to do exactly what I want, when I want it. We're going to have to work to find our equilibrium."

"You'll get there. I've got a ton of faith in you."

Catherine got up and opened her arms, then Jamie rose and slid into her hug. Even though she was a couple of inches taller and twenty pounds heavier, she still felt a little like a child when her mother hugged her. And that's just how it should have been. The door swung open and Ryan stood there. As Jamie released her hold it hit her that her mom hadn't been trying to make sure Jen didn't hear them. She didn't want Ryan there. Probably a good idea. It was going to take a little salesmanship to get Ryan to babysit for a week without complaint.

At 6:30, Jordan sat in the car at the Rockridge BART station, scanning the crowd. A curly head popped out of the group, and Jordan gave the horn a quick beep. Mia turned and waved, giving Jordan a full minute to watch her. She looked remarkably cute in one of Jamie's dresses and a fashionable pair of heels. Ryan's platinum necklace caught the light from a passing car and Jordan hoped fervently that no one ripped it from Mia's neck. Besides injuring her, replacing it would empty their savings account.

The door opened and Mia slid into the seat before leaning over to place a long kiss on Jordan's lips. "The working warrior returns," she said before sitting upright. "I looked at the clock at three, certain it was seven." Wiping her brow dramatically, she added, "I've never been in one spot for more than eight hours…upright, that is."

"Was it really bad?" Jordan asked, having exactly the same amount of work experience—none.

Mia's usual sunny expression bloomed. "Nah. It was kinda fun. This guy…Chris something-or-other was my babysitter. He showed me how to prepare a press kit for a law firm that's opening a San Francisco office, and I cranked 'em out until I noticed people start to leave. Then I grabbed my purse and skedaddled."

"Were people nice to you?"

"Sure," she said breezily. "Nice enough. Carly and Chris and a woman named…Lori, I think, took me to lunch. Well, they didn't pay, and it was just a salad place, but they invited me to tag along."

"How many people are in your office?"

"Mmm…fifteen? Something around there. Most of them are women only a few years older than me. I'm not sure why there's so many women. That must mean the field doesn't pay great."

"But you're going to be paid great, 'cause you're gonna kick ass."

"Well…" Mia showed the smile she reserved for when she was boasting a little. "Chris was pretty amazed at how quickly I caught on."

"That's because you're really, really smart."

"Right," she chuckled. "That's because I'm smart enough to keep my questions to myself until I can't possibly figure something out. Then I ask someone who isn't a supervisor, or I look it up on the internet."

"That's what makes you smart," Jordan said. "You know how to work around problems."

"It's a gift." Mia leaned over and placed another kiss on Jordan's cheek. "Have you spent the afternoon cooking for me?"

"Wouldn't that be nice?" she asked, chuckling. "No, I spent the afternoon at volleyball practice. But," she added brightly, "I called Zachary's and ordered a pizza to go. Then I stopped and bought a bottle of wine. Isn't that better than scrambled eggs, the only thing I can competently cook?"

"Significantly. Take me home. Feed me. Then make love to me." She smiled when Jordan turned her head to make eye contact. "Your evening is all planned out."

On Friday evening, Ryan had a hard time convincing her feet to attack the stairs to her home in her usual manner. She would have felt like a wimp about being so bushed, but she was behind Jamie, who was almost crawling. They'd both had a tough day at the OFC, with Jamie doing surface prep in the bathrooms, while Ryan dug post-holes for the new wooden fence they were installing. After gobbling down the carryouts they'd picked up on the way home, neither had the energy to take Duffy for a long walk. Luckily, the dog park was always a good alternative for the rambunctious pooch, and let him socialize with everyone.

They didn't go often, but people tended to remember you—or your dog. They stood and chatted with several people, then a woman they'd met a few times came over to say hello. Ryan liked her. She was a psychologist who worked for the VA and had always been friendly. "Hi…Judy, right?" Ryan said.

"Right." She reached down and patted Duffy, who'd raced over the minute he saw his people talking to someone. "I could act like I remember your names from meeting you here, but I'll be honest and tell you I remember you from your…incident last year."

"Yeah. Our incident." Ryan gave her a sick-looking smile. "That was a lot of fun."

Judy clapped her on the back. "You're both alive and well. You can bounce back from psychological injuries a lot easier than…" She shrugged. "I'm not doing a good job of saying I'm glad to see you both."

"We're glad to be seen," Jamie agreed.

"You've had a big year," Judy continued. "With your dad unexpectedly running, things must be…interesting."

"Yeah. I wouldn't have chosen a public life for him, but he seems to like it."

"I know he doesn't need it, but he's got my vote," she said, smiling. "I'm gonna split this time. I hate to let one party have a monopoly, so I'm going with Bush."

"What?" Ryan said, the hairs on the back of her neck rising.

"It doesn't matter," the woman said, clearly oblivious to Ryan's flushing skin. "There's no real difference between the two parties any more. I'm going with Bush mostly because he has more charisma than Gore. He's almost a flatliner."

"Charisma?" Ryan's ire began to rise as she felt Jamie's hand grip her bicep.

"Sure. A politician's got to be able to relate to people. That's his main role, when you get right down to it. He sets the mood for the country, and I think Bush is more optimistic."

"Optimistic?" Ryan knew she was going to lose it, but she didn't know how to pull back. "He does a whole hell of a lot more than set the mood. He appoints judges to the supreme court, the federal courts, all of the heads of departments, most of the people who really impact people's lives." She was building up a head of steam, and it was about to explode. "He's the one who decides how we educate our kids! You want to vote for a guy who slashed the education budget in Texas? Because he's got *charisma?*"

Jamie's hold grew firmer. "Excuse my fiancé," she interrupted. "She's very invested in politics."

"It's not politics!" Ryan fumed. "It's our lives! If Bush wins, we can kiss our chance of having an anti-discrimination bill away. Abortion will be illegal, food stamps will be cut. He's a dope! A slightly charismatic dope!"

Jamie started to drag Ryan away, apologizing the whole time. Judy was clearly too stunned to respond, but she looked like she'd just stepped onto a beehive.

They got to the gate, with Duffy stuck to them like glue. "You've upset your dog," Jamie soothed, bending to pet Duffy.

"Charisma?" Ryan shouted, drawing curious looks from everyone within fifty feet. "She's got a Ph.D., and she thinks charisma's the most important trait in a president? What the fuck?"

"Ryan, you've got to calm down," Jamie said, trying to keep her voice low. "You know I agree with you, but you can't go around shoving your opinion down other people's throats. You won't change a single mind, and it'll ruin your day."

"It's already ruined," she groused. "When well-educated, gay-friendly people in San Francisco think they should vote for an anti-gay

Republican just because he's got a better smile—we're fucked!"

On Saturday, Ryan spent the whole morning taking the GRE at a test center in the city. Jamie spent it helping Colm cut tile. She wasn't sure which of them had worked harder, but she was definitely dirtier. Ryan cruised into the job site at around one, bringing a very healthy salad for Jamie. They sat outside together to eat while the rest of the guys got back to work. Lunch was always brief—unlike the after-work beer bash they usually enjoyed.

"How was the test?" Jamie asked as she munched on a piece of red pepper.

"Same as all standardized tests." Ryan swiped a green bean and nibbled on it.

"No lunch for you?"

"Oh yeah," she chuckled. "I'm all about skipping lunch. No, I got a big Italian sandwich and ate the whole thing while they made your salad. I just handed the cashier the label to pay for it. He acted like I was a freak."

"Well, you kind of are." She leaned forward and kissed Ryan's cheek. "You're my freak. So…? Nothing more to say about the test?"

"Nope. Multiple choice for the most part. My favorite kind of test." She got up and brushed off the seat of her jeans. "I'm gonna go help do—something. Take your time. I'll fill in for you until you're finished."

"Colm will be disappointed, but thanks."

Ryan bent over and kissed her on the head. "I wish that wasn't as true as it is."

November the seventh, election day, was near-perfect in terms of weather. By the time Ryan finished priming the new plaster walls it was seventy degrees, sunny and dry. A great day to go for a long bike ride or lie on the grass at the Marina. But she was inside, working, while Jamie spent the day at Jim's San Francisco office, helping to get out the vote. Ryan could have easily tagged along, since they weren't going to paint the interior until the weekend, but she thought it best for her mental health to stay as far away from the actual election process as possible.

In her view, Gore had run a bad campaign. He hadn't used Clinton much, seeming to prefer not to be connected to him. She got that. Clinton had been so tarred with his impeachment and all of the other scandals that had dogged him since the moment he took office that it would have been nice to have a clean slate. But no one could argue that Clinton wasn't a good campaigner. Nor that Gore was a bad one. But it was all over now. By tonight the country would have a new president—and she hoped with all of her might that new president was the unglamorous but seemingly intelligent Al Gore. A guy who appeared to respect science and technology and the climate. The clock was ticking, and if someone didn't step up to the plate and do something about climate change... She couldn't bear to think of the repercussions.

After work, Ryan went home to shower and get into her uniform. The last thing she wanted to do was go to a big dinner and celebration at a hotel. But Jamie wanted to support her dad and Ryan had to step up to the plate. The polls were closed in the East and things weren't looking great for Gore. But it was still early. She hoped.

Watching an election without having to have information filtered by TV networks was kind of cool. They were ensconced in a huge suite at the Mark Hopkins, watching as half a dozen aides and consultants peppered Jim with numbers and predictions. The polls in California had only been closed for ten minutes, but Jim's guys were confident he'd won. By a big margin.

Ryan watched him prowl around the interconnected rooms, an unlit cigar in his mouth. He seemed to use a cigar like a baby used a pacifier, with no real purpose other than to calm him. But it seemed to work. Or maybe it was the numbers that turned his smile brighter. Not long after nine, the networks declared him the victor, one by one. When the talking heads at Fox finally admitted the truth, he opened the window, stuck his head out and lit his cigar. He looked like a kid sneaking a smoke so his parents didn't catch him, sitting in the open window, blowing the stream into the still night. Kayla walked past him, put a hand on his shoulder and gave it a squeeze, sharing a smile as she moved past to talk to another aide. Boy that must have sucked. To be having an affair that everyone knew about, but you had to act like you were simply an aide—even with the people who were supposed to be one hundred percent on your side.

An hour later, Ryan was sweating through her suit jacket. Sometimes she had to admit she was as dumb as a post. How had she not guessed she'd have to be on stage with the newly elected senator? She certainly wasn't going to abandon Jamie—their relationship deserved recognition. But standing on the dais, trying to listen to Jim's speech while TV cameras and flashes burst all around her, made her wish she'd had a few more drinks at the party. Like a dozen. Then Jamie slipped her hand around Ryan's and linked their fingers. Ryan turned to look at her, seeing a mix of pride and pleasure on her beautiful face. This meant something to her. And if it meant something to Jamie—Ryan would tolerate the fear of having an outright panic attack. She kept repeating her mantra: This would only last a few minutes. They were cameras, not hand grenades. People could take her picture, but they couldn't take anything important from her. She was safe. Jamie was safe. This would only last a few minutes…

At three a.m., Ryan sat on a long sofa in the hotel suite. She'd taken off her jacket, as well as her shoes, and had her stockinged feet braced on a sturdy table. Jamie was out cold, her head on Ryan's lap.

On another sofa, set at a diagonal, Jim almost perfectly mimicked her posture. His shoes were also off, his tie had gone away hours earlier, and his shirt was untucked. Kayla was still awake, but only barely. She leaned against him heavily, occasionally opening her eyes, grumbling something about the state of Florida, then closing them.

Other than the four of them, the big room was empty. The Jim Evans campaign machinery had done its job and had disbanded for the night.

People would probably wait until morning to start vying for the plum jobs the properly elected senator could parse out. In just a few hours time, she'd noted that people were sucking up to Jim in ways they hadn't earlier. Before, he'd been an interim appointee. Now he was a true member of the club.

She and Jamie should have gone home hours ago. But she was too keyed up to rest, and she couldn't very well turn on the TV in Conor's room at this time of night. Watching this shit-storm with another political addict was somehow soothing.

"Makes you a little embarrassed when we insist on being election monitors for 'undeveloped' countries, doesn't it?" Jim asked, rolling his eyes at Ryan.

"I don't have words to express how I feel about our many levels of hypocrisy. What were the odds that the governor of a single state could be the guy who has the power to hand the election to his brother? We'd step in in two seconds if this happened in…some place we thought we could manhandle."

Jim was chewing on another cigar, and he took it from his mouth and pointed it at her. "I didn't know you were so… What's the term? Jaded? Bitter?"

"Both," she agreed, nodding. "I wish I wasn't, but the system seems so permanently screwed up." She could feel her blood pressure start to rise. "We've got *so* much. We could be such a good example. We could lead the world into a better place." Feeling the air go out of her, she added, "We won't."

"I wish I could disagree with you, but I can't. Everyone's in it for themselves. I don't know how to make the system better, but I swear I would if I could."

"Would you really?" She looked at him curiously.

"I would. I didn't fully realize how things worked until I got to Washington." He shook his head slowly. "It's not good."

"We've let lobbyists take over the country," she grumbled.

He waved his hand in the air, his cigar moving around like a bird in flight. "I thought the same thing. But, to be honest, lobbyists don't come to us with bags of money. We go to them."

"What?"

"Yeah." His head moved up and down again. "Since I wasn't going to run for the job, I didn't have to play the money game. My first months were a breeze! But these last two months have opened my eyes. All I've done," he stressed, "*all* I've done is raise money and campaign. It took tens of millions to win this race."

"That's nuts," Ryan said. "Just nuts."

"You don't have to tell me that. I went to a crummy room at the Democratic National Committee three times a week, making calls to people I thought might give me five thousand or ten thousand bucks. *All* of us do that. Every single one of us. And we're supposed to do that—year-round—forever. We're either raising money for our own campaigns or for people who can't raise as much. I'll have this job for six years, but I'm supposed to raise money like the election is six months from now."

"Why do you have to go to the DNC?"

"It's illegal to ask for donations from your office. So we all trot over to a phone bank at the DNC. After we panhandle from the usual suspects, we call the lobbyists, begging for a few thousand bucks. If they like my voting record they might have a fundraiser for me. Yet another breakfast or lunch with the pork producers of California or the agricultural workers union or the technology billionaires. Anyone with money who's willing to part with it."

"And if they don't like your voting record?"

"That goes without saying. I thought they bought the votes. I truly did. But what they do is toss you a few bucks to help keep you around if you've been good. The majority of lobbyist dollars go to people who support big tobacco, the NRA, and every type of anti-regulation group. The liberal list is a hell of a lot shorter."

"We've really screwed this up," Ryan said, feeling as bad as she ever had about politics.

"I think it was always screwed up. I certainly don't know what system would be better, though. Maybe you can't have a great system when there are humans involved."

"I think we're stuck with us. Regrettably."

Jim pointed at the latest numbers from Florida. "This isn't going to be decided tonight. We should shut this off and get some sleep."

Ryan turned and looked at him. "You can sleep?"

He let out a ghost of a laugh. "Hell, no." He grabbed the phone next to him. "If we're going to be up all night, we might as well eat."

"Best suggestion I've heard all night. A turkey club, please. A beer wouldn't hurt either."

"Sounds good. Fries?"

"Why the hell not?" She rested her chin on her folded arms and glared at the screen, wishing she could make the numbers change by the force of her personality.

On the morning after the election, Ryan was up and out of the house before Jamie could form sentences. They'd been at the hotel until the wee hours of the morning, and Jamie wasn't at all sure Ryan had even been to bed. If she turned into a political junkie, Jamie wasn't sure they'd be able to live together. She understood how important politics was. She truly did. But taking elections as personally as Ryan had taken this one was beyond the pale. If they had to go to couples counseling to find the tipping point, she was more than willing to invest the time. Getting Ryan to go would be another issue, but Jamie was not going to have her acting like the end was near during every national election. She had far too many obsessions. Another was untenable.

They had a couple of very brief conversations through the day, with Jamie finally realizing that Ryan had gone to work just to avoid having to interact. Jamie had an afternoon appointment to look at a house Ray was pretty excited about, and given Ryan's mood, Jamie almost didn't ask her to ride along. But she needed another set of eyes, and even grumpy ones were better than nothing. If she had her way, they'd hop on a plane and go to Eleuthera for a few days. Ryan would cheer up in minutes if they were away from this election mess. But the chances of that were slim and none.

The good news was that the house was close to home. Noe was where the yuppies they were trying to appeal to wanted to live. And taking one of the old Victorians and tricking it out to suit yuppy taste was the way to make some money.

Ryan was glumly riding in the passenger seat, the news channel humming in the background. It was clear the mess in Florida was going to take some time to iron out, but she seemed to think cooler heads would prevail and simply declare Gore the winner. Good luck with that.

The car climbed up Twenty-Third, going as far as one could go without falling over onto Grand View.

"Nice," Ryan said, nodding appreciatively.

"The view should be great," Jamie agreed.

"I hope that yellow house isn't the one, but I bet it is."

Jamie checked out the house Ryan was pointing at. "Ooo. That has… potential." She turned and added, "That means it's a true dump."

While they were talking, Ray pulled up in his small truck. "How's it going?" he asked when he got out and approached them.

"Good." Jamie pointed at the yellow house. "That one, right?"

"Right. You don't mind that someone died in it, do you?"

"Last night?" Ryan asked, her eyebrows raised.

"Nah. A couple months ago. But it's not in probate, so that's not an issue. I just have to tell people about the death. California law."

"Our public servants at work," Jamie said. "Hard at work on the important issues of the day."

"Hey, is that your dad who's a senator?"

"Uh-huh."

Ray laughed. "Somebody in the office told me that, but I thought they were kidding."

"Nope." She got out and started to walk towards the house. "This looks like it's from the nineteenth century."

"Yeah." He pulled out the listing sheet. "1891."

"Cool," Ryan said, eying the fish-scale shingling on the top floor. "Let's see what's going on."

They went inside and Jamie stepped back out in less than a second. "I don't like the way it smells."

"It's been closed up for a while," Ray said. "I think that's just mildew from the refrigerator or something."

Ryan was standing by the door, and Jamie handed her the camera. "Take photos. I'll be right here."

"Seriously?"

"Yeah." She turned and sat on the front steps. "Wouldn't be prudent."

That night, they reviewed the photos. The house was a wreck, but the last owner had been in it since the seventies, and hadn't painted the woodwork or ripped out the original floors. There was a rickety addition in back, but if they tore that off and added one with a big kitchen and a master suite, the place could be 2500 square feet, a perfect sized home for a family with two kids—their prime demographic.

The house was overpriced, as was everything, but Jamie was fairly confident they could make it into a showpiece—with a ton of work. Conor agreed to swing by and see if the bones were good, and if they were Jamie was going to make it happen. Relying on the cousins to come to an agreement on the prior property had been a waste of time. If Conor gave the go-ahead, she was going to notify the boys instead of trying to reach consensus. The group needed a leader and she was the only one ready and willing to take on the title.

Ryan sat on the loveseat in their room, engrossed in the latest issue of PNAS. She'd thought Catherine was wasting her money when she'd subscribed to a number of academic journals for her, but they'd been a thoughtful, helpful gift. She was so busy she never would have taken the time to go to the library to read for a few hours. Now she could keep up on the latest developments in her field, while not having to leave her room.

For a change, Jamie wasn't reading a book. "Whatcha doin'?" Ryan asked, after checking the clock to see that it was bedtime. Time really flew when you were reading about prime type III factors.

Jamie swung around on the desk chair and gave Ryan a sly smile. "Stalking you."

"Hmm... How can you be stalking me when I'm right behind you?"

After pushing the chair across the floor, Jamie was now right in front. "I'm choosing what classes I'm going to take. I'm trying to find ones that match the days you're going to be on campus so we can ride together."

"You're taking classes just to be together?" Ryan wasn't sure how to frame the question, knowing it sounded very dismissive. But... "Uhm, are you really interested in computer science? The classes I'm going to take have a lot of prerequisites..."

Jamie grabbed a piece of her cheek and gave it a pinch. "Are you nuts? Not only couldn't I get *into* the classes you want, I'd be asked to leave by the end of the first class meeting." Leaning forward, she kissed the spot she'd just pinched. "No, baby, I haven't lost my mind. I'm going to take some more real estate courses."

"Really?" Ryan sat up straight and gazed at her, puzzled. "Why?"

Jamie planted her feet on the floor, pushed off, and rolled all the way back to the desk. Then she started to close the windows she'd been using. "I've decided I'm not getting my money's worth with Ray. His firm gets three percent of every sale, but he's not giving me three percent of value. I'm going to get my license and do it myself."

"You have to go to Cal to get a real estate license?"

"No, of course not. To get a license to sell you just need three college-level courses, which I have. But to get a broker's license you either need additional coursework, then you have to work for a broker for two years, or you have to have a major or minor in real estate. She made a dismissive gesture with her hand. "No way I'd work for a broker, so I'm going to take enough courses for a minor. If I take a full load, I can finish in a semester."

Ryan got up and walked over to stand next to the desk. "Uhm, not to ask the obvious question, but why not just get the license to sell?"

"Because, my sweet babboo, I'd have to pair up with a broker and give him or her one and a half percent of my three. Not gonna do that. I wouldn't think of paying someone one and a half percent just to let me use a license."

"Wow." Ryan smiled, her admiration for Jamie's business sense growing all of the time. "You've really thought this through."

"Of course I have." She grabbed Ryan around the waist and forced her to sit on her lap. "Urg. Heavy."

Ryan put her hands on the desk and pushed, lifting at least half of her weight off Jamie's lap. "Better?"

"Much. On a million dollar house we'd have to pay sixty thousand bucks to sell it. That's crazy."

"I know math isn't your thing, but three percent is thirty thousand." A sharp pinch made Ryan jump to her feet. "Math doesn't lie, baby!"

"You pay six percent total. Usually, the selling broker gets one and a half, the selling agent gets one and a half, the buying agent gets one and a half...etc."

"Ohh. So you'd get the whole three since you'd be both the broker and the agent."

"Yes, but I wouldn't get anything since I'd be doing it to save us money. Ideally, I'll be the listing and the selling broker. Then we'll save sixty large for every million we turn over."

"Sixty large." Ryan bent over and kissed her. "You sound like a bank robber."

"Real estate. Larceny. Same thing in this crazy market. If we buy the house we looked at today Ray's gonna get like…nine thousand bucks, and all he had to do was take me to see one house. That's not gonna fly. Jamie Evans doesn't pay big bucks for little work."

"I've never been more turned on," Ryan said, unable to keep from laughing. "Your sex appeal goes through the roof when you're trying *not* to spend money."

Chapter Twelve

On Thursday afternoon, Ryan was hand-sanding all of the woodwork in the apartment. It was a dusty, tedious job. A job she wouldn't be thrilled with any time. But she was so cranky about the election that she was actually muttering to herself as she moved about the space.

Jamie was prudently keeping her distance, following behind her with the wet/dry vac, just keeping the dust down. A loud "thunk" reverberated through the place and Jamie turned to see Conor enter with his arm around Rory, who had his accordion case in one hand and a huge duffel bag in the other. Squealing with delight, Jamie reached over and stuck the hose of the vacuum on Ryan's butt. After swatting it away, Ryan turned, caught sight of her brother and ran to him, leaping into the air—where Conor stepped in and caught her.

"The man's got his hands full!" Conor yelped.

"I'd gladly break my neck to give my sister a hug." Rory dropped his bags and wrapped his arms around Ryan. Jamie got in line, but Ryan dropped one arm from Rory's waist and pulled her in. "We've missed you," Jamie said, rising on her toes to kiss his cheek.

"Not as much as I've missed all of you. It's so good to be back home." When he was free, he looked around, clearly amazed. "How did you manage to turn this dump into such a showplace?"

"Hard work and time," Conor said. "But tonight we'll put the work on hold. We've got some drinking and singing to get to!"

By seven, all of the cousins were in the back yard, drinking beer and demanding that Rory tell them every mildly interesting thing that had happened during his months in Ireland. But Rory was one of the quietest of the whole bunch, and he kept turning the question around, getting the boyos to explain their roles in bringing the old apartment building back to life. Eventually, some of the aunts brought food, then Conor went home and returned with his mandolin and a guitar. Both Brendan and Ryan played, but neither expertly nor often. They passed the instrument back and forth when their fingers got tired, but they managed to keep up with Rory, who was clearly playing slowly for the amateurs.

Jamie didn't know any of the songs well enough to sing along, but she didn't mind a bit. Watching the siblings play together always brought tears to her eyes. They frequently squabbled like any set of closely-related adults, but you could see their fondness for each other from a mile away.

At one point, Jamie looked up to see people in the adjacent building sticking their heads out of their windows. They probably hadn't enjoyed the dilapidated apartment building that blighted the corner. It was an open question on whether they'd trade that blight for a yard full of men—drinking, playing and singing at full volume.

The party didn't break up until after midnight. After making sure Rory had everything he needed, Ryan led the way to their room. She flopped onto the bed, grinning from ear to ear. "Isn't it grand?" she asked, Irish accent in place. "Home is never homier than when my beloved brother is back in the fold."

Jamie sat next to her and started to play with her hair. "I'm very, very glad he's back. Sorry he missed your birthday, though."

Ryan waved a hand. "He usually does. It's fine. He's always home for Mama's. That means more to me."

"I'm really glad he makes sure to be here then. I know it means a lot to you to have all of your family together to remember her."

Ryan looked up with such a sweet, melancholy smile that Jamie's heart clenched with feeling. "I remember her every day. Every single day." Her voice grew quiet when she added, "I hope I never stop."

Bending to kiss her, Jamie whispered, "You won't. Not a chance." She shifted around until she could lie next to Ryan. They were both on their backs, staring up at the ceiling. "I don't know if you realize this, but I try to emulate you."

Ryan turned and looked into her eyes, an unasked question lurking there.

"Seeing how losing your mom has affected you makes me try hard to be as supportive of mine as I can possibly be." Ryan's head cocked slightly. "To support her even when she's doing something that I'm not one hundred percent in favor of."

Ryan sighed heavily. "She wants to visit Giacomo."

"Yeah. She's going to New York to meet him on Monday. I said we'd stay at her house and watch Jen." She grasped Ryan's hand and held it to her chest. "I know you're probably less enthusiastic than I am, but for different reasons."

"Do you want me to…" Ryan sat halfway up and braced herself on an arm, gazing at Jamie for a long minute. "Just support your decision? Or is this up for discussion?"

"I said I'd watch Jen. If you don't want to go, you certainly don't have to."

Moving her arm, Ryan fell back onto the bed. "Support only. Got it. I'll pack my toothbrush and be ready to go on Monday morning."

Jamie rolled over and tucked her arm around Ryan's waist. "Thank you. You're a very good girlfriend."

Ryan chuckled a little bit. "And you're a wily one. Don't think I didn't notice that you sprang this on me when I was in a good mood."

"*Finally*," Jamie said, giving her a pinch.

On Monday morning, Ryan's small bag was packed and waiting by the front door. Agitated, she checked her watch for the fifth time. "I'll go alone," she called downstairs. "You can come over when you're finished with…whatever it is you're doing."

Catherine had scheduled her flight to New York for the crack of dawn, and Ryan thought she knew why. Skipping away early in the morning saved her from having to leave with an audience. Ryan wasn't sure how Jen felt about Catherine's taking off for a week, but Ryan sure wasn't a fan.

Jamie's light tread sounded on the stairs. "I'm on time. We said we'd be there at eight, and it's twenty 'til."

"I wanted to walk," Ryan said, trying hard to keep the grumpiness from her voice.

"You didn't say that, baby. And I want a car at mom's. I don't want to have to walk to the Mission to work on the project."

"Your mom's car's home. She won't mind if you use it."

Jamie stopped and stared into Ryan's eyes for a few seconds. There were storm clouds brewing in those green depths and Ryan knew she was going to get a lecture. "Look. I'm not forcing you to go with me. I made the commitment, and I can keep it alone. So either suck it up or stay home. I'm not going to listen to you whine for a whole week."

"I just wanted to walk!"

"Then walk. I'll drive and take your bag for you." She opened the door and pushed Ryan through it. "Don't rush. Actually, stay outside until you've worked through whatever's bugging you."

They were both on the deck now, with the heavy fog making Ryan wish she'd worn another layer.

"I wanted to walk over, take Jen to school, then go work on the apartment. I had a *plan*."

"That you didn't share with me. Now it's too late to execute your plan, so let me take Jen to school. You go to work and unleash some of your bad vibes onto an inanimate object. The apartment building won't want to wring your neck for being such a grump. I will." With that, Jamie picked up both bags and started for her car.

Ryan started after her. "I'll go," she said, her voice too grumpy for even her to stand. "I said I'd go, so I will."

Jamie stopped and looked at her. Troubled eyes ranged all across Ryan's face. "I'd really rather you didn't. I want you to figure out what's bothering you and either be prepared to talk about it tonight or stay here. I'm serious, Ryan. I've been very patient with you, but my patience is at an end." She put a hand on Ryan's shoulder and pulled her close for a kiss. "I love you, sweetheart, but you're driving me crazy." With that, she turned and headed for her car, determined strides soon absorbed by the thick fog.

Jamie didn't hear from Ryan all day, but for a change, she didn't mind the silent treatment. She knew something was deeply bothering her partner and was finally beginning to understand that Ryan simply *couldn't* talk before she was ready to. Jamie was sitting in the library, trying not to listen to Jennie hacking away during her clarinet lesson, when a quiet knock preceded the door opening. "Who's this?" Jamie asked, smiling as Ryan entered. "Is my sweet-tempered girlfriend back? Or is this the grouchy-bear who's been prowling around for a week?"

Ryan smile sheepishly. "I'm not sure I'm sweet-tempered, but I'm ready to talk."

Jamie patted the seat next to her. "Come."

With a few long strides, Ryan stood next to the sofa, then sat down and put her arm around Jamie's shoulders. "I'm sorry I've been so grouchy. I thought it was about your mom's leaving, and I didn't want to bring that up, so I just stuffed it away." She shrugged. "Ineffectively."

"Ryan, you don't have to do that. I can handle your criticizing my mother. I don't *like* it, but I can handle it."

"No, no." Ryan held a hand up. "I figured out that wasn't it. Well, maybe it was a tiny piece of it. Anyway, my bigger problem is this friggin' election. I've let myself get way too involved, and it's making me nuts."

"I know you've been following it pretty closely…"

"Not even close. I've been obsessed. Every morning, I've woken an hour after we go to sleep. Then I get online and read message boards. People are *so* angry, Jamie. And their anger is firing mine! I've got to let go. I just don't know how to." She let her head drop into her open hands. "I feel like I'm watching the destruction of the democratic process. It's…I can't explain how it makes me feel." She sat up and slammed a fist into an open hand. "I'd like to bring the founding fathers back to life to show them what a fuck-fest the electoral college is. Gore won the damned election! More people voted for him!"

"I know, sweetheart, but that's not how the system works." She reached over and pulled Ryan against her body, shocked by how stiff and unyielding she was. Her body was like a steel wire, completely filled with tension.

"Listen," Jamie soothed. "You've got to get out of this mindset. Here's what I've done." She took in a breath and let it out slowly. "I've decided that one way or the other, Bush is going to win. I've made my peace with that. If you value your sanity, I'd urge you to do the same."

Ryan sounded like she was on the verge of tears. "But it's not fair. The process—"

"Shh," Jamie said, covering her mouth with her fingers. "Politics is a dirty game, and our side is going to lose this match. But I think we can both imagine a set of circumstances where we'd be top dog. And we wouldn't lose a lot of sleep over it if a contested democratic state swung the election our way. If Gore had done a better job campaigning, he'd have won."

Slowly, Ryan's body relaxed and she eventually cuddled close. "Sucks," she grumbled.

"It does. But you have to let it go. You *have* to."

"All right." She sat up and gave Jamie a resigned smile. "After we take Jen to school in the morning, can we do something fun? I need to knock some of this mood out of my head."

Jamie kissed her gently, then urged Ryan to lie down and put her head in her lap. Rhythmically, she threaded her fingers through Ryan's hair, soothing her. "We certainly can. Let's put our drysuits on and go sailing. Nothing cleans the cobwebs out like doing something wet and wild."

"You're on. And do me a favor. If you see me go near a computer, slap me. I'm going on radio silence until this is over."

"It's a deal," Jamie said, smiling at the sincere tone in Ryan's request. "After the way you've been moping around it'll be a pleasure."

On Tuesday afternoon, Jamie picked Jen up at school and they walked home together. "Good day?" Jamie asked.

"S'okay. No tests."

Laughing, Jamie agreed, "A day without tests is a good day. Oh. My mom called and said to tell you she might not have time to call before you go to bed. She's got something going on." She put her arm around Jennie's shoulders and gave her a hug. "But she wanted me to tell you she's thinking about you."

Jen gave her an odd look. She was either puzzled or dubious—Jamie couldn't tell which. "She doesn't need to worry about me. You guys are watching me just as close as she does."

Mentally rolling her eyes, Jamie said, "She wasn't calling to check up on you. She just wanted you to know she cares for you."

"Mmm." Jen nodded, looking unconvinced. "What's she doing, anyway? She doesn't have a job or anything, does she?"

Stunned, Jamie shook her head. Where did the kid come up with these questions? "No, she doesn't have a job. Today she and Giacomo were going to look at some art, then they're going to the opera."

"Who's Giacomo?" Jennie's gaze was sharp, further shocking Jamie.

"He's…Giacomo," she said, knowing she sounded like a dunce. "Her…friend. I think you met him down in Hillsborough."

"Don't remember," she said dismissively. "Is he like a boyfriend?"

"Well, he's definitely a boy, so…"

Jen seemed satisfied with that answer. But after just a few seconds she gave Jamie another narrow-eyed look. "Why does she have a boyfriend in New York?"

It was too late to pull back now. Jamie wasn't sure if her mom didn't want Jen to know about Giacomo or just hadn't thought to explain the purpose of her trip. Either way, she wasn't going to go through a bunch of verbal gyrations to hide the facts. "He doesn't live in New York. He's Italian. I'm sure you met him when he was here last spring."

"Lots of people were at those parties." She was staring straight ahead, then once again her head snapped to the side. "She's not moving to Italy, is she?"

"No, of course not." Jamie reached down and took Jen's hand in hers. The poor kid was always waiting for the other shoe to drop. "She has an apartment in Italy, but she doesn't go there very often. I'm certain she has no plans to move, Jen."

"Do you think she'd take me with her if she did?"

Jamie stopped, put her arms around Jen and gave her a long hug. "She's your guardian, Jen. Think of what that term means." Releasing the girl, she stepped back so she could see her face. "She's legally required to give you a safe, secure place to live. Nobody made her do that. She *wanted* to. She really, really wanted to. She, and I, and Ryan, and everyone else consider you a part of our family. If she goes anywhere—you're going with her."

"But she's not going anywhere." Suspicion still clouded the girl's face.

"No, she's not." Jamie took a breath and let it out. The kid needed to know the situation. "She loves Giacomo, but he lives in Italy and needs to stay there. My mom needs to stay here. So they try to see each other as often as they can—but that's not very often."

"Does your mom need to stay here just because of me?"

"No, not at all." Jamie smiled at her. "I think it's mostly because of me. She made the decision to stay here long before she became your guardian." She draped her arms across Jen's shoulders and smiled as she thought of her mom's decision. "She's trying to be a good mom—for both of us. But she needs to make herself happy too, so she needs to visit Giacomo once in a while. When that happens, Ryan and I will come over and fill in. Gladly."

"Okay." Jen nodded, looking a little more convinced. "So she's just hanging out this week."

"Right. And knowing my mom, she'll come back with a piece of art."

"That's what we've been doing," Jennie said as Jamie released her hold and they started to walk again. "Going to art galleries when I don't have too much homework."

"That's cool. You might like Giacomo. He's an art dealer."

"Really?" she said, clearly surprised. "Every guy we've met at a gallery is way, way gay."

Jamie laughed. "I'm pretty sure Giacomo's not gay. He's…" She stopped herself from talking more about him, afraid her antipathy might shine through. "You'll meet him one day."

"Does he have new stuff or old stuff? I like new stuff better."

Jamie stopped to think, realizing she had absolutely no idea of what kind of art Giacomo sold. "I'm not sure. We'll have to ask." *Maybe if one of us stops being a big baby we can ask all sorts of questions. Maybe we should give a damn about someone who's really important to someone we love.*

On Wednesday, Ryan knocked off early to go pick up Jen. She hadn't had time alone with the kid in ages, and since Jamie and Maeve went to dinner and their bible class on Wednesdays, this was the perfect time.

Ryan was still in her work clothes, and she was slightly out of breath when Jen found her standing under a tree.

"Hey," Ryan said. "I had to huff it to get up that last hill. Guess I should have driven."

"Who's making you do this?" Jen asked as they started to walk home. "Ms. Smith or DCFS or a judge or what?"

Ryan stopped on a dime. "Making me do what?"

"Supervise me like this." She hoisted her heavy back pack over a shoulder, then started to walk again.

"What are you talking about?"

"I live like half a mile from here. When I was ten I was riding my bike across Oakland to get to school. Ten! Now I'm a sophomore and I have to have a police escort."

"Whoa!" Ryan grabbed one of the straps of her backpack and pulled her to a halt. "Do you honestly think Catherine doesn't trust you to walk home?"

"Why else?" the girl glared at her insolently.

Ryan swiped at her, hitting her backpack. "You've lost your mind." Draping an arm around Jen's shoulders, she started to walk. "She cares about you, you dope. She goes out of her way to make sure her calendar's clear so she's available. And she made it perfectly clear to us that we were to take over and do the same." Bending over, she kissed Jen's head. "And we're happy to do it. But only because we thought you liked having someone to walk home with." Shaking Jennie gently, she added, "I'm perfectly happy to leave you alone if you don't want me here."

Jen looked up at her. "I think it's because she thinks I'll run away again."

"No way! Granted, she almost lost her mind when you did that, but she trusts you plenty. She's just trying to show she cares."

"My mom never walked me to school," Jennie said quietly. "Not even first grade."

"Well, I think it's pretty clear that Catherine's fixated on making your life better than it was before. But if you'd rather walk home alone— just tell her."

"Nah." Jen shook her head briskly. "I don't wanna hurt her feelings. A lot of kids get picked up. Nobody knows I just live a couple blocks away."

"Not even your friends?"

"Yeah, they know, but they've got stuff after class. They're never outside when I'm there."

"Want me to cross to the other side of the street? Or I could run ahead…"

Jennie obviously saw that Ryan was teasing. "You can stay. And as long as you're here…" She lowered her shoulders and her heavy pack slid down her back and hit the sidewalk. "You can carry my books."

"Happy to." Ryan grabbed the bag and hefted it over her shoulder. "What are you carrying? A set of encyclopedias?"

"What's that?"

"Books. A big bunch of books."

"I go to high school, Ryan. All we do is carry books around."

"Got it," Ryan nodded, trying not to laugh. "It's been a while. I forgot."

Jordan sat up in the stands of the gym, watching the volleyball team warm up for that night's game. Normally, she stood on the court, able to offer a correction or a compliment. But changing her angle, and being able to see the arc of the ball from a different perspective gave her some added insight into individual players' skills.

She didn't honestly think she was helping much, but Coach kept telling her she was contributing, so she kept coming. Plus, it was fun to watch people play for kicks. Not that the players thought they were just having fun. Playing for a major college program was a big deal, and she was sure all of them felt the pressure of competing for their team as well as their school. But that pressure was nothing compared to traveling the world for your country, knowing your games were being broadcast to hundreds of millions of people. Just thinking about it made her body start to tense up. She was so lost in thought that she levitated a little when someone dropped into the chair beside her.

"Ashley!"

"Hey." She got up and moved down a few seats. "The trainer told me to stay away from everyone until this sore throat gets better." She started to laugh, then grasped at her throat and shut her eyes tightly. "I guess I should show you the same courtesy."

"I didn't know you were sick. Got a fever?"

"Little bit. But the throat's killing me."

"Maybe you ought to head home and get some rest."

"I will." She leaned forward and rested her chin on her hands. "I hate to miss a game," she said wistfully.

"I get that. But it's better to miss one than three." She reached across the seats and popped her on the shoulder. "We probably would have made the tournament if Ryan hadn't gotten the flu. Don't let that happen to you."

"Don't even say that!"

Even in the bad lighting of the gym, Jordan could see her turn pale. "I'm not putting a spell on you, just reminding you to take it easy until you're better."

"You're right. I'll take off." She got up, but continued to look down at the court. "Will you be here until practice is over?"

"Yeah. Why?"

"Tell Heather you guilt-tripped me into going home. I don't want her to think..." She rolled her eyes. "You know she's gay, right?"

Jordan looked up at her, unsure how to respond. "She's never told me that," she finally said.

"But you guessed, right?" Ashley was looking at her like she wasn't in the mood for playing games.

Jordan shrugged. "I wouldn't be surprised. But if you told me she's got like six girlfriends—I'd be amazed."

That made Ashley laugh again, and her eyes slammed shut one more time. Pointing at her throat, she whispered, "It's killing me."

"Go home! Why are we talking about Heather and whether or not she's gay?"

"Last night, she finally told me that she thinks she is, and she's been watching me like I'm going to move out or something ever since. So just tell her I'm going home to chill."

After looking up at her for a moment, Jordan said, "You're okay with it, right?"

Ashley shook her head briefly. "I'm pissed. I guessed she was gay the day I met her, but it's taken her over two full years to talk about it? I'm supposed to be her best friend."

Jordan could see the hurt in her eyes. She got up and put a hand on her shoulder, resisting the urge to hug her. She couldn't afford to bring home a virus to the family breadwinner. "I wasn't kidding when I said Heather's never said anything to me, and she knows I'm gay. I don't think she's confided in Ryan either. Give her a break. This is probably hard for her."

"It's hard to be shut out, too," Ashley said. Her chin started to quiver, and Jordan ignored her self-preservation instincts to give her a hug.

"I know. But I can guarantee Heather's just frightened. She's probably had a hard time admitting this to herself, much less her friends." When Jordan moved away, their eyes met. "I was paralyzed with fear when I was coming out. And I don't mean to brag, but I think I'm gutsier than Heather."

Ashley let a half smile show. "Yeah, you are." She grabbed her throat as a short, quiet laugh came out. "But just a little."

"Be patient with her, Ash. When she knows you're on her side, she'll start opening up."

"I've always been on her side," she insisted, her temper flaring again.

"I know. But when you're in the closet, you assume everyone will turn on you. It's irrational, but really common. This is about her fears, not your relationship. That's solid."

"Yeah, yeah, it is." She took in and let out a breath. "I'll try to be more patient." As she started for the aisle, she smiled and added, "I'll give her until the weekend to get this all figured out."

At seven, Ryan and Jennie sat in the stands at the gym at Cal, watching the Golden Bears take on the Washington Huskies. Jordan was down on the bench, making Ryan just a little jealous. If she'd had time, she'd have been there helping out in the afternoons too. But she had to admit she had limitations—limitations she hated.

"They're not as good as they were with you and Jordan," Jennie said. "But they're still good."

"They are. There's a chance they'll make the NCAA tournament." She put her arm around Jen and made a promise. "If they make it, we'll follow them through—no matter where they play."

Jennie looked up with surprise, which quickly turned to caution.

"Yeah. Okay."

"I mean it," Ryan said. "The games will be on the weekend. School won't be an issue."

"But something else will be." Jen rested her elbows on her knees and settled her chin in her hand.

Ryan clapped her on the back. "The only thing that'll stop us going is if they don't make it. You and I are a lock."

On Wednesday afternoon, Catherine and Giacomo stood in a lavishly decorated apartment in a building on Central Park West. A real estate agent, a good-looking, glib gay man in a suit more expensive than Giacomo's, could not stop talking. Catherine had finally had enough. "We both know New York well enough, Carter. If we buy a place, it won't be to enjoy the city as much as to have an apartment that we can both get to in about six hours."

"But we love your city," Giacomo said, unable to be brusque, even to an overly-chatty real estate salesman. "We would enjoy all of the things you speak of; the museums, the park, the Lincoln Center. They are all fantastic."

"Yes, they are, but it sounds as if your...friend is more interested in the apartment than the city. Luckily, this building can't be beat. It was built in 1928 by the pre-eminent architect of the period—"

"I'm quite familiar with Emery Roth," Catherine interrupted. "And I like the unit. But I'm not interested in doing a lot of renovation, so buying in a new building has some appeal. The plans for 15 Central Park West are very impressive."

"If you want to wait for five...or six...or ten years," Carter said dismissively. "You know how construction delays can add up. They've barely broken ground."

"Still..." She walked over to the windows and admired the view of the park. "I like this unit. It's just..." She shook her head. "It would have to be redone. Completely. I don't like the kitchen or the baths and the master bedroom is too small. I need less space in the living and dining rooms and more in the bedrooms and baths. This unit was designed for people who entertain." She shot a quick look at Giacomo. "That's not our interest. We want a—"

"Nest," he said, smiling at her. "We want a place for just the two of us. A place to be all alone with the city swirling around us."

Catherine cleared her throat and tried to remain businesslike. With Giacomo giving her that love-sick look she could be talked into anything. "That's it exactly. We want a modern apartment to use as a pied-à-terre."

"I can find you a contractor who can revamp this place into any configuration you wish," Carter said decisively. "You can't do any major construction until August, but by the time you completed the purchase, and worked with an architect, and ordered all of your materials…"

"August?" Catherine gawped.

"You'll find that in all of the good buildings in the city. Most people are gone for the month." He laughed. "The only people in New York in August are tourists and construction workers. So you'd have the exact space you want, sparkling new and ready to go in September." His eyes grew wide. "If you want to do this, you'll have to move quickly. All of the best contractors are snapped up by January."

"I've never had work done when I'm not there to supervise," Catherine said.

"I guarantee that the firm I recommend needs no supervision. You'll pay for it, but Anthony hires only union workers. Craftsmen. I can show you some of the work he's done if you're interested."

"How can you possibly arrange that? I can't imagine letting anyone into my home just to see what a wonderful job my contractor did."

"He did my home," Carter said. "And my boyfriend's. I can show you a two-bedroom on the Upper West Side, and a studio in Chelsea. You'll be amazed."

"Hmm…" Catherine walked over to the French doors that led to the balcony. "Could we be alone for a while?"

"Of course. How long do you need?"

"An hour?"

He blinked, but did what all good real estate salesmen did. He agreed. "Of course. I'll go return some phone calls. I'll be…" He frowned. "At the Starbucks on Fifty-Ninth and Broadway."

"We'll come find you," Catherine said, waving as he put his topcoat on and exited. She took Giacomo's hand and led him to the balcony. It was windy, and the grey skies were so low it seemed they'd be able to touch them. "I'm not sure how much I'll like this weather," she admitted, chuckling.

Giacomo stood behind her and wrapped her in a hug, with his body immediately helping to warm her. "I want this building," he said, his breath tickling her ear. "I love the architecture of New York in the 1920s. So much optimism! Let's make an offer. We'll each pay half."

"That's not necessary, Giacomo. I'll probably use it more than you will, and there might be issues with your not being a citizen. It's easier if I buy it alone."

The hurt in his voice was painfully obvious. "Do you not trust me to own this with you? For many years?"

Catherine turned in his embrace, then spent a few moments looking into his warm brown eyes. "I trust you completely. But you shouldn't spend money on a place you'll use so infrequently. You have your family to consider."

His mouth quirked into a grin. "You don't know how much money I have. This might be like buying a cappuccino for me."

"This is true." She nodded. "I still think it would be easier if just one of us had our name on the title. I'm not sure if it's difficult for a foreign national to own property—"

"Fine. I will not argue," he interrupted. "You will buy the apartment and I will pay for the remodeling. How does that seem?"

Sputtering, she said, "You can't do that! You wouldn't have any protection."

"Protection?" His head cocked.

"What if we...stop seeing each other? I'll own the apartment outright."

His head shook slowly. "First, if that happens, the last thing I will care about is my money. Second, if you were to stop wanting me, you would pay me back—even though I wouldn't ask for you to. You're a very honorable woman, Catherine."

She snuggled into his embrace, touched by his words. "What if you decide you don't want to see *me* anymore?"

"That will not happen," he said, his voice taking on a steely quality he didn't show often. His arms closed more tightly around her body. "I want this place. Some day I want our grandchildren to come with us to New York." He tilted his head and kissed her cheek. "At Christmas. We'll take them to see the wonderful Neapolitan crèche at the Met, and to The Nutcracker at the ballet. They will love New York! It will be so different for them."

Looking up at him, Catherine tried to stay centered, to think of the present and the near-future. But she desperately wanted to abandon her more pragmatic self and follow along into Giacomo's fantasy world. "They will love it. I want a dozen grandchildren. How many do you want?"

"Two dozen!" he said, laughing. "Or maybe three. A man cannot have too much love in his life, and no one ever loves you as much as your grandchildren."

"Don't be so sure of that," she said, her voice taking on a sexy purr. She took his hand and led him back into the apartment. "I'll call Carter on the way to the hotel. I have plans for you this afternoon. Big plans that I'm sure you will love."

"What about the apartment?"

"We can settle that tomorrow. Today is for fun."

Mia got home at six, drained from a day spent making calls and following up on details for the more important people in the office. She'd stripped out of her dress and heels and was just about to put on her pajamas in anticipation of Jordan bringing home Chinese food after volleyball practice. Her phone rang and she answered it without looking at the display. "Hello?"

"Hello, my darling little wage-earner. How was work?" Anna Lisa said.

"It's going good."

"Well," her mother corrected.

"I know the right word, Mom. I choose not to use it. I like to sound like I'm in my twenties."

"That's a nice way to defend your laziness as well as take a swipe at me. Good job."

"One of my best traits. What's up? Did you just call to remind me my salad days are over?"

"Salad days," Anna Lisa scoffed. "You don't even know what that means."

"Did I use it right?" Mia waited a beat, knowing she had.

"Yes, I suppose you did."

"Then maybe I know what it means. Did you call for a reason—other than busting my chops?"

She could hear her mother take in and let out a long breath. "Let's start over. Are you having a good week?"

"Yeah. Sure. I'm not doing anything exciting yet, but I can tell they're happy with me."

"That's wonderful, honey. How can you tell that?"

"Uhm…stating the obvious, I'm good at reading people. Carly perks up when I poke my head in her office, which I don't do very often. Bosses don't like to have to waste their time on you."

"You can perk anyone up. Or drive them crazy. I hope she doesn't learn about that side of you."

"I don't think it's a whole *side*, Mom. More like a part. I think it's genetic…from your mother's side, if I remember my biology."

"Nice. Another zinger."

"Just lobbing them back. I haven't served once."

"Speaking of serving," Anna Lisa said, speaking over Mia. "I'm serving Thanksgiving dinner at two p.m. You don't have to bring anything."

"Oh. Right. It's next week. I haven't talked to Jordy about it yet…"

"I'm sure she'll want to come. She seemed to enjoy our little dinner last month."

"Yeah, yeah, she probably will. But what about Nonna?"

"It's just going to be the five of us this year."

"Oh, come on! You're skipping Thanksgiving with your parents just so they don't find out about Jordan?"

"You're not the number one topic in the family you know. Nonna's arthritis is flaring up and she doesn't want to cook this year. She and Poppi are going to his sister's house."

"Why aren't we going with them? Great Aunt Marcella can seat twenty at that massive table of hers."

"They're all starting to slow down. They can't deal with a big crowd anymore, so they want it more low-key this year."

"Are you being serious? This was their idea?"

"Of course. Thanksgiving doesn't have much meaning for Italians. I think it's just an excuse for them to get together and play briscola. It's not a big deal."

"All right. I assume Jordy will want to come, so put us down as a yes. I'll call if she's rabidly opposed."

"Sounds lovely. I'm sure we can count on her. She's got very good manners."

"It's all in the breeding, Mom. She obviously comes from better stock. See you!"

At 6:30, Jordan called to say she was running late. Mia went upstairs and had just a tiny hit of weed. Luckily, she didn't have to be as careful as she'd been in Colorado, with the threat of random drug testing hanging over Jordan. Now she tried to smoke only when she was alone, even though Jordan never complained or even commented on her pot use.

A cold beer had her feeling relaxed and ready for the weekend. She paged through her phone, looking to see who she could call, stopping when she got to "Giovannetti."

She hit the button and in a few rings her grandmother answered, "Yeah?"

Mia smiled at the way her grandmother answered the phone. She barked her greeting, as if she expected to be harassed or bothered in some way. "Hi, Nonna. It's Mia."

"I know who it is. You're the only girl who calls me nonna."

"Good point. I just called to see how you're doing. I miss you guys."

"Us guys are right here almost every day. If you miss us, you wouldn't ignore us for months at a time. I see Peter more often and he's thousands of miles away."

"I'm sorry, Nonna. I know I've been a jerk, but I'm going to be better. Promise." The fastest way to get back into her nonna's good graces was to accept responsibility. Calling yourself names didn't hurt.

"Oh, you're busy," she said, already over her pique. "It's all right. Just promise you'll come when you get back, okay?"

"Back?"

"From your trip."

Mia's brows shot up. Maybe her mother was right. If Nonna was having memory problems... "My trip?"

"You're leaving for Italy next Wednesday, Mia. Given that you're breaking my heart by not coming for Thanksgiving, the least you can do is remember you're going!"

Oh, fuck!

"I'm sorry, Nonna. Since I started working, I've been distracted. I have to admit I completely forgot about going on a trip." *Because I'm not!*

"I'm not happy about this, honey. You know I love to cook a big meal for everyone, so you'd better have a wonderful time."

"I will. And I hope you know how much I love to eat your cooking. I'll truly miss it."

"I know that, angel, but your mother says this might be the last year you'll be able to have a holiday trip. Peter will have a job next year, you know."

"Yeah, I guess he will. Well, I'll miss seeing you and Poppi over Thanksgiving. It won't be the same without you."

"I know, my little angel, but we'll all be together over Christmas. There will be no excuses then."

"Can't wait!" Mia said. They'd never had fireworks for Christmas, and that was about to change.

Mia picked up the phone on her desk the next morning and put in a call.

"Hello?"

"Have I called you from this number yet?" Mia asked.

"Nope. I'll put it on my speed-dial list right now. How's it going?" Jamie asked.

"Okay. Hey, do you have time to come down and have lunch with me?"

"I've got nothing but time. Ryan's working, and I don't have to start dinner for hours. What time?"

"Not sure. I like to wait until Carly leaves, then even if I get back well after she does, she's not sure how long I've been gone."

Jamie let out a laugh. "You spend as much time thinking about things as Ryan does, but she's always trying to figure out how to make *more* work for herself."

"An attribute you will never be able to…attribute to me. That was a fucked up sentence. Wasn't sure where that one was gonna wind up."

"It made perfect sense to me. Call me when Carly leaves and I'll grab a cab."

"A cab? Really?"

"It's either that or I'll have to pay Embarcadero parking rates. A cab's a bargain."

"Deal. It'll be around noon. See you then."

They met up in the lobby of Mia's massive building. Even though Jamie had just been hanging around the house, she looked like a million bucks.

When Mia reached her, they hugged and kissed each other like it had been years since they'd seen each other. Nothing better than having your best friend act like she dug the hell out of you. "What are you in the mood for?" Mia said. "I've put on a couple of pounds and want to stay right where I am, so I usually have a salad or soup for lunch. But we can get whatever."

"A salad's fine with me. I have to make substantial dinners, so I tend to eat light at lunch too."

"Tablecloths and napkins?" Mia asked.

"Preferably. If you don't know of a spot, I've got one."

Mia turned and stared, open-mouthed. "You know a good restaurant? Really?"

Jamie flicked her right on the cheek, making it sting. "Hey! You've gotten a lot more physically abusive since you've been with those rough and tumble O'Flahertys."

"All too true."

Mia linked her arm through Jamie's and they walked down the clogged sidewalk, then turned left and continued through the throng. It was hard to talk while dodging all of the people, so Mia just let herself be led.

Jamie stopped in front of an elegant little spot, one of the many old school places San Francisco tended to favor. It was a high end tea room, and a guy in a suit rushed over with menus. "For lunch?" he asked.

"Correct," Jamie said. He seated them, left them with the menus, and rushed to get them water.

After the glasses were delivered, Mia said, "Guess what I think I'm going to do tomorrow night?"

"Hmm." Jamie closed her eyes halfway, clearly thinking. "Is it sexual?"

"I wish. No, I'm thinking of going down to visit my grandmother and come out to her."

"What?" You knew you'd gotten to Jamie when she spoke too loudly for the venue. "I assume you mean your mom's mom."

"Right. The Lucchesi Lunatic."

"Not your grandfather?"

"Nah. He goes to his club on Thursday to hang with his paisans. Nonna will be home alone from seven until nine. That's Poppi's curfew," she added, smirking. "I've got about thirty hours to talk myself out of it."

Their server came by and Jamie ordered for both of them, even though Mia hadn't seen her look at the menu. Reaching across the table, Jamie gripped Mia's hand and gave her a long look. "Do you want to be talked out of it?"

"I don't think so." She took in a breath and found herself almost crying. "My mom made up a huge lie about all of us going to Italy for Thanksgiving. I'm finished with playing that game. I want to be honest."

"I can understand that. You've always loved spending time with your grandparents. Having a bunch of lies you have to tiptoe around must make that hard."

"Impossible," Mia said. "I haven't seen them for months, leaving them to think I'm a flake."

"Oh, right," Jamie said, wincing. "They couldn't know you were in Colorado. Or all over Europe. Or Australia."

"My mother wants me to act like Jordy doesn't exist," she said, once again feeling a tightness in her throat that wanted to turn into tears. "I can't do that any more."

"But if your mom already lied…" Jamie made a face. "I hate to be on her side about this, but you could let it go until after the holiday. Maybe your mom will come around by Christmas."

Their salads were delivered, and Mia took a look at the seared tuna atop perfectly arranged baby lettuce. The place looked old school, but they weren't stuck in the past. Mia took a bite and nodded her approval.

"Good," she said. "You're still batting a thousand." After she swallowed, she said, "I'd give my mom a pass if she'd made any progress. But she insists my grandparents don't need to know something 'like this.'"

"Ever?"

Nodding, Mia said, "Yeah. That's her plan. I'm supposed to ignore Jordy for every holiday just so my grandmother doesn't get upset." She rolled her eyes dramatically. "It's like my mother's never *met* me!"

"I sure can't see you going along with *that* plan."

"No. Not gonna happen." She took a sip of water, trying to guess at her mother's motivations. "It's like my mom doesn't *want* to get past this. She's stuck. At this point I think I have to save her from the turmoil she's putting herself through. She'll kill me for doing it behind her back, but she'd never give me permission to be honest. I'm kinda screwed no matter what."

"Ooo, that's tough. Really tough. But what'll happen if you tell your nonna and…" She made a cutting motion at her throat.

Mia could feel her resolve build. She was going to do this, no matter what advice Jamie offered. "I can't guarantee she'll still love me, but I'd be a fool if I let that stop me."

Jamie put down her fork and studied Mia for a minute. "I understand your point, but it's not that easy for a lot of people. I don't think people are foolish for being in the closet if the reward isn't worth the risk."

Frowning, Mia said, "What price would you accept to lose your integrity? I don't want to sound like a jerk about this, but if my grandparents only value me as a straight girl, they don't truly love me."

"I don't think that's fair," Jamie said, being annoyingly reasonable. "They're from a different era, a different country. They could truly love you but not be able to get used to your being…whatever you are."

"Nope." Mia shook her head, her mind made up. "If their prejudices and preconceived notions are more important than our relationship—I'm willing to lose them. I won't *like* it," she added. "In fact, it would hurt like hell, and it would take me years to get over the pain. But I *would* get over it." Her expression softened when she thought of her motivation. "The thing I couldn't get over is hurting Jordy by acting like I'm ashamed of her." She swallowed around the lump in her throat. "And it *would* hurt her," she added, tears coming to her eyes. "That's something I will not risk."

To make sure she didn't lose her nerve, Mia took the train directly from work to San Bruno. Once there, she found a cab and sat in the back seat, preparing herself for the worst.

Her grandfather was a pushover, the kind of guy who'd shrug his shoulders at nearly every question you asked him. Living with her grandmother for over forty years had drained away whatever fight he'd ever possessed.

Her grandmother, on the other hand, was like a tiny Mt. Vesuvius. She could be loving, caring, sweet and amazingly thoughtful. And no one was more generous with the needy—so long as their needs suited her beliefs. Hard-working, low income people from their parish, or anyone who'd suffered a catastrophic loss might find a basket full of housewares or linens or enough canned goods to last a month on their front porch—without ever knowing who it was from. She hated to have anyone indebted to her, or to even thank her, which Mia had always thought cool. But if you were at all responsible for your hard times—good luck. She wouldn't have thrown water on you if you'd been on fire.

Her views on most social issues were the same. Either supremely understanding or "you're dead to me." And even though they'd talked about many things through the years, Mia had no idea how her grandmother felt about gay people.

The family home wasn't too far from the train station, and as Mia paid the guy and got out, her knees turned rubbery. The lights were on, and she was going to have to suck it up and spit this out—minutes from now.

After ringing the bell, Mia stood in the golden porch light and waited, hearing her grandmother's quick steps cross the floor. "Who is it?" she demanded, in a voice harsh enough to make the most hardened criminals take off.

"It's Mia."

"Mia?" she said as she unlocked each of the bolts and threw the door open. "What are you doing here?" She peered out at her, dark eyes narrowed. "With a dress on, no less."

"Can I come in?" Mia said, grasping the storm door handle.

"What's wrong? You haven't shown up without warning for ten years. Did something happen to your mother?" She craned her neck to see the street. "Are the police here?"

There was every chance the old woman wasn't going to let her in! "Why would the police be here?"

"How do I know? Maybe you got arrested and they won't let you go unless you have me sign something."

"Nonna," Mia said, trying not to let her frustration show, "the police aren't here, my mother's fine, and I'd really like to come in."

Warily, she opened the door, now scanning the driveway. "Where's your car?"

"I took a cab from the train station."

Suddenly, her ear was gripped and she was bodily hauled into the room. "When did you find out? How long have you known? Is it too late to get an abortion?" She yanked hard, sending Mia flying from one direction to another. "You know I don't approve of abortion, but I'm not going to have you raising some little bastard with no father!"

"I'm not pregnant! Jesus Christ, let me go!"

A pair of strong, age-spotted hands landed on her shoulders and she was held still, with her grandmother's laser-like eyes boring into her. "Then why are you here?"

"To talk to you. I have something to tell you."

"You're not pregnant?" Those vise-like fingers gripped her painfully. "You don't have AIDS, do you?"

"God, no!" Pulling away, Mia moved until she was certain she'd be able to outrun her grandmother if necessary. "I want to have a simple conversation with you, Nonna. The world isn't coming to an end."

"Go. Talk," she said, crossing her arms over her chest.

If the Cosa Nostra needed an enforcer, a very promising recruit was right in front of Mia's eyes. She was nearly seventy, weighed around a hundred pounds and topped out at five feet, but she could kick anyone's ass and not suffer a scratch.

"Can we sit down? I feel like I'm testifying, rather than talking."

"Am I stopping you? Sit."

Taking a chair past her grandmother's reach, Mia sat and tried to get her thoughts in order. She hadn't planned this well, not having rehearsed exactly what she'd say. But she knew the message she wanted to deliver, so she started with that.

"I wanted you to know that I've fallen in love."

"Huh? Is this some kind of joke? Why would you come all the way down here to say that?" Her eyes narrowed again and Mia covered her ears just in case.

"What's wrong with him? Does he beat you? Is he the one who won't let you come visit?" She leapt to her feet, amazingly spry for her age. "That's it! He's...what do they call it? A domestic violence!"

"No, that's not it," Mia said, trying to keep her voice calm and clear. "I'm not in love with a man, Nonna. I'm in love with a woman. That's why I haven't been visiting. My mom doesn't want you to know."

"What? *What?*" Her pitch had hit a new high. One that would have the neighborhood dogs howling. "What are you talking about?" The little old lady hovered above her, glaring at her with fire in her eyes. "What do you mean, your mother doesn't want me to know?"

That threw her for a loop. *That* was the question?

"Uhm, well, she's upset about it, and she assumes you will be too. I guess that's her motivation."

"I've never heard anything more stupid in my life." She sat down again, then cocked her head in question. "What could it hurt?"

"What could *what* hurt?"

She shrugged, having the ability to almost cover her ears with her dramatically rising shoulders. "So you've got a little crush on a girl. You'll make eyes at each other for a while, then some bum will catch your attention and we'll all be worrying about you getting pregnant again."

"First off," Mia said, working hard to keep the edge from her voice, "if I did get pregnant, it wouldn't be an accident. I'm twenty-two, Nonna, a perfectly reasonable time to start a family."

Her grandmother didn't respond, merely waving a hand in the air as she turned her head and stared at the wall.

"Secondly, I'm not just making eyes at Jordan. We love each other, and we're going to make a life together."

"You can't make a life with a girl," she said, starting to chuckle. "But if thinking that makes you happy, you just go right ahead."

"It does," Mia said, her voice firm and strong. "She makes me very happy."

"What's this girl's name? Jordan?" One eye closed halfway. "Isn't that a boy's name?"

"It's both, but she's a girl. I'm a hundred percent sure of that."

"I'll just bet you are. God knows what you get up to." She stood and started for the kitchen. "What do you want to eat? I've got some ?? I can warm up. Maybe a glass of wine?" She started to laugh again. "We can toast to your new love. What's her name?"

"Jordan," Mia said, rising to follow her grandmother into the kitchen. "Her name is Jordan, and I promise you're going to be seeing a lot of her."

Jamie and Ryan sat in the living room of the Berkeley house with Jordan that night, anxiously waiting for Mia to return. They'd had dinner together, mostly to try to keep Jordan calm, but the plan hadn't worked. Jordan had been distracted and fidgety, spending more time looking at her phone than her food.

"She said she'd call the second she could get away," Jordan said, her face a map of anxiety. "What could they be doing?"

"Hiding the evidence? Did anyone go through the house to remove sharp objects?" Ryan asked. "From the stories I've heard…"

"Knock it off, Boomer! Don't freak me out more than I already am! I can't let myself start to worry about Mia actually being *killed*. I've seen the woman's picture. She's small, but she looks wiry." She tilted her head to see the clock. "It's eleven! Mia said she'd be ready for me to pick her up by ten at the latest. What in the hell is going on?"

Jordan got up and started to pace. They'd gotten her to sit and try to relax at least three times already, but Jamie figured it was a wasted effort at this point. She was about to join her when the front door opened and Mia stood in the doorway, leaned her head back and took in a dramatic breath.

"I've never been so happy to be home."

Jordan dashed over to her and wrapped her in a hug. "How'd you get here?"

"Took Nonna's car. When it was time to leave, I wanted to get out of there as quickly as I could."

"Are you all right?" Jordan stroked her face, her shoulders, her back, as if looking for signs of trauma.

"Yeah," she said, smiling up at her. "Exhausted, but all right."

"Why didn't you call? You said you'd call!"

"Shh…" Mia put her arms around Jordan and patted her back. "I'm sorry. But I had the opportunity to leave, and I took it. I was so distracted, I didn't trust myself to talk and drive." She looked up. "Forgive me?"

"Yeah, yeah, of course. Come sit down and tell us what happened."

"Liquor?" Mia asked. "I'll take whatever we've got."

Jordan ran into the kitchen and came back with a beer. "It's warm," she said, making a face.

Jamie got up and went towards the library. "I've got all sorts of stuff in here." She opened a cabinet and assessed her stockpile. "I can make you a real drink. How about a vodka gimlet?"

"I have no idea what that is, but I like vodka," Mia called back.

"I think I'll join you. Ryan? Jordan?"

"No thanks," they said in tandem.

Jamie quickly made the simple drinks, then detoured to the kitchen to add some ice to the cocktail shaker. She came out a few seconds later, heading back to the library to fill a pair of cocktail glasses. "I used to make these for my dad when I was a kid. I got pretty good at it, if I do say so myself."

"If I don't hear what happened right now I'm gonna burst!" Jordan exclaimed.

Jamie came back into the room, handed Mia her drink and patted Jordan on the shoulder. "Nothing bad happened. Guaranteed."

Mia nodded, then smiled as she took a sip. "Damned fine cocktail, James. You have the knack."

"Tell me!" Jordan demanded.

Mia kicked off her shoes and cuddled up next to Jordan on the sofa. "You've become very impatient since we've been together. Is it something I've done?"

Jordan let her head drop, then started to laugh. "I give up. Tell me or don't. Either way, I've got to get to bed soon. My shift at the coffee shop starts awfully early."

"Okay." Mia took another sip of her drink then set it on the table in front of her. "I surprised the heck out of her by showing up. I mean, it's been months since I've seen her."

"Right," Jordan said, nodding. "Your mom's been keeping you at a safe distance."

"Absolutely true. I went along with not telling them about being in Colorado, making them think I was blowing them off. That's over now. We can be honest." She took a breath. "I'm going to try to keep this brief since my sweetie has to go to bed."

"You could have started ten minutes ago," Jordan said, a playful grin lighting up her expression.

"True dat. Okay. It started off rough. Showing up unannounced was a mistake. A big mistake."

"You just showed up? Out of the blue? I wouldn't have done that," Ryan said thoughtfully.

"Knock it off!" Jordan fumed. "Let her finish. No interruptions!"

"Sorry. Sorry." Ryan held both hands up in surrender. "Proceed."

"Of course, she guessed I was pregnant."

Jordan nodded. "Odd, but…"

"I quickly brushed away any unplanned pregnancies, arrests or time spent in rehab, and she settled down. Then…I just told her."

"Told her what?" Jordan asked, her cheeks pink.

"That I was in love." Mia gripped her shoulder and pulled her close to place a soft kiss on her lips. "That's what matters, right? I'm in love with the woman I'm going to be with for the rest of my life. That's what I wanted her to know."

"Nice," Jordan said, grinning vacantly. "That's really nice."

"It's not about sexual orientation for me. It's about who I love. And I love you." She tapped the tip of Jordan's nose. "Just you. Only you."

"What did she say?" Ryan asked. "I don't see any obvious bruises."

"No bruises." She reached up and felt around her ear, then took another drink, a thoughtful expression on her face. "She was pretty dismissive, as I thought she might be. She wouldn't have been so calm if Peter had told her he was gay, no doubt about that."

"What's that mean? How was she dismissive?" Jordan asked.

"She doesn't seem to think women can do much together. Like we just hold hands and write each other sonnets."

"*Please* tell me you didn't make it clear just how much we do," Jordan pleaded.

"Of course I didn't. If she wants to think we just stare at the moon together, it's fine with me. So I guess the bottom line is that she thinks this is a phase, she thinks we're not able to really have sex, and she thinks I'll go back to men in a very short time."

"And you're happy with that?" Jordan asked.

"Sure. Very, as a matter of fact. This is the best I'd hoped for. But then she surprised me."

"Gonna tell us how?" Ryan asked, her head supported on her fist. "I've never had a tooth pulled, so I can't say from experience, but this is…"

"Yes, Ryan, I think I will tell you. My grandfather came home and my nonna said, just as casual as you can imagine, "Salvatorre, our little one thinks she's like Margherita Pardini." Mia blinked. "I was like…say what?"

"Who in the heck is…who?" Jordan asked.

Mia turned to her and said, "My nonna is from Lucca, a decent-sized town in Tuscany. Poppi's from Barga, a much smaller place on the outskirts of town. Nonna has always thought she was the big city girl. You know…the sophisticate. She's always trying to make my grandfather seem like a hick. Well," she added, her excitement growing, "this girl from her town had a crush on her at the same time my grandfather was trying to get with her. I'm sure she was freaked out at the time, but now that she's lived here for a zillion years she can act like she was totally chill about the whole thing."

"A girl hit on her? That's amazing," Ryan said. "And cool."

"Yeah, it really is cool because she actually knew a lesbian. And when you know someone who's gay…"

"It's easier to accept a relative who is," Ryan finished for her. "That's excellent!"

"It really is." She put her hand on Jordan's leg and added, "I didn't totally come out. It was easier to let her think I was gay. Trying to get her to understand my Mia-sexuality was too much for me."

"That's fine," Jordan said. "You're never going to get the opportunity to demonstrate you still like guys, so it's not a problem."

"This is true." She picked up and drained her drink. "Let's hit the rack, girls. My sweetie has to get up at the crack of dawn."

"Are we going home or staying?" Jamie asked.

"Gotta go home. We're parents this week."

"Oh, shit! I totally spaced."

"One more reason we're too young to have kids of our own. Forgetting about them can land you in jail." They all got up and exchanged hugs. "We're proud of you," Ryan said, holding Mia in a loose embrace. "You showed a lot of guts tonight."

"She always does," Jordan said, beaming at her. "That's why I love her."

Ryan left the job site on Monday afternoon, dirty and tired. She and Brian had spent the afternoon putting in toilets, and that meant she'd been on the floor, screwing in bolts while he held the fixtures level. She was sure that wasn't his norm, but he was good at tasking people with the things he didn't like to do.

After going home to shower and change, she walked over to Catherine's, using the long walk to get her head on straight.

Marta answered the door, offering a hug. "I haven't seen you for hours, Ryan. Welcome home."

"Not home today, Marta. We're visitors again."

"I will miss you and Jamie. I get to cook more when you're here."

"We'll come for dinner more often. Jamie loves your cooking almost as much as I do."

"Catherine and Jamie are in the kitchen," she said. "Can I make you a snack?"

"No, I'm good."

"There's a plate of brownies on the table. They're so much better when they're warm."

"Couldn't agree more," Ryan said, grinning. "I hope you're not trying to save any for tomorrow."

"I can make more when they're needed. Have your fill."

They went into the kitchen together, then Marta veered off to go to her room. Ryan bent and kissed Jamie, then Catherine. "It's good to see you both, but particularly you, Ms. Smith. You're looking very well."

"Why thank you, Ryan. Sit down and eat these brownies before I'm tempted to have two."

"Two," Ryan scoffed. "Child's play." She pulled the platter over in front of herself. "I could polish these babies off in two minutes flat."

Jamie reached over and pulled two brownies away, placing them on a napkin. "I'll save two for Jen."

"Where is she?" Just then, a tortured clarinet emitted a few notes. "Nice," Ryan said. "Remind me to make sure our children have no musical interests."

Catherine put her hand on Ryan's arm, rubbing it gently. "I missed you two. You make every day a little brighter."

"You do the same for us."

"Hey, guess what Mom bought," Jamie said, giggling.

"Can't guess. Her bank balance and her imagination combine to make the possibilities endless. Just tell me."

"An apartment."

"What?" Ryan's eyes popped open. "Another house?"

"A co-op on Central Park West." Catherine cocked her head. "That's right by Central Park if the name wasn't a giveaway."

"What in the hell?" Ryan asked in mock outrage. "It was our turn! You promised you'd get busy finding us a house, but you've bought two in the meantime!"

"I know, I know," Catherine said, laughing softly. "But I couldn't resist. It's a great building, one of the big, beautiful white limestone towers they built right before the stock market crash. It's not at all what I want in its present shape, but I'm going to work with an architect to create three bedrooms with attached baths. There will be plenty of room for you two and Jennie to visit."

"Cool. I've always wanted to leave JFK. That's the only place I've ever been in New York."

"It's nicer outside of the terminal," Catherine assured her. "We're...I mean...I'm going to work with an architect to plan the space, then I'll have the work done in August." She picked up her hand and waved it. "Don't ask."

"Arcane co-op rules," Jamie said. "Mom has to go back for a board interview. If they don't like her..." She made a cutting motion across her throat.

"Who wouldn't like you?" Ryan demanded.

"I told mom all about our new purchase," Jamie said. "Although we won't get to live in it, at least I'm getting the hang of buying houses—in the right city," she added, playfully glaring at Catherine.

"It sounds exciting," Catherine said. "But you'll need an architect for this one. Do you have anyone?"

"Conor knows a guy that he's worked with and likes," Ryan said. "I suppose we'll try him. I sure wish Jordan would hurry up and get her license. We're gonna need an architect on board if we keep doing this."

"You'll have a broker, an architect, tradesmen of every stripe, attorneys… I can't imagine why you wouldn't keep doing it," Catherine said. "I'd think the boys could quit their regular jobs and do this full time. Goodness knows they work well together."

"That's not something I'm going to suggest," Ryan said. "We need to make sure we can make money over time. If not, they'd be crazy to give up the security of government jobs."

Jamie cut in. "Only a few of them work for the city, but not many of them would be good at finding individual jobs on their own. They need structure."

Ryan wiped her hands to make sure there was no chocolate on them, then grasped Catherine's hand and gave it a good squeeze. "Speaking of structure, I was a little worried about your being gone for a week."

Catherine started to speak but Ryan continued. "I thought your being gone would make Jen feel unsafe, but it was a good experience for all of us. Jennie handled it really well, and it let each of us have some time alone with her."

"I'm so glad to hear that," Catherine said.

"It was good. We went to a volleyball game and had a great time. She acts…I don't know…a little different when it's just the two of us. She treats me more like a peer when we're alone."

"I can see that," Catherine said. "Or like an older sister."

"Yeah. Exactly. So it's good to have some time alone." She held Catherine's hand a little tighter. "I know you need some time alone too. And to be with Giacomo. So when you need to go—go. Jamie and I are happy to sub for you."

"Thank you." Catherine got up and pressed Ryan's head to her hip. "You made a very good choice here, Jamie. As I'm sure you know, you're a very, very lucky woman."

Mia pulled into the driveway that evening, looking forward to an evening of Jordan's undivided attention. Distracted by her plans of how to get her sweetie to bed before dinner, she didn't notice her visitor until she hit the front step of the porch.

"Mom!"

"Guess where I've been?" Anna Lisa purred, her voice as cold and lethal as a serial killer's.

Mia steeled herself for the onslaught. "San Bruno," she said, not wanting to play the game.

"Correct. Would you like to guess what I was doing in San Bruno?"

"Getting your ass chewed." She put her key in the door and stepped inside. "We don't have to play cat and mouse." After dropping her purse on the table, she turned to face her mother, who'd followed her. "I know you're pissed, but I did what I thought was best for us as a family."

"You're the one who decides what's best for us? You're the child! You don't jump two generations to make decisions that affect all of us!"

After kicking off her heels, Mia went into the library. "I'm having a drink. Would you like one?"

"You know I only drink wine with dinner."

Looking around the very well stocked bar, Mia called out. "I've got Cabernet, Cotes du Rhone, Barolo, Beaujolais…"

"You must be making a very good salary if you can afford to keep nice wine in the house."

"Do you want a glass of wine or not." Her mom was standing in the doorway, looking around the sumptuously decorated room. She had to admit it looked more like an English gentlemen's club than an extra room in a recent college graduate's home, but Jamie liked having a room that reminded her of her childhood home—and Mia was polite enough to not tease her about it.

"Yes, I'll have a glass of wine. You don't have to waste the expensive stuff on me, though. The Beaujolais is fine."

"Got it." She opened the bottle and poured two glasses. A cocktail was what she'd had in mind, but it was silly to waste a nice bottle of wine. As she handed her mother a glass, she touched their rims together. "To honesty."

"Oh, yes, you're obsessed with honesty. That's the first word I'd use to describe you."

Mia took a gulp of wine, hoping it would calm her down if she chugged it. "I learned from the best. I'm surprised Nonna knows your address. You keep her so in the dark she should have Vitamin D deficiency."

"I'm considerate!" Anna Lisa sat on the overstuffed leather sofa. Mia watched her shift around a bit, probably wondering how the piece looked so broken in while being so supportive. She could have told her about the envelope of down that covered the springs, but didn't want to get off track. "I try to protect my mother from things that don't concern her."

Mia sat close, so close she could see that her mom's mascara had run. She'd probably been crying. Trying to gentle her voice, she said, "I'm her only granddaughter. I've chosen my life partner, Mom. How can you say that doesn't concern her?"

Jordan's key slid into the lock. Mia'd been waiting for her, but Anna Lisa was too hyped up to let it register.

"You're having sex with a woman, Mia. You haven't chosen your life partner. I'd be amazed if Jordan's here for another year. Some guy with more muscles than brains will catch your eye and you'll be—"

Jordan stood in the doorway, her normally ocean blue eyes cold and stormy gray. "That's a terrible thing to say...to both of us."

"Oh, shit." Anna Lisa stood and moved over to Jordan. "I'm sorry you heard that."

"But not sorry you said it?" A blonde eyebrow rose, making her look even more imposing. Mia had never seen her stand up for herself like this. Then it hit her. She was standing up for Mia, not herself. That gave her strength she normally wouldn't have shown. *Cool.*

"I'm sorry to be so blunt, I'm operating on years of experience, Jordan. Mia's been in love half a dozen times, and each time she was sure he was 'the one.' She hasn't learned what love is at this point of her life." She patted Jordan on the shoulder, and added, "Why don't you leave us alone for a while. We need to discuss some private things."

Jordan turned and gazed at Mia for a moment, then cocked her head slightly.

"Stay," Mia said, patting the sofa beside her. "These 'private things' are all about us."

"They are not!" Anna Lisa moved to a wingback chair and stared hotly at Mia. "They're about my relationship with my mother—which you've stomped all over."

Surprisingly, Jordan spoke, her voice clear and strong and confident. "I probably wouldn't have done what Mia did." She turned and gave her a smile so filled with love it almost took her breath away. Shifting her gaze back to Anna Lisa, she added, "If you were my mom, you'd intimidate me too much to even consider going behind your back." Taking Mia's hand, she pulled it onto her lap, the gesture just intimate enough to make Mia's heart swell with love. "But she's not like I am. It's hurt her to be so distant from her grandmother, to go along with the lies you've asked her to tell. You obviously can't see this, or you wouldn't be here yelling at her, but she only did what she did to make things easier—especially for you."

"For me? Come on, Jordan. I know you're in love, but if you think Mia does things for anyone but herself, you don't know her very well."

Jordan's voice grew as cold as ice. "If you can say that... You don't know her at all." She grasped Mia's hand more firmly and pressed it against her chest. "She's the most generous person I've ever known. She stayed with me in Colorado, in a crummy apartment with people she didn't like. She was far away from her friends and family, with almost nothing to do and no one to talk to. She got up at five a.m., changed every part of her diet, cut her spending down to nothing! And she did that *only* for me." Her eyes traveled back to Mia, then they slid down to take an appreciative look at her dress. "Just like she's gotten this job for me. She'd be happy to have you support her until she was through with law school, but she gets up early every morning and sits in an office all day just so I don't worry about spending my savings." Turning back to Anna Lisa, she said, "She's generous to a fault."

"I'm not saying she's a bad person. I'm only saying she's immature. She hasn't had time to learn how to put other people first. I'm sorry, Jordan, but I'm confident she'll break your heart. She's got a long way to go until she learns how selfless you have to be to make a relationship work."

"How much do you like volleyball?" Jordan asked, giving Mia a sidelong glance.

"I love it when you're playing it. But now that you're finished, I'll never watch another minute. Why?"

"How many hours have you sat in cold, drafty gyms, watching me play?"

"I have no idea. But I enjoyed every one of them. Seeing you do something you loved was a real thrill for me. But the thrill is gone…and I can't say I miss it." She patted Jordan's leg. "I'll start liking whatever you take up next. Just make it something outside. I'm sick of gyms."

Jordan raised that pretty blonde eyebrow again, and Anna Lisa didn't have the nerve to reply—which might have been a first.

Mia stepped in. "You were a nervous wreck, Mom. I know you didn't want me to tell Nonna I was in love, but you certainly weren't going to do it."

"It's none of her business who you have sex with! Why can't you see that?"

At her breaking point, Mia's voice rose when she said, "Why can't you see this isn't about sex? Jesus! Is that all Dad is to you? A guy you fuck?"

"How dare you!" She leapt to her feet, hands balled into fists. "Don't you dare disrespect our relationship like that!"

Mia got to her feet, nearly chest-butting her mother. "How does it feel? That's what you do to me! You want people to know you're *married*. Not because of sex, but because you love him. You want the people you care about to support your relationship. To honor it. That's all I want." She dropped back into her chair, clamped her hand around Jordan's arm, and tugged her close. "I want the same thing you want. Support and respect for someone who means everything to me."

Anna Lisa closed her eyes for a few moments, sank into her chair, then took a hearty swallow of her wine. "It was wrong to go behind my back. You've undermined my relationship with my mother."

"I tried to strengthen my relationship with my grandmother!" She scowled, still mad at herself for one thing she'd done. "I went along with the lie about Italy. If I'd wanted to undermine you, I would have told her you made that up. Then the fur would have really flown."

"I'm surprised you were able to restrain yourself," Anna Lisa sniffed. "You're the standard bearer for honesty now."

"I'm happy to call her," Mia said, narrowing her eyes. "I'll tell her all about Colorado and going to the Olympics."

"You don't have any idea what it's like to deal with her," Anna Lisa growled. "I can't talk back to her like you do to me. I *respect* her."

Mia held her hands up. "If that's what you want, I'll change. I'll keep my life completely private and lie to you when I think you're not going to like something I do. Is that how you want it?"

"Of course not! I want to be closer to you, not more distant. I feel like I'm dodging land-mines every time I'm with Nonna. It's exhausting."

"Yeah, I wouldn't know anything about feeling like I've been beaten after a lovely visit from my mother."

Jordan put her hand on her leg and squeezed gently. "Is this productive?" she asked, her voice just loud enough for Mia to hear.

"No," she admitted glumly. "I'm sorry for that," she added, with her voice carrying across the room. "I don't want to fight. I really don't."

"And you think I like it?"

Mia looked at her mother for a moment, seeing the fire in her eyes. She did, in fact think she liked to fight. It let her clear her feelings out— to let some fresh air in. But Mia didn't enjoy their battles any longer. They were unproductive. And she didn't get over them as quickly as her mother did. They had to stop.

"I don't know how it feels for you. I can only speak for myself." She got up and went to sit on the arm of her mom's chair. Reaching down, she took her hand and caressed it for a moment. "I'm sorry I went behind your back, but I'm not sorry I told Nonna about Jordan. I knew you'd never give me permission, so I did what I thought was best."

Anna Lisa looked up at her for a long time, her dark eyes gliding over Mia's face like she was studying someone she didn't know well. "You're right. I never would have given you permission. I got the lecture to end all lectures today: how I've never learned to control you, how I let you do anything that comes into your head, how you're probably going to start wearing leather and riding a motorcycle in the Gay Pride Parade... I heard it all."

"I wish they wouldn't televise that damned parade," Mia grumbled. "You should have to drag your butt down to Market Street if you want to see it. Having it broadcast lets a bunch of straight people think we only care about sex."

"Well?" Anna Lisa said, giving Jordan a run for her money in the pointedly raised eyebrow competition. "You don't see straight people having a parade."

Mia dropped her mother's hand and walked back toward Jordan. "Every day is straight people's day. You shout your sexual orientation from the rooftops. But we're not going to go down that path. I'm tired."

She flopped down and put her feet up on the table. "I'm also hungry." Turning her head, she asked, "Do we have any food in the house?"

"No. Sorry. I worked a double shift today. I thought we'd just have soup."

Anna Lisa stood and smoothed her wrap dress out. "I'll take you two to dinner. Jordan still looks like she just escaped from a refugee camp. She needs more than soup."

"Are we going to argue?" Mia asked, staring at her mother.

"We're not. You may choose the topics of conversation."

"Great. We can talk about our upcoming trip," she said, unable to restrain herself from getting in a final dig. "Rome's lovely in the fall, but it might be tough to find a good turkey dinner."

Ryan rose early on Wednesday morning and got ready to go for a run. Her cardiovascular fitness had suffered since she'd been working on the OFC project, but if she'd gone on a run long enough to really get the cobwebs out, she'd be ready to call it a day by three. But today she was less concerned with her physical reserves than the emotional ones.

It was going to be a tough day. Her mother's birthday always was. She was in better emotional shape now than she'd been in a year, but it never hurt to be prepared. Being alone to reflect might do the trick.

Her plans changed quickly. Just a few blocks from home she spied her aunt heading into St. Philip's for the seven a.m. mass. She surprised herself by following her into the church. Maeve gasped when Ryan slid into the pew.

"I know I don't go to church very often, but you look like the devil himself just sat next to you."

Maeve let out a short laugh. "You're such a silly girl." She put her arm around Ryan, pulled her close and kissed her cheek. "I'm very glad you're here."

Ryan nodded, then grew quiet and tried to concentrate. The early mass was the choice of the parish's oldest members, the ones who'd never gotten used to offering the sign of peace or even acknowledging each other's presence. Today, she was grateful for her fellow worshipers' stand-offishness. This wasn't a day for chit chat with strangers.

They must have had a special class in the seminary to teach priests how to whip through early morning services. Just a half hour after he'd begun, the priest urged them all to go in peace. Ryan had been concentrating on her own thoughts and hadn't noticed that her aunt was saying the rosary. She wasn't quite finished, so Ryan sat quietly until Maeve crossed herself, kissed the tiny silver crucifix, and put the rosary away in a little silken case.

They walked out together, holding hands. When they got to the stairs, Ryan said, "I'm keeping our deal. I haven't told anyone, especially Da, that you're still worshiping here."

"I've been coming less frequently," Maeve said. "I'm really very happy with Charles's church. But today…"

"I understand. Given how Mama felt about the Church, I'd guess you'd want to pray for her here."

"That's part of it, of course." Her watery smile almost made Ryan shed her first tears of the day. "But it's more the memories I have of our being here together. Every Sunday that she was well enough, and most weekdays for…" her eyes closed slightly as she seemed to think. "Fourteen years. I'd feel like I was leaving her behind if I stopped coming here on days like this." Sniffling, she wiped at her eyes and said in a raspy voice, "She's here for me. I can feel her presence as well as I could when the whole pew behind us was filled with your family." She grasped Ryan and hugged her tightly. "I don't know why you always sat behind us. You were always trying to snatch the hat right off my head."

"I could use a cup of tea before I go to work." Ryan took in a deep breath, slightly amazed she wasn't crying. "Care to join me?"

Charles's church had a regularly scheduled Wednesday evening Eucharist, and the entire family gathered to commemorate Fionnuala's birthday. It was the first time all of them had attended as a group, and while it felt very different, it was nice to be together as a family. After the service, Ryan managed to get Charles alone for a moment. She kissed him on the cheek and gave him a long hug. "I can't imagine how long it took you to figure out how to tailor your homily around such a depressing epistle. How you took 'My days are like a passing shadow, and

I wither away like the grass' and turn it into such a soothing image defies explanation."

Charles leaned close and whispered, "It takes a lot of practice to pull a bit of hope out of some of the readings. But I'm persistent." He kissed her cheek and she almost giggled when his trimmed beard tickled her. "Your family made up seventy-five percent of the congregants tonight. I thought you deserved special treatment."

"You're coming for dinner, right?"

"I am. Just let me get changed and I'll drive right over."

"I'll give you a ride. You deserve chauffeuring for your efforts."

The dining table seated eight, but they managed to squeeze nine in. Maeve had thought ahead and had made her great-grandmother's stew earlier in the day, saving them from having to cook with a full house. At the end of the meal, Martin cleared his throat, immediately drawing everyone's attention. His pale blue eyes scanned around the room, with a ghost of a smile that seemed like it would disappear in a moment. But he controlled his emotions and spoke. "If you live long enough every one of us will lose the people who have the biggest impact on your life. If you're lucky, you won't regret any of the years you spent loving that person." His smile grew stronger, and he looked more confident.

"Some of us, through no fault of our own, have fate shine on us. While I lost my beloved wife, she left me with four of the greatest gifts a man has ever received." The confidence that had thrummed from him just moments before began to crumble. "Every day I see her patience and steadfastness in Brendan, and her playfulness and big heart in Conor. Rory's the luckiest of you all, as he resembles her so much, both physically and in temperament. And Siobhán, even though she bears few of her physical traits, sometimes takes my breath away when she sings or turns a phrase in a certain way." His chin was quivering now, and Ryan was sure he was going to lose it, but Maeve put a gentle hand on his arm and that seemed to give him a second wind. "She'd be proud of each of you. As I am. And she'd love both Maggie and Jamie as if they were her own. I only wish you'd been able to know her." Tears rolled down his cheeks as he managed to say, "She was extraordinary. In every way."

He leaned over and buried his head in Maeve's shoulder, crying audibly. Every other member of the family seemed to be frozen—none of them ever having seen him so fractured. Ryan's instinct, almost undeniable, was to comfort him, to whisk him into the living room so he could collect himself. But that was her aunt's place now. Jamie's hand was in hers, squeezing it tightly, probably ready to pull her back if she made a move.

Then Charles made a small noise, sniffling as he reached for his handkerchief and dabbed at his eyes. "Isaiah's words give me comfort when I need it most. 'Do not fear, for I am with you. Do not anxiously look about you, for I am your God. I will strengthen you, surely I will help you, surely I will uphold you with my righteous right hand.'" He let his gaze fall on every face, slowly going around the table. "No one can take away the pain of a great loss, but we can lessen it by being here for each other. All we can hope for when we leave the earth is that those we leave behind will hold us in their hearts and their memories. Fionnuala is *very* well taken care of in that way. She was a lucky woman."

"She was," Martin said, struggling mightily to regain control. "And we have to remember that. We've lost her on earth, but she'll be waiting for us in heaven. Of that, I have no doubt."

As Ryan watched her father speak, an ache hit her in the solar plexus—a physical need to once again share his unshakable faith. But hers was lost, and she was almost certain it would never return.

After taking Charles home, Ryan and Jamie immediately headed for bed. It was still early, but Ryan was wrung out. She flopped down onto the bed, feet still planted on the floor. "I don't know if I can take another big family get-together tomorrow. I truly wish my mother had been born in the summer."

Jamie sat next to her and tenderly rubbed her back when Ryan turned onto her side. "I know it's tough for you, but you did very well this year. You seem stronger, more resilient." She bent over and kissed her cheek. "I didn't know what to do when your father started crying. That's so unlike him."

"I'm not sure why he lost it," Ryan said thoughtfully. "Maybe he's feeling funny about retiring. At least I hope that's all it is." Her stomach started to knot as her vivid imagination began to run through the laundry list of things that could be wrong with him.

"I hadn't thought of that," Jamie said, "but it makes perfect sense. He's moving onto a new path in his life, one that he's forging with only Maeve."

"It's still weird for me," Ryan admitted. "I'm so glad they have each other, and I see how in love they are. I'm even certain that Mama would be happy they were together. But…"

"I get it. My only analogy is if my mother married my grandfather." She started to giggle. "I'd have to leave the country."

"That would be one way to get me to travel more," Ryan said, a laugh breaking through her sadness. "I'd have to visit you in your exile."

Jamie snuck her fingers into the back of Ryan's slacks, making her squeal. "That might be the *only* way to get you to travel."

"That might be true, but please, please don't let it happen!"

Ryan moved about the house on Thanksgiving morning, making sure every inch was dusted. There would be so many people gathered later that the most unused corner would have a body pressed into it. Jamie was in the dining room, wrapping napkins around cutlery.

"What's our total count?" she called out.

"The O'Flaherty eight, all cousins, all aunts, all uncles, your mom and Jen, your dad and Kayla and… I guess that's it."

Jamie batted her eyes. "And that's…how many?"

Ryan walked over to her and kissed the back of her neck. "You can't do arithmetic?"

"Of course I can, but you've already done it."

"True. Thirty."

"Wow. I'm glad I bought enough napkins. I just wish we didn't have to use paper plates. Why wouldn't you let me splurge?"

"Because we don't have anywhere to store that many plates. Our cabinets are stuffed as it is." She picked up one of the shiny, new spoons. "It's bad enough we'll have to find some closet space for all of this stuff."

"It's Thanksgiving, Ryan. You should have cloth napkins and real cutlery."

"We've done fine with paper and plastic all these years."

Jamie stood, turned and placed a gentle kiss on her lips. "I didn't just buy them because they look better, even though they do. I'd prefer not to add a load of plastic to the landfill." She grasped Ryan's nose and tugged on it. "As would you."

"You've got me there. My cheapness collides with my environmentalism and I get all confused. Thanks for straightening me out."

After another hug, Jamie released her. "Something I'll never be accused of. I like you as non-straight as I can get you."

Ryan took a napkin from the pile and started to help. "I wish the children were going to be here. It doesn't feel right without them."

"I know. But it's good they're going to be with Mia's family. I'll miss Sara and Ally too, but I can't blame them for wanting to go away to celebrate the anniversary of the day they met." She grinned, showing her teeth. "We've been good matchmakers."

Conor emerged from his room, looking a little hungover. "You haven't done squat for me. Or Rory, for that matter. What good does it do to be related to two pretty girls, neither of whom can hook us up?"

"Tough break for you," Ryan said. "We'll keep our eyes peeled."

"Are those chicks from your volleyball team gonna come?" he asked. "The blonde's cute."

"No, they're not. And I'd rather you didn't hit on Ashley. She's…not very experienced."

"Mmm." He started to walk into the kitchen. "Anybody make coffee?"

"I did," Jamie said. "I can make you breakfast too."

"No she can't," Ryan said. "You can make your own."

He stopped in the doorway and turned to give her a narrow-eyed look. "Did she make yours?"

"No comment, but even if she did, she's my fiancé. It's allowed."

Conor rolled his eyes and went into the kitchen, where he banged dishes around for a few moments.

"Why'd you say Ashley's inexperienced?" Jamie asked, standing close so Conor wouldn't hear.

"Because I don't want him to get his grubby hands on her," Ryan whispered. "He's too lazy to find a decent girl, and that means he's too immature to screw around with someone I like."

"That's what people probably said about you not that long ago," Jamie teased. "Maybe he just has to have the right girl fall into his lap."

"That sounds like what will have to happen. Literally."

Mia delicately placed feather-light kisses all across Jordan's neck. She knew she was awake, and that Jordan was playing with her. This was a game they played all the time. When Jordan was sufficiently turned on, she'd flip over and pounce.

From right outside her door, Mia heard her mother loudly say, "I'd love some help in the kitchen. I suppose I'll have to wait until Mia wakes up, whenever that is."

Jordan turned over and started to speak, but Mia put a hand over her mouth. "She'll go away in a second. Be as quiet as a mouse."

Pulling the hand away, Jordan whispered, "But she needs help. We should get up."

"It's eight o'clock in the morning, and the turkey's already in the oven. She just doesn't want us to do what we're about to do." Moving forward, she caught Jordan's lips and proceeded to kiss them.

"Mmm…" Jordan pulled away, a worried frown on her face. "We should probably help."

"She *never* lets me help. And if I'm going to be honest, limiting the time we're together will help keep the fights to a minimum." She kissed Jordan again, lingering even longer on her full, sumptuous lips. "This is *my* Thanksgiving. Showing you how much I love you."

"Really?"

Mia knew she had her. Desire was practically glowing in those lovely eyes.

"Really. This is our first Thanksgiving as a real couple. I want to spend some time merging with you." She moved so she could look right into Jordan's eyes. "Because you're what I'm most thankful for."

"Me too," Jordan said, her voice a mere whisper. "I love you with all my heart. You mean everything to me."

"Then show me," she said, trying for a sultry smile.

"With pleasure." She kissed her, escalating the heat slowly. Then Jordan pulled away and looked deeply into Mia's eyes. "And restraint. I don't want your parents to hear us. I *mean* that."

"It's a deal. I'll quietly show you how you make me throb." She took Jordan's hand and moved it down under the covers until it hit the right spot. "Feel that? That's where you start."

"Mmm," Jordan said, beginning to lose her ability to speak. Her good arm slid around Mia as she pressed her to the bed. "*This* is something to be thankful for."

Ryan and Jen sat on the floor of the second floor hallway, looking down on the gathering crowd below. "I really wish Heather and Ashley had been able to win a few more games," Ryan said. "If they'd done just a tiny bit better in the PAC-10 they probably would have gotten to the NCAAs."

"They matched your record last year. Almost good enough."

"Maybe next year."

"They'll be juniors then. And so will I. Maybe Ms. Smith…Catherine will let me go to their games by myself."

Ryan bumped her on the shoulder. "You should make a decision about what to call her. It's been a while."

Shrugging, Jennie said, "I think I should call her Catherine, but that sounds funny to start all of a sudden."

"I get that. I still refer to my Aunt Maeve, even though she's invited me to call her by her first name. But you adjusted to Catherine going from Evans to Smith pretty quickly. This is just one more tweak."

Jennie looked up at her quizzically. "Do you think it bothers her?"

"What? That you go out of your way not to have to refer to her by name?"

"Yeah. That."

"She hasn't said so, but it might."

"Okay." She nodded decisively. "I'll start today. She's Catherine from now on."

"Good choice. I think that sounds better. She'll like it."

"I don't have to start calling your dad Martin, do I?"

"Not unless he asks you to, and I don't think he will. I was surprised when he told Jamie to call him by his first name. He doesn't see anything wrong with being formal."

⚜

The house was about half full, with Patrick and Francis's families not yet arrived. Jamie was surprised to see her father and Kayla picking their way through the crowd.

"You're getting into the O'Flaherty habit," Jamie teased when she met them in the living room. "It's not like you to arrive early."

"I told him this was rude," Kayla said, frowning slightly. "But he insisted."

"We're taking the red-eye back to Washington tonight, and I was hoping we'd have some time to chat if I got here early enough."

"That's a good idea. Do you want to go out to the backyard? There's a little sun back there to take the chill off."

"Great."

Surprisingly, Kayla said, "I'll stay inside. Maybe I can help."

"Are you sure?" Jamie asked. "I think we're in good shape."

"I'm sure. We brought wine," she said, holding up a pair of bottles. "I'll get them chilled."

It was clear she wanted them to have time alone, so Jamie took her at her word. She led her father through the kitchen, then paused at the landing. "Mmm. Malachy and Martin are fussing with the turkeys." Knowing her father didn't want to make small talk with the O'Flaherty brothers, she said, "Let's go for a walk. You can have a cigar if you want."

"Great idea." They trooped back through the house and as they got near the stairs that led to the front door Jamie saw Ryan heading for her.

"Going out for a walk," she mouthed and Ryan stopped and turned back to chatting with her aunt. She was a very good watchdog.

They started to walk down the street, with Jim taking out one of his cigars and fussing with it. "I've got news," he said, his attention on his work.

"Good news, I hope?"

"I think so." He flicked his lighter and spent a moment getting the cigar properly lit. "I'm buying an apartment."

"You too?" As soon as she said it, she regretted her outburst. "Uhm… seems like everyone's buying apartments these days."

"You've never been a good liar, cupcake. Where is your mother's real estate empire expanding to?"

"New York." The less said, the better.

"That's odd." He took a couple of puffs, then blew out a smoke ring. "Why would she want to live in New York?"

"I'm sure she has her reasons." Jamie knew her father would understand she was trying to close the subject.

"Right. You don't want to be in the middle. Sorry," he said, shaking his head.

"Tell me about your apartment. I didn't know that was something you were considering."

"Well…" He finally smiled and she noted how happy he looked. "I convinced Kayla to stay on my staff. She'll be one of my policy advisors."

"Nice," Jamie said. "That's a big job, right?"

"It is. Everyone knows about us, so we're going to be more open about our relationship. It's silly to pay for two rooms at the hotel, so moving in together will make it clear we're committed to each other while saving a lot of money."

"Wow. I'm…pleased." As she said that, she realized it was true. "It'll look much better for her to be more open."

"I'm sure people think she's just a plaything, but if they have to work with her they'll quickly learn that's not true."

"I'm happy for you, Dad. Tell me about your new place."

"It's ultra-modern. Three bedroom, three bath. Big pool and roof deck. Plenty of room for you and Ryan to come visit."

"Thank you. I'd love to come."

"Not Ryan?"

"You know she's not much of a traveler, but I might be able to pry her out of the city." She pulled him to a stop and kissed his cheek. "But whether or not she wants to go, I'll come visit. Soon."

When they returned to the house, the whole family was packed inside. Even through the mob, Ryan caught Jamie's eye and lifted one eyebrow. Jamie gave the "ok" sign and Ryan resumed playing with the baby. It was a good thing she had no intention of ever cheating on her eagle-eyed partner. She'd be caught within ten minutes.

After the dinner platters were cleared, Maeve and Deirdre started to put the pies on the dining room table. Once everything was set out, Martin called everyone to attention and said, "It's time to speak of our thanks. Is everyone here?"

A general murmur of agreement went through the crowd, even though Ryan could easily spot at least five of her cousins missing. The boyos really hated having to say what they were thankful for, and she didn't blame them. It was a nice tradition, but it would have been nicer with a smaller crowd. She and Jamie were near the kitchen, and she blinked when her father started with her. "My darling daughter can get the ball rolling. What are you most thankful for this year?"

"Uhm… As always, I'm thankful for my family. Every one of you," she said, letting her gaze pass over the crowd. "And I'm also thankful I wasn't more involved in this ridiculous election. This recount has fried my last nerve!"

"You couldn't have been more involved if your name was Gore," Jamie teased.

"That's a short list, sweetheart, but we'll move on. Jamie?"

Ryan watched her swallow, then look like she might tear up. This was exactly what she was trying to avoid by being flippant during her turn, but Jamie didn't have enough experience with the tradition to know you could slide by if you kept it light.

"I'm thankful I'm alive," she said quietly. "And to have my wonderful partner here by my side." She turned her gaze to the crowd, picking Caitlin out, secure in her father's arms. "And to see that adorable little two-year-old, without a hair on her head harmed. Every day since the carjacking has been a gift." She bit at her bottom lip, then turned and buried her face against Ryan's shoulder.

Martin's voice caught as he said, "Every one of us feels the same, darlin'. Thank you for reminding us of how lucky we are to all be here together. Every day is a gift."

It took forever to go through the whole throng, but when Niall, the last to go, mumbled something about, "Thankful for…everything," Ryan took Jamie's hand and led her out to the front deck. It was surprisingly cold, but they didn't need to stay long. She put her arms securely around Jamie's waist and looked into her eyes.

"As much as I love my family, I can't say what I'm feeling in front of a crowd that big." She dipped her head, slightly embarrassed. "I'd never hear the end of it if I showed what a sap I am."

"You're not a sap," Jamie said, looking up with a very sweet smile on her face. "You're a romantic, which is even worse."

"Yeah, I guess I am." Ryan took a breath, settled her thoughts and said, "You're what I'm most thankful for. Every single day. I wake up in the morning, so amazed to have you lying next to me. It's like Christmas," she murmured, feeling her eyes begin to cloud with tears. "You're the greatest gift I could ever wish for, and I look forward to spending every day of my life with you." She moved close and captured Jamie's lips with her own. "I love you more than I'll ever be able to tell you, but I'm going to keep trying."

"You're the perfect woman," Jamie said, her eyes so filled with love it made Ryan's heart skip a beat. "I know I don't always show I believe that, but you really are."

"I'm not perfect and you know it." She gave her a long, sweet kiss. "But we're perfect for each other. We're a matched set, Jamers. You and I."

"I'd like to see the fool who'd try to split us up." She pulled Ryan down and gave her a heartfelt, lingering kiss. "What a dumb wish. Why ask for trouble? Let's keep on loving each other just like this for the rest of our lives. Better?"

"The very best," Ryan said, leaning over to place another tender kiss to her lips. "Now let's go enjoy the people who give us the greatest pleasure available on this earth—our family."

Jamie looked up into her eyes, shining in the soft light that illuminated the deck. "What you really want is another piece of pie. Don't even try to lie to me, O'Flaherty."

Ryan barked out a laugh. "You caught me. But I sincerely want to eat it while surrounded by kith and kin." She opened the door and held it for Jamie to pass in front of her. "My favorite holiday, spent with my favorite person. Life doesn't get much better than this."

As Jamie slipped by, she placed a gentle kiss on Ryan's cheek. "Dream bigger, baby doll. We've only just begun."

The End

By Susan X Meagher
Novels

Arbor Vitae
All That Matters
Cherry Grove
Girl Meets Girl
The Lies That Bind
The Legacy
Doublecrossed
Smooth Sailing
How To Wrangle a Woman
Almost Heaven
The Crush
The Reunion
Inside Out
Out of Whack
Homecoming
The Right Time
Summer of Love

Serial Novel

I Found My Heart In San Francisco

Awakenings: Book One
Beginnings: Book Two
Coalescence: Book Three
Disclosures: Book Four
Entwined: Book Five
Fidelity: Book Six
Getaway: Book Seven
Honesty: Book Eight
Intentions: Book Nine
Journeys: Book Ten
Karma: Book Eleven
Lifeline: Book Twelve
Monogamy: Book Thirteen
Nurture: Book Fourteen
Osmosis: Book Fifteen
Paradigm: Book Sixteen
Quandary: Book Seventeen
Renewal: Book Eighteen
Synchronicity: Book Nineteen
Trust: Book Twenty

Anthologies

Undercover Tales
Outsiders

Information about all of Susan's books can be found at
www.susanxmeagher.com or www.briskpress.com

To receive notification of new titles, send an email to
newsletters@briskpress.com

facebook.com/susanxmeagher
twitter.com/susanx